A Better Place

Gay Youth Chronicles

A Better Place

Mark A. Roeder

Writers Club Press
New York   Lincoln   Shanghai

A Better Place

Writers Club Press
an imprint of iUniverse, Inc.

For information address:
iUniverse
2021 Pine Lake Road, Suite 100
Lincoln, NE 68512
www.iuniverse.com

ISBN: 0-595-17176-1

Printed in the United States of America

This book is dedicated to Ronald Donaghe, one of the greatest writers alive today; to Ken Clark, for all his continued help; and to Ralph, who is finding his way.

This book is also dedicated to my late Grandmother, Ardelene (Selby) Rogers and to all the memories I have of sipping hot tea with her at the kitchen table, and of her garden.

Foreword

Up until the publication of this book, Mark A. Roeder's body of work included *The Soccer Field Is Empty, Someone is Watching*, and *Someone is Killing the Gay Boys of Verona*. Beyond the fact that Mr. Roeder wrote three books within less than two years, his work is remarkable for bringing to an enthusiastic audience of young gay men stories that are no doubt relevant to their lives. Further, his work is remarkable in that he captures what must be the language and nuance of feelings present-day "gay boys" experience as they come out of the closet and come out to their peers. Not so many years ago, it was unheard of for gay men and women to come out of the closet, and even more remarkable for gay teenagers to do so; and sadly, not too many years ago, as well, violence against gay people was relatively rare.

Mr. Roeder's stories, however, give credence and substance to both—that a significant number of teenagers regularly come out to their peers and that they are the objects of violence and hatred as a result. In the order that Mr. Roeder's books have appeared, he has written about gay teen suicide (*The Soccer Field Is Empty*), courage in the face of terrorism and hatred (*Someone is Watching*), and religious bigotry and persecution of gay teens (*Someone is Killing the Gay Boys of Verona*). Further, in the same order, these novels are a romance, a suspense, and a ghost story.

Now comes his fourth novel, *A Better Place*. It is distinct from his others, in that it is a story of the cruelty of attempting to cure homosexuality through aversion therapy and other medical and psychological quackery. Like the three novels before it, however, *A Better Place* is also a story of high school age gay teens, and it should also appeal greatly to a young gay audience.

While Mr. Roeder's novels reveal the ugliness of homophobia, they reveal equally strongly the heroic struggle that present-day teens are involved in, as they attempt to make sense of their lives and to learn to love themselves and each other.

I would recommend that readers enjoy the books in the order that Mr. Roeder has published them, beginning with *The Soccer Field Is Empty*, then moving through *Someone is Watching* and *Someone is Killing the Gay Boys of Verona* and, then, reading *A Better Place*. But if you have picked up this book and have not read any of Mr. Roeder's previous novels…go ahead and read this one. Be certain, however, to pick up the others. You will gather within your heart a satisfying number of characters to get to know and to return to time and again.

> Ronald L. Donaghe
> Las Cruces, New Mexico
> Author of "Common Sons"

Acknowledgements

I'd like to thank Ronald Donaghe, author of "Common Sons" for editing this book, and Ken Clark for all his suggestions, corrections, and all the hard work he puts in as my "highly unpaid publicist".

Chronology

Historical Note: "A Better Place" takes place during the same time as "The Soccer Field Is Empty" and "Someone Is Watching."

Introduction

This novel is fictional, but it represents the real world all too well. Unfortunately, places like the fictional *Cloverdale Center* do exist, although what is done there is unthinkable. Very real horrors are inflicted on children and young adults in an attempt to "cure" them of homosexuality. What is done in such places is nothing more than medical and psychological quackery, not unlike that practiced in mental hospitals of centuries past.

Just as there is evil in the world, so is there good. Despite those filled with prejudice, hate, and intolerance, acceptance and understanding are becoming more commonplace. The ignorance and lies of the past are disappearing and a new world stands before us. Friendship, understanding, and compassion are more powerful things than hate, and will one day lead us all to a better place.

PART I

Fall 1980

Casper

I put my tray down and took my place beside Stacey. She was my best friend, my only friend really. I liked her because she was nice to me, and she didn't look down upon me because of my worn clothes the way most people did. She talked to me like a real person, like I was worth knowing. I liked that.

I wasn't sure why she liked me. Maybe because I didn't drool all over her like the other boys. I just talked to her. I didn't try to look down her shirt. I didn't stare at her chest. I just talked, and I listened, really listened. Stacey knew I was really interested in what she had to say. The other boys just pretended they were interested, so they could be near her and check her out. I was different though, and she knew it. She knew I was real, and not a fake like the others.

The only thing I didn't like about Stacey was that she treated me like a little boy sometimes. I don't mean that she treated me bad, or ordered me around or anything; it's just that sometimes she acted more like a babysitter than a friend. I didn't like that, I wasn't a baby—I was fifteen. I was pretty short and thin, however, and looked younger than my age. I always had to wear my brother's old clothes too, hand-me-downs from my dad, which were too big for me and made me look even smaller.

Stacey stopped talking when Brendan Brewer walked toward our table. Her eyes devoured him. She wasn't the only one who followed him with her gaze either. I noticed that the other girls sitting near were watching him too, even though most of them were pretending not to watch. The boys watched him as well, with an envious look in their eyes and a touch of jealousy too.

I frowned. I knew it was stupid, but I didn't like it when Stacey paid a lot of attention to another guy like that. It wasn't because I thought of her as my girl-friend or anything. We were friends, just friends. I guess I was afraid that if she started dating that I wouldn't get to talk to her. I was also kind of protective. I knew what most boys at school wanted from her.

Brendan smiled at her as he passed our table and went to sit with his football buddies. Stacey sighed. I guess I could understand that. Brendan was the captain of the football team. He was a living, breathing advertisement for tall, dark, and handsome. He was smart, good looking, and athletic. He had muscles bulging in all the right places. Every girl wanted to be his girlfriend and every boy wanted to be him.

Brendan seemed like a pretty nice guy, but I still didn't like him too much. He'd never done anything to me, but then he'd never even bothered to talk to me. I didn't really expect him to talk to me. He was from a whole different world. He had looks. He had money. He had everything. I had nothing.

I watched Brendan as he sat down with all the football jocks. I guess I was like the other boys. I kind of wanted to be him too. I wondered what it was like to be tall and muscular, and to wear new clothes that actually fit and looked good. Brendan was wearing his letterman's jacket. It was maroon and cream and made him look like a real jock. I felt my heart grow a little tighter. I'd never have a jacket like that. I'd never have anything that Brendan had. Life just wasn't very fair.

I pushed it out of my mind and tried to enjoy my lunch. We were having cheese burgers and fries, with corn, and apple cobbler. It was really good. Most of the kids complained about the food in the cafeteria, but I thought it was great, well, most of the time anyway. Of course, most of the other kids knew they'd get something to eat when they got home. I didn't.

Stacey grilled me about our reading assignment for English. We were supposed to be reading *The Lord of the Flies*, but I don't think Stacey so much as picked up the book. She just asked me what it was all about.

"You know, I think you're just using me for my brain," I said, teasing her. "If I wasn't around you might actually have to read something."

"Don't ever leave me, Casper, I couldn't live without you," she said laughing. "Now tell me what happened in chapter 3."

I filled her in on all the details. Unlike Stacey, I always read the assignments. I really liked reading *The Lord of the Flies*. It was a good story and I couldn't wait to see what happened next in it. I had to fight myself to keep from working ahead. Sometimes I didn't have much to do after school, so I rationed out the things I enjoyed to make them last longer. We didn't have a television and I didn't have any money to do anything, so that left me with little to do.

Lunch was over all too soon and Stacey and I went our separate ways. School became a much more unfriendly place when she wasn't around. When I was with Stacey, no one bothered me. They wouldn't dare because she'd lay into them. When she was gone things were different. When I was alone I tried to be as invisible as possible and not draw any more attention to myself than I could help. That was the best way to survive in high school. The more invisible I could be, the less I got picked on. I was real good at it. I thought of myself as the "invisible boy."

I looked around the hall, carefully checking it in both directions, then quickly slipped to my locker and worked the combination. I jerked on the latch. It was stuck, of course. The old lock was tricky. If I didn't do the combination exactly right, it wouldn't open. If the dial was so much as a millimeter off it would hold fast. I quickly worked the combination again. I pulled. The latch opened. I opened the door just a crack and then a hand slammed it shut again.

"Having trouble with your locker again, Casper?"

Even before I looked up, I knew who was standing there. Brent Bairstowe was one of my least favorite people in school. He and his buddies, George Winters and Jimmy Pearson, made up what I called "the terrible trio." They lived to make life difficult for boys like me and I was their favorite target of all. I looked around, but Brent was alone. At least I didn't have all three of them to deal with.

I didn't answer Brent. I knew he'd twist anything I said and use it against me. I swallowed the small knot of fear rising in my chest and reminded myself that there was only so much he could do to me there in the hallway. Mr. Vanmeter, my science teacher, was on hall duty and was only a few feet away.

"Huh, Casper? Answer me! You think you're too good to talk to me do you?"

I hated it when he called me Casper, although everyone did. My real name was Clint, but I got tagged with the nickname Casper in grade school and it stuck. Jimmy was the one who started it. He said I was so thin and pale that I looked like Casper The Friendly Ghost. He started calling me that and so did everyone else. I didn't really mind it when others called me that, even Stacey called me Casper. I think most people thought it was my real name. I hated the way Brent, George, and Jimmy said it, however, like an insult. I especially hated it when they called me "Casper, The Friendly Runt."

"Answer me you little punk!"

Brent was getting mad. There was no way to win with him.

"My locker is fine," I said.

"So now you're calling me a liar," he said and pushed me up against my own locker. The knob dug painfully into my back. I don't know how he figured I was calling him a liar. It didn't matter really. Brent would find one excuse or another to hurt me. Like I said, there was no winning with him.

"I try to be nice and you treat me like shit," he snarled at me.

The bell rang. Brent gave me one last glare, and then ran off to class. I worked the combination to my locker again and finally managed to get my science book out. I dumped all the books I wouldn't need and picked up the ones I would. Science was my last class of the day and I intended to make a break for it as soon as school was over. I knew Brent would be looking for me, probably with his buddies.

* * *

I dodged my way through the halls after Science and quickly slipped out the front doors.

"Hey you little punk!"

My heart skipped a beat in my chest and I prepared to run. I looked to my right, in the direction of the voice. It was Brent all right, but he wasn't talking to me. He and his buddies had cornered another kid and were giving him a hard time. I wished I could do something to help him, but I was way too small to take on the terrible trio. If I intervened, all I'd do is get myself roughed up too. I hated being small. I slipped away quietly and quickly, before they could spot me.

When I felt I was safe, I slowed down, walking as slowly as I could. I wasn't eager to go home. I didn't like it there. It was a bad place. I was afraid when I was there. It hadn't always been like that. When I was little I always rushed home to my mom, to tell her what I'd done at school. She'd always give me a cookie and sit with me at the kitchen table and talk to me. My family had been poor then, too, but Mom had a way of brightening things up. She kept everything as neat as could be and decorated with flowers and things she could find that didn't cost anything. Life wasn't so bad then, but then mom got sick. She got real sick and had to go to the hospital. Dad complained about how expensive it was, how it used up all our money. I couldn't believe he talked like that, like money was more important than Mom. I'd have spent everything I had to make her well, no matter how much I had. I even gave dad the few pennies I had saved up, but he just laughed at me and called me stupid. He was only nice to me when Mom was around. I knew he was ashamed of me because I was puny. My older brother, Jason, was tall and strong. He was dad's favorite. I'm sure my father wished that I had never been born.

Mom didn't get any better. She just got weaker and weaker. Every time I went to see her she was worse. She promised me she'd get better, but she didn't keep her promise. She died. I was mad at her for a long time for that, but later on I understood. I was little when it happened, but I could still remember lying on my bed and crying. I didn't really know what it meant to be dead, but I knew I wouldn't be seeing her again.

That's when things started to get bad. There was less to eat after that, and often nothing. Dad acted like I wasn't even there. I felt like I'd lost both parents instead of just one. When he did notice me, it was even worse. He was always angry with me, like it was my fault that we were poor, like it was my fault that Mom died. And then, some nights when he came in late and drunk…I closed my eyes and blocked the pain from my mind.

I wished I had somewhere else to live. I dreamed about a nice family coming to take me home with them. We'd live in a big house and I'd have my own room. There would always be lots of good things to eat, and there would be a television, and maybe even a pool. I knew it was a fantasy that would never come true, but sometimes I liked to think about it and pretend. Sometimes I managed to lose myself in my own little world. I could be happy there for a while, even though I knew it wasn't real.

I could see the overgrown grass in our yard before I even got close. The neighbors were always complaining about how horrible our yard looked. I didn't blame them. The grass was knee high and dad's old pickup truck was sitting up on blocks in the front, rusting away. I'd have mown the lawn myself, but the mower hadn't worked in ages and Dad was in no mood to repair it. I didn't even bother asking him. I avoided him as much as possible. I tried to remain invisible at home, just like I did at school. If Dad didn't notice I was there, he wouldn't yell at me, or hit me.

I waded through the yard and opened the front door. It was hanging on just one hinge. There was no lock, but then we didn't need one. We sure didn't have anything worth stealing, except maybe dad's liquor.

The house was quiet, no one was home. I knew Dad would probably still be at work, if he bothered to go to work that is. My brother Jason wasn't home either. He usually didn't come home until late. He spent most of his time after school running around with his buddies. That was fine by me. I didn't like him. He was two years older than me and a lot stronger. He picked on me and called me names. He was a lot like Brent or George or Jimmy, only worse because I couldn't get away from him. I lived in the same room with him. Jason did his best to make me feel unwelcome. He made it clear that he didn't want me in his room. That's what he called it, *his* room, not *our* room. Jason was never nice to me. I was afraid of him, even more afraid of him than Dad.

I went into my bedroom and sat at the old kitchen table that served as a desk. It was rickety and squeaked. I opened up my books and worked on my homework. I wanted to get it done when no one was around. I wanted to finish before Jason got home so I could hide it somewhere. Sometimes Jason thought it was funny to rip up my homework so I had to do it all over again.

I was sure I'd have plenty of time, however. It was barely four and Jason would be out for hours yet, getting into trouble with his friends. I sat and worked, scribbling out an essay for English, reading a chapter for science, and doing a bunch of problems for math. I was done in less than an hour. All I had to do was read some in *The Lord Of The Flies* for English and I could do that later.

I was hungry. I got up and went into the kitchen. I found some left over macaroni and cheese in the refrigerator. I heated it up on the stove and ate it right out of the pan. It was really good. I always had to find myself something for supper and most of the time there was nothing there at all. Sometimes, when I got really hungry, I'd slip into dad's room when no one else was home. I knew where he kept a jar of change hidden. He threw his change in there whenever he came back from the bars. Sometimes I stole a couple of dollars out of it and went somewhere and bought something to eat. I knew it was wrong to steal, but when I was really hungry I didn't care so much. Besides, parents were supposed to take care of their kids.

I didn't have to steal that night, however. I ate every last bit of the macaroni and cheese. I washed up the pan when I was done, so my brother wouldn't see it sitting there. If he did, he might yell at me for eating it. He considered everything to be his and I got hurt if I touched stuff.

I went back to my room and lay down on the bed. It wasn't even my bed, it was Jason's. I didn't have one. We were supposed to share, but Jason had claimed it as his. I'd put up a fight for it at first, but as always, Jason's muscles got him what he wanted. He was a lot stronger than me and I didn't stand a chance against him. I'd gone to Dad and complained, and I was instantly sorry. He just glared at me and told me to stop being a pussy and stand up for myself. Dad made me feel really worthless. Maybe he was right. I never could stand up to my brother, or anyone else for that matter. Maybe I deserved to be treated the way I was.

Jason wasn't home, so I lie on his bed and read. I didn't dare defy him when he was home, but I could get away with a few things when he was gone. The bed was soft and cozy, a lot more comfortable than the foam rubber mattress I slept on. It wasn't even a real mattress, but a thick piece of foam rubber like they use to make sofas. Luckily I was small, so I fit on it pretty well.

I turned the pages of my book and lost myself in *The Lord Of The Flies*. There was something rather pleasant in reading about boys running around wild in only their underwear. There was something uncomfortable about the book too. It seemed a little too much like my own life. Sure, I lived in a boring little town in Kentucky instead of a tropical island, but life at school, and at home, wasn't all that different from life in the book. Sometimes I felt just like Ralph, frantically hiding as Jack and the other boys searched for me, a stick sharpened at both ends. I tried not to think about that too much and just concentrated instead on the more pleasant parts of the novel. I wished I could live on an island like that; it must have been wonderful to be in a place so beautiful…

I awoke with a start. Someone was shaking me roughly. They were gripping my shoulders so tightly they hurt.

"Wake up, you little wuss."

My eyes opened, Jason was on top of me, glaring at me. The room was dark except for the bare bulb overhead. I must've fallen asleep reading.

"What do you think you're doing on my bed? Huh?"

Jason climbed up on me, digging his knees painfully into my chest. He started slapping the sides of my face with his hands, one then the other, harder and harder.

"What-have-I-told-you-about-messing-with-my-stuff!" He smacked me once with each word for emphasis. My cheeks were hot and stung painfully.

"I'm sorry," I said, tears welling up in my eyes. He was hurting me.

"I'm sorr-ee," he said mocking me, pretending he was crying. He smacked me harder. It made me mad. I tried to push him off, but couldn't budge him.

"Oh, baby's gonna cry," he said.

I bit my lip and tried to keep the tears out of my eyes. I couldn't help it. He was hurting me. Finally, he grew tired of tormenting me and stopped. He lay down full length on top of me and stared into my eyes.

"You know, I might let you stay in bed with me, but there's a price," he said.

I swallowed hard, my eyes darting around. I tried not to look at him. I didn't like the look in his eyes. I'd seen that look before. I knew what it meant. Jason pushed himself hard against me. I could feel the bulge in his pants.

"Wanna sleep with me, Casper? Huh?"

I wiggled and squirmed, trying to get out from underneath him. He grabbed my arms and held me in place, pressing harder against me. He was starting to breathe hard. I was scared.

I struggled against him, but he was too strong for me. I grew more terrified with each passing moment. I cried and shrieked and screamed, but there was no one to hear. In my terror I did something I normally would not have done. I spit in my brother's face. He jerked back and I used the opportunity to bolt from the bed and run down the hall. Jason was hard on my heels.

"Get back here you little bastard. You'll pay for that!"

I ran into the bathroom and only just got it locked before he slammed himself against it. He pounded on the door and called me horrible names. He acted more like a vicious animal than a human being. He terrified me when he was like that.

I wasted no time, but lifted myself up and climbed out the window. I ran into the darkness, swiftly, silently. After a little while I stopped. I listened, but there was no sign of pursuit.

I rubbed my arms to warm them. It was a little chilly and I was wearing only a thin t-shirt. It was late, past midnight. I walked along the sidewalk toward the cemetery. I couldn't go home yet. I had to at least wait until Jason had fallen asleep. Then maybe I could slip in without him knowing, and wake up early and get out of the house before he got up. Jason didn't like getting up in the mornings, not for anything, not even to hurt me. The longer I could keep away from him, the better it would be. I knew he'd hurt me for spitting in his face, but it was better than what would have happened if I'd stayed in that bed. Jason didn't bother me like that very much, but when he did…I shivered.

I didn't want to think about it. I blocked it from my mind and pretended it had never happened.

I walked on past the cemetery and onto the park. The moonlight was bright and made it almost like day. The park was empty. I curled up on a bench and wrapped my arms tightly around my body, trying to be my own blanket. I shivered. It was fall and it was chilly, not too bad really, but I wasn't comfortable. The bench was hard and hurt my shoulder, and my head. Compared to the bench, my little foam rubber mattress was luxurious.

I tried to forget about what had happened, and about being cold. I imagined that I was sleeping under a great palm tree, on a warm tropical island, just like in *The Lord Of The Flies*. I was tired. I kept thinking of the waves lapping at the beach and the warm sand releasing all the heat it had sucked up during the day. I drifted off to sleep listening to the gulls.

I did not sleep easy. My life invaded my dreams. I was standing on a beautiful beach, a spear in my hand, wearing only a loin-cloth. The sun felt warm on my tanned torso. I was happy but it didn't last…

"There you are you little bitch!" yelled Jason. He was running toward me, followed by Brent, George, and Jimmy. All of them were wearing nothing but underwear. They all carried spears, except for Jason; he carried a long stick sharpened at both ends. I bolted, running as fast as I could. They were hot on my heels.

I was Ralph and they were going to cut off my head and impale it on the stick. I tore up the beach trying to get away, but I couldn't do it. Jimmy dove at my ankles and sent me crashing into the hot sand. They all piled on me; Jason held a sharp knife to my throat. I screamed.

I jerked upright on the bench, shivering from fear, and a chill in the air. It was early. I didn't have a watch, so I wasn't quite sure how early. I guessed about six or so in the morning. I thought about going home to clean up, but then thought better of it. Instead I pulled off my shirt and washed myself in the fountain. The water was cold and made goose-bumps on my skin. I washed my face and wet my hair down. I ran my fingers through my hair, hoping I wouldn't look too bad at school.

My stomach growled, but there was nothing to eat. I was used to that, however. I reminded myself that I'd get something to eat at lunch, and then maybe I could find something else when I got home after school. Being hungry wasn't too bad really, not when you got used to it, unless it lasted a long time. When I went without anything to eat for a long time I got all shaky, and my stomach hurt.

I flicked the water off my chest and arms with my hands, wishing I had a towel. I put my shirt back on and walked to warm myself up. I didn't really have anywhere to go, so I went ahead and walked to school. It was well before time for school when I got there, but the doors were open and I went in. It was a lot warmer inside. I began to lose the chill that had seeped into my body. I found myself a corner in the cafeteria and sat down in a chair. I put my head on the table and closed my eyes. I hadn't slept well on the hard park bench.

I must have fallen asleep, for it seemed only a few minutes later when I heard people walking by. I was still tired, but I felt better. I stretched and looked at the clock. I still had plenty of time. I walked to my locker and worked the combination. For once it opened on the first try. I was glad it did, because I caught site of Brent out of the corner of my eye. I grabbed what books I needed and headed for first period English before he had a chance to spot me and start trouble. He didn't always come after me when he saw me. Brent had a lot of boys he picked on and he couldn't always get around to us all. I made sure to stay out of his way, however, just in case it was my turn.

I nearly made it to the relative safety of English class without incident. Just before I got there my brother came out of nowhere and shouldered me, nearly knocking my books out of my arms. I know that's what he meant to do. He looked a little disappointed because he hadn't succeeded. I smiled inwardly.

"I'll be seeing you later, bitch," he snarled at me, and then went on. I knew what he meant. I knew I'd have to pay for spitting in his face. Whatever he did to me, it was better than what would have happened.

I didn't have my copy of *The Lord of the Flies* for class. I'd left it at home along with a few other books. I didn't really need it anyway. I'd already read the chapters we were covering and I had a good memory. Stacey sat down beside me and asked me to fill her in on what we were supposed to have read. I picked up where I'd left off at lunch the day before and brought her up to speed.

"You'd better be glad we're friends," I said. "Without me you'd be going to summer school."

She laughed. I noticed a couple of girls looking at me, like they thought that Stacey and I shouldn't be friends. I knew they thought she was too good for me, and that I was nothing, just a poor boy. I tried not to let that kind of thing get to me, but it did. I self consciously covered up the hole in my shirt and stuck my feet under the desk in front of me so they couldn't see my shoes.

I felt a wave of sadness wash over me. My clothes embarrassed me. I got a lot of looks from the other kids in school. Most of them were too nice to say anything, but I knew what they were thinking. I got looks from the teachers too. I think those looks were the worst, because what I read there was pity. I couldn't stand it that they actually pitied me. It made me depressed. Sometimes it was hard just to walk down the hallway, wearing clothes that were little better than rags. The kids with nice clothes didn't know how easy they had it. I'd never had a new shirt, pants, or pair of shoes in my entire life. All I got was hand-me-downs from my dad, and my brother.

The teacher started asking questions about our reading, and I lost myself in the discussion. I didn't speak out a whole lot, but when he called on me I could answer. In that, at least, I was as good as everyone else. I didn't have nice clothes, or live in a nice house, but I wasn't stupid.

By the time lunch rolled around I was starving. I was so hungry that I said "yes" to everything the lunch lady offered me. I think she could tell I was really hungry, because she gave me more than anyone else. I didn't turn it down either.

I took my usual seat beside Stacey and tried not to wolf down my lunch. I felt like shoveling it in as fast as I could, but I didn't want anyone to notice me eating like that. Besides, I wanted to make it last. I ate the lima beans first, because they were my least favorite. I usually saved what I liked best for last. I'm not quite sure why I did that, but I always did. I guess maybe I did it because it was something to look forward to, like the lunch that was coming up on Friday. We were having pizza. I loved pizza. I'd been thinking about lunch on Friday for days.

Brendan Brewer walked toward our table and Stacey and the other girls practically drooled over him. I heard one of them say "He's sooooo cute." He sat down not far from us. A few of his football buddies followed him and it changed the way everyone acted at the table. All the girls were stealing glances of him and talking to him. All the guys looked like they were trying to be impressive. It was like he was some celebrity or something. I guess he was, at least in our school. Everyone knew him and admired him. Not only was he captain of the football team, he was, without doubt, the best looking guy in school. He was handsome and had really nice muscles. Just looking at him made me breathe a little funny, but I didn't like to think about what that meant.

Yeah, he had nice muscles. I liked the way they bulged with his slightest movement. I froze, and then looked around quickly when I realized what I was thinking. I turned a little red in the face, even though there was no way anyone could tell what was going through my mind. I suddenly felt sick. Not physically sick, but emotionally sick, well, maybe a little physically sick too. I knew something was wrong with me. I knew I shouldn't be thinking things like that. Boys weren't supposed to notice such things about other boys. It was bad, unnatural.

I ate slowly, but lunch didn't taste so good after that. I didn't like to be reminded that there was something wrong with me. I didn't like it when I lost control and let myself think things about other boys like that. Sometimes I couldn't seem to help it and that really scared me. I didn't know what I'd do if someone found out.

I thought about Jason and how much I hated him. I think he's the one who did it to me. He's the one that made me like that. He gave it to me, like a disease. I hated it when he got like that, it terrified me, and yet some little part of me didn't hate it. Maybe some part of me even wanted him to do what he did. I shuddered. I pushed it from my mind. I just wouldn't think about it.

I knew deep down that what was wrong with me wasn't Jason's fault. It was me. The other boys were right when they called me names. Even though they didn't know for sure, something gave me away and made them treat me like they did.

"Hey kid, um…"

"Casper," said Stacey.

"Casper, can you pass me that salt?"

I looked up. I'd been totally lost in my own little world. I was shocked. Brendan Brewer was actually talking to me.

"Um, yeah sure," I said and did as he asked. I had to stand up and stretch way over to pass him the salt. His fingers brushed mine. I felt a tingle pass through my entire body. His eyes locked on mine for that brief moment and I felt like he could read my mind. My face grew hot. I turned my attention back to my lunch and hoped that no one was looking at me. When I looked up, I knew I was safe; all attention was focused on Brendan.

Brendan kept looking in my direction. At least I guessed so. He might have been looking at Stacey, which would have made more sense, but I think he was looking at me. I wondered why he was looking at me. I was afraid that maybe he really did know what I'd been thinking. I sure hoped not. I didn't need yet another guy who was twice my size hunting me down to beat the shit out of me. I didn't look in Brendan's direction anymore, just in case. I didn't want the coolest guy in school to know what a total freak I was.

Brendan

I put down my tray and sat near Stacey Gibson and the cute little blond boy that always sat with her at lunch. I'd noticed him around school. He seemed nervous and afraid almost all the time, withdrawn and quiet, except when he was with Stacey. He talked more around her, and even laughed.

He was especially cute when he laughed, but he was cute all the time. I found myself drawn to his boyish good looks. He looked really young and I felt a little guilty about my attraction to him, but he was a freshman, so he couldn't be *that* young.

"Hey kid, um…" I realized I didn't even know his name. I hoped he didn't think I was a jerk for calling him kid.

"Casper," said Stacey.

"Casper, can you pass me that salt?"

Casper looked up. He seemed lost, like he didn't even quite know where he was. He looked surprised too, like it got to him that I'd spoken to him. I was accustomed to that look, but usually from girls. Seeing the expression on Casper's face made me hopeful.

"Um, yeah sure."

Our fingers brushed, and I smiled at him as I took the salt. I put a little on my lima beans, since I wasn't going to eat those anyway. I didn't want anyone noticing that I'd asked for the salt and didn't use it. I knew I was being paranoid, but I wasn't going to take the slightest risk that someone would find out about my secret.

I stole a few glances of Casper as I ate. Looking at him made me feel warm inside. There was something about his shyness that really attracted me. I was surrounded by jocks most of the time; loud, boisterous boys that thought they were God's gift to women. Seeing a boy who was actually modest was a novelty. Casper could easily have been conceited as hell. He was beautiful, with light blond hair and the bluest eyes I'd ever seen. He was nearly too beautiful to be a boy.

I flirted with the girls some, and kept stealing glances of Casper. He was so slim that it looked like the wind could blow him away. I found myself wanting to put my arms around him and hold him tight. I liked the way being near Casper made me feel. I'd never felt like that before. There were a lot of guys that turned me on, like just about all of my team-mates, but something stirred in my heart when I looked at Casper. He was a boy that I definitely intended to get to know better.

I thought about Casper as I walked to PE. I wondered if maybe I'd better think twice about getting to know him better. He was a boy that I could really fall for. I'd done a really good job of keeping my sexual orientation a secret, but if I got involved with Casper, I might not be able to keep it up. What if I opened up to him and he told everyone? Or what if I forgot myself and did something to give myself away in front of others? I knew how everyone thought about homosexuals at my school, or at least I thought I knew. Being called a "fag" was about the worst put-down there was.

I had a lot to lose. I was popular. I was Captain of the football team. I'd worked my ass off to become captain and I finally did it, even though I was just a junior. If people found out about me, they might take that away from me. Hell, my team-mates might not even want me on the team, period. I could just imagine what they'd think of showering with me if they found out.

I wasn't ashamed of being gay, not at all. I was proud of it. It was part of me. I knew the hicks in my little Kentucky town wouldn't see it the same way at all. I also knew that I had enemies. I tried to be nice to everyone and treat them with respect, but I knew there were guys that didn't like me, just because I was a success. I'd heard the grumbling when I'd been made captain. I saw the looks some guys gave me when the girls stared as I walked past. They were jealous. Jealousy could lead to some bad things. I wasn't exactly perfect either. I was a pretty nice guy, but I could be a dick now and then. I was sure I'd made a few enemies.

The more I thought about it, the less sure I was that I wanted to get to know Casper better. It might be wiser to keep my distance. If I allowed myself to get close, I probably would fall for him. If I did so, I was a goner.

I changed into my PE uniform. A maroon shirt and gold shorts. It didn't look as bad as it sounds. In fact, a lot of the boys in my class looked damned hot in that uniform. I stole a look at Derek Allen as he pulled his gold shorts up over his jock. He was fine. He was a little like Casper in a way, except taller and better built. He was blond though, and had blue eyes. That was a combination that always got to me.

I wondered if Derek ever thought about what we'd done. Derek was the first guy I'd experimented with. Okay, he was the only guy. It was just two years before, but it felt like it was ancient history. It was during summer break. Derek and I were pretty tight back then and I had a crush on him. It was the first time I realized that I was gay. I'd had some minor crushes on guys before, and I'd been attracted to a lot of guys, but up until Derek, I'd just thought I was going through a phase. I'd heard that a lot of boys had homosexual urges when they were young. When Derek and I began to pal around I knew that what I wanted with him wasn't just a phase. I knew I was gay.

That realization never bothered me. It just seemed natural that I be gay, so I never thought about it all that much. What I did think about was Derek. We spent a ton of time together that summer, when we were both fifteen, and it drove me crazy. I was totally head over heels in love with that boy. Just being around him made me happy. I was always trying to do nice things for him and made any excuse I could to be near him.

Derek seemed to really want to be around me too. I was already popular at school and had a reputation as a jock. A lot of guys wanted to be around me, but only because I was part of the "in" crowd. I felt like Derek wanted to spend time with me for other reasons. What I hoped was that he felt the same way about me as I did about him.

It was with Derek that I learned how to steal glances of other boys when they weren't looking. It was hot that summer and it seemed like neither of us ever wore a shirt. Derek had a slim, firm chest and was nicely muscled for a fifteen year old. Just looking at his bare chest was enough to get me breathing hard. A lot of nights he stayed over at my house and we thought nothing of sleeping together. Sometimes I'd lain there awake for hours as Derek slept beside me, both of us clad only in boxers. He was so beautiful he made my heart ache. A few times, I even worked up the courage to run my fingertips over his chest as he slept. Touching him like that made my cock strain against my boxers. I considered touching him elsewhere while he slept, but I never had the courage to do it.

And then came *the* day. My parents were gone and Derek and I had been out swimming and sunning. We went to my room where it was a little cooler, and sat on the edge of the bed. We talked about something, I don't remember what. All I could think about was Derek. I'd been hot for him for weeks and I was about to explode. The sight of him sitting there on my bed, wearing nothing with a bright blue swim-suit, was just more than I could take. I'd been stealing looks at his beautiful chest and cute little butt all day and my arousal was at a fever pitch. I couldn't believe I had the balls to do it, but I put my hand on his leg as we talked and started moving it up and down, real slow.

Derek didn't think anything about it at first; at least he gave no indication that he did. That didn't surprise me. We touched each other a lot. We were always wrestling around, punching each other, or even giving each other back rubs. All that made me hopeful that Derek wanted more.

I ran my hand to Derek's inner thigh. I was so nervous I was shaking. I'd never touched him so intimately before. Derek noticed what I was doing. I remember his voice faltered a little as I rubbed my hand back and forth across his inner thigh, coming ever so close to his swim-suit. Derek turned to me and our eyes locked. That's when I did it. That's when I touched him—there.

Derek closed his eyes for a moment and lightly moaned. He opened his eyes again and stared into mine. We sat there looking at each other as I continued to grope him. Derek reached over and began feeling me up. I moaned then too.

We both stood and pulled down our swim-suits. We grasped each other and stroked. It didn't last long. It probably wasn't more than two minutes before both of us lost control and made a sticky mess on the carpet. We pulled our swim-suits back up right after we were done. I remember that Derek looked kind of embarrassed, but I'd never been so happy in all my life.

That happiness didn't last long. I leaned over to kiss him, but he pushed me away.

"That's gay," he said.

I very nearly said "Yeah, so?", but there was something in his eyes that warned me not to do it. The next day I put my hand on his leg again and looked at him. He pushed my hand away.

"We can't do that again," he said.

"Why not?" I asked.

"Because it's queer. We shouldn't have even done it once."

"But it felt so good," I said. There was a lot more that I wanted to say, but he had that look in his eyes again. He just stared at me suspiciously.

"You're not a fag, are you, Brendan?" he asked, looking more than a little disgusted at the very idea.

My heart broke at that moment. I was in love with Derek, but it was quite clear that he didn't feel the same way about me at all. What had happened between us was a one time thing for him. Something he felt guilty about. Something he wanted to forget. I thought it was the beginning of something wonderful. I thought that Derek would be my boyfriend, but there he was, asking me if I was a fag. The very words he chose warned me of his opinion of gay boys.

"No, of course not," I lied. I should have told him the truth. I should've told him that I was gay and that if he didn't want to do anything else with me that was fine, but I still wanted to be his friend. Instead, I lied and denied what I was. I felt like a traitor to myself. It was the beginning of more lies than I could even begin to count.

Nothing else ever happened between us. I knew better than to even try. Things were never quite the same between us either. We still spent time together and were still friends, but it just wasn't the same. When school started that fall we grew apart. We were still friendly, but no longer really friends. I wondered if Derek ever thought about that day when we touched each other. I know I did.

My experience with Derek made me think seriously about Casper. I was afraid it would be the same situation all over again. Hell, maybe I was even so taken by Casper because he reminded me of Derek. Maybe I was trying to recapture what I'd lost. I didn't know if I wanted to go through all that again. What happened with Derek had really hurt. I still hadn't gotten over it completely. I still bore a secret hope that he'd come to me and tell me he'd been thinking about us. I knew that wasn't going to happen, however.

I closed my locker and headed for the gym. We were playing basketball that week. I was glad. I needed to lose myself in some physical activity. I was doing way too much thinking. Try as I might, however, I couldn't quite get Casper out of my mind.

Casper

I walked home after school. There was no sign of the terrible trio, so I didn't have to run for it the way I had the day before. I crossed the overgrown yard and walked into the house. I listened. Silence.

I walked into my room. I'd barely passed through the doorway when Jason pounced on me. Before I knew what was happening, I was face down on the bed, my arm painfully twisted behind my back.

"So are you going to do it again you little bitch?" asked Jason. "You going to EVER spit in my face again?" He twisted my arm harder and I cried out in pain.

"No!" I screamed into the mattress.

"Huh? Huh?" said Jason, twisting my arm harder still. It hurt so bad I was crying. I thought he was going to break it. I knew it was close to snapping.

"No! No!" I screamed. "I'll never do it again! Please, what do you want? Please stop!"

"Please stop!" Jason mimicked me, but he let go of my arm.

I crawled off the bed and stood, my arm felt pretty much useless right then. Jason closed on me. He grabbed me by the shirt and twisted it so hard it ripped.

"Don't fuck with me Casper. You fuck with me and I'll fuck you up so bad you'll wish you were dead."

I sometimes wondered if Jason knew another word besides "fuck." I was too scared to think about it right then, however.

"I'm not fucking with you, Jason," I said, holding my hands out in front of me, trying to placate him. "I'm sorry. I'm really sorry."

"Fucker," he said with a snarl and slugged me in the face. I tasted blood. He shoved me back into the closet doors and I fell to the floor and groaned. I felt like I'd been kicked in the back and blood was trickling from my mouth.

Jason left me laying there without another word. I didn't dare move until he was gone. When I heard the front door close, I got up and went to the bathroom and cleaned up. I looked at my face in the mirror. I knew I'd probably have a bruise on my jaw the next day where he'd hit me.

I tried to never cross my older brother. If I did, I paid dearly for it. I'd learned that lesson long ago. Whatever I did to him, he gave it back to me twice as bad. I didn't dare try to stand up to him either. I'd done it once, after I'd complained to dad how Jason treated me and dad told me to stand up to him and not take any crap. My courage had earned me the worst beating I'd ever had. No, it was much better to crawl. It made me feel like shit, but it was a lot better than getting my ass kicked. If I said whatever it was that Jason wanted me to say, he usually went a lot easier on me.

* * *

"No I'm not," I said.

"Yes you are," said Stacey.

"No, I'm not!"

"Yes you are!"

It was just after school on Friday and Stacey and I were standing near the parking lot. She was trying to convince me, or rather make me, go to the dance that night with her. She was being extremely persistent and I was getting a little cross, although for reasons that had nothing to do with her demanding tone.

"I don't know how to dance," I told her.

"Yes, you do."

"Okay, I don't like to dance then."

"Come on, Casper, go with me. It'll be fun."

"You can find someone else," I said, in yet another attempt to get away.

"I want to go with a friend, someone who won't be pawing me all night."

"There are plenty of guys who have no interest in pawing you I'm sure."

"Oh thanks a lot, Casper."

"You know what I mean!"

"I want to go with you. We're friends. It will be fun. Come on."

"No."

The truth was that I really would've liked to have gone to the dance. Even as I argued with Stacey, I was thinking about the music, and the food, and the dancing, and the food. It did sound like a lot of fun. There were reasons that I couldn't go, however, and it made me sad, upset, and angry.

"Please Casper."

"Just let me alone!" I practically screamed at her, and then turned away. My eyes filled with tears.

I tried to hide that I was crying, but I knew she could hear me. I knew she could see my shoulders moving.

"Casper, I'm sorry. I didn't mean…" Stacey put her hand on my shoulder. "I'm so sorry. I'm so stupid sometimes."

I turned around and faced her. There was no use in facing away from her anyway. She knew I was crying.

"You're not stupid, Stacey, and it's not your fault. It's just…"

"What is it, Casper? Does it have something to do with that bruise on your face?"

It was the first time she'd mentioned my bruise, although I'd seen her looking at it. I'd hoped she wouldn't ask.

"It has nothing to do with my bruise."

"Then what is it, Casper?"

I really didn't want to tell her, and then again maybe I did.

"Look at me," I said.

"You're very cute," she said. I smiled shyly and I'm sure I turned a little red.

"Look at my clothes," I said, and nearly started crying again. I was wearing the same old jeans and shoes I wore every day. I was wearing the same old shirt, too, except that now it had a tear in it, thanks to Jason. "Stacey, I don't have any other clothes. I can't wear this to a dance. Everybody dresses up for a dance. I'd look like a fool."

"You would not look like a fool."

"I'm still not going."

"But you want to…" she said, peering at me.

I didn't answer.

"I could get you some of my brother's clothes."

"I'm not a welfare case," I said. "I'm not taking anything from you."

"You could borrow some then, just for tonight."

"I don't think that's a good idea."

"Come on, he's off at college, and I'm sure there's some of his old clothes that are about your size. He's never thrown anything away. He'll never know, and he wouldn't care if he did. Please Casper, for me. I really want to go and I really want you to go with me."

Damn, she was looking at me with those puppy dog eyes of hers. I hated it when she did that. I felt like I owed her a lot too. Stacey was really nice to me when others weren't. She was the one person who didn't care if I was poor or not. She liked me, for me.

"Okay," I said.

"Let's go!" She practically dragged me toward her house.

A few minutes later, we were in her brother's bedroom. Stacey was digging through his closet.

"Here, try on these jeans."

I started to take off my pants, and then looked at her.

"Oh for heaven's sake, don't be so modest. I've seen my brother without pants lots of times."

I still felt a little self conscious as I slid my pants off. I quickly tried on the pair Stacey had tossed to me.

"Yeah, those fit well. How about this shirt?" she said, holding a blue polo shirt up to me. "No, not quite right...here, this one." She handed me a red plaid shirt—a really expensive looking one.

I pulled off my shirt, feeling even more self conscious than I had before, even though Stacey was nice enough to look the other way. I slipped the shirt on.

"Oh, you do look nice," she said when she turned back around.

I looked at myself in the mirror. I did look pretty good. I wondered what it must be like to have nice clothes like that.

I changed back into my clothes as Stacey and I talked. She faced the other way while I was changing pants, but turned around just as I was taking off her brother's shirt. She looked at my bare torso.

"Casper, has someone been hurting you?" Her tone was serious.

I had bruises on my chest and back where Jason had beat me. I hadn't even thought about the bruises until Stacey was looking at them. Stacey walked over to me. She turned me around, examining my bruises. She also took my chin in her hand and turned my face to get a better look at the bruise on my cheek.

"Has someone been hurting you?" she repeated.

"No," I said. I didn't want to talk about it.

"Casper, it's me, Stacey, you can tell me. Does your dad hit you?"

"No," I said.

"Well, somebody has hit you."

"Just drop it okay?"

"No, I care about you, Casper. If your dad is hurting you, I want to know about it. You can get help if he's hurting you."

"It's not my dad okay?" I said, a little cross. "It was just some boys at school. It's no big deal."

"It is a big deal if they're leaving bruises like that. How long has this been going on Casper?"

"Just drop it," I said. "I can take care of myself. It's not my dad. It was just some boys at school. It's over with and I don't want to talk about it."

Stacey looked like she didn't quite believe me, in any respect, but she accepted my story, at least for the moment. I felt bad lying to her, although it wasn't completely a lie. Some of those bruises had come from the terrible trio, although most of them had come from my brother. Stacey quit bugging me about it and talked about the dance instead. I was relieved. Stacey put her brother's clothes in a bag for me. A few minutes later I walked home.

No one was there when I arrived, luckily. I hid the bag of clothes where Jason wasn't likely to find them and looked for something to eat. There was nothing. Well, that's not quite true, but the mustard and mayonnaise I found in the refrigerator weren't exactly what I wanted for supper, especially considering that the mayonnaise had green fuzz on it. There would be food at the dance. I'd wait.

I was really excited about going to the dance. I never got to do anything like that. I showered and made myself presentable long before it was time to go. I changed into the clothes I was borrowing from Stacey's brother and left the house. I still had an hour or so to kill, but I was too excited to sit around the house. I also wanted to wear those clothes while I had a chance. They made me feel good. I felt like I wasn't so poor when I wore them.

I walked to the town park and sat under the trees, dreaming about what it must be like to wear nice clothes all the time. Someday I would know. I was good in school. After I graduated, I'd get a job, and then maybe some day I could even go to college. Maybe I'd even have my own house. It would be a nice one, and I'd keep the yard mowed and trimmed and all the neighbors would be jealous because it looked so good.

The smile that had formed on my lips faded. I was dreaming. None of that would come true. I was pretty good at school work, but I'd never be able to afford college. Any job I could get would be minimum wage. It would take me forever to save up enough for college. Some kids parents actually paid for their tuition. They were lucky. I think if my mom had lived, then maybe she and dad might have sent me to college, but she was gone, and there was no way my dad would pay for anything.

I pushed the thoughts from my mind. Tonight, I would have fun. I wasn't going to let myself think of depressing things. All that mattered was tonight. The future was yet to come. If I could be happy in the present, then that's all that mattered. That was all life was after all, one present after another. The future never really came. By the time it got here, it was the present too. If I could manage to enjoy the present, I'd have it made.

I walked to Stacey's house. She met me at the door. She was looking very pretty all dressed up. She took my arm and we walked side by side. I almost felt like she was my girlfriend. I nearly laughed at that. Stacey and I were close friends, and the thought of her as my girl was just plain funny.

We walked through the doors to the cafeteria. The whole room was filled with loud music and dancing lights. It was beautiful and wonderful. All the tables had been pushed back to create a large space for dancing. The dance was just getting started and no one was dancing yet.

"Let's get something to eat," said Stacey.

I was starving. I was so hungry I was getting kind of shaky. There were soft drinks and potato chips and candy, and all of it was free. Stacey and I talked as we ate. I tried not to scarf down chips and candy like I was starving, but it was hard. I never got anything like that. I couldn't even remember the last time I'd had candy. I'd never tasted anything so good in all my life. The soft drinks were good too. All we got with lunch at school was milk, and at home there was only water. I loved the way the soft drink bubbled on my tongue.

Some kids started dancing, but Stacey and I stayed by the food and ate and talked. I was already having a blast. For the first time in a long time I got to eat as much as I wanted. I sipped on my drink and watched the lights play across the ceiling and floor. I listened to the beat of the music and moved in time with it.

"It looks like you're ready for a dance," said Stacey.

We walked out onto the floor and began dancing together. Stacey acted real crazy and made me laugh. I acted crazy too. Everyone danced around us and everyone was having such a good time. It sure beat sitting home doing nothing.

The next dance was a slow one. Stacey and I drew close together. I wrapped my arms around her. It was a little difficult because I was quite a bit shorter than her, but we managed. I saw some people looking at us, but Stacey ignored them. She didn't care what anybody thought. She was having fun. So was I.

My eyes fell on Brendan Brewer. I didn't even know he was there, but I felt someone looking at me. When I turned, he was watching me. He looked quickly away. I watched him as he danced with a beautiful girl. I didn't know her name, but she was a cheerleader. Brendan could have any girl he wanted I'm sure. Brendan was handsome and strong. He was a stud.

As Stacey and I danced, I kept looking at him. He was everything I wanted to be. He had it all; looks, height, money, popularity. His life must have been a dream.

I had to keep looking away because Brendan kept looking at me. He probably thought I was some kind of freak or something for looking at him. He didn't act like he thought that, however. He had a slight smile on his face. He seemed friendly. I started having some warm and fuzzy thoughts about Brendan. Before I knew what I was doing, I was dreaming that I was dancing with him, my head on his shoulder.

I frowned. I felt a little sick to my stomach. Maybe it was all the junk I'd been eating. Maybe it was the images that were entering my mind unbidden. My old sickness was back, trying to ruin my evening. Why couldn't I just be normal? Why couldn't I get those unnatural, disgusting thoughts out of my head? I had enough problems to deal with, without thinking perverted and disgusting things about other boys. I was sick, sick in the head.

Brendan

I was slow dancing with Sara Davidson when my eyes fell on Casper. I hadn't been able to get him out of my mind for a moment. There was something about that boy that just drew me to him. He was so beautiful he made my heart flutter in my chest. I was surrounded by guys that were a lot better built than Casper, but, to me, he had them all beat. I think his shyness and modesty added a lot to his physical appeal. When I looked at him, I could somehow feel what was inside him, at least partially.

Casper was dancing with his friend Stacey. He was holding her real close. I wondered if maybe they were more than just friends. That possibility disturbed me. What if he wasn't even interested in guys? I knew that most guys weren't, but something told me that Casper was a gay boy just like me. What if I was wrong? The possibility that he might be straight made me more fearful than ever about approaching him.

Straight, I hated that word. If heterosexuals were straight, then what did that make me? Bent? Crooked? It made it sound like being gay was some kind of deviation. I didn't like that. I wasn't a deviant. I just liked boys.

I tried not to be too obvious, but it was hard keeping my eyes off Casper. I wanted him. I needed him. I'd been alone with my "gayness" for too long. I needed someone flesh and blood to share it with. I longed to take Casper in my arms and kiss him. I'd just stand there holding him, kissing him forever.

"What? Oh, sorry Sara, what did you say?"

"I said you seemed distracted. I guess I was right."

"Oh yeah, I guess I am a little. I was just thinking about our game against the Buccaneers next week." I lied. "They are a tough team."

"Don't you think about anything besides football?" asked Sara.

"Oh yeah, I think about a lot of things," I said, stealing yet another glance of the boy of my dreams.

* * *

Sara and I sat in the back of my parked convertible necking. I made out with a lot of girls. At first, I thought that was kind of odd. I was gay after all, but making out with a girl could still be hot. The first few times I did it, I even began to wonder if maybe I wasn't bisexual. That would have certainly had its advantages. It would've doubled my chances of getting some action. I knew I wasn't bi, however. I enjoyed the kissing, the entwining tongues, but that was as far as it went. When I thought about taking things further, I got a kind of sick feeling in the pit of my stomach. There was something definitely un-sexy about girls. The thought of pulling a girl's top off filled me with revulsion.

Sara's hands started wandering. It made me nervous. If she touched me in the wrong place she'd find out something I didn't want her to know. It was sexy kissing her, but I wasn't excited. There was nothing happening in my jeans. There would have been something happening down there if I was a straight boy. If Sara groped me, she'd know something was wrong. I tried to think up something I could tell her to explain it if she did. Maybe I could tell her I was on some kind of medication or something? Or maybe I'd just say I was all stressed out about something. I'd heard that could cause impotence.

I got off lucky, however, Sara didn't touch me there. Instead, her hands wandered over my shoulders, chest, and arms. It felt kind of good, really. She worked her hands up under my shirt and felt my naked skin. Her touch felt good. I closed my eyes and imagined she was a boy. For a few moments the fantasy held, and I felt myself getting excited. Her breasts brushed against me and that was the end of that. We made out for a few minutes more, then I make up an excuse about having to be home soon. I didn't want to take any chances. I was afraid that Sara wouldn't be happy with a little necking. I was afraid she'd want more.

It was kind of funny, really. I feared the very thing most boys dreamed about. I couldn't think of a single straight boy that wouldn't have drooled over the prospect of getting some action with Sara Davidson, and there I was making up excuses to make sure nothing happened between us. It seemed kind of crazy. Then again, if I was in the back seat with a boy instead of a girl, I'd have stayed right where I was as long as I could manage. Yeah, that would be it. That was my dream, making out with a cute boy in the back of my convertible. If I got the chance to do that, there would sure be no excuses about why I had to go home. I'd have defied any curfew for some action with a cute guy.

Casper

I held Stacey close as we danced the last of the slow dances. It had been a wonderful night. I felt like I was somebody. I felt like people weren't looking down on me for the first time in my life. I loved feeling like I belonged, instead of like some outsider who wasn't good enough to be there. The dance was near its end, however, and soon I'd turn back into a pumpkin.

Brendan Brewer kept looking at me. I could tell he was trying hard not to look like he was looking, but he was definitely looking. I thought that maybe he was just surprised to see me not looking like a beggar for once, but somehow I knew that wasn't it. He seemed pleasant enough, but I wondered if maybe he guessed the things that were running through my mind. I shivered to think that anyone else might even suspect I had such thoughts. They were disgusting and perverted. I pushed it out of my mind. It didn't make any sense anyway. Why would he be smiling at me if he thought I was some kind of pervert?

I was still a little frightened. I hoped that Brendan wouldn't come looking for me after the dance to beat me up. I planned on sticking close to Stacey just in case. It's not that I expected her to protect me, that would have been embarrassing, it's just that I thought it less likely that I'd get attacked if she was there.

The dance ended and Stacey and I each grabbed one last soda and a bit more candy. I was so stuffed that I couldn't even eat it. That was a new feeling for me. I stuffed it in my pocket for later. I'd have to find a good hiding place when I got home or Jason would take it from me. I could just hear him gloating "Like taking candy from a baby."

Stacey and I walked back to her house. I breathed a sigh of relief. Brendan Brewer didn't try to slug me. Maybe being with Stacey kept him off, or maybe he'd just never intended to come after me. He probably didn't. I was being stupid. Like he could really tell what I was thinking by looking at me. Where did I get a dumb ass idea like that?

Stacey left me alone for a few minutes to change clothes. I was glad. I was really uncomfortable with her standing there while I was changing at the beginning of the evening. I didn't like anyone to see me without clothes. I was too short, too scrawny. I didn't want any more questions about my bruises either.

I talked with Stacey for a little bit and then left for home. When I got there, the lights were on in my bedroom. I crept up and peeked through the window. Jason was already home. He had his shirt off and was standing in front of the mirror flexing his muscles. I watched him for a little bit. He looked pretty silly standing there admiring himself, although he did have a pretty nice build. I wished he didn't. He used those muscles to hurt me.

Jason pulled down his shorts and boxers. He stood in front of the mirror naked, still flexing, still admiring himself. He reached down and groped himself, making himself hard. I backed away from the window. I had to go somewhere. It wasn't a good time to be at home. I was afraid of what might happen. I stashed my candy under the porch and walked down the sidewalk.

The moon was full and bright, making it seem almost like daylight. The stars looked so close I felt like I could reach up and grab one. I walked a lot at night. I loved to walk under the stars. Most of my walks weren't for enjoyment, however, even though I did enjoy them. Mostly I walked when it wasn't safe to be home with my dad or brother. Sometimes when Dad was drunk he could get real mean and it was best not to be around him. Sometimes Jason was about the same. And then there were those times when Jason got that look in his eyes, the look that made me draw back in revulsion. I'd seen that look as he gazed at himself in the mirror. I was afraid of what would've happened had I gone inside. I always checked out the situation before entering the house. I'd learned long ago not to take any chances. If things didn't look good, I just didn't go in.

My mind drifted back to the thoughts I had about Brendan at the dance. I didn't really want to think about it, but if I didn't, it would just keep coming back at me. I liked to get unpleasant things out of the way as soon as possible, just like I liked to save good stuff for later. Anticipation could be either a good or bad thing, depending on what was being anticipated. This time the anticipation was unpleasant, so I wanted to get to it and get it over with.

Ever since grade school, the other boys had made fun of me and called me names. I was one of those boys that always got picked on and was always picked last for teams. Even back in grade school the other boys called me sissy and queer. I knew I wasn't a sissy. Sissies were afraid and weak. I was afraid a lot of the time, but I wasn't afraid to do stuff, like learn how to roller skate or play football in gym. Then again, maybe I was a sissy, because I was afraid a lot of the time. I was afraid every day. I was afraid someone would call me names, which they always did. I was afraid I'd get picked on and hit, which happened almost every day. I was afraid of my dad when he got mean, and my brother. Maybe I was a sissy for that, but was it really my fault?

The other name bothered me more—queer. For a long time I didn't even know what that meant. I'd figured it out, however. The dictionary said it meant "a strange person, someone different from normal." I knew that queer meant a lot more than that, however. It meant pervert. It meant boys that did stuff with other boys, or at least wanted to do stuff with them.

For a long time, I didn't think that name applied to me, but then things began to change. I'm not sure when they began to change, but now that I looked back; I could see that the change had taken place. I felt it when I was in the locker room or showers with the other boys—sometimes looking at them made me breathe funny. Sometimes it made me feel funny. Sometimes it made me get hard, like my brother when he had that look in his eyes. Sometimes I just couldn't keep from looking at the other boys, even though I knew it was wrong, even though I knew it was queer.

A tear rolled down my cheek, followed quickly by another. It was painful to think the thoughts I was thinking. It hurt. I didn't want to think about it, but I wanted to get it over. I cried more as I openly admitted to myself that I was queer. I'd been trying to hide it from myself, but no one could really do that, not for long anyway.

I think I know what made me queer. I think I know what did it, or rather who did it—my brother. I hated him. He's the one that did it to me. He's the one that made me queer. I shivered. My train of thought had become far too painful. I shifted it.

"Okay, so I'm queer," I thought to myself. "Now how do I get rid of it? How do I cure myself, make myself unqueer?"

I decided that the first thing I needed to do was not look around in the showers and locker room. I mean, why was I doing that anyway? It was disgusting. It wasn't like I really wanted to do anything with any of those other boys. I'd never do that stuff. It was too gross, thinking about it just about made me sick. So there was no reason to be looking. So I wouldn't look.

There were times when images came into my mind, images that disturbed me. That was something else I had to work on. When those thoughts entered my head, I just had to force them out and think of other things. I didn't want those thoughts, they were bad, and so I'd just keep myself from thinking them.

And then there was the thing I did when I was alone. The thing I'd caught my brother doing. The thing he was starting to do as I looked through the window. The unwanted thoughts and images that invaded my head were the worst when I was doing that. I was disgusted with myself for touching myself there. It was gross. It was something my brother would do. It was a bad habit that I had to quit. I was sure it was a big part of what was making me queer. It had to go.

I was feeling a little better about myself. Yeah, I could handle this. I could get rid of my queerness. I thought about Brendan, and the way he made me feel. Most of what I felt when I looked at him didn't seem so bad, but then again other things that I thought were worse than bad. Maybe it would be best if I didn't look at Brendan either, at least not until I got the whole queer thing under control. There was no real reason to be looking at him anyway. I mean, it's not like we'd ever be friends. He was a jock, he was popular, and he was captain of the football team. I was nothing. He'd spoken to me, but all he'd done was ask me to pass the salt. That was nothing. I was nothing.

A twig snapped behind me. That wasn't all that significant in itself, but I could tell something was wrong. Someone was there. I turned and looked just in time to see Brent lunging for me, Brent and his buddies. I tore down the sidewalk, running for my life. The terrible trio was hot on my heels. I usually did a pretty good job of avoiding them, but I'd let my defenses down. I'd been too busy thinking to pay attention. They must have spotted me and closed in on me while I wasn't looking. If it hadn't been for that twig snapping, they would probably have grabbed me before I even knew what was happening.

I ran as fast as my legs could carry me, which was pretty fast. I wasn't athletic, but I was a good runner. I think it probably came from having to run so often. It seemed like someone was always chasing me, someone who would kick my ass if they could catch me. I tried my best not to get caught, of course, and was successful more often than not.

I was tired, so I wasn't exactly at my fastest. I was keeping ahead of Brent, George, and Jimmy, but I wasn't pulling away from them. They were whooping and hollering, having a great time. I wasn't. I knew they'd beat me senseless if they caught up to me. I was their favorite punching bag. They were bullies, and picked on whoever they could, but they liked picking on me best of all.

I ran and ran. I was getting tired. My breath was coming hard and fast and my side was even beginning to hurt a little. I could hear the terrible trio huffing and puffing right behind me. I hoped that I could outlast them. All three of them were a lot bigger than me. They were loaded down with a lot of heavy muscle. They had longer legs though, more powerful legs, so maybe I didn't have an advantage. One thing was for sure. I wasn't going to stop running until I collapsed. I knew what they'd do to me when they caught me, and the pain of running was far more pleasant.

I spotted the graveyard up ahead. It was filled with big old trees, tomb stones, and mausoleums. Maybe I could lose my pursuers in there. Maybe I could dart around and lose them in the darkness of the trees. I ran through the gates, and into the cemetery. I couldn't hear the boys running behind me any more. Their heavy breathing grew farther away.

I risked having a look behind me and saw them standing at the gate. They were gasping for breath. George was holding his side. I moved into the deep shadows and watched them. They stood there, looking into the grave yard, but they didn't enter. I smiled. They were afraid. They stood there a few moments longer, then turned around and left. They gave up and went in search of easier prey.

I couldn't believe it. The terrible trio was afraid of walking into the graveyard at night. I'd just discovered something valuable. The cemetery was like a base where I was safe, at least at night. I stored away the information for future use. If ever the terrible trio came after me near the graveyard, I knew just where to run.

I looked around me. It was spooky in there. The shadows were deep and I was surrounded by tombstones and old, old mausoleums. There was no telling how many dead people were in there. I wasn't afraid, however. The dead seemed a lot less frightening than the living. The dead were just bodies; the living could beat me up. There was nothing to fear in that cemetery. There were things to fear beyond its gates.

The real reason I wasn't afraid in the cemetery is that my mom was there. When she'd died, she was buried among all the other graves. I visited her grave a lot, even though I knew she wasn't there. It was just her body in that grave.

Maybe her spirit did still hang around though. Sometimes I felt like she was there with me.

I walked slowly to my mother's grave. I sat down and leaned up against a tree, pulling my arms up close about me. It was chilly and I was getting cold. I looked at the tombstone, and, as I had so many times before, I felt my mom there with me. I rested my head on the tree and closed my eyes. I was safe. My mom was watching over me, just like she did when I was little. I'd wait for a while until I was sure the terrible trio was gone, and that my brother was asleep, before I'd leave the safety of the graveyard. In only a few moments, I was fast asleep.

Brendan

Alex Fleming slammed me to the ground, a fraction of a second after I'd passed the ball. I landed flat on my back and it knocked the wind out of me.

"You okay, Brewer?"

"Yeah, Coach."

"Simmons! Grant! Where were you?" yelled Coach Howell. "You let the Cougars break through like that on Friday night and we don't stand a chance! Fleming just missed sacking Brendan. You guys have got to get your act together!"

The coach continued going off on the linemen. It didn't bother them too much. We were all used to it. Coach was always yelling at someone.

I passed the ball back and forth with Brad Sawa. He was my best friend and took my place as quarterback if I was injured and couldn't play. Brad and I had been together forever. Even so, I'd never shared my biggest secret with him. I often wondered what he'd do if he knew I was gay. It's something he'd never know, however, so I guess I didn't really need to think about it. I trusted Brad more than anyone, but I could not trust him with that. I knew friendships ended over such things. I didn't want to lose Brad, and I didn't want to take the risk that he would out me if he knew.

I was scared that Brad would get really pissed if I told him I was gay. I'd done some things in the past that I shouldn't have, things that he thought nothing of now, but would look at in a whole different light if he found out I was into guys. Some of it was simple stuff, like how I liked to wrestle with him and how I used any excuse to pull off my shirt, so he would take off his as well. Then there was more incriminating evidence, like the way I always got him to sleep in my bed when he stayed over. I knew all that would take on a much greater significance if he knew I was gay. He'd instantly think I'd been taking advantage of him, and maybe he wouldn't be completely wrong.

I had done some things I should not have. Sometimes I gave Brad a back-rub. That wasn't bad in itself, Brad gave me backrubs too. I used the opportunity, however. Getting the tension out of his muscles wasn't my sole reason for rubbing his back. It was my chance to touch him, to feel him. I used the opportunity to run my hands all over his firm, young body. Sometimes I was even bold enough to work my hands out onto his butt a bit. I always had to hide my arousal after I'd rubbed Brad's back. Touching him like that aroused me like crazy.

If Brad found out I was gay, then he'd remember those back rubs. He'd remember how I'd touched him. He'd know what I had done. That wasn't the worst of it, either. Sometimes, on rare occasions, Brad and I even jerked off together. He'd start talking about girls and I'd act like I was into them too. Pretty soon Brad would get a big bulge in his shorts. Seeing him would give me a bulge too. We'd push our shorts down and stroke ourselves. We never touched each other, but I sure did plenty of looking. It was something a lot of boys do, but I knew what Brad would think of that if he discovered I was gay. He'd feel used.

I wished that I could tell Brad I was gay, then I wouldn't have to wonder anymore if he would still be my friend if he knew. I hated not knowing that. I was very popular, but I didn't really know if any of my friends were really my friends. Would they remain my friends if they knew I lusted after other boys instead of girls? I doubted it. I could just imagine how they'd all freak out if I was in the locker room or the showers with them. They'd be afraid I was looking at them, checking them out. It wouldn't exactly be an unjustified fear either.

I looked at Brad as he passed me the ball. He sure looked good in his foot-ball uniform. Sometimes I just wanted to grab him and rip his shirt off. His smooth, firm muscles drove me insane with desire. My thoughts turned to Casper. What about him? There was something about that boy, and unlike Brad, I had a feeling that Casper was attracted to other boys just like me.

"Brewer! Sawa! Let's get going!"

We ran back and took our places on the field. I kept thinking about Casper. He wasn't built like Brad and my team-mates, but he had a nice body. He was cute too, way cute. I just about melted when I looked at him. That blond hair and those blue eyes were so dreamy. I could picture myself taking him in my arms and kissing him.

Alex Fleming smashed into me again. It was my fault this time though. I hadn't been paying attention.

"Brewer! Get your head out of you ass son! Come on!"

"Sorry, Coach," I said.

I tried to push Casper out of my mind. I had to concentrate on practice. I wasn't very successful, however. He was never far from my thoughts.

Casper

I closed my locker and looked around. I knew they'd be after me. I'd escaped from the terrible trio the night before and I knew that would only make them that much more determined to get their hands on me. I'd somehow managed to stay out of their way all day, but I knew the odds of escaping were slim.

Instead of walking out the front entrance the way I usually did, I headed for the back, the one next to the gym and the parking lot. I didn't like to go that way because I had to pass through some areas outside where there weren't many people. There was safety in numbers. If the terrible trio were waiting to ambush me, however, they'd probably be waiting out front. It was a calculated risk.

I made it out the doors. There was no sign of Brent, George, or Jimmy. I smiled at the thought that they were probably waiting out front. I knew they'd get me eventually, but at least I'd have this little victory.

I was wrong. There would be no little victory. I was just passing the gym when I saw George running up behind me. I'd been spotted. I accelerated into a full run, flying across the grass. All I had going for me was speed. My only hope was to outrun him. That hope was in vain, however. As I dashed past the corner of the gym someone stuck his foot out and I went crashing to the ground, scraping my forearms on the grass. Jimmy grabbed me by the collar and pulled me to my feet.

"Well look. It's Casper, The Friendly Runt. Out for a little run, Casper?"

George caught up with us and each of them grabbed one of my arms. They pulled me behind the gym. I struggled against them, but it was useless. I had no chance at all against their powerful muscles. They dragged me over to Brent, who was standing there punching the palm of his hand with his fist.

"Thought you could outsmart us, huh Casper?" said Brent smiling. It wasn't a nice smile at all.

The three of them stood around me in a circle, glaring, just daring me to do anything to get away.

"You're so pathetic," said Jimmy. "If I was you, I'd kill myself."

I tried not to let on that his words hurt me, but they did.

"You're such a fucking little queer," said George, smacking me hard in the back of the head.

"I'm not a queer," I said quietly.

"Of course you are," said Jimmy, shoving me toward Brent. Brent shoved me toward George and that started a game of "Shove Casper." It was a game I didn't like at all. I hated those guys. I hated the way they picked on everyone.

"Get off me!" I yelled. "Get the fuck off me!" I was screaming at them.

George backhanded me in the mouth. It hurt, it hurt a lot.

"Shut up you little faggot!"

"I'm not a faggot," I said through clinched teeth.

"Yeah right," said Brent. "Your brother says you are. He told us what you do for him."

I was on the verge of bawling. It was too much to take. I couldn't handle it.

"Why don't you do that for me? Huh Casper?" said Jimmy.

He had the same look in his eyes that I saw in my brother's when he was in that mood, that mood that terrified me more than any other. Jimmy reached down and unfastened his belt. Brent and George tried to force me to my knees. I went out of my mind screaming and kicking, but they were too strong for me. I couldn't get away. I couldn't keep them from forcing me to my knees. They slugged me, but I kept right on screaming and fighting. I was hysterical.

"Get off him."

I looked up. I knew that voice. He was standing there, not five feet away. It was Brendan Brewer. The terrible trio backed away, leaving me standing on my knees in the grass, crying and bleeding. I felt embarrassed and humiliated to have Brendan see me that way, but at the same time I wanted to clasp my arms around his knees and thank him for saving me. I looked into Brendan's eyes, they were aflame with anger.

"If any of you so much as look at Casper cross-eyed again, I'll fuck you up so bad your mother's will cry when they see what I've done to you," said Brendan.

I could tell he meant it. The terrible trio could tell too. They didn't even offer to talk back to Brendan. There were three of them, and only one of him, but they didn't dare to even speak. I had no doubt that Brendan could have kicked all their asses at once if it came down to it.

"Now get out of here," he said. I don't think I'd ever seen Brent, George, and Jimmy run quite so fast before.

"You okay?" asked Brendan, once they'd gone. He extended his hand and pulled me to my feet without effort. He was so strong.

"Yeah," I said and started crying. I felt stupid for crying in front of him, but I couldn't help it.

"Hey, it's okay," said Brendan. "I won't let those guys hurt you again. They do anything to hurt you and you just tell me okay?"

"Okay," I said.

I was all shaky and kept crying.

"I'm so embarrassed," I said.

"About what?"

"About them beating me up."

"Hey, dude, there is nothing to be embarrassed about. You had three guys on you. Those aren't good odds for anyone."

"Seemed pretty good odds for you," I said.

"Well, that's a little different. They know I have big friends."

I smiled at him. He was being modest. He did have a lot of friends, and most of them were certainly big, but the terrible trio had run from him, not his friends.

"Hey, come on. I'll buy you some ice cream."

"You don't have to do that. You've done enough. Thanks for saving me from those guys."

"I want to, and you're welcome. You seem like a pretty cool guy to me and I'd like to get to know you better."

I wanted to start dancing right there on the grass. I couldn't believe that Brendan Brewer had just told me that he thought I was cool, and that he wanted to get to know me better. He was the most popular guy in school. Stacey would absolutely die when I told her.

We walked together to the *Dairy Queen* and he bought us each a huge banana split. I couldn't even remember the last time I'd had ice cream. It was the best thing I ever tasted.

"So what are you into Casper?"

"I like running."

"You must be tough then" said Brendan. "Coach makes us run before practice and it kills me."

I smiled when he said I was tough. No one had ever called me tough before. I knew I wasn't, but I liked Brendan calling me that.

"Being light helps," I said. "My legs don't have much weight to support, so I can run pretty fast. It comes in handy when George, Jimmy, and Brent are around."

"Yeah, I bet. I meant what I said about those guys. They bother you at all and you let me know. I'll take care of them for you. I'll have a little talk with them the next time I see them to make sure they understand."

"Thanks a lot, Brendan."

"No problem. No one should have to put up with shit like that, especially not a nice guy like you."

"Thanks." I was smiling from ear to ear.

We kept talking. I really liked Brendan. I think what I liked about him most of all is that he treated me as an equal. He didn't look down on me because of my height, or my clothes. He just treated me like a regular guy. Some kids from our school came in while we were sitting there and Brendan just kept right on talking to me. He didn't even pay them any attention. He made me feel special.

"You're really nice," I said.

"So are you."

"I can't believe you're talking to me."

"Why not?" asked Brendan. He was truly perplexed.

"Well, you're the most popular guy in school; you're the captain of the football team and all that. I'm just nobody."

"Hey, no one is nobody. Everyone is somebody. Yeah, I'm popular, and I'm captain, but I'm just a guy you know. It's not like I shit gold or something."

We both laughed. It was the most wonderful afternoon of my life. We sat and talked long after we'd devoured all the ice cream. For the first time in my life, I felt I had a real friend. Stacey was my friend of course, but that was different. She was a girl. Not that there is anything wrong with being a girl, but no guy had ever talked to me like Brendan. He acted like I was cool.

"Hey, how about I walk you home?" said Brendan.

I immediately grew afraid. I didn't want Brendan to see where I lived. I was ashamed of my home, and its horrible front yard. I was ashamed that I didn't have anything better.

"Thanks, but that's okay. I'll just walk home by myself."

"I'll see you tomorrow then," said Brendan. "At lunch?"

"Yeah, sure," I said. "Thanks for saving my ass, and for the ice cream."

"Don't mention it, Casper."

We got up and left, each going our separate ways. I had a smile on my face. I felt better about myself, about everything, than I had in a long time. For the first time ever, I actually looked forward to going to school the next day.

Brendan

I'd taken the first step, and it made me so nervous I thought I'd hurl. I had but-terflies in my stomach as I sat and talked with Casper as we had ice cream. I don't think that boy had any idea of how cute he was. He seemed totally unaware of his good looks. As we sat there, I wanted to reach out and take his hand, but I was afraid. Just asking him out for ice cream was a major step for me.

I stiffened for just a moment when some kids from school walked in, like I thought they'd know I was working up the courage to put the moves on Casper. I relaxed almost immediately, however. All we were doing was eating and talk-ing. It's not like I had my arm around him or anything. It did make me think twice about what I was doing. I'd decided to approach Casper because he seemed approachable. He seemed like he might be interested. I didn't really know much about him, so it was still a risk. My greatest fear was being outed. I could just imagine what would happen if word got out that I was gay. The school paper would probably run the headline BRENDAN BREWER IS A HOMO. Okay, maybe not, but whatever did happen would be just as bad, or worse.

As Casper and I parted, I felt a tug at my heart. I hadn't just approached him because I thought he might be safe. There was a lot more there. I felt something for Casper. I cared about him. I had a crush on him. I couldn't think of much besides being with him. I was scared, but I wanted to go on. In fact, I didn't see how I could do anything else besides proceed.

I made sure to sit near Casper every day at lunch. I tried not to be obvious about my interest in him, but I wanted to keep our relationship, such as it was, going. I had to keep from looking at him too much. When I looked at Casper, I felt a hunger within me. It was part emotional, part physical. I wanted to take Casper in my arms and hold him close. I wanted to kiss him, make love to him. It wasn't just sex either. Sure, I wanted sex, what boy didn't? But I wanted something more. I dreamed about just being with Casper, talking with him, laughing with him. I had it bad for him in every way imaginable.

I was terrified at the prospect, but I wanted to get closer to Casper. I knew what a dangerous risk that could be, but my heart, and my body, ached for him. I felt like I'd waited forever to be with another boy and I just couldn't wait another minute. I felt like I was going to explode.

Another dance was scheduled for Friday night and I wanted to go with Casper. I couldn't take him as my date of course, but I wanted him there so that we could talk and spend time together. If I could work up the courage, maybe I could even approach him after the dance. Maybe something would happen between us.

I caught up with Casper after school. I had a few minutes before football practice.

"Hey, uh, Casper, are you going to the dance on Friday?"

"Um, well, I don't really know. I hadn't thought about it much."

"I'd like you to go."

"Why?"

I practically froze. It was a lot harder approaching the subject that I'd thought, and that was saying something because I expected it to be hard. I should have just told him right then and there that I was interested in him, but I was too big of a chicken-shit. It was just too risky, too frightening. So instead, I lied to him.

"Well, uh, there's this girl. I really like her, but she's doesn't want to go out with me."

"I can't imagine any girl not wanting to go out with you," said Casper. I smiled.

"Well, uh, she seems to think I have a reputation. She doesn't want to go alone with me. I was thinking though, if we could double date, then maybe she'd go with me."

"I see."

"So would you like to go? I'd really appreciate it."

"I don't know who I'd take. I don't have a girl."

"How about Stacey? You were with her at the last dance. She your girl-friend?"

"Well, maybe. She's not my girlfriend. We're just friends."

I breathed a sigh of relief. I don't know what I would've done if Casper had told me that Stacey was his girlfriend. It would have broken my heart. As the words had come out of my mouth to ask him, I realized just how much it would hurt if she was his girl.

"Could you ask her?"

"I'll ask," said Casper, "Just for you." He smiled at me. It made my heart melt. I had it bad for that boy.

The dance was all I could think about that entire week. Casper told me the next day that he'd asked Stacey and they could go. I asked Jennifer Atkins out and she immediately said "yes." I felt kind of bad, like I was using her. I really wasn't interested in her. Then again, I wasn't interested in any of the girls that I dated. I just did it so no one would suspect I was gay. The girls I took out always seemed to have fun. I was always nice to them, and showed them a good time. I guess I did use them in a way, but it was just a date. It wasn't like I was promising to marry them or something.

Friday evening finally arrived. I picked up Jennifer, but was hardly aware of her presence. My thoughts were on Casper and what might happen after the dance. I wasn't exactly sure what I was going to do, but I wanted to let Casper know that I liked him, a lot. I didn't know if I could go through with it. I was so nervous I was actually shaking. Even Jennifer noticed that I was edgy.

We picked up Casper and Stacey at Stacey's house. Casper was looking very sharp. He was wearing the same clothes he did to the last dance. I didn't care what he wore. Casper was cute in anything. I realized as I looked at him that not only did I not care how he was dressed, I didn't even care what he looked like. I liked Casper for Casper, and not his looks. I was first drawn to him because he was cute, and possibly available, but my feelings had already grown past mere lust. Sure, the lust was still there, I was seventeen after all, but there was far more involved than there had been the first time I laid eyes on him.

It was only a short drive to the high school, but it gave the impression of a double date. I wanted to continue the impression that Jennifer wanted others close because of my "reputation." Actually, I didn't even have a reputation for pawing girls, although I'm sure a few did suspect I might be that kind of guy. Over the years I'd let rumors start, and grow. It helped me to remain hidden.

I felt kind of lousy for lying to Casper, but I was sure he would understand. The path I was treading was so terrifying that I had to take things one step at a time. If I didn't, I'd never make it. I wasn't so sure I was going to make it in any case. I'd had butterflies in my stomach many times in my life, but now I felt like I had pigeons or doves flying around in there. I was afraid I was going to be sick.

We hit the dance floor almost as soon as we got there. I loved to dance and it helped put me at ease. I tried to just lose myself in the movement, and the music. The dance was a familiar and comfortable environment for me. I was surrounded by friends and teammates. I was popular, even admired, and envied. It was my turf. Still, I wasn't completely at ease. I couldn't get my mind off Casper, or what I wanted from him. I guess I didn't really want to get my mind off him. I just wanted my nerves to calm down. I'd never been so nervous about anything in all my life.

"I'm really glad you asked me out," said Jennifer as we danced.

"Well, you seem like a fun girl."

"I can be a whole lot of fun, Brendan." She reached out and touched my chest as she said it. That, and her tone of voice, left no doubt as to her meaning. Suddenly, I was nervous for a whole new reason.

I looked into Jennifer's eyes and saw the look there that I'd come to recognize, and fear. I'd never been out with Jennifer before, but I'd seen that look in more than one girl's eyes. Some of the guys complained that girls never wanted to do anything, but I didn't have that problem. I wished I did. It was another way that I could be exposed. I never dated the same girl for very long because I was afraid she'd start talking about how I never tried anything with her. I generally didn't date any girl for more than two or three weeks. A month was the absolute cut off point. It was just too dangerous to go beyond that. They were usually happy with a kiss now and then, especially if it were deep and long. I didn't mind kissing girls. I liked to kiss. It was sexy. I was glad that I didn't have some kind of aversion to it; otherwise my life would've been much more difficult. Making out with girls was like camouflage, it kept my gayness well hidden.

I looked at Casper dancing with Stacey. I gazed at his beautiful red lips. I wanted to kiss him so bad I could taste him. My situation would have been funny if it weren't so frustrating. I was dancing with a girl that would let me kiss her any time I wanted. I had the feeling Jennifer would let me do anything I wanted, period. I didn't want anything with her, however. I wanted Casper. I wanted a boy who might not even be interested in boys. I wanted someone who might be disgusted by my desires. That thought made me more uneasy. I wasn't at all sure if I could let Casper know how I felt about him.

I gazed at Casper as I danced. I looked at him with longing. I felt something for him, and it felt a lot like love. I had a crush on him at the very least. I thought more about how I felt about Casper. Yes, it was love. I did love him. The more I thought about it, the more certain I became.

The next dance was a slow one and Jennifer pressed herself hard against me. I took her in my arms and held her close. I gazed at Casper yet more as I danced with Jennifer. He was so beautiful he made my heart ache. I fell into a daydream. I imagined that I was dancing with him instead of Jennifer. I imagined that he was pressing his firm little body against my own. The thoughts began to excite me. The bulge in my jeans made my arousal obvious. Jennifer looked into my eyes deeply, giving me the look that frightened me. She held my eyes with hers as she ran her hand over the front of my jeans. I closed my eyes. When I opened them again, she was still looking at me, still pressing her hand against the front of my jeans. She kept it there for a few more agonizing moments.

I swallowed hard and tried not to think about Casper anymore. Jennifer was getting the wrong idea about me. There would be no dating her for a month. I wasn't sure it would be safe to ever date her again. I wasn't even sure if it was safe to have this one date with her. I was afraid she was expecting a lot more from me than she was going to get. Any other boy would have been beside himself with excitement and lust. I felt faintly nauseated. I hoped that I could get through my night with Jennifer gracefully, without giving my secret away. Girls like her were dangerous.

My mind was only partly on my fear of Jennifer. It was much more on Casper. I kept stealing glances of him as we each danced with our girls. I was glad we were friends. He wouldn't think anything unusual about me looking at him since we were friends. I almost laughed at myself. I was planning on telling Casper how I felt about him after the dance, but I was still busy protecting my secret, as if I'd never reveal it to anyone. Old habits died hard. For a long time, I'd been hiding the real me. I'd never been sure that I'd ever reveal the real Brendan, that I'd ever let anyone see me as I truly was. I knew that my secret could destroy me.

I wondered how many boys I'd looked at with longing while trying desperately to hide what I was feeling inside. How many times had I gazed into another boy's eyes, hoping to find someone like me? My stomach churned. The day that I would reveal myself had come at last. Casper was the one. I'd show him the real me. I prayed that I was right about him. I prayed that his feelings were the same as my own. I don't think I'd ever been so terrified before in my entire life.

* * *

I breathed a heavy sigh of relief as I let Jennifer out at her house. I'd survived the evening without having to spend even a moment alone with her. I thanked God that Casper and Stacey were there. Without them, the situation would have been awkward. I'd have found myself in the position of having to explain why I didn't want to mess around with Jennifer. I know that's what she wanted. I could tell by the way she looked at me, and by the way she acted. She was pretty free with her hands, even with Casper and Stacey right there in the car. I don't know what I would've done if I was alone with her. I don't know how I'd have gotten out of that situation gracefully. I pushed it from my mind. There was no reason to think about it. I was safe.

I asked Casper to stay with me when I dropped Stacey off at her house. He seemed slightly uncomfortable with idea, although I'm not sure why. We drove around town while I worked up the courage to tell Casper that I liked him. The truth was, I loved him. I'd come to realize that my feelings for him were deeper than I thought. I didn't just have a crush on Casper. I wasn't just interested in getting into his pants. I felt something for him, and that something was love. He wasn't just another boy that I lusted after. He was far, far more.

Revealing my secret to Casper was about a million times harder than I thought it would be, and that was pretty amazing because it didn't seem possible that it could be harder than I thought. I must have started to tell him fifty times as we drove around, but I didn't have the balls to do it. Well, maybe it wasn't fifty times, but it sure felt like it. I kept edging the conversation in that direction, but it was just too hard to speak the words.

I pulled into the parking lot by the park. I'd practically run off the road a couple of times because I was so busy thinking about Casper, and trying to work up the courage to tell him what was on my mind. I thought it best to park the car. There were a lot of other kids parked there too. It was a hang out place for everyone on Friday and Saturday nights.

We sat and watched cars cruising by on the street. I knew just about everyone in those cars. It was a warm night, so I had the top down on the convertible and we could hear the radios in the passing cars and guys calling to each other. I didn't pay much attention to any of that. I was far too absorbed in what I had to tell Casper.

I was trembling and my voice shook a little. I'd never before experienced such nervousness. I wanted more than anything to just run away, but this was far too important to me. I knew I had to go through with what I'd planned.

Putting it off would only prolong the torment. Procrastinating would only serve to keep me isolated and alone. I turned to Casper, and looked into his eyes.

"Casper, I really like spending time with you." It wasn't quite what I'd meant to say, but it was a start. I wanted to be cool about the whole thing, but I knew that was beyond me. I'd just have to stumble through it.

"Spending time with you is really cool," said Casper. "You're the best!"

"You really mean that?"

"Yeah, of course I do. I've never really had anyone to do stuff with before, you know? I don't really have any friends, except Stacey, and it's different with her."

Casper's words were putting me at ease a bit. He obviously liked me. The expression on his face and the way his eyes lit up said even more than his words. I could tell that he meant what he said.

"I'm glad we've become friends," I said. "I hope we can become a lot closer friends." My words were filled with far more meaning than they seemed. I had a feeling that Casper wasn't getting that.

"That would be great," said Casper. There was a certain expectancy in his voice. He seemed to sense that I was going somewhere, but it was clear he didn't know where I was going at all.

I wanted to just take him in my arms, hold him close, and tell him I loved him. That was out of the question. Too many people could see us. Instead I moved a little closer to him. I ran my eyes over his body. Casper was small, compact, and firm. He was the cutest boy I'd ever seen in my life. I felt familiar urges and yearnings stir within me. It wasn't just lust I felt as I looked at Casper. I loved him. I was in love with him. I don't know how it had happened, but there it was. The love I felt fanned the flames of my passion into an inferno. I was trembling, with fear, love, and lust.

I wanted to scream and run away. What I was experiencing was nearly too intense to bear. I plunged ahead. I knew that if I stopped, I'd never be able to go on. If I even slowed down, I'd never again be able to work up the courage to approach another boy. Casper wasn't just any boy either. He was the one. I just knew it.

I ran my hand onto Casper's thigh and rubbed it back and forth. I was trembling, breathing hard. I think it would've been easier to jump to my death from a cliff. The amount of courage that it took to reach out and touch Casper was beyond belief. I didn't dare stop, or even pause. I ran my hand over the front of his jeans; touching him in a place I'd never touched another boy.

It was the biggest mistake of my entire life. Casper pushed me away with every ouch of force he could muster. He went nuts. He freaked out. He swung at me hard and fast with his fists, hitting me in the face and chest and stomach, anywhere and everywhere he could reach. He was screaming, yelling, shrieking, and crying. He was out of his mind with anger and fear. I could read both clearly in his eyes as he attacked me. He was like a cornered beast.

"Get off me! Get off me!" he shrieked. "Get off me you fucking faggot! Get off me!"

He clawed and climbed his way out of the car, punching and scratching and kicking me. He kept screaming at me in sheer anger and terror, calling me horrible names. His eyes were wild with terror, as if I were some crazed psycho trying to kill him. In moments he was out of the car, running as if for his life.

I sat there in an absolute daze. Everyone was staring at me. I hadn't paid them any attention until then. I was so shocked by Casper's reaction that I wasn't even aware of those around me. When I became aware, I wished I hadn't. I'd created quite a scene. I turned the key in the ignition and tore out of the parking lot. I couldn't stand everyone looking at me. I couldn't stand what they might be thinking.

I didn't drive far. I was too upset. I knew if I kept going I'd ram the car into a telephone pole, perhaps on purpose. I pulled the car onto a side street and parked. I sat there, crying, breathing so hard I was hyperventilating. I was shaking with fear. More thoughts were racing through my head than I could handle. People had seen Casper freak out in my car. People had heard him call me a fag, over and over. And Casper, in my worst nightmares I'd never dreamed he would react like that. I knew he might reject me. I knew he might be upset, call me a fag even, perhaps slug me, but I never expected him to totally freak out right there in my car. I don't think I'd have gotten a more violent reaction if I'd have pulled a knife on him and started slashing. I'd seen the look in his eyes. He looked like he feared for his life. He looked at me like I was going to rape and kill him. That look, I'd never forget it. It hurt me far more than his words, or the blows that he had rained down upon me.

I felt a trickle of blood running from the corner of my mouth. My chest and abdomen hurt in a few places. There was a dull ache in my groin. I'd been so shocked by Casper's outburst that I'd barely registered the blows, painful as they were. I guess I deserved what I got. I'd meant to tell him that I loved him, but instead I ended up groping him. How was he supposed to react to that? It was obvious now that he wasn't gay and I'd gone and felt him up in my car. I was such a fucking moron.

I broke down and cried, not just cried, bawled. I'd messed up everything, but the worst thing of all was knowing that Casper didn't love me. Hell, he hated me. The thing was, I still loved him. I couldn't stop loving him. I loved him more than anything and he hated me. I couldn't stand that. I couldn't take it. I closed my eyes, but all I could see was the look of sheer terror and hatred on Casper's face. His beautiful features were contorted by rage and fear and I'd done it, I'd caused it.

I bawled my eyes out. My life was over. After all these years I thought I'd found someone like me, but he was just like the rest. They'd all hate me if they knew. I was a fake. The Brendan Brewer that everyone saw each day was nothing but a fictional character. His popularity, all that he had, was just an illusion. I was nothing. All those girls that flirted with me, all those boys that patted me on the back and told me how awesome I was, they'd all hate me if they knew—all of them. And my parents, they were so proud of me, they were so proud because I was such a stud, because I was captain of the football team. They wouldn't be proud if they knew what I really was. They wouldn't be proud if they knew I was a fag.

I kept on crying, although I knew there was no use in crying about it. It was all over. Everyone in the park had heard Casper screaming at me, calling me a fag. By Monday morning it would be all over school, all over town. I was finished. I cried more. I knew what I had to do. There were no options left. I started the car. It was all over. I'd never live to be eighteen.

Casper

"Get off me! Get off me! Get off me you fucking faggot! Get off me!" I screamed hysterically.

I punched and kicked at Brendan, fighting my way out of the car. I was terrified, and all the more so because I wasn't expecting that from him. I never thought he'd be like my brother. I never suspected that he was one of *those*. I was shaking with terror as I jumped out of the car and bolted. Everyone was staring at me, but I didn't care. Brendan was the faggot. He was the one who put his hand on my leg and tried to feel me up. I didn't care if everyone stared at me or not. I was glad they were there. Who knows what would have happened if I was alone somewhere with Brendan? He didn't try to stop me as I fled from the car. If we'd been alone, I'm sure things would've been different. God only knows what he would've done to me.

I ran and ran and kept running. I was pretty sure that Brendan wasn't following me, but I ran anyway. I ran all the way to the cemetery and took refuge in its comforting darkness and solitude. I collapsed on a stone bench, my heart pounding in my chest like it wanted out, my breath coming in gasps. Tears flowed from my eyes. I sobbed. My whole body shook with fear.

It wouldn't have been as bad if I'd seen it coming. It wouldn't have shaken me up so much if I'd suspected it. I had no clue, however. It blind-sided me completely. I thought Brendan liked me. I thought we were becoming friends. I was wrong. All that time he'd just been getting close to me, waiting his chance. All that time he'd just been working up to what he really wanted. He made my skin crawl.

"Fucking faggot," I said to myself. "Molester."

That's all he was, a molester, just like my brother. How could I have been so taken in by him? How could I have been so stupid? I felt like a fool as I thought about it. What else could Brendan Brewer have wanted from me? Why else would the star of the football team hang out with the smallest, poorest, most pathetic boy in school? He probably thought he could do whatever he wanted with me and I wouldn't say anything because he could snap me like a twig.

I couldn't stop shaking. I kept thinking about what he could have done to me. If he'd got me somewhere alone, he could've raped me, killed me. I'd gotten off lucky. All he'd managed was a quick grope. Brendan was way stronger than me. He could have made me do anything he wanted. He could've done anything to me he wanted. My stomach churned at the thought of what could have happened. I tried to calm myself, tell myself that I was safe, that I'd escaped.

I looked around me. The graveyard was lit by moonlight. Sometimes I envied the dead. They didn't have any worries or troubles. No one could hurt them. They didn't have to run. They didn't have to hide. Sometimes I wished I was dead. At that moment, I just wished I could stop shaking.

Life was cruel. I thought I'd been gaining a friend, the coolest I'd ever had in my life. Brendan Brewer himself was talking to me, doing things with me. I was practically cool just by association. People weren't bothering me as much anymore. The terrible trio was afraid to hurt me. Everything was looking up and then, BAM, life smashed me upside the head with a two by four. I hung my head and cried some more.

After a good long time, I stopped crying. I began to think about what might lie ahead. I began to think about what I was going to do about Brendan. I thought about telling everyone just what he'd tried with me. Who would believe me though? I'd just get laughed at. No one would believe that the quarterback of the football team had tried to molest me, me, Casper the Friendly Runt. I knew they'd just say I was crazy. They'd say that if Brendan was gay he could sure do a hell of a lot better than me. Hell, the whole thing seemed crazy to me. I wouldn't have believed it myself, but there was no denying it. Brendan's hand had been on my leg, he'd rubbed it, and he'd touched me…there.

I wondered what Brendan would do. If I told anyone about what he'd done, he'd kick my ass for sure. He'd hunt me down and beat me senseless. Brendan was strong. Those muscles of his weren't just for looks. He could rip me in half if he wanted. He wouldn't even have to touch me; he could get someone else to do it for him. Any of his football buddies would work me over with just one word from Brendan. He could get the terrible trio to do his dirty work too.

They'd be delighted to beat me into a bloody pulp. Any way I looked at it, I was screwed.

I waited until it got really late, and then made my way home. It was Friday night, or really Saturday morning I guess. At least I had the weekend before I had to go back to school and meet my fate. I wasn't so sure I was going to go back. I'd get my ass kicked for sure. I'd thought that my life couldn't possibly get any worse. I'd been wrong.

Brendan

"Hey, Brendan!"

My head snapped around. It was my best friend Brad. I turned away from him, shoved the car in gear. I had to get away. I couldn't let him stop me from doing what I had to do. I couldn't face him.

Brad wasn't going to be so easily left behind. He lunged for the car, caught my arm. Before I knew it he was inside sitting by me. I turned off the motor. I couldn't do what I wanted to do with him in the car.

"What's the matter with you?" said Brad. He was out of breath, he'd been running. I realized that he must have been in the park. He must've run after me on foot. I looked at him for a moment. His eyes were filled with concern. Mine were filled with tears, there was no hiding that.

"Leave me alone," I said. "Just get out of the car and leave me alone."

"And what are you going to do if I do that, Brendan? Huh?"

I looked at him. I couldn't bear to be near him. I just knew what he must think of me, how much he must hate me.

"I'm going to do what I have to do," I said flatly.

"You're scaring me, Brendan."

"Get out."

Brad dove for the keys and jerked them from the ignition. I lunged for them, but he jerked back and kept them out of reach. I was furious.

"Give me the fucking keys Brad or I'll..."

"You'll what? Huh? Are you going to hit me, Brendan?"

I was on the verge of doing just that. I was on the verge of attacking my best friend. There was something in his voice, however, some edge of concern, some memory of our friendship, that wouldn't allow me to attack him. My rage turned to pain. I broke down and bawled right in front of Brad. It must have shocked him. I'd never cried in front of him before. I didn't allow myself to cry.

Brad took me in his arms and held me while I cried. He didn't say anything. He just held me and petted my hair. I'd known Brad forever, but we'd never hugged, not once. It felt weird in a way, but it also felt right. I could feel Brad's friendship flowing through me. I could feel that he cared about me, even after what had just happened. It gave me hope.

I don't know how long I cried on his shoulder, several minutes at least. All the pain and fear came pouring out of me. It wasn't just the torment of the last few minutes; it was the anguish of a life-time. Finally I leaned back and rubbed the tears from my eyes.

"Brendan, what's wrong?" asked Brad quietly.

"You saw what happened, didn't you?"

"Well, yeah."

"Well you saw it, you heard it. Doesn't that explain it?"

"No, it doesn't, not really. I mean, that boy started screaming at you and shit, but…"

"You heard what he was saying didn't you?"

"Well, yeah. I heard, but…"

"I can just guess what everyone is saying about me."

"What do you mean?"

"Oh come on, Brad. He was calling me a fag."

"Yeah, so?"

"So?" I said, as if the answer was obvious.

"What? You think everyone is going to think you're a queer just because some boy was calling you a fag. Fuck Brendan, I've been called a fag plenty of times. It's just one of those things guys say when they get mad. It doesn't mean anything. Hell, everyone knows you're no queer Brendan, if that's what you're worried about."

I was balanced on the edge of a razor, so precisely positioned between two possibilities that I was trapped in indecision. Part of me wanted to tell Brad my secret, part of me wanted to bury it deeply and hold it as close as I ever had. We'd just shared one of those rare moments between friends when emotions and feelings that were long hidden, but forever there, were brought into the light of day for a moment to remind both of what was really between them. I looked into Brad's eyes. He was my oldest and dearest friend. We'd shared everything; except for that part of myself I could not share. Did I dare trust him now, at the very moment when I'd need his friendship the most? What if he turned on me, called me a fag as Casper had done, and bolted from me as if I were some kind of unspeakable monster?

The few moments before I spoke reached out into an eternity. I felt as if years, even millennia, were spinning past as I sat there, poised to dive in one direction or the other, indecisive, terrified beyond the ability to speak or move. I was perfectly balanced, unsure until the very last moment which direction I would chose.

I looked into Brad's eyes, searching, seeking a connection to all the years of our friendship. I sought out his heart, and his friendship.

"Brad, I..." The words I wanted to speak caught in my throat. I loved Brad, as a friend, I trusted him more than anyone, but when it came right down to it I couldn't open up to him. I just couldn't.

"Brad, we both know I'm no queer, but when someone starts saying shit like Casper did it doesn't matter if it's true or not. Being accused is just as bad as being queer."

I nearly started bawling again. The loneliness fell on me like a mountain, crushing me under its weight. I'd come so close to sharing the real me with Brad. I'd actually started to tell him, but I couldn't. I just didn't have the balls to reveal my true self to him and risk the loss of his friendship. I felt more alone at just that moment than I ever had in my entire life.

"Dude, you're overreacting. It's not all that bad."

"Come on, Brad, everyone in the parking lot was staring at me."

"Okay, they were all looking, but that doesn't mean they think you're a queer."

"Doesn't it?"

"Look Brendan, if you're so worried about it, let's do a little damage control. I'll spread some rumors about you and some girl. Or, better yet..." Brad laughed to himself. "Yeah, that's it; Kate Beckner is over in the park right now. She's always had a thing for you. Fuck, if you snapped your fingers she'd get on her knees and dive straight for your zipper. Let's go back, you talk to Kate, make out with her or some shit like that, right in front of everyone. Or better yet, try somethin' serious right there in the park. I guarantee no one will even remember what that little shit said to you."

I wasn't sure, but it sounded like a reasonable plan. If I didn't do it, or something like it, I'd be up to my ass in rumors Monday morning at school.

The only way to fight it was to start more rumors that would make everyone
forget about the first ones.

I drove Brad back to the park. I got out and leaned against the car. I felt like
everyone was staring at me. I was shaking. Kate was there all right, standing
with some other girls, and a couple of guys. I wandered over in her direction.
Her eyes latched onto me. She devoured me with those eyes. I let her.

"Hey, Kate."

"Hi, Brendan." I could practically feel her ripping off my shirt with her
eyes. I was playing with fire.

"What was up with that kid?" asked Eric.

"He your new boyfriend or something Brewer?" asked Scott, and then
laughed.

"I didn't know you were funny," I said, not cracking so much as a smile. I
looked Scott up and down, like I was considering kicking his ass all over the
parking lot. I was. He stopped laughing fast enough.

"Ah, you know Brendan's no fag," said Eric.

"Yeah, fags don't do this," I said, grabbing Kate and giving her the most passionate kiss of her life. Eric and Scott started whooping and soon everyone was
looking at us.

I pulled my lips from Kate's. She looked like she was about to faint. I think
I shocked the hell out of her. She was smiling, though, and I hadn't failed to
notice her hand wandering down onto my butt as we kissed. No one else had
failed to notice it either.

"You need a ride home, Kate?" I asked.

For an answer, she grabbed my arm and pulled me toward my car. We were
giving birth to a dozen rumors at least, all of them the kind that would make
everyone think I was just as girl-crazy as my buddies, and far more successful
at bagging them.

Kate slid over next to me as we pulled out of the parking lot. Eyes followed
us as I drove the convertible down the street. Brad was right; it was just the
thing to make everyone forget about the whole scene with Casper. It would
cover my ass nicely, and make Casper look like a little freak. I felt guilty about
that. I didn't want to hurt Casper. I loved him. I was in love with him. But what
could I do? I had too much to lose if I didn't crush the rumors that I was gay
before they had a chance to get started. Besides, Casper wasn't likely to have
anything to do with me after what had passed between us. I'd seen that look in
his eye. He was terrified. He looked at me like I was going to rape and murder

him. That look shook me to my very soul. No doubt he hated me now. That didn't change the way I felt about him, however. I still loved him. I didn't know if anything could ever change that.

Kate wasn't wasting any time. She cuddled up against me and put her hand on my leg. It didn't surprise me. I knew that Brad was right about what he'd said about her. Kate had a reputation. Most of the stuff guys said in the locker room was bull-shit, but I knew for a fact that some of it was true. I'd been at the party where she went upstairs with three guys. I'd walked in on them by mistake. I was looking for the bathroom and instead I found Kate, on her knees with all three guys around her. After seeing that, I didn't doubt much of what was said about her. I didn't like calling a girl that, but Kate was a slut.

Kate rubbed my leg. She was getting me excited, even if she was a girl. I still had no interest in her, however. I drove around town a few times, making a big circle, passing the park so everyone could see Kate practically sitting in my lap. When I thought we'd been seen enough, I drove home and pulled up in front of the house. The lights were on.

"Shit, my parents are home," I said. I knew they'd be home, but I wanted Kate to think I didn't. I wanted her to think I'd planned to take her in and do the things she expected of me.

I looked at her like I was disappointed and upset that my plans were ruined. It wasn't too hard to look upset. I was upset about a lot of things. I wasn't feeling very good about using Kate like that either. She had a reputation, but she was still a person. She didn't deserve to be used.

"Ah, this isn't right away. I can't use you like this," I said out loud. I hadn't really meant to say that. I quickly thought up lies for cover.

"What do you mean?" asked Kate.

"I'm not looking for a girlfriend," I said. "I was just planning to…"

Kate didn't look too upset, hell, she didn't look upset at all.

"I didn't think you were looking for a girlfriend, Brendan. I'm not looking for a boyfriend either. I'm just looking for some fun." She rubbed my jeans some more, right where it counted. I was getting excited, and uncomfortable.

"We don't have to go in," she said. "We can do something right here in the car." She started unfastening my belt. I stopped her.

"Are you crazy? My parents are right inside!"

"Then let's go somewhere. There are lots of places. I'll show you."

"I, uh, can't…"

I thought about telling her my parents expected me home, but I'll already acted like I was surprised they weren't gone. I thought about telling her I was going with someone already, but how could I explain kissing her in the park?

"Why not?"

I was really sweating it. I was in a bad situation and I needed out.

"I'm not feeling very good." Now there was the truth. "I feel like I'm gonna hurl." From the way I felt just then, I'm sure I did look like I was about to blow chunks. I was feeling sick, but not in the way I was explaining to Kate. "Mind if I just drive you home? I'm sorry about this."

"It's okay, Brendan. We'll get together some other time, soon." She kissed my cheek and ran her hands all over my chest. Her hands wandered a lot as I drove her home. I was glad to get her out of the car.

Casper

I woke up on the stone bench. I was shivering and damp with morning dew. My hair stuck to my face and felt oily. I sat up and rubbed my arms, trying to get some feeling of warmth back in them. My side hurt where I'd slept curled up on the bench. My neck was stiff and popped like crazy when I twisted it. I was damp, and cold, and hungry, but that wasn't the worst of my problems. My first lucid thought was of Brendan, and what he'd tried to do to me. The betrayal was too much to bear. I bowed my head and cried.

I hurt so bad inside I thought I'd die. I'm not talking about physical pain or hunger; I'm talking about the hurt I felt because of Brendan. My life sucked. I was poor, unpopular, weak, puny, and pathetic. The only thing I had going for me was Brendan. When he'd started spending time with me, it made me feel like I was somebody, like I wasn't such a total loser after all. If a guy like Brendan Brewer, captain of the football team and all that, thought I was cool enough to hang with, then there must be something to it.

Every morning when I got up, I had Brendan to look forward to. I hadn't known him long, but he was the one thing in my life I valued. He was the one thing about my life that didn't suck ass. My mom was dead, my dad didn't care about me, and my brother beat me, and worse. Being buds with Brendan Brewer was the one thing I had to hold onto. I didn't know how I'd made it before he came along, and now, before we'd barely got started, he was gone. Worse than that, it had all been a fake. Brendan didn't think I was cool. He didn't like me. He just wanted to use me. He was a fucking pervert and he tried to molest me. I was nothing to him.

I sat there and cried for a good, long while. As I was doing so, one thought came to my mind that made me feel just a bit better. There was something else in my life that didn't totally suck—Stacey. She was my friend, a real friend. She

63

cared about me. She was the only one, but she cared about me. One was a whole lot better than zero when it came to that.

I rubbed the tears out of my eyes and walked home. I entered cautiously, but I knew I was safe. It was about ten on Saturday morning and both Dad and Jason would still be asleep. Dad didn't usually get up before noon on Saturdays and it was a safe bet that Jason would sleep until at least two in the afternoon.

I walked into the bathroom and pulled off all my clothes. I turned on the water and stepped under the warm spray. It felt better than anything. The cold that had seeped into my bones began to leave. I soaped myself up as the hot water beat down on me, easing the tension in my shoulders, bringing me back to life.

I thought about what Brendan had tried to do to me. I thought about his hand on my leg, and the way he groped me. I started to get excited standing there in the shower, thinking about what Brendan had done. If felt good being excited, but it disgusted and scared me. I was afraid that the things Jason had done to me were making me like him, and now Brendan was doing it to me too. I quickly turned off the water and got out.

I dried off, feeling clean and warm. My clothes were still a bit damp, and a little smelly, as I put them on, but not too bad. I guess I should say Stacey's brother's clothes; I was still wearing the ones I'd borrowed for the dance. I was clean anyway, and my hair wasn't oily anymore. I combed my hair in the mirror, making myself as presentable as possible. I was going to go and see Stacey. I had to return the clothes I was wearing and pick up my own. I also had to explain why I hadn't returned to her house after the dance. I wasn't sure what I was going to tell her about that. I didn't really want to admit what had happened. I was embarrassed and ashamed, even though I hadn't done anything wrong.

* * *

"What happened to you last night?" asked Stacey as soon as she opened the door.

I stood there in my borrowed clothes, wanting to tell her everything, willing to tell her nothing. It was too humiliating. My lower lip began to tremble. I bit it to keep it still. I clinched my fists trying very hard not to cry. Tears welled up in my eyes.

"Oh Casper," said Stacey hugging me. "What happened?"

She pulled me inside and took me up to her room. I sat on the edge of her bed, staring out into space. Stacey looked at me with concern. I was fighting as hard as I could manage to keep back my tears. Her sympathy made it hard not to cry. I'd planned to pretend that everything was cool, but when I heard her sympathetic voice, I cracked. There was something in her soft voice, something that reminded me of my mom.

"Casper, what's wrong?"

I looked at her, the tears streaming from my eyes. I was so embarrassed, so humiliated.

"I can't tell you."

"You can tell me anything, Casper, you know that."

"No, there are some things you don't want to hear, some things you can't."

"Casper," she said, sitting by me and taking my hands in hers "I do want to hear, tell me."

"You'll think I'm nasty. You'll think I'm a pervert. You won't be my friend anymore." I broke down and cried in front of her. Stacey took me in her arms and held me as I cried. It made me cry even more. My mom used to hold me like that when I was upset.

"Brendan…" I said, between sobs "after the dance….he…." I cried even harder.

"He didn't hit you did he?" asked Stacey confused. She was no doubt remembering my bruises.

"No."

"I didn't think he'd do something like that."

"Worse," I said. "Much worse."

"Tell me," said Stacey. She was seriously concerned. I could tell I was scaring her.

"We were in his car, in the park. He…." I had trouble getting the words out. It was so hard. Even if I hadn't been crying, it would still have been hard. "I thought…he was my friend. I…thought he liked me. But he was just….using me. He…" I broke down and cried even harder than before. Stacey did her best to comfort me.

"You're okay, Casper. I'm here. Tell me what happened."

"He put his hand on my leg," I said, tears still flowing from my eyes. I looked at Stacey. "He rubbed my leg." I could see the horror began to rise in her eyes. "He…he grabbed me…he tried to…" I cried some more.

"Casper, are you sure?" asked Stacey. She looked like she just couldn't believe what I was telling her. I became angry.

"You think I'm making this up?!"

"No. No, Casper. It's just…it's just hard to believe. Brendan Brewer?"

"Yes, Brendan Brewer. Brendan Brewer molested me," I said flatly. Tears were still in my eyes, but I wasn't crying. I hated him.

Stacey became very angry. I half expected smoke to come from her ears.

"That bastard! That fucking bastard! The next time I see him, I'm kicking him right in the balls! Oh, Casper, I'm so sorry."

I could read the anger in her eyes, the pity, and the horror. She really hated Brendan just then. She was frightfully angry. I wondered about what she thought of me though. I knew I must disgust her.

"You think I'm nasty don't you?" I asked.

"Why would I think that, Casper?"

"Because I…because he…"

"Casper. There is nothing wrong with you. I don't think you're nasty. I think you are sweet, and kind, and wonderful. You didn't do anything wrong. You didn't cause this to happen. Brendan did it. He tried to take advantage of you. That fucking bastard!"

I told Stacey the whole story. She knew parts of it. She knew I'd been hanging out with Brendan, but I told her how nice he'd been to me, how good he made me feel. I told her all about what happened in the car. How Brendan touched me. How I fought my way out and ran. Stacey kept taking me in her arms and holding me. Her eyes smoldered with hatred for Brendan. She switched back and forth between concern for me, and contempt for him.

I felt a lot better by the time I left. I'd told Stacey what had happened and she still liked me. Before I talked to her, I felt like maybe I'd done something to cause it, that maybe I'd brought what had happened on myself. I knew now that I hadn't. At least there was that. There was no changing what had happened, however. There was no undoing what had been done. Brendan had betrayed me in the worst way. The best part of my life was gone.

Brendan

I got in the shower as soon as I could get inside and get my clothes off. Kate's scent was still on me. It repulsed me. I hated having to put on an act for the sake of everyone else. I'd always hated it, but I had to do it, especially now, especially after what had happened with Casper. I needed to look like a straight boy now more than ever. I had to cover my tracks, make it look like I was as obsessed with girls as my team-mates.

I let the hot water flow over my muscles, relaxing them. I was tense. It had been a difficult night. I kept asking myself the same questions over and over. How could I have been so wrong about Casper? How could I possibly undo what I'd done? What would I do when Monday morning came and I had to face the rumors that were surely already circulating about me? I knew the little act I'd put on with Kate would quash most of the rumors about what had happened between me and Casper, but I still worried that it wouldn't get rid of them all. Any doubt in the minds of my classmates was dangerous. I felt my mask slipping and it terrified me.

One miscalculation, one fuck-up, and my life was turned upside down. I felt like I didn't even know which way was up. In one swift move I'd managed to unmask myself, to one boy at least, and destroy what I had going with Casper.

I closed my eyes, trying to forget the look of horror and betrayal on his face. I couldn't get it out of my mind. It was etched there—permanently. As frightened as I was, knowing what I'd done to Casper was the worst of it all. He'd scrambled from the car as if I was some kind of axe murderer. He was terrified and hurt. I didn't want to hurt him. I didn't want to hurt him at all. I loved him, and I wanted him to love me.

Any possibility of a relationship with Casper was destroyed. It was beyond clear that he didn't want to have anything to do with me. I'd dreamed of holding him close and kissing him. I knew now how that would repulse and disgust him. It had taken a long time for me to accept what I was. It had taken a long time for me to feel good about myself, and now even that was slipping. If Casper was so disgusted by my advance, then maybe there was something wrong with me after all.

I let the water beat down on my muscles. I stuck my head under the shower and just let the water fall on me. Why did my life have to be so fucking complicated? Why couldn't I just be open about who and what I was? Why couldn't I just flirt with boys in the halls at school and have a boyfriend and have everyone not think a thing about it? Why was the world such a screwed up place? Why was being gay such a big fucking deal?

I got out of the shower, dried off, and slipped on some boxers. I lay back on my bed, my hands behind my head, staring at the ceiling. Images of the night haunted me like ghosts, but eventually I managed to fall asleep.

* * *

I walked into school with tremendous dread. I had no idea what awaited me there. I half expected everyone to start pointing and yelling "fag." It was oddly normal, however. No one said anything about what had happened in the park on Friday night. I even ran across a couple of people that I knew were there, and they looked like they didn't think a thing about it. It was like it hadn't happened at all. I was surprised, and relieved.

Between second and third period I met Brad in the hall. He pulled me aside so he could talk to me in private.

"How's it going, Brendan?"

"Pretty good really. No one has said anything to me about what happened."

"I told you."

"You heard anyone saying anything about me and Casper?"

"All I've heard is people talking about you and Kate. There is a rumor that you fucked her on the football field."

I nearly laughed out loud, with relief and at the absurdity of the rumor.

"Maybe it's going to be okay," I said.

"Of course it is. I told you dumb ass, every guy gets called "fag" by someone, sometime or other. It don't mean shit. It really doesn't mean anything coming from that little piss ant. I don't even know why you hung around with him anyway. What did you do that got him so pissed? You never told me."

Luckily, the bell rang and saved me the trouble of making up a lie. I could hardly tell Brad that Casper got mad because I ran my hand up his leg and felt him up.

I hurried to class, relieved that my life might not be over after all. There was still Casper to deal with, however. The worst of the whole situation was still there. I'd hurt him and I didn't know how to make it right. Knowing I'd caused him pain was even worse than living in fear that I'd be marked as a fag.

Casper and I crossed paths after third period. I met him in the hall. His eyes were smoldering when he looked at me. I wanted to tell him how sorry I was, but I knew I'd likely get a fist in the face for my trouble. I knew for sure Casper would make another scene. I didn't want that. I'd gotten off easy after what had happened on Friday. My luck wouldn't hold if there was another scene with Casper. I was afraid of him.

The anger in his eyes wasn't the worst of it. What really hit me was the pain and fear. He was hurt, hurt bad. He looked at me like I'd betrayed him. That look was like a dagger in my gut, twisting and turning while I writhed in agony. I deserved it, every bit of it.

I think the fear was what hit me the hardest. Casper was afraid of me, that much was certain. He unconsciously shrank away from me, even surrounded by dozens of others in the hallway. He was afraid I'd hurt him, that I'd try something with him again. I can't describe how much it pained me to see him fear me like that. He looked like he was afraid I'd attack him. It made me feel about two inches tall.

In mere moments he was gone, but the pain remained. How had I managed to screw things up so badly so fast? The one person that I loved the most was the one person who hated me the most. I didn't know how long I could go on like that.

Lunch was the worst. I'd been sitting with Casper and Stacey for several days, but I sure couldn't do that anymore. I stiffened as I passed their table. Out of the corner of my eye I could see Casper frown, and Stacey glare at me. It made me feel like a rat. I was a rat, worse than a rat. I joined my teammates at a table about as far away from Casper as I could manage, but I knew he was there, afraid of me, hating me. My friends laughed and joked with me as always, but nothing was funny anymore. All the joy had been sucked out of my life. I pretended that nothing was wrong. I laughed. I joked with my friends, but I was crying on the inside. My life was over.

Casper

I'd been trying to avoid Brendan, but I passed him in the hall just before fourth period. The hair on the back of my neck stood on end as I neared him. He looked so handsome, so clean cut and nice. It seemed impossible that he was the same guy who molested me. He looked so innocent, but God only knows what he would have done if I hadn't gotten away. I was glad we were in a crowded hallway. I knew he wouldn't hurt me there.

I lived in fear. I had not told anyone what had happened besides Stacey, and I'd made her promise not to tell anyone, but I was still afraid Brendan would come after me, him or his buddies. I knew if I talked, he'd beat me worse than I'd ever been beaten before. I knew he'd make me pay if I told what he'd done to me. I wasn't going to tell. Maybe I should have, but it just wasn't worth it. No one would believe me anyway. Brendan was like a god at school. I was nothing.

I wondered if he'd tried the same thing with other boys. He probably had. He'd tried it with me, so he'd probably done it before. He probably did it a lot. Who knew how many boys he'd taken advantage of, the mere thought made me sick. I wondered if I shouldn't come forward and tell one of the school counselors or teachers what he'd done. If he was doing to other boys what he'd tried to do to me, then someone needed to do something about it.

I knew they wouldn't believe me. Then again, maybe other boys had reported him too. If enough did it, then someone would have to believe it. Then again, maybe I was the first. If that were so, then it was less likely they'd believe me. I thought that maybe I should still tell. Even if no one believed me, maybe they'd believe the next boy who reported him. Guys like him needed to be stopped.

My thoughts were brave, but I was not. I knew I should say something, but I just couldn't do it. It was too frightening, too humiliating. I knew I should report Brendan anyway, but I just didn't have the balls to do it. I felt like a coward. I just couldn't summon the courage to report him, not yet.

I wasn't going to tell, but I was still scared. I was afraid he'd rough me up just to give me a little taste of what would happen if I did talk. I was screwed. Brendan had all the power. One word from him and I'd be dead meat. I was sorry our paths had ever crossed. I never once guessed that I was in such danger hanging out with him, but then again, I never suspected that he was a disgusting perv.

Brendan

I walked to my convertible after football practice. I knew I was in for it before I even got close. Stacey was standing there waiting on me, her arms crossed, her expression angry and determined. I swallowed hard as I drew near, looking around to see if there was anyone else around. Luckily, we were alone.

"What kind of sick monster are you?"

"I can explain," I said.

"Save it! Casper told me what you did. There is no explanation for that. How could you do that to that sweet boy? You make me sick."

"I didn't mean…"

"I'm warning you. You stay away from Casper. You don't go near him. You don't touch him. You don't even talk to him. If you try what you did again so help me I'll make you wish you weren't born."

"Just let me…"

"Your little secret is safe, Brendan. I don't know why, but Casper hasn't told anyone what you tried to do to him. If I was him I'd have gone straight to the police. He made me promise not to tell either, and I'll keep my word, unless you try something with him again. You touch one hair on his head and I'll tell everyone."

Stacey was really scaring me. My greatest fear was being found out. I lived in terror of my team-mates and friends discovering I was gay. What Stacey was threatening was even worse. I could end up in jail. If only I could get her to listen to me, then she'd understand, but she wasn't having any of that.

"Please Stacey, I'm begging you. Please let me explain."

"I don't want to hear anything you have to say. I can hardly stand being near you. You are the worst kind of filth. It's one thing to be gay, Brendan; it's another trying to force yourself on an innocent boy like Casper. Remember what I said, stay away from him or you're finished."

With that she was gone. I hadn't been able to explain anything to her. She hadn't given me the chance. I guess I couldn't blame her. In her eyes, I was little better than a rapist. I was a little surprised she hadn't gone to the authorities herself.

I got in my car and drove around town. I was so upset, I was practically in tears. How had everything gone so wrong? I was so stupid. Why hadn't I just told Casper how I felt about him instead of putting my hand on his leg like that? Why hadn't I told him I was in love with him instead of groping him? I was an idiot, a fucking idiot.

I felt like I was going to explode. I was scared. No one was talking about what had happened in the park. Stacey had told me that Casper was keeping his mouth shut, and that she would too, but how long would that last? How many days did I have before the end? If either Casper or Stacey told what they knew, I was finished, and there was nothing to stop them, nothing.

I drove around for hours until sunset came and my mind was numb from turning my problems over and over in my head. The strain was too much. I couldn't take it. Something had to give.

As I neared the far edge of town, I saw a blond boy walking down the sidewalk. I recognized him immediately, even in the growing darkness. It was Casper. He turned and saw me at almost the same moment I noticed him and bolted as if the hounds of hell were after him. He ran away from the street, toward the old town cemetery. I stopped the car and ran after him.

He was a lot faster than I anticipated. Casper could really move. My longer legs and all that running in football practice gave me the advantage. I slowly closed in on him.

"Casper! Wait! I just want to talk!" I yelled after him. He refused to listen and kept on running.

I knew I was scaring him, but I had no choice. I had to talk to him. I had to make him listen. I had to make him understand. I knew I was taking quite a chance. If he got away, he'd tell Stacey and she'd destroy me. Even if he didn't, I might not be able to make him see reason. I couldn't live with all that was hanging over my head. I couldn't live with knowing that Casper hated and feared me. I had to try, even if it cost me everything.

Even as I ran, I knew what I would do if I failed. I couldn't face what would happen. I couldn't take everyone knowing I was gay. I certainly couldn't take everyone thinking I'd tried to rape another boy. It didn't matter if it was true or not, just having everyone think that about me would be too much. If I failed, I'd make sure I didn't have to face any of it. I'd be dead by morning.

I caught up with Casper in the cemetery. I lunged for him and caught him around the knees. He went down hard but fought like a wildcat trying to free himself. I forced him onto his back. He kicked and screamed and beat on my chest with his fists. He was out of his mind with panic and sheer terror. I worried that he'd have some kind of seizure or something.

I clapped my hand over his mouth to silence his screams. The action struck fear into my heart. It made me feel like a rapist. It made me sick to my stomach. Casper kept fighting me for all he was worth, but I held him down. He couldn't get away.

"Casper, I just want to talk. I just want to explain. I'm not going to hurt you."

He didn't believe me. He kept struggling. Tears were flowing from his eyes. He was terrified. It made my heart ache. Finally, he stopped struggling. He knew he couldn't break free.

"If you promise not to scream, I'll take my hand off your mouth. I just want to talk, Casper."

After a few moments he nodded his head. The look in his eyes tore into my heart. It was a look of hate and fear, all the more devastating because it came from the one I loved.

"I'm not going to hurt you," I repeated. I wanted to get that point across to him. "I just want to talk, to explain. When we're done talking, you can go, no matter what."

I could tell he didn't really believe me, but he didn't have much choice in the matter. I was several times stronger than him.

"Friday night, in the park—I didn't mean to scare you. I wasn't going to hurt you, or do anything you didn't want. I know I shouldn't have touched you like that, but I thought, I thought…"

Tears welled up in my eyes and I started crying. It was too much to bear. The reality of my situation bore down upon me. It wasn't the fear of being exposed either, it was the knowledge that the boy I loved didn't love me back. I felt utterly alone.

"I'm so sorry, Casper. I'm so sorry I scared you like that. I didn't mean to. I'd never hurt you, Casper, never. I…" My sobs halted my voice yet again.

When I could once again see Casper through the tears, I saw a look of profound confusion on his face.

"I've never told anyone this, but…I'm gay, Casper. I've been so alone. All I want is someone to love, but I can't…" I cried some more. I was doing a really lousy job of telling him what I needed to, I kept getting sidetracked. Maybe there were just things in me that I needed to say to someone. Casper already hated me. He already knew about me. In that he was safe.

"I really, really like you Casper. I wasn't faking our friendship. I know you have no reason to believe me, but the times we spent together were the best."

Casper listened, but remained silent. I wished that he would say something, anything. His silence terrified me.

"I made a mistake, Casper. You see, I thought you were like me. I thought you liked boys too. I thought you were interested in me the way I was you. I love you, Casper. I'm in love with you. I'd never hurt you, not ever. I'm so sorry I upset you. I'm so sorry for what I did. I'd do anything to take it back, but I can't. I know you don't trust me. I don't blame you. But nothing would have happened, Casper. If you told me to stop, I would have stopped. I'm so sorry." I started crying once more.

Casper looked confused, but still suspicious. I think he suspected that I was playing some kind of sick game with him. It made my heart ache to know he didn't trust me.

"I don't know how to prove to you that I'm telling the truth. If I was what you think I am, I could have you right now. No one is around to help you. I could do whatever I wanted. But I'm not what you think I am, Casper, I'm not."

I released my grip on him, stood, and backed a couple of steps away.

"I told you the truth, Casper, about everything. It's up to you to believe me or not. I'm going to leave. I'm not going to hurt you. It would have been the same Friday night. I wouldn't have hurt you. I'd never hurt you. Please believe me. I'm sorry."

I turned and walked away, leaving him lying there on the grass. I didn't look back, I just walked. I was still crying. I was shaking. I knew my fate was in his hands.

I hadn't taken more than five steps when I felt something hard smash into the side of my face. I fell, clutching my jaw. I could feel it slick with blood.

"You fucking son of a bitch! What did you do to him!? What did you do to him!?"

It was Stacey. She'd come out of nowhere. I tried to get to my feet, but before I could do so, she swung the tree branch she was holding full force across my abdomen. I cried out in pain and doubled over, clutching my stomach.

"I didn't touch him!" I half yelled, half moaned.

"Bull shit!"

"Stacey! Stacey! Stop!" It was Casper. He came running up. "He didn't hurt me. He didn't do anything."

I started to get up, but Stacey speared me with her eyes.

"You stay right where you are or I'll take your fucking head off!"

I had no doubt she was serious. I did as I was told. She was sure a lot tougher than she looked.

"Are you okay, Casper? He didn't hurt you did he?"

"No. I told you he didn't. He just wanted to talk to me."

Stacey still eyed me suspiciously. I sat there on the grass, her prisoner.

"What about Friday night? Huh? What the fuck were you doing then?" she asked me with spite.

I looked at Casper. He didn't say anything. It was a nightmare. I had to explain everything to Stacey, just like I had to Casper. I had to speak the most difficult words of my life, again.

When I finished, I was bawling. I was sitting there on the grass bawling and bleeding. Everything was so fucked up. So much for the tough football quarterback, a girl had kicked my ass and a boy half my size held my fate in his hands.

"Get up."

I stood.

"Now leave," said Stacey.

I looked at Casper, wanting to tell him yet again how sorry I was about everything. I still didn't know if he really believed me or not. I turned away and limped to my car. A trickle of blood was running down the side of my face and I felt like someone had torn my guts out. As bad as the physical pain hurt, it was my heart that hurt the most.

Casper

I lay in bed, staring up at the ceiling. Jason was out carousing with friends, so I was safe for the moment. The events of the night were still buzzing through my head. I was lost, and confused. When Brendan had spotted me, I'd thought it was all over. I thought he was either going to beat me, or rape me, or both. He had done neither, however, and he'd told me things that made my head spin.

I wasn't quite sure what to believe, but some things he said made sense. If he wanted to hurt me, if he wanted to have me, he could have, right there in the cemetery. Stacey had shown up at the very end, but neither Brendan nor I knew that was going to happen. Brendan was a lot stronger than me, and we were alone, in an isolated place. He could have made me do anything. He could have done anything to me he wanted. But he didn't. He just said he was sorry for everything and walked away.

I was beginning to think that maybe I'd been wrong about a few things. On Friday night, I'd assumed he was going to do something terrible to me. I thought he was going to use me like my brother did sometimes. But that didn't really make sense. If that is what he was going to do, then why would he try it in a public park where there were lots of other people around? Why didn't he take me somewhere isolated where no one could hear me scream? It would have been easy enough. I'd have gone with him, and he knew that. And then, just tonight, he'd had me in such an isolated spot, but he didn't try anything. Sure, he'd chased me, knocked me down and held me, held his hand over my mouth, but he didn't hurt me. He didn't try anything with me. If he was after me on Friday night, why didn't he finish the job tonight?

I thought about Brendan's tears. Those were real tears. He wasn't just crying a little for effect, to gain my sympathy and make me believe he wasn't such a bad guy after all. He was bawling, that tough football jock was bawling his eyes out as he told me how sorry he was, and how it was all a big mistake. I heard the regret in his voice. I felt his pain. He wasn't faking.

But he was a fag. He'd admitted it to me, and to Stacey. He was just like my brother, a disgusting fag. He'd even told me how he wanted me. That was so fucking sick. He was a pervert, one of those guys that everyone hated.

He'd told me how he loved me. I didn't understand. Being a fag was all about sex. It was all about taking advantage of someone weaker. What was this about love? Fags didn't love, they just molested. And yet, when he said it, I felt that he meant it, he really meant it. I felt something in me too, and, for the first time ever, it didn't fill me with revulsion. I felt the same friendship I'd felt for Brendan before everything went wrong on Friday night, and I felt something more. I liked him. I really, really liked him. I...I couldn't even let myself think the words. It was too queer, too disgusting. It wasn't natural. My brother had done it to me. He'd made me feel things for Brendan that I shouldn't be feeling.

I was disgusted by the feelings rising within me, but there was something within them, something that I'd been needing and missing.

I tried to put the contradictions together. Brendan was gay. He was a fag. Fags were bad. They were evil and disgusting. They raped and abused. But Brendan had never hurt me. He'd put his hand on my leg, he'd rubbed it, he'd touched me. That was disgusting, but he hadn't hurt me. He hadn't tried to rape or abuse me. I'd thought that was within his mind, but I knew I was wrong. It didn't add up. Fags were bad, Brendan was a fag, but Brendan wasn't bad. Even as I thought about it, I grew uncomfortable calling Brendan a fag. It was such a harsh and hurtful word. It didn't seem to apply to him. Brendan was gay, but calling him a fag was wrong. I was beginning to wonder if I hadn't been wrong about a lot of things.

Brendan

"What the fuck happened to you?" asked Alec. We were standing in the school hallway before school. He was looking at the big bruise on the side of my face, and my black eye. A lot of people were looking. I had an even bigger bruise across my abs where Stacey and smacked me with a branch, but that one was hidden by my shirt.

"I got into a fight," I lied. I sure as hell wasn't going to tell Alec that I'd gotten my ass kicked by a girl. It wasn't just Alec either. A crowd had gathered.

"Who was it?" asked Dan. "He must have been big if he was able to do that to you."

"I know who it was." I turned at the sound of the voice. I froze in terror. It was Stacey. I was about to get caught in my lie, but worse, much worse. Stacey knew things that could destroy me, and she hated me for what I'd done to Casper. I turned to her, swallowed hard, and waited for my life to end.

"I was there. I saw it. Two football players from Calvert City were picking on my friend Casper. Brendan jumped on them both. You should see those guys. He really messed them up."

My huge sigh of relief was lost amid all the congratulations. I'd thought I was a goner. I looked into Stacey's eyes and she smiled at me. I smiled back. My chest suddenly felt warm. I felt warm all over. I felt like I was consumed by happiness. Stacey believed me. She believed I'd never meant to hurt Casper. She'd have told everything if she didn't. She believed me. More importantly, if she believed me, then Casper did too. I felt as if I'd received a stay of execution right as I was stepping up to the gallows.

I wanted to talk to Stacey just then, but there was no way. I was surrounded by people wanting a look at my bashed up face and wanting to know what had happened. Stacey stepped away and I stood there trapped in the crowd, making up answers to questions about the fight.

* * *

At lunch, I took a deep breath and walked to Casper's table. I sat down near him and Stacey. Casper looked at me oddly. He didn't smile, but he wasn't angry either. He looked more confused than anything. We didn't talk, but it was nice to be near him again. It hurt, too, however. I kept stealing glances of him and my heart ached for him. I didn't know how it had happened, but there was no doubt I was in love with him.

Why did I fall in love with this boy? Why not some guy on my team? Why not one of my friends? I knew lots of good looking boys. I knew all kinds of guys who were taller, better built, and even better looking in their way. Well, maybe not better looking. Casper was cute, he did have that. He wasn't very big, however. He was small, and frail, and downright puny. There was something about him, however, something that drew me to him. Maybe looks didn't matter or maybe I just liked his looks, even if they weren't what everyone else thought of as good looking. I sure thought he was good looking. The mere sight of him drove me crazy.

I smiled, but the smile soon faded from my lips. Casper didn't love me back. He didn't feel the same about me. Looking at me didn't drive him crazy. I was taller and way better built, but he wasn't interested in me, or any guy. Why did I have to fall for a straight boy? I felt like I was cursed, but there was no helping it. I loved him and I couldn't stop loving him.

I looked at him again and almost cried. Some people searched their entire lives for someone to love and never found them. My love was sitting right across the table from me, but he might as well have been a million miles away. Maybe it was better never finding someone, at least then you didn't have to look at them and know you could never have them.

* * *

Practice was nearly over when I looked up and noticed Casper sitting quietly in the stands. I didn't know how long he'd been there. He was watching me and my eyes met his. I smiled cautiously. He smiled back, but I couldn't tell what kind of smile it was. I couldn't tell if it was real, or just a polite smile, like you give to strangers sometimes.

As soon as practice was finished, I walked over to Casper. I walked slowly. I didn't know what was going to happen.

"Hey," I said.

"Hey."

"So what do you think?"

"About what?" asked Casper.

"About the team."

"Oh, they look good."

There was a pause, an uncomfortable silence. I don't think either of us knew quite what to say.

"Uh, listen…" said Casper. "I thought about what you said. I thought about it a lot. I don't know how comfortable I am with this whole gay thing, but I know you didn't mean to hurt me. I thought…Well, I thought you were going to do something really, really horrible to me, but I know I was wrong."

"I'm glad," I said. "I'm so sorry that I scared you. I didn't think it would freak you out like that. I guess I was just stupid, but…I don't know how to approach another guy you know? Well, maybe you don't, but you know what I mean. I'm just sorry I scared you, and I'm even sorrier it almost ruined our friendship. We are still friends…aren't we?"

I looked into Casper's eyes. I was afraid, afraid he'd tell me "no."

"Yeah, we're still friends. I've missed doing things with you. Not many people are nice to me, but you were. I liked that."

"Everyone should be nice to you, Casper. You're a great guy."

Casper shrugged with his eyebrows.

"I like spending time with you, Casper. I can be real with you. I don't have to be something I'm not. I don't have to act. I can just be me." Saying those words brought me back to my problem.

"You think you can handle me being gay?" I asked.

He didn't answer right away. He looked down at the ground, then back up at me.

"I'm pretty confused about the whole gay thing. I've always thought gay guys were…well, not nice. But you're nice. So…I don't know. It makes me kind of uncomfortable you know, but I still want to be friends. I mean, you've never said one thing about how poor I am, or the clothes I wear. You don't put me down like a lot of others. You see the same things, but you don't put me down because of it. You do that for me, so I can try to do the same about you being gay. At least I'll try."

"That's all I could ask, Casper," I said, and smiled. The smile faded from my lips. "Just one thing, Casper—please don't ever, ever tell anyone what you know. And tell Stacey not to tell either okay? If people found out I was gay, I don't know what would happen, but I think it would be pretty bad."

"Don't worry, Brendan. I'll never tell. Stacey won't either."

"So are you hungry? I'm starving. Want to go to Phil's and get something? I'm buying."

"Yeah," said Casper. "I'd like that. I'd like that a lot." He smiled at me. I smiled back.

Casper

Brendan dropped me off in front of the house. We'd gorged ourselves at Phil's. We'd laughed and talked and everything seemed like it did before the incident in the park. Well, things weren't quite the same. Brendan was gay—knowing that made things different and difficult.

"See you at school," said Brendan.

"Yeah, bye," I said.

Brendan drove off in his fancy convertible. I felt mildly ashamed of letting him see where I lived. He was a rich boy. I was dirt poor. I'd never let him take me home before. I never let anyone know where I lived, except Stacey. When he asked if he could drive me home, I said "yes" because we were friends. I knew Brendan was gay and I accepted him anyway. Being gay was just part of him. Being poor was just part of me. I let him take me home so he could better know the real me, just like I knew the real him.

He didn't say anything about the overgrown yard, or the dilapidated house. I knew he wouldn't. He was too polite. I knew what he must be thinking, but even that was okay. I knew Brendan would still like me. It made me feel good inside.

In the coming days, things went back to normal. Brendan and I hung out a lot. He was busy a lot of the time with football practice and games, but we still found time to do stuff together. I started going to the football games. It usually cost students $1.50, but Brendan got me a season pass for free. Knowing the quarterback had a few perks.

I liked to watched Brendan play. He was so strong and powerful, and yet graceful too. I marveled at the way he ran through the guys on the other team. He could weave in and out, just nicking past them as they all tried to take him down. Sometimes they did of course and I wondered how he could survive getting knocked around like that. Getting hit like that would have killed me. I was also amazed at how cool he could be passing the ball. I mean, there were all these guys just waiting to pounce on him. He knew he had only seconds to pick out a receiver and pass the ball, and yet he looked so calm and focused. He even looked like that when the guys from the other team were flinging themselves at him. There he would be, calmly passing the ball as if no one else was around, when three or four guys were a half second away from colliding with him. Brendan was amazing.

One Saturday, Brendan brought a picnic lunch and we ate in the park at a table. I'd been thinking a lot about Brendan and his secret. I'd been thinking a lot about me too.

"Brendan, what made you gay?" I asked him as we sat and ate. I knew my question wouldn't anger him and I was eager to hear his answer.

"Well," he said, chewing slowly, "nothing made me gay, at least nothing like you are thinking. At first, I wondered what made me gay too, so I did a lot of reading on it. Guys like me aren't made gay, we are born that way. It's genetic. My genes made me gay. It's something I got from my parents."

"You mean your parents are gay?" I asked. "How could they be? I mean, they had to have sex to have you."

Brendan laughed for a moment.

"My parents aren't gay. They could have been and still had me, but they aren't. When I say I got it from my parents, I mean I got it the same way I got my eye color, my hair color, and all that. There's some gene somewhere that made me gay. Just like there's some gene that made my eyes brown. Me being gay doesn't mean my parents are too. Just like me having brown eyes doesn't have to mean my parents both have brown eyes. In fact, neither of my parents does. My dad has green eyes, my mom blue, and yet mine are brown. It's in the genes, like me being gay."

It was all news to me. I always assumed something made boys gay, like what my brother did to me. It seemed there was another way.

"But most gay guys are made gay aren't they?"

"No, nothing can make someone gay, Casper. You either are, or you're not. Saying something made someone gay is like saying that someone is tall because they got bullied in grade school. It doesn't work that way."

"You sure?"

"I'm sure."

"But what if, what if a boy forced another boy to do something, couldn't that make him gay?"

"What boy are you talking about, the one forcing, or the one being forced?"

"Okay, let's say that a boy forced you to do something, like something sexual. Maybe he did it a few times. Wouldn't that make you gay?"

"No, it wouldn't," said Brendan. He looked at me concerned. "Casper, are you trying to tell me something? You can tell me anything you know."

"No, no, I'm just sayin'. I was just trying to understand. I'd heard that stuff could make you gay, especially stuff like being forced into doing something with another boy, that's all. I just wanted to know what made you gay," I lied coolly. I gave no outward sign, but inside my heart was racing. I knew I shouldn't have been so direct, but I had to know and who else could I ask? I'd been giving certain things a lot of thought and I was realizing that I'd been wrong about practically everything.

I steered the conversation away from gay issues. Brendan didn't usually like to talk about stuff like that anyway. He was always afraid someone would hear. Sometimes he did talk to me about it, but he always seemed afraid that I'd get mad, or that someone would find out. I started talking about football, and that got him going. I hardly listened; however, too much was running through my mind.

Brendan

I knew I should have been happy that things were back to normal with Casper, especially after how bad things had been, but I wasn't. Hanging out with Casper was great, but it was also a constant reminder of what I really wanted from him. Try as I might, I couldn't stop loving him. We were once again good friends, and that was cool, but it only served to make my problems worse. The more time I spent with Casper, the more fun I had with him, the more it made me want him as my boyfriend.

I tried to be happy with what I had, and not be unhappy about what I didn't have. I couldn't help but want more. Casper was a lonely boy. He needed a friend. He desperately needed someone to love him. I did love him, but he couldn't take the love I had for him. He couldn't accept it, because I was another boy. The world was so unfair. Why was I made to love someone that couldn't love me back? It shouldn't have been like that. If you loved someone, they should love you back, period.

Spending time with Casper was almost too painful to bear. I treasured every moment with him, and yet each of those moments tormented me. I began to wonder if maybe it wouldn't be better if we weren't friends. Maybe it would be better if we didn't see each other at all. The thought of that made a sob rise in my throat, however. The thought of not being with Casper was more than I could bear. I was trapped, cursed to have what I wanted always before me, but never being able to reach it.

Casper

I walked alone in the moonlight. My brother was prowling the house with that look in his eyes, so it wasn't safe there. I'd walk until he left, or finally went to sleep. I had a lot to think about anyway. Brendan and I had been spending a lot of time together. I loved being with Brendan. He made every moment special. It didn't even seem to matter what we did together, we just had fun. We'd only known each other for a few short weeks, but I felt like we'd been best friends forever.

I'd always dreamed about having a friend like that—all those years when I was alone. I hoped and prayed for someone like Brendan, and there he was. My friendship with him was causing me problems, however. I didn't even want to admit to myself what those problems were, but if what Brendan said was true, and I had no reason to doubt him, then maybe what I was feeling inside wasn't so bad after all.

I'd always heard the other boys at school say bad things about homosexuals. Being called a "fag" was about the worst insult ever. Guys like that were prissy and girl-like. They did disgusting things with each other. They were pillow-biters. Brendan was gay, however, and he was about as far from prissy and girl-like as anyone could get. He was tough, tough as nails, and he was strong. Brendan had muscles bulging out everywhere.

I'd seen him take pain too. I remembered last fall, when he broke his leg during a game. It was the only game I went to that year and I'd seen it. Not only that, I'd heard it. I was standing down close to the field because I felt uncomfortable sitting in the stands. I was there by myself and I blended in better standing around with everyone near the field. I was right there when he got tackled by practically the entire opposing team. I saw his leg bend back the wrong way, and I heard it snap. Brendan yelled when his leg broke, but after that, he didn't make a sound. I could see the pain in his face. I knew it had to hurt worse than anything, but he didn't let on. He just took the pain.

Brendan was nothing like what I'd heard about gay boys. He was strong and brave and tough. If he was gay, then maybe it wasn't so bad after all. Maybe a lot of the stuff I'd heard wasn't true. Maybe it wasn't so bad being gay.

I'd always believed what I'd heard because of my brother. He wasn't prissy or girl-like either, but he did things to me, things the other boys said fags do with each other. My brother was mean. He liked to hurt me. He liked to make me do things I didn't want to do. He used me, sexually, and so I'd thought that what I'd heard about gay guys was true. I thought all of them were sick bastards, when the truth was; it was just my brother that was sick. The more I thought about it, the more I doubted he was even gay. I'd seen him with girls. I'd found his girlie magazines. If he was gay, he wouldn't have been having sex with girls, or looking at magazines like that. My brother wasn't gay. He was just a bastard.

I had so many things to sort through, so many thoughts about Brendan, and me, and me and Brendan. I had a lot of feelings inside to sort out. It was a big job. In a way, I was faced with an entirely new world, a world where a lot of things I'd thought were true weren't, and a lot of things I didn't think were true were. I had to rethink everything.

It wasn't so bad, however, having to rethink everything that is. My new-found understanding put a lot of things in place. It changed a lot of things for the better. I'd been getting more and more worried about some parts of myself, about some things that I'd been feeling. I was beginning to realize that maybe I didn't need to worry about those things at all. What I'd thought was so bad wasn't really bad. I'd just thought it was because I didn't understand. Now that my eyes were opened, a whole new world was before me.

Brendan

Casper met me in the park on Saturday morning. I knew right from the beginning that it was going to be a great day. We hopped into my convertible and sped away. It was fall, but the day was bright and hot, Indian Summer my grandfather had called it. I looked beside me at Casper's blond hair flying in the wind. He was standing up, catching the breeze as he held tightly onto the windshield. He turned and smiled at me, then sat back down.

"The only thing I don't like about doin' that is getting bugs in my teeth," he said.

"I don't see any," I told him.

"Didn't happen this time, but I think I swallowed one." He laughed. "This sure is a nice car."

"Yeah, but it's not really mine. Well, it is, but my dad paid for it."

"Wow, I can't even imagine my dad giving me a car, even if we had money like that. Yours must love you a whole lot."

"Well, I guess he does. Yeah, he does, I just don't get to see him as much as I'd like. He's always working or something."

"At least he's nice to you when he is there."

"Your dad isn't?" It was a question, but I was pretty sure I already knew the answer.

"Not really. I mean, he's usually not too mean. It's just that he really doesn't want me around, me or my brother."

"You never talk about your brother much."

"No, I don't like him."

"Why not? I think it would be cool to have a brother."

"It isn't, believe me, at least not with a brother like mine."

90

I could tell that Casper didn't want to talk about it, so I didn't press him. It was too fine a day to ruin.

"Here we are," I said.

I pulled off into an abandoned drive at the edge of a large forest. There had been a house there once, but there was nothing left but the foundation. I wondered for a moment about who had lived there.

"So where are we going anyway?" asked Casper.

"I'm going to show you the old Highland farm. It's a long hike into the woods. Rumor is it's haunted."

"You're foolin' me," said Casper.

"No, I'm not really, but I've never seen a ghost there. I think you'll like it, it's cool."

I hefted a backpack out of the convertible and slipped a strap over my shoulder. We started walking toward the trees and were soon surrounded by them. The sounds of insects were everywhere and frogs croaked out their songs in the distance. I loved the forest.

It only took a few minutes to get hot and sweaty. I stopped, pulled off my shirt, and stuffed it through a loop in my backpack. Casper looked very hot, but he didn't take his shirt off. I was a little disappointed because I was curious to see what he looked like shirtless. I would have doffed my shirt if I was him. We'd barely started and he was already so sweaty that his shirt was clinging to his slim torso. It stuck to him so closely that it was almost like he wasn't wearing a shirt.

Casper was painfully thin, as if he didn't get enough to eat. That made me wonder if maybe he didn't get enough sometimes. It put a knot in my throat. I didn't like the thought of anyone doing without.

Despite being terribly thin, Casper was very good looking. His small body was firm and well proportioned. He was beautiful. I had to fight myself to keep from looking at him too much. Having him so near brought to the surface the same problem I experienced every time we were together. Casper and I had quickly become the best of friends, but I couldn't help but want more. Even after what had happened, I couldn't make myself not love him. I knew he couldn't love me back like I wanted. I tried not to feel as I did for him, but I couldn't help it. It was something in me and I couldn't get it out. It made my time with Casper a bittersweet pleasure. The more fun we had together, the more of a reminder it was that I could never have the boy of my dreams.

I thought that things would grow easier, that I'd get used to the idea that Casper could be my friend, but not my boyfriend. It was getting harder instead. The pain inside me increased with each passing day, and it was at its worst when I was with Casper. I wasn't about to avoid seeing him, however. He brought me my greatest pain, but also my greatest joy. I couldn't think of anything more wonderful than being with him.

"Hey, look at that!" said Casper, pointing off to the side.

I looked up in time to see three white tails disappearing into the distance. I'm sure Casper's shout ensured that that was the last we'd see of those deer, but we'd probably spooked them before that anyway. Casper was smiling, his eyes wide with wonder.

"Haven't seen many deer huh?" I asked.

"No, I've seen some just a couple of times, near the cemetery."

"There's lot of them out here, deer and all kinds of animals. There are even wild turkeys sometimes."

Casper looked about as if expecting to see something else interesting just then. I loved the way his eyes sparkled when he was curious about something. He looked at everything like he was seeing it for the first time ever. In many ways, he was very innocent.

"When we went to Tennessee, we saw big herds of buffalo," I said. "We even saw a couple of eagles at Land between the Lakes, and a rattlesnake. You ever been down there?" I asked.

"I've never been much of anywhere. I've never been very far outside of town."

"You're kidding right?" I said, smiling, thinking Casper was making some kind of joke.

"No," he said.

"Not even Paducah, or Madisonville, or Hopkinsville?"

"No, I never been anywhere like that." He was suddenly very quiet and the smile faded from his lips.

"Well, we'll have to go places then, lots of places. There's a lot to see outside of our dinky little town."

"I'd sure like that, but I bet I'd be scared in a big town."

"You'll be fine. We'll be together. There won't be anything to fear."

I liked the thought of taking Casper to see new things and new places. I knew he was poor and didn't have the opportunities that I did. I was happy to be able to share new things with him. Taking Casper to all the places I loved would be like getting to experience them for the first time all over again.

What was I thinking? I had to watch myself. I kept acting within my own mind as if Casper was my boyfriend and we were going to be living our whole lives together. I got lost in my own little fantasy world and then got hurt all over again when I woke up from it. It was kind of like having a wonderful dream only to wake up and find that I didn't have what I thought I did.

I shoved the unhappy thoughts out of the way, as if they were linemen standing between me and a touchdown. I wouldn't let them stop me. I was determined that today was going to be a great day and I wasn't going to let myself ruin it by crying over what I wanted and couldn't have. Instead, I'd focus on what I did have, and that was a very dear friend.

We walked on and on through the forest. It was as if it had no end. There was little breeze under the great canopy of leaves and sweat streamed down my torso. I didn't mind. I liked to sweat. There was something about it that made me feel vital and alive.

"You do know where we're going right? I mean, we're not going to get lost in here, are we?"

"Don't worry Casper. I know where we're going. We couldn't get lost in here if we tried. Even if we missed the farm and kept on going beyond it, we'd hit another road within an hour. There's a large stream to the south, and another road to the north. We're in a big square bordered by something in every direction. An hour's walk in any direction and we'd hit something that would get us home. And anyway, we aren't going to get lost. I've run around in these woods for years."

"That's good; we could get awfully hungry out here."

"I'm getting hungry right now. Why don't we stop and have some lunch?"

We halted under the shade of a giant oak tree. It looked like it had stood there for time out of mind. I couldn't even have begun to reach around it. I slipped the backpack off my shoulder and pulled out sandwiches, chips, soft drinks, and all kinds of snacks, including my favorite, chocolate chip cookies with pecans in them.

We sat on the grass and gorged ourselves. We sat in silence for several minutes. We were far too busy eating to talk. Instead we just enjoyed each other's company and the beauty of our surroundings. I loved being out in the woods. Sometimes I slipped off by myself and walked there alone under the great trees. It was so quiet and peaceful and the trees didn't care who I found attractive, or who I dreamed of at night. They weren't judgmental like people. I often felt that I wanted to live out there, just me and the trees, then I wouldn't have to pretend to be something I wasn't. I guess that wouldn't have been the best, however. There would have been no need to hide my attraction to other boys because there would've been no other boys. I didn't think I could handle that. I had way too much fun looking at them.

I realized that Casper was staring at me as I was lost in thought. I turned to him and smiled.

"What are you thinking?" I asked.

"Can I ask you a question?" he said.

"You just did," I teased "but sure, go ahead and ask." I was a little nervous. I was afraid he was going to ask me something about being gay.

"What's it like to be so handsome, so muscular, and so popular?"

"I'm not sure how to answer that," I said. I could feel myself turning a little red with embarrassment. I thought for a moment. "It's really cool, but I guess saying that makes me sound conceited, like I'm agreeing with you that I'm handsome and all that."

"Well, you are good looking, Brendan. Why is that so hard to admit?"

"You're even better looking," I told him. Casper blushed and ducked his head. "See. It's hard to take a compliment isn't it? You are the cutest boy I've ever seen in my life, Casper, so I think you should know what it's like to be handsome."

Casper could hardly look at me. I don't think I'd ever seen him so shy before. It made him cuter than ever.

"I never thought of myself as cute," he said.

"Well, I don't really think of myself as handsome. I just look the way I look is all. I mean, I know I'm not ugly, but I don't think I'm all that special looking, you know?"

"Yeah, I understand, but you are. Maybe it just takes someone else to see it. So, answer my question."

"Well, I guess it's cool, but it's kind of a pain too, looking like I do that is. I have a lot of girls looking at me all the time, and I don't really like it. It puts pressure on me. I feel like everyone knows they are looking and like I'm expected to do something about it. The thing is, I don't like girls. I mean, I'm not attracted to them, so having them think I'm good looking just causes trouble."

"I guess I can see that," said Casper. He seemed much more at ease talking about me being gay. That made me feel really good about myself. "How 'bout being built? I'd give anything to be built like you. Now don't get all modest on me, just answer."

I smiled. "Okay, it feels really good to be honest, but I'm not talking about looking built, I'm talking about feeling strong. I love to feel strong. It just makes me feel good about myself. I started working out because I wanted to look muscular, but I kept doing it because of the way it made me feel."

"I wish I could feel like that."

"You can, Casper."

"Yeah right! You know what everyone calls me, 'Casper The Friendly Runt.' I could never be built like you."

"But you could, Casper. You just have to work on it. Tell you what; if you're interested, I have a weight machine at home. I work out three times a week. You can come and work out with me."

"I'd be embarrassed."

"Why?"

"I couldn't lift anything I bet."

"It doesn't matter where you start Casper, just that you start. If you get into it and keep going, you'll get real big muscles. I think you look just fine like you are, but if you want to be stronger, then I can help you."

"I would like that."

"Then let's do it, Casper. It'll be fun."

"Yeah, right!"

"No really. I know it looks like work, and it kinda is, but when you get into it, it's enjoyable. I look forward to it. It will be twice as much fun with you there. So what do you say?"

"I say 'yes,'" he said.

"Great! Just you wait and see."

We gathered up the wrappers and bottles and stuffed it all in my backpack and headed out once more. Far to the southwest we could hear a distant rumbling that warned of bad weather, but in the forest it was still fine and hot. We followed a faint trail under the trees, probably made by passing deer and other animals. We passed through open meadows with great bunches of blackberry bushes. It was too late in the season for blackberries, however.

The rumble to the southwest grew ever nearer and within minutes seemed to be almost on top of us. The sky darkened and the wind got up. The warm, moist air in the woods was colliding with a mass of cold air heading our way. I knew that a terrific thunderstorm was bearing down upon us. We pushed on; the only shelter for miles was the abandoned farm ahead.

The clouds burst as we walked into a great clearing. There was the farm before us, partially obscured by the falling rain. In the distance was a large barn and various outbuildings, before us was the big, two story farmhouse with most of the windows of the lower story boarded up.

The cool rain felt good on my naked chest, but it was beginning to soak my shorts. The sky quickly darkened further and great flashes of lightning added sudden brilliance to our newly dimmed surroundings. Suddenly, the lightening was terrifyingly close and we scurried for shelter.

I ran around the back of the farmhouse, with Casper close on my heels. There was a window where the boards had fallen off and we pulled ourselves inside. We were safe from the elements for the time being.

"It sure is dark in here," said Casper fearfully.

"Hold on," I said and rummaged through my pack. I pulled out a large flashlight. "See, I'm not just a big, dumb jock, I can think ahead," I said with a laugh and turned on the light.

We were in what must have once been the kitchen. There was a rusting hulk of a wood stove in one corner and built-in cabinets along one wall. There was even an old table still sitting in the middle of the room. It was rickety and would soon be like the ruins of chairs that lay on the floor where they had collapsed under their own weight long ago. There was an old sink with a pitcher pump for water along another wall. I gave it a try, but nothing came out except dust and rust. Remnants of old wallpaper clung to the walls.

"This is pretty cool," said Casper.

"There's lots more, let's explore," I said.

I led Casper through an open doorway and into a hall. Directly across the hall was what must've once been the living room or parlor, but it was empty. There were water stains running down the outer wall and we couldn't walk too far into the room because the floor creaked and threatened to collapse on us. We returned to the hall and followed it until we came to a closed door. I opened it and there was nothing but darkness within. A stair led down.

"Let's not go down there," said Casper. I could tell he was scared. Something about the basement made the hair rise on the back of my neck and I was no more eager to go downstairs than Casper.

"We couldn't if we wanted to," I said, casting light on the stairs. About a third of the way down, the stairway stopped. The bottom section had broken away.

I closed the door and we headed back the way we had come. It was very dark inside, because it was cloudy out and the windows were boarded up, but it must have been quite a nice place to live at one time. I'd been there before with my uncle long ago, but we'd only looked from the outside, peeking in the cracks in the windows. I'd always wanted to get inside that place and have a real look around. I was glad I was not alone. It was kinda creepy in there.

We found the stairway that led to the second floor. Luckily it was far sounder than the one leading into the basement. We followed it upstairs. The second floor hallway was littered with fallen plaster and wallpaper. It was lighter than downstairs, however. The storm outside kept things dim, but the windows on the second floor weren't boarded up like they were on the ground floor and some light got in. There were rather large windows at either end of the hall and I imagined it must be quite a bright place on a sunny day.

The wind rattled the old windows. An occasional rumble of thunder shook the house and flashes of lightning lit up the interior like day every few seconds. The rain began to really hammer down and there was a constant drip, drip where the roof was leaking. I felt kind of sad that the old home was in such disrepair. I wondered about the family who had once lived there. They were likely dead and gone, but it seemed a shame for their old house to become such a ruin.

The upper floor was all bedrooms. Most of them were empty, but in one there was still an old bed. It had collapsed and lay where it fell. It looked like no one ever went into that old house.

Casper and I sat down on the mattress and rested. We'd been walking for at least a couple of hours and it felt good to get the weight off our feet. The light was dim, but we could see well enough. The rain fell down ever harder outside and it felt all warm and cozy inside the old farmhouse.

I stretched out my legs. My tired muscles were glad of the change. Casper stretched out beside me. I could tell he was tired.

"This place wouldn't be too bad fixed up," said Casper. "I wonder who owns it."

"My parents," I said.

"Really?"

"Yeah, they bought all this land as one of their investments. The farm came with it, not that it's worth much. It's sure interesting to explore, however."

"Yeah," said Casper. "I like this place. I don't think I'd want to be here at night, but I like it in the daytime."

"Don't worry, we'll leave long before dark."

"Good."

We dug some more cookies and chips out of my pack and sat in the middle of the room munching on goodies. As we talked I found myself getting lost in Casper's face. There was just something about it that made me want to keep looking. If my dreams could have come true, he would have suddenly looked at me and told me that he loved me, but I knew that wasn't going to happen. Life wasn't a dream and dreams didn't come true like that. There were no magic lamps that granted wishes.

It was cooler now, but the moist air still felt warm on the bare skin of my chest and back. I looked at Casper's slim torso. It was easy to make out his build under his wet shirt. He was unbelievably thin. He was beautiful, however, so beautiful that it made my heart ache with longing. I think I would've loved Casper no matter what he looked like. He was attractive to be sure, but it was something within him that really drew me to him.

Without thinking I leaned over, drawing ever nearer to Casper's delicate, red lips. I'd dreamed of kissing those lips so often that I felt as if I was within a dream. I think I could have died happy if I could kiss him just once. I was head over heels in love with that little blond boy and nothing in the world would ever change that. I leaned in, pressed my lips to his, and kissed him.

I jerked back, my eyes wide. I felt all the color drain from my face as I realized what I'd just done. A wave of remorse and self-hatred swept over me.

"Casper, I'm so sorry. I didn't mean…"

I didn't have time to finish. Casper grabbed my face with both hands, pulled me to him, and gave me the most passionate kiss of my life. When his lips parted from mine, I just sat back and stared at him, my mouth hanging open, stunned.

Casper

I almost laughed out loud at the look on Brendan's face just after I kissed him. I don't think there is anything I could've done that would've shocked him more.

"But why?" he asked, exasperated. I could tell he was thoroughly confused.

"We need to talk," I said.

"No fuck," he said, smiling. The smile instantly faded from his lips, however. "Just one thing, Casper, you're not messing with me are you? Please don't mess with me. You have no idea how cruel that would be." He looked as if he were ready to cry. It was such a sudden change that it seemed unreal.

"No, Brendan, I'm not messing with you." The smile was back in an instant.

"Then why, Casper? Don't get me wrong, there's nothing I could have wanted more, but I don't understand."

"It was me that didn't understand, about a lot of things," I said. "I've kinda suspected that I was into boys, that I was gay, for quite a while now. Okay, I didn't suspect it, I knew it. I just didn't want to admit it, even to myself. I've always thought it was something really gross and disgusting. I didn't think there could be anything worse. So when you put your hand on my leg that night and, you know, I just couldn't handle it. I thought you were going to do something to me like my brother…"

My voice faltered as I realized what I'd just said. I hadn't meant to tell Brendan about my brother. I guess I had such trust in him that my guard wasn't up.

"What about your brother?" asked Brendan. There was concern and fear in his voice.

"Fuck." That was all I could say. I'd screwed up big time. I'd let slip the very thing I didn't want Brendan to know about.

"Casper?"

I didn't say a word. I just looked down at the floor.

"Casper?"

"Just forget I said it, okay?"

"No," said Brendan, shaking his head. "Your brother has done something to you, hasn't he? Something bad."

"Just let it go."

"No. I can't just let it go. If he's hurting you, if he's doing something bad to you, I'm not going to stand by and let it happen. Tell me." He spoke so earnestly that I wanted to tell him everything, but it was hard. I was ashamed.

"Please." With one word I begged him to let me off the hook.

"No, Casper. You can't keep a secret like that. Not if he's hurting you. He is hurting you, isn't he? You've got to tell me, Casper. I can't bear the thought of anyone hurting you. I love you."

I looked up into his eyes. They were filled with tears. He had said that he loved me, and this time I believed him. I could hear it in his voice. It seemed too good to be true. Was it even possible?" I think he could read the question in my eyes.

"Yes, Casper, I love you. I've loved you since the first time I saw you. You don't know what you mean to me." He hugged me tight and cried onto my shoulder. Brendan, the captain of the football team, the popular jock with muscles bulging out everywhere, had just told me he loved me and was crying on my shoulder. It seemed like a weird dream, and yet a dream better than any I could have dreamed. I wrapped my arms around him and held him close.

"I, I love you too, Brendan." I didn't know it until I said the words. I didn't realize I loved him until that very moment. The feeling had been with me for I don't know how long, but it was disguised as friendship and more. Tears filled my eyes and I smiled with a happiness that I'd never felt before.

Brendan leaned back and looked into my eyes. "Then you must tell me, Casper. Tell me what he's done to you."

The smile faded from my lips in an instant.

"I can't. It's too terrible. I'm so ashamed."

"Casper, tell me." Brendan took my chin in his hand and gently, but firmly, made me look into his eyes. For a long time I didn't say anything. It was just too hard. Finally, after what seemed like forever, it burst from my lips.

"He beats on me," I said. There was a long pause before I spoke again. "He molests me." I swallowed hard, pausing even longer. "Sometimes, he rapes me." I started crying. I turned my back to Brendan. "I'm so ashamed, don't look at me!" Brendan grabbed my chin again and forced me to look at him.

"You have nothing to be ashamed of Casper. You haven't done anything wrong. You hear me? This isn't you fault. You didn't cause this. It isn't your fault, Casper. It's your brother, that sick bastard."

Brendan's eyes narrowed with hatred. I think he would have ripped Jason to pieces if he'd been there just then. I started crying again. It was all too much. I felt a great weight lifted from my shoulders as I shared my deepest, darkest secret with Brendan. Part of me was glad I'd told him. Part of me just wanted to crawl under a rock and hide. Brendan and I sat there, crying into each others shoulders. It felt good to be held like that. It felt good to have someone care about me again. No one had cared about me since my mother had died. I felt like I wasn't alone anymore.

Later, when the tears stopped, we stood and looked out the window. The rain had slacked and was nearly over. We made our way downstairs and out the window. It was still cloudy and dim outside, but the light seemed blinding after the darkness of the old farmhouse. We walked toward the barn, passing an ancient well. It looked like one of those wishing wells you see in books.

"So that's why you freaked out in the park that night, isn't it? You thought I was like your brother. I'm so sorry, Casper. I didn't know."

"It's all right, Brendan. How could you have known? No one knows. Well, my dad might, but he doesn't care. I did think you were like my brother that night. That's why I fought you, and got out of that car as fast as I could. I was so scared, and so hurt. I was so happy we'd become friends, and then…"

"You thought I was just using you."

"Yeah, I did. But then later, in the cemetery, and after, I got to thinking how it didn't make sense. If you'd wanted me like that, you could have had me. I couldn't have stopped you in the cemetery, but you didn't do anything. And in the park before that, if you'd wanted to do something to me, you wouldn't have tried it there. You'd have taken me someplace where there was no help. I'm sorry I ever thought that about you, Brendan. That was horrible of me."

"No, it wasn't. I shouldn't have come onto you like that. I should have used a little more sense. It's just that I wanted you so bad. I wanted to be with you. I couldn't control myself anymore. I've had these feelings for all these years and I've never been able to do anything about them, and then you came along. I fell for you on the spot. I thought I'd finally found someone. I should have just told you how I felt. Maybe I am just a dumb jock sometimes."

I smiled at Brendan. It was hard to take it all in. So much was happening so fast. I felt like we'd lived a whole year in the last few minutes. We both grew silent as we neared the old barn. It was weather-beaten, but still had traces of red paint. It was amazingly well preserved. We walked in the open door. The sky above was beginning to clear and shafts of light fell through the cracks in the walls. The barn still smelled faintly of hay. I almost expected to find horses or something in there.

"Listen, Casper," said Brendan, "about your brother. I know that was really hard to tell me. It took a lot of courage. I can't even imagine how bad things have been for you, but all that's over. I'll take care of you. I won't let him hurt you anymore."

I smiled sadly and hugged Brendan tight. It felt so good to be hugged. I leaned back and looked at Brendan. We just stood there looking into each others eyes for a few moments. He looked like he wanted to kiss me again, but he didn't. Brendan was a little shy about doing that. So was I. I knew things would get easier with time; we'd just have to take it slow.

We explored the barn a little. There were a few old tools still hanging on square nails. The timbers that framed the barn on the inside were huge, hand-hewn out of great logs. They were all held together by wooden pegs. I couldn't imagine how anyone could build such a thing.

We climbed a worn ladder into the loft, but Brendan had barely stuck his head above the floor when there was a horrible screech that just about caused me to go in my pants. We both jumped down and bolted outside. My heart tried to fight its way out of my chest and my breath came in gasps. I turned to Brendan; he was holding his hand to his chest. We looked into each others eyes and laughed.

"Aren't we a couple of cowards?" said Brendan.

"What was that?"

"An owl, I think. I thought it had me. Don't tell anyone!"

"Your secret is safe with me. I 'bout had an accident in my pants." We laughed at ourselves again.

We stood there for a few moments looking around us at the old, overgrown farm. Everywhere there was evidence of what once had been; unkempt lilac and snowball bushes near the house, half broken down fences trailing away into the distance, old farm machinery rusting away, a battered weather vane still clinging to the top of the barn. It was a spooky place with its stillness and absence of life, but I felt an attachment to it. It was peaceful and beautiful, even in its dilapidated state. I could just imagine how wonderful it must have been when it was a working farm. I wished that Brendan and I could live someplace like that, where everything was quiet and beautiful, and there were no bullies—a better place.

"We'd better start back. It's a long hike and I sure don't want to be out here when it starts to get dark," said Brendan.

"Me either."

I took one last look at the old farm and then followed Brendan back into the forest. My head was spinning with all that had happened on our trek into the woods.

* * *

Just after school on Monday, I walked out the back entrance to meet Brendan. We were going to spend a little time together before he had football practice. I'd also asked him to talk to the coach about something for me.

I looked up and saw Brendan standing there. He wasn't alone, however. He was facing my brother Jason and the two of them were exchanging heated words. I couldn't make out what they were saying, but I had little doubt as to what they were arguing about. By the time I got near, things were getting violent.

"You fucking son of a bitch!" yelled Brendan as he punched Jason in the face.

In a flash Brendan and Jason were all over each other. They were a big blur of flying fists, rolling around on the ground, looking like they were trying to kill each other. A few guys ran up and watched with me. I felt helpless just standing there, but I was sure Brendan didn't need any help from me. My brother was tough, but Brendan was even tougher. I was sure that Jason had met his match at last.

It wasn't long before Jason was on his back with Brendan kneeling on his chest, beating the shit out of him.

"You ever touch him again and I'll fuck you up so bad you'll be begging me to kill you! You hear me? Just once fucker and you're finished!"

Brendan was slugging him in the face the entire time he was threatening him. He was pounding him so hard I thought he'd break Jason's neck. Jason was cowering, trying to fend off the blows. He wasn't even trying to fight back anymore.

Brendan stopped hitting Jason and slowly got up off of him. I could tell by the look on his face that he would have rather kept pounding on Jason. Brendan was pissed and I knew it was because of what I'd told him my brother had done to me. I had no idea he was going to hunt Jason down and kick his ass, but I guess it shouldn't have surprised me. After all, Brendan had told me he'd take care of Jason. He'd done it. As I stood there, I started to feel safe for the first time in my life. I knew that Brendan wouldn't let my brother hurt me, ever again.

Brendan limped a little as he walked toward me and there was a scrape on this face. Other than that, there was no evidence he'd just been in a fight. My brother looked much worse. He was lying on the grass moaning, with a busted lip and eyes that were about swollen shut. Brendan put his hand on my shoulder and we walked away.

"If he gives you any trouble, Casper, you let me know. I'll take care of him. Don't let him try and pull any shit on you either. If he threatens to hurt you if you tell, just tell him you know he won't because I'll kick his ass. And if he tries to bring in friends to get me, I've got friends too. I'll have the whole football team after his sorry ass if he hurts you again."

"Thanks, Brendan," I said, smiling. I wanted to hug him right then and there, but I knew that wasn't wise. I also knew that Brendan didn't want it. We'd talked and he'd made it clear that we couldn't let on we were boyfriends in front of anyone else.

We walked back into the school and headed for the gym.

"I talked to coach and he said he could definitely use you as an assistant for football season, kind of water boy/gofer type of thing. You sure you want to do it?"

"Yeah, I am. This way I can spend more time with you. I don't have anything else to do anyway. I sure don't want to be home." Brendan looked at me meaningfully. He knew just what I meant.

"Okay then. Let's go see the coach."

Brendan

My fingers brushed Casper's as I accepted a cup of water from him on the sidelines. Our eyes met and we smiled at each other. Having a boyfriend was the best feeling in the entire world. I glanced at Marc Thayer, who was just heading back to the field, and then back at Casper.

"Nice ass, huh?" I said beneath my breath. Casper smiled and rolled his eyes. I crushed my cup and headed back to practice.

I felt like I had my life back, only better. Those few days when I thought Casper hated me were the worst in my life, but they were worth it for what I had now. My life was pretty sweet overall, but I'd always felt like I was missing something, and I knew that something was Casper. I felt complete for the first time ever.

I glanced over at Casper now and then during practice. The mere sight of him made my chest swell with happiness. I made sure not to look at him too much. I didn't want my team-mates to see me looking at him with a big dopey smile. That was the only bad thing about me and Casper, the danger of being found out. Before Casper came along, it was fairly easy to hide my desires from my friends and team-mates. I just had to make sure I didn't let my eyes rove too much. I'd even dated a few girls, so no one would suspect that I was a gay boy. Now that Casper was in my life, that secret was going to be much harder to keep.

All the guys really seemed to like Casper. Of course, all of them knew we were friends and the fact that I liked him made the others think that he must be pretty cool. I know that sounds conceited, but that's the way popularity worked at my school. Casper was popular by association. Well, maybe not popular, but well liked by the guys on my team. They all knew that anyone who gave him shit had to answer to me.

Casper seemed surprised that he was accepted by the guys. It made my heart ache to watch him as he looked at them with a kind of awe. He had such a low opinion of himself that it was like he didn't think he deserved to be liked or something. I loved Casper, but he had really lousy self-esteem. I guess that was understandable. Being that poor had to have an effect on him. I knew I couldn't really understand what it was like; my family had always been rich. I didn't know what it felt like not to have nice clothes or a nice house. The only time I was ever hungry was when I was too busy to eat. Casper and I came from different worlds.

Maybe I couldn't understand what it was like to be poor, but I was determined to make Casper see in himself what I saw when I looked at him; a kind, loving, wonderful boy with a lot to offer.

I stole another glance at Casper. I loved him, I really loved him. It felt good to love someone. Sure, I loved my parents, and I'd loved pets I'd had in the past, but this was completely different. This was another kind of love. I can't begin to describe how good it made me feel inside. The best part was that Casper loved me back. I could see it in his eyes every time he looked at me. It was the best feeling in the entire world.

Casper

I was in my room, sitting at the rickety old table studying, when Jason walked in. I was so busy getting my homework done that I didn't even hear him coming until he was opening the door. My instincts kicked in and I made ready to run for it the first chance I got. Then I remembered that I didn't have to run anymore.

I looked up at Jason. His face was bruised and blood had dried on his lip. He looked like he'd been hit by a truck or something. He'd been hit by something far more dangerous, he'd been hit by my boyfriend.

"You told him, didn't you runt?"

I looked straight into his eyes without flinching.

"Yes, I told him."

"You know what I said would happen if you ever told anyone." His voice was menacing, the threat hung heavy in the air. I slowly stood.

"If you hurt me, Brendan will kick your ass," I said.

"Oh, little brother has balls now. Or I guess he's just borrowing someone else's."

Jason was being as big a jerk as ever, but he made no move toward me.

"You touch me and I'll tell him," I said. I knew Brendan was my only protection. Jason was way bigger than me, but Brendan was even stronger than Jason.

"What is it with you two anyway? Why is Mr. Bigshot suddenly your friend? You doin' all his homework for him or somethin'?"

"No, we're just friends is all."

"Bullshit, there's something more goin' on here." He stared at me as if he could make me tell. "You can't be paying him, since I know you don't have any money. He wouldn't need it anyway. He's a big kiss-ass and gets whatever he wants from his daddy."

"He's not a kiss-ass!" I shouted. Jason laughed.

"He's getting somethin' from you I bet. You might as well tell me, you know. I'll find out what it is sooner or later."

"Even if there was something to find, you're not smart enough."

"You know, if I was you little brother, I wouldn't be such a smart-ass with me. Mr. Football Stud won't be there to protect you forever. He'll get tired of you soon enough and then it's just you and me baby. You can bet I'll remember every single thing you say to me. I can't wait until it's pay back time." Jason sneered at me. I was afraid. It was the first time in a long time that I'd made the slightest effort to stand up to him. I knew that Brendan wouldn't leave me, but what Jason said still scared me.

"Yeah, I'm gonna find out what's up, little brother, and then I'll take care of you good. Or maybe I'll just take care of your boyfriend."

I tensed at Jason's use of "boyfriend," but tried not to let my fear and surprise show. I knew he was just trying to insult me. Then again, maybe not, maybe he was fishing for clues.

"He's not my boyfriend."

"I'm sure he's not. Even if shit for brains was a fag, he sure wouldn't want you for a boyfriend," he laughed. "I bet he would use you though. You Mr. Football's little bitch, Casper? Huh?"

"I'm gonna tell him you said that." I put as much threat into my voice as I could manage. Jason was getting a little too close to the truth. If he really did begin to suspect that I was Brendan's boyfriend, then it would be harder than ever for us to date without anyone knowing. My greatest fear was that Brendan would get scared and not want to see me anymore. I didn't let Jason see my fear, however. I knew he'd just feed on it. I had to maintain control.

"I'll figure it all out, little brother. Then I'll get rid of dick-head, and then your ass is mine."

Jason left me alone, but I was practically shaking. Even with Brendan protecting me, I was still afraid of him. My brother was capable of just about anything.

Brendan

I pulled the convertible up in front of the library. Casper was sitting on the steps, waiting for me. He wore the same clothes he wore to school every day, but he was as clean as could be. He'd told me some about his life at home and I was amazed at how he even survived.

"Hungry?" I asked as he settled into the passenger side.

"Trick question?" he asked. We both laughed.

I drove us to the local smorgasbord. It wasn't my favorite place to eat, but I went there for two reasons. First, Casper could eat as much as he wanted without feeling self-conscious about it. Eating as much as you could was the goal at a smorgasbord after all. And second, I knew that Casper felt out of place at the restaurants I usually ate at. I took him to my favorite once, but I could tell he was uncomfortable. Everyone else, including me, was dressed in really nice clothes and Casper was wearing the same clothes he did every day. I didn't want to do anything to make him uncomfortable, so the smorgasbord was just the place. I kind of liked it myself. It was different.

We both started out with big plates full of fried chicken, mashed potatoes, meatballs, shrimp, and everything else we could fit on them. We ate and talked and ate some more. Casper didn't realize it, but I made sure we ate whenever he was with me. He hadn't come right out and said it, but I knew he didn't get much at home. I couldn't imagine anyone having to live like that. It was unthinkable that some people went to bed hungry, while others had plenty. It pained me to think of Casper going without.

"You really shouldn't keep taking me out all the time," said Casper.

"Why not? Have another boyfriend hidden away somewhere?" I said quietly and smiled.

"No, it's just that you always pay for everything and I can't. It makes me feel bad."

"Hey, I like taking you places. It's sure a lot more fun than going alone. And don't feel bad about me paying. My family has a shit-load of money. They've always had it. They just keep passing it down from one generation to another. You know what I do for my money?"

"No, what?"

"Not a damn thing. So don't feel bad about it. I know you'd pay if you could. If our situations were just the opposite, I wouldn't feel bad about you paying at all. And besides, what you give me is worth a lot more than any old money."

"What do I give you?"

"You're the best friend I've ever had Casper, and you're more than that. I wished for you all my life and here you are. You're my dream come true."

Casper blushed and I could feel my own face going red. I felt kind of corny saying that, but I meant it with all my heart. He was the boy of my dreams.

"I'm ready for some more!" I said. "Let's bankrupt this place! We'll just keep eating until they run out of money buying food for us." Casper thought that was funny. I loved to see him laugh.

When we returned to our seats, a few of the guys from my team walked in. They came over and talked to us for a little bit. I was somewhat uncomfortable with my team-mates there. Casper and I spent a lot of time together at school and I didn't really like anyone seeing us together outside of school more than was necessary. I was keenly aware of what could happen if my friends and team-mates started getting suspicious. My one great fear was being outed.

"What's wrong?" asked Casper. He could read my thoughts on my face.

"Just me being stupid," I said. "I'll tell you later when we're alone."

* * *

We hopped in the car and drove away. I was so full I was about to burst.

"So what was wrong in there?" asked Casper. His beautiful young face was etched with concern.

"I just get worried sometimes. I'm afraid someone will find out about us. I'm afraid the guys will find out I'm gay."

"Oh, that would be bad I guess."

"There's no guessing to it, Casper. I'd lose everything. You think they'd let me be captain of the football team if they knew I was gay? They'd kick my ass out as soon as they found out about me. Hell, I'd probably get kicked off the team."

"Oh they wouldn't!"

"I bet they would. People are like that. They don't understand. They think all this weird shit about us gay guys."

"It'll be okay, Brendan. No one is going to find out." Casper looked very thoughtful.

"What is it, Casper?"

"Well, this might not be the best time, but maybe I'd better tell you. My brother suspects something is up between us."

"Like what?"

"He doesn't know, but he said there must be some reason you're being nice to me and sticking up for me. He said he's going to find out what it is."

"Shit, we're really going to have to be careful."

"Yeah, my brother is dangerous. I don't think there's much he wouldn't do."

"Well, we'll handle him. We're going to stick together no matter what."

"You really mean that, right?"

"Of course I do. Why?"

"Well, Jason said you'd get tired of me pretty soon. He said you'd dump me and then he'd make me pay for everything."

"That's never going to happen, Casper, never! I love you."

"I love you too, Brendan." Casper smiled at me, but I could read a mix of fear and relief on his handsome face. He had a lot bearing down on his young shoulders.

"Hey, we'll always be together, Casper, always. Don't let anyone tell you any different, especially your brother. He's just trying to scare you."

Casper nodded and I could tell he felt better.

"After we've driven around a bit, what do you say we go to my house and I'll start teaching you about lifting weights."

"Sure, if you think that's okay."

"Of course it's okay."

"Your parents won't mind?"

"Of course not. They probably won't even be there. They won't care if they are anyway. I have friends over all the time."

"Cool."

"I have someplace I want to stop before we head home," I said.

"Where?"

"You'll see."

A short time later I pulled up in front of *Anthony's Squire Shop*. It was a clothing store. I took Casper in.

"What do you think of this?" I asked, holding up a shirt that I thought would look really hot on Casper.

"I think you'd look good in that," he said.

"It's not for me silly, it's for you."

"For me?"

"Yeah, I'm going to buy you some new clothes."

"That's really nice of you, Brendan, but you shouldn't."

"Shhhh," I said. "No arguing. I'm bigger than you remember. Don 't make me have to rough you up." I smiled. Casper smiled too.

I could tell he was a little uncomfortable that I was buying him things, but I made it clear that I wanted to do it. Casper resigned himself to the situation. I picked him out several nice shirts, some jeans, and lots of boxers and socks. I would have let him pick out what he wanted, but he was too shy and reluctant to do so. I was sure he'd like what I picked out anyway. Casper's eyes just about popped out of his head when the cashier told me the total, it was a little over $700.

"I can't believe you just spent that much money on me," said Casper, as we got back into my convertible.

"Don't worry about it. My dad probably made more money than that during the time we were in there." I wasn't bragging, I was just letting Casper know that the money meant nothing to me. Money wasn't important, Casper was.

Casper

Brendan and I pulled up to his house in his fancy convertible. I'd only seen pictures of houses like that in magazines. I couldn't imagine actually living in one. I knew Brendan's family had money, but I had no idea how much. They were beyond rich.

Brendan led me inside. The first thing I noticed was how clean everything was. There wasn't a bit of dust anywhere to be found. The floors were covered with thick, comfy carpeting, and everything was so beautiful.

I followed Brendan back to where he kept his weight machine. I looked around wide-eyed. It was a whole workout room. There wasn't one machine, but several. There was an exercise bike and other machines I didn't even recognize. Brendan had more different kinds of machines than the school gym.

"I need to change, so do you. You can wear these." Brendan tossed me a pair of shorts. He pulled off his clothes right in front of me, stripping down to his boxers before pulling on a pair of soccer shorts. He kept his shirt off and he looked so fine. Looking at his bare chest, with all of its muscles, made me breathe funny.

I slipped out of my old jeans and put on the shorts. I kept my shirt on. I felt more than a little self conscious. I also wasn't keen on Brendan seeing my bruises. He knew Jason had beaten me, but I didn't want another conversation about it starting up.

"Okay, let's get started. When I'm done with you, you're going to be buff."

"I doubt that," I said laughing.

"I don't," he said. I could tell he wasn't kidding.

"We'll start with the bench press. It works the muscles of your chest. Watch me do it, and then you can try."

Brendan lay back on the bench and grabbed the handles of the machine. He pushed the handles up and a big stack of weights rose in the air. I could see all the muscles in his chest and arms flex. Brendan was beautiful. He was so built. I couldn't help but drool over him. He lowered the weights back down, and then pushed them up again. He did it ten times in all, and then stopped.

"Okay, it's your turn."

"I can't do that! It's too heavy!"

"You're not going to do the same weight I use. I've worked out for a long time. You can't expect to lift what I do, at least not until later."

Brendan pulled a peg from the weight stack and moved it up several weight plates.

"Here, try this weight. If it's too much of a strain tell me and we'll lower it."

I lay back on the bench and grabbed the handles just like I'd seen Brendan do. I pushed up hard and was surprised when the weights lifted off the stack. I could feel the muscles in my chest and arms flexing. I liked it. It made me feel good. I pushed the weight up all the way until my arms were fully extended, then I lowered the weight back down. I did it ten times, just like Brendan.

"How was that?"

"That was great!" I said.

"Like the way it feels, don't you?"

"Yeah. The last three times were kinda hard, but I could do it!"

"I told you. Most guys think you have to strain your guts out to lift weights, but you don't. You just use the weight you can handle. I usually do three sets of each exercise, but we'll start you out with just one. Next time you can do two sets, then three after that."

Brendan showed me how to do lats, butterflies, ab crunches, barbell curls, and dumbbell curls. While he was doing it, he explained weight lifting to me.

"I always work out three times a week and always allow for a full day of rest between workouts. So like if I work out on Monday, I don't Tuesday."

"Why not?"

"Because of the way the body builds muscle. You see, when you lift weights, you aren't building muscle, you're straining the muscles you already have. That makes them grow. The first thing your body does is repair any damage you've done."

"Damage?"

"Yeah, there's usually a little damage, but not much. It's nothing to worry about. Anyway, after repairing the damage, your body adds on new muscle. It builds you up so you can handle the weight you are lifting. After that it needs to rest. It takes more than twenty-four hours to do all that, so I always rest a full day in between workouts. Some guys work out every day, but you actually put on muscle faster if you don't. It sounds like it doesn't make sense, but it does when you know how muscle is built."

"Okay, got it," I said.

"The next important thing is how much weight you use. It should be heavy enough to strain the muscles, but not too heavy. If you are straining your guts out, you're using too much weight. If it's too easy, you need more. After you've worked out for a while the weight you are using will get easy to lift, so then you lift more weight and your body keeps getting stronger. The idea is to keep straining the muscles a little so your body will keep adding on more muscle."

I really liked all the different exercises Brendan showed me. I don't think I'd ever felt so good before. I had my doubts about what I could do, however.

"You really think I can work out like you? I mean, look at me."

"Sure I do. Here, take a look at this." Brendan took a notebook off a table and showed me a photo taped to the inside of the front cover.

"That's me four years ago, when I started lifting weights."

"That's you?" I asked.

"Yeah, kind of skinny, huh?"

"You look almost as skinny as me!"

"And look at me now," he said. "I wasn't born looking like this. I started working out and I stuck with it. I know you can do it, Casper. I did." Brendan started laughing. "I sound really hung up on myself don't I?"

"Nah, you're just explaining things to me. Anyway, you sure look good." I smiled at him. Maybe I really could do it. I sure liked the idea of being built like Brendan some day.

After our workout, Brendan led me out to the hot tub. I'd never even seen one before. I blushed when Brendan stripped completely naked and got in. I didn't fail to check him out, however. I couldn't help myself. Brendan saw me look and he just smiled.

"It's best if you strip. Be careful. It's not called a hot tub for nothing."

I pulled off my shirt, feeling a little self-conscious. I felt stronger after my workout, however. Brendan's eyes fell on my bruises, but he didn't say anything. I was afraid he would, but he didn't. I guess he knew I was uncomfortable talking about the things that had happened with my brother. Brendan had taken care of the situation, so maybe he didn't feel that he needed to ask about the bruises.

I turned red as a beet when I pulled off my shorts and briefs. I'd never gotten naked in front of Brendan before. He looked me over and smiled when I looked back at him. I blushed even more. I slipped into the water.

"It's hot!" I said.

"Told you."

The hot water felt really good on my tired muscles. The workout had worn me out and made me feel kind of tense.

"This will help you feel less sore tomorrow. You'll probably feel a little sore anyway, since this was your first workout, but pretty soon you won't be sore at all."

We sat across from each other, with our arms over the sides of the hot tub. I was thinking to myself how gorgeous Brendan was when I felt his foot running up my leg. He rubbed my leg and kept going higher and higher until he was nearly touching my groin. I got excited. I was glad he couldn't see my lower half clearly through the water. The way he grinned I think he knew what he was doing. I slid my foot up his leg too. From the look on Brendan's face, he liked it.

Sitting there naked in the hot tub with Brendan brought thoughts to my mind that I'd long suppressed. We'd kissed a few times, but we hadn't done anything more than that. I think Brendan was taking things real slow with me because of what my brother had done to me. I was glad because it was kind of scary. I knew it would be different with Brendan than it was with my brother. Brendan wouldn't hurt me. His concern for me was obvious. I had a feeling he wanted to do a lot more with me than just kiss, but he was waiting patiently until I was ready.

I was getting pretty ready. I was having warm fuzzy thoughts about putting my hands on Brendan's body, and about having his hands on mine. I edged closer to Brendan until our shoulders were touching. Feeling his muscular arm pressed up against mine filled me with desire. I turned and looked into Brendan's eyes. He leaned down, ever so slowly, and pressed his lips to mine. He kissed me and I melted.

We broke our kiss and sat there gazing at each other. I cautiously reached out, stretching my fingers toward his chest. Brendan's chest was tanned and smooth. My fingers brushed it. His smooth, silky skin was such a contrast to the hard muscle underneath. I ran my hands over his pectoral muscles, feeling the power in his chest. It was as if Brendan's masculinity were kept there. Gay boys were supposed to be soft and effeminate, but Brendan was about as far away from that as it was possible to get. It was Brendan that made it possible for me to admit to myself that I was gay. Well, I already knew I was gay, but Brendan made me feel that it wasn't a bad thing. Brendan made it possible for me to accept what I was. If a boy like him was gay, then it couldn't be bad at all.

I sat there by Brendan for the longest time, just running my hands over his chest, his shoulders, and his arms. He just sat there and let me touch him wherever I wanted. After quite a long time, Brendan reached out and put his hand on my shoulder. He did it ever so slowly and gently, like I was a wild animal that he didn't want to frighten. He moved his hand slowly to my chest. I tensed, but willed myself to relax. I reminded myself that there was nothing to fear. Brendan loved me and I loved him. He'd never hurt me.

Brendan ran his hands over my chest. It felt good to be touched like that. The fact that it was another boy touching me made it that much more intense. I was trembling, but it wasn't from fear, it was from pure joy.

Brendan stood and pulled me up with him. We stepped out of the hot tub and gazed at each other. For the first time ever, I didn't feel awkward or self-conscious about being naked in front of someone else. I knew that Brendan accepted me just as I was.

I placed my hands on his chest again as he kissed me. I let them trail lower until my fingers traced the hard rows of Brendan's abdominal muscles. Brendan placed his hands over mine and guided them lower. I drew in a sharp intake of breath as I felt his hardness. Brendan pulled his hands away, but mine stayed.

Brendan slowly moved his hands down my body until he was touching me in the same way I was him. His touch was exquisite and maddening at the same time. Our breath grew rapid and our hearts pounded in our chests. I wanted the feeling to last forever, but it was not possible. My entire body shivered as I experienced the most intense pleasure of my young life. Brendan's beautifully muscled form tensed and flexed as he too experienced the ultimate pleasure.

Brendan

I was late getting into the showers after football practice. Coach wanted to go over some plays, so pretty much everyone else was gone when I got in there. By the time I made it to the locker room, the whole place had cleared out, except for Casper. Part of his job was picking up all the towels the jocks left behind in the locker room. He didn't seem to mind. I could tell Casper really liked helping with the football team. He was proud of helping out. I smiled to myself with the knowledge that the main reason he helped out was to be near me. I was glad he was there; the very sight of Casper filled me with happiness. There was no more wonderful feeling in all the world than having someone to love, especially when he loved me back.

When I'd pulled on my boxers and jeans, I walked over to Casper and put my hand on his shoulder. He smiled at me. I looked carefully around the locker room, then pulled him to me, leaned down, and kissed him. I wrapped my arms around him, holding him tight against me. We closed our eyes, our mouths opened and we kissed with the passion of two young men in love. Kissing Casper, just being with him, filled me with utter joy.

"What the fuck?!"

I opened my eyes and gasped. Ben Woolsey was standing there gaping at us with his mouth hanging open in shock. He'd stopped dead in his tracks as he'd come around the corner. Casper looked around and saw him too. I could feel my heart racing in my chest. All of us stood there in complete silence. Ben swallowed hard, turned on his heel, and ran.

I collapsed on the bench between the lockers. I was too shocked to even cry. I knew it was all over. I was screwed. I just sat there and stared blankly into space.

"Oh Brendan!" said Casper and held me close. Part of me wanted to push him away. Part of me was angry with him, but I knew it wasn't Casper fault. My own lack of caution had exposed me. What had happened was my own fault. I was the one who had just ruined my entire life.

"What are we going to do?" asked Casper. I just looked at him with sorrow in my eyes, unable to answer.

"Maybe you should go after him, talk to him before he tells anyone. Maybe he won't talk."

I shook my head, but at the same time, I wondered if it wasn't worth a try. I pulled on my socks and shoes. I got up and ran from the locker room, putting on my shirt as I went. Ben was nowhere to be found in the gym. I hurried outside, Casper scurrying to keep up with me. Ben was standing near his truck in the parking lot, talking to two other boys from the team. All three looked up at us and I knew it was already too late. The look of shock on their faces made it clear that our secret was already out. We just stood there looking at each other for a moment. I turned toward my convertible. Casper and I climbed in, and sped away.

I had to concentrate hard to keep the car on the road. It was probably a good thing Casper was with me, or I might have wrecked it intentionally. Actually, there was no maybe about it. I'd have accelerated to top speed and slammed into a telephone pole for sure. I knew I couldn't face what was to come; it would just be too humiliating, too horrible.

Casper kept looking over at me with a very worried expression on his face. Tears streamed down my cheeks. I wasn't even trying to hide how upset I felt. My whole world had come to an end.

"Drive to the cemetery," Casper instructed me. I did as he said. I could barely think for myself.

We got out of the car and walked into the cemetery. We sat on a little stone bench in the midst of great cedar trees and mossy tombstones. Tears kept flowing from my eyes. Casper hugged me tight and I broke down and bawled in his arms. He was supposed to be the frail one, but he was obviously much stronger that I was.

"It's all over, you know," I said to him when I could finally speak.

"What do you mean?" he said.

"Everything. It's all over. By tomorrow, everyone at school will know about us. By this time tomorrow evening, I won't have any friends. I'll have lost everything. Everyone will hate me and look down on me. I can't take that, Casper. I won't!" I looked at him with fear in my eyes.

"You're scaring me, Brendan."

"I'm sorry, Casper. I don't mean to scare you, but that's the way it is. There's only one way out now."

"Please, don't even say it, don't even think it," begged Casper. He was crying.

I just shrugged my shoulders. It was time to give up on life. My greatest fear was about to be realized and I couldn't face it. I didn't have the balls to take what was coming. I had no intention of sticking around so everyone could laugh at me and spit on me and hate me for what I was. I'd been unmasked and now everyone would know what I really was.

"It won't be that bad, Brendan. I know it's going to be hard, but we can get through it, together."

I just shook my head. I couldn't face it.

"So you're just gonna quit, huh?" said Casper with anger in his eyes. "What was all that you said about never leaving me, huh? What was all that about us staying together forever? You didn't mean any of it, did you?"

"You're not being fair," I said.

"You're a coward," said Casper flatly.

I jumped to my feet and turned on him in anger. I drew back my fist to slug him. I saw the fear in his eyes. Casper feared me. He didn't shrink from me, however. He held his ground. He just sat there, even though he expected me to hit him in the face.

"Go ahead, hit me!" he shouted at me. "It doesn't matter! When you're gone my brother will do much worse! He said he'd make me pay and he will! I'll be worse than dead! But you don't care! You're a selfish coward! You're just going to leave me. You're going to go off and kill yourself and leave me all alone because you're too big of a coward to face what's happened!" Casper was angry, but he was crying.

"I thought you loved me," he said quietly. "You said you loved me and I believed you." Casper bawled like his heart was broken. It was.

I kneeled down by him. I took his head in my hands and forced him to look into my eyes.

"I do love you, Casper. I love you more than anything. I just…I'm so afraid Casper. I can't…" We were both crying. Casper held me in his gaze.

"Don't leave me, Brendan. I love you. We can get through this. I know it will be hard, but we can do it. If you love me, you can't kill yourself, Brendan. If you do that, you'll be hurting me worse than my brother ever did. You'll be taking from me something that means more to me than anything else in the world—you. Please. If you love me, promise me you won't do it. Promise me you won't kill yourself, Brendan."

I was so terrified that I was shaking. I couldn't bear to face what was to come, and yet, I knew that I couldn't leave Casper like that. I was being selfish like he said. I was thinking only of me. If I killed myself, I'd be dooming Casper to the same fate, either that, or to a fate more horrible still. I loved him so much it hurt. I couldn't bear the thought of hurting him.

"I promise," I said, then kissed him deeply. I held him tight in my arms and kissed him, shutting out the entire world. I never wanted to let him go. I just wanted to keep on holding him and kissing him forever.

Casper

I walked into my room and there was Jason waiting on me. He was smiling, and it wasn't a nice smile at all.

"Guess what I heard, little brother?" he said.

I didn't say anything. I swallowed hard. The hair rose on the back of my neck. I was afraid.

"Mr. Football Jock was caught in the locker room, kissing another boy. He's a faggot. Your hero is a fag, Casper. But I guess you know that don't you? I guess you'd have to know it since he was kissing you." Jason laughed at me.

"I told you I'd find out about you two," he said. "I knew something was going on. I can't believe he'd sink low enough to do it with you, but I guess fags just don't have good taste. I guess queers will just do it with anyone."

"Shut up."

"I wouldn't be so brave if I was you little brother. The fag won't be protecting you anymore. He's gonna be way too busy getting his ass kicked." Jason smiled again. I wanted to knock that gloating smile right off his ugly face.

Jason grabbed me by the chin and forced me to look into his eyes.

"I told you Brendan would be gone someday. I warned you, didn't I?"

I was trembling with terror. I knew what was about to happen. I tensed, ready to run for it if I got the chance. Jason licked his lips.

"I can't wait to see what happens tomorrow. I can't wait to see Mr. High and Mighty fall."

Jason pushed me roughly away, and then crawled into his bed.

"You'd better get your sleep, little brother. You're going to need it. Tomorrow is going to be a long, hard day." He lay back, and then leaned up on one elbow. "I haven't forgotten all the shit you said to me, Casper. Don't think you're getting off the hook. I'm just giving you a little time to think about what's going to happen. Sleep well." He laughed to himself, a cruel wicked laugh.

I wondered what had made Jason into such a bad person. He hadn't always been like that. I guess it didn't matter. I couldn't change him. I lay down and tried to sleep, but the fear within me was too great. I was afraid of Jason. I was afraid for Brendan. And I was most afraid that Brendan wouldn't be able to handle what was to come. I was afraid he'd snap and that I wouldn't be there to catch him when he fell. I was afraid his promise wouldn't hold. I was afraid I couldn't keep him from ending his own life.

Brendan

I tried to steady my breathing as I sat in my convertible and stared at the back of the school. I didn't know how I was going to summon the courage to walk through those doors. I could only imagine what awaited me there. Classmates were already giving me curious glances as they walked past. A group of girls looked in my direction, then giggled and started talking excitedly among themselves. There was no doubt about it, the word was out.

Someone smacked the driver-side door hard, causing a bang that sounded like a shotgun. I jumped and snapped my head around. It was Brad. He smiled at me. I got out of the car.

"I thought maybe you could use some company," he said.

I looked him in the eyes for a moment thoughtfully.

"You know, don't you?"

"Yeah, I know, Brendan. I don't think there's anyone who doesn't know by now. Is it true?"

"Yes, it's true." I swallowed and stood there looking at him. Tears tried to well up in my eyes, but I fought them back.

"So uh, where do we stand, Brad?" He didn't seem belligerent, but I was still afraid, afraid of losing my best friend.

"We stand where we always have," said Brad, putting his hand on my shoulder. "I've got to admit, it shocked the hell out of me. I'd never have guessed it, not in a million years. It doesn't change anything, however. Well, I guess it's got to change some things, but we're still buds. We are still best friends. If you think that's going to change, then you've underestimated me, Brendan."

"I was so afraid of losing you."

"Don't be afraid of that. It's not going to happen. Hell, I kind of like it that you're gay. With you out of the game, I've got a lot better chance to score with the ladies!"

"And you need all the help you can get," I said smiling. Brad hit me hard in the shoulder for that.

"Come on. Let's go in," said Brad as he put his arm around my shoulder and walked me toward the school. I felt good inside. I was still afraid of what was to come, but at least Brad was sticking by me. At least I hadn't lost him.

"What's everyone saying?" I asked, as we drew ever closer.

"They're surprised, like me. You're the talk of the whole school of course, but then you always are. Some girls are kind of disappointed. Some guys don't believe it."

We were almost at the doors. I stopped. Brad turned and looked at me.

"I'm afraid to go in," I admitted.

"Hey, Brendan, I don't think it'll be as bad as you think. I'm sure a few jerks will give you shit, but you've got lots of friends."

"Do I? You think they'll still be my friends?" I asked, almost desperate.

"Yes, I do, Brendan. I really do."

Brad put his hand on my shoulder and guided me inside. Despite his reassurance, walking through those doors was the hardest thing I'd ever had to do in my entire life.

When we got inside, everyone was looking at me. They weren't all standing there gawking, but they were stealing glances whenever they could. I caught bits and pieces of whispered conversations as I walked past, but few were derogatory. I did hear "gay" and "queer" a couple of times, but that was about the worst of it. I guess even that wasn't bad. It was true after all, I was gay.

As we passed Casper's brother and one of his friends, I heard Jason mutter "faggot." Brad spun on his heel and grabbed Jason by the throat.

"What was that fucker? You have a problem?"

Suddenly, everyone was looking at us openly. We were the center of attention. That made me uncomfortable, but I had to suppress the smile that wanted to form on my lips. Jason looked like he was ready to wet his pants.

Brad stared into Jason's eyes, giving him a menacing look. He released him and Jason rubbed his throat.

"The word is 'gay' Jason, not 'faggot'. I don't want to hear you say 'faggot' again. Got it?"

"Why are you taking up for him? You know what he is. Hell, he's been doing it with my little brother!"

"I'm taking up for him because he's my best friend, and he doesn't need to hear stupid shit from losers like you. And as for your brother, well, if he's Brendan's boyfriend, then I'd say that he's pretty damned lucky."

We walked away amid a few cheers and "yeas." I really did have to smile then. Jason tried to dis me and no one took his side. I was almost afraid to even hope it, but it was beginning to look like my greatest fear wasn't nearly as terrible as I'd always imagined.

We stopped at my locker and I picked up my books. A few of my teammates passed and said "Hey, Brendan." I could tell from the look in their eyes that they too were surprised to learn about me, but they were friendly, they greeted me just as they did every day.

"I need to get going. You going to be okay?" asked Brad.

"Yeah," I said. "I think I am. Thanks, Brad."

"What for?" he said smiling. "Catch you later."

"Bye."

I closed my locker and walked to my first period class. People were looking at me, but it wasn't at all like I thought it would be. I'd imagined them pointing and snickering. I'm imagined them all looking at me in disgust and calling me horrible names. It wasn't like that, however. I felt very self-conscious about the whole thing, but it wasn't a tenth as bad as I'd expected. Hell, it wasn't a thousandth as bad. And to think that I'd nearly offed myself out of fear. The next time I thought of killing myself, I was going to remember that. This made twice I'd almost done it, and both times what I'd feared turned out to be far less terrible than I'd expected.

At lunch, I sat down by Casper and Stacey. I was soon joined by a bunch of my football buddies. Everything felt really weird, but it felt weird because it was so normal. I was on the receiving end of a lot of curious glances, but there really wasn't much more to it than that.

Casper looked at me with concern on his young features. It was clear that he was very worried about me. It made me love him that much more.

"You okay, Brendan? He asked quietly. "You sure you want to sit with me?"

I looked around at my team-mates sitting near. They were trying to act as if they weren't straining to listen, but there was a certain expectancy in the air.

"Yeah, I'm okay," I said in a normal voice. "And why wouldn't I want to sit with my boyfriend?"

Casper looked scared and his eyes darted around as he waited for everyone's reaction. The result was anti-climatic, however. A few of the guys seemed a little taken back that I was being so open, but no one really had a problem with it.

"I think you two are really cute together," said Stacey smiling. Her smile was genuine. Stacey had known about my gayness longer than just about anybody. "I guess I'll have to stop dreaming about you asking me out on a date." That made me laugh.

"Hey Stacey," said Brad "some of us still like girls. So if you're looking for a date…"

"I'll think about that," said Stacey.

I knew Brad wasn't knocking me. His humor even served to put me more at ease and everyone else as well. There were more than a few laughs at our table. It wasn't just a joke, however, Brad was hitting on Stacey, and from the look in her eyes I think it was a successful hit.

"Think you can lower your standards that much?" asked Marc Thayer. "I mean it's a long way down from Brendan to Brad." Everyone laughed at that.

"Hey!" yelled Brad, but even he was laughing.

It made me feel real good inside that everyone was taking the news about me so well. I'd never have dreamed that I'd be sitting there like that, being open about being gay, and having my friends and team-mates accept it so easily.

* * *

Just before football practice, a boy I didn't know came up to me as I was heading for the gym. He was young, probably a freshman.

"Hi, I'm Tommy," he said.

"I'm Brendan." I could tell he wanted something, but he seemed kind of afraid.

"Yeah, I know. Is it true about you? That you're gay?"

"Yeah," I said, "it's true. I'm gay." Something felt right about saying it out loud. Something felt good about not having to hide it anymore. I felt like I could be myself at last.

"That's really cool." Tommy paused. "I'm gay too. I never told anyone that. I've always been afraid, but if a guy like you is gay, well then maybe it's okay."

I smiled.

"Maybe, maybe we could talk sometime," he said.

"Sure, I'd like that Tommy." He smiled.

"Well, I'm sure you're busy. I just wanted to say thanks."

He turned and left. I thought his gratitude a bit misplaced, since I had hardly come out by choice, but I appreciated it anyway. Maybe some good could come out of me being open about being gay. Maybe I shouldn't have been so afraid. Maybe I should have come out on my own long ago.

* * *

Coach pulled me to the side as I entered the locker room. He took me into his office and closed the door.

"We've got a problem," he said.

"What?" My heart was racing. Everything was going so well that it seemed too good to be true. I feared that it was, and that the ax was about to fall.

"Ben's mother called me this afternoon. She's the president of the PTA. She has expressed concerns about your, uh, sexual orientation."

I looked at coach. My heart fell. This was it. This is what I'd feared. I braced myself for it.

"And?"

"She doesn't think you are the type of boy who should be captain of the football team, or on the football team at all. She thinks that will send the wrong message."

"And what do you think, Coach?"

"I think she's a bitch," he said flatly. I smiled. "That's off the record of course. I know you, Brendan. You're the best quarterback this school has ever had. You're also the finest young man I've had the privilege to coach. I'll support you in whatever course you choose. So I'm asking what you want to do."

"I think we should ask the team, Coach."

"Fair enough."

Coach led me out of his office. We were met outside by Ben.

"Can we talk for a moment?" he asked. He looked extremely uncomfortable.

"Okay," I said, none too friendly. He was the one who outed me after all. It was his mother who was trying to get me removed as team captain, and maybe kicked off the football team.

"You can use my office," said Coach.

We went inside and closed the door. Ben turned to me. There were tears in his eyes.

"I'm sorry," he said. "I didn't mean to cause you any trouble. I was so stupid. It's just that I couldn't believe it when I found you kissing Casper. I mean...you. I just...I should have kept my mouth shut, but I wasn't thinking. I blurted it out to the first guys I came across. They didn't even believe me at first. I didn't mean to out you like that. I mean, I don't think it's bad at all. It's just...different. I don't have anything against you, man. I know you probably hate me, but the best I can do is say I'm sorry. Please forgive me, Brendan."

Ben's face was filled with anguish. Tears were rolling down his cheeks. I had no doubt he was sincere.

"I forgive you," I said. "Maybe you even did me a favor. Who knows?"

"My mom," said Ben "she's going to cause trouble. She's like that. She doesn't even want me near you, but fuck her. When she tries to get you removed as Captain, I'm going to stand up myself and speak against her. What she's trying to do isn't right. I'm so sorry."

"Hey," I said, "it's okay. You made a mistake. We all do. Let's just forget about it okay?"

"You're a better person that I am, Brendan."

"Well, I don't know about that, but we're cool."

"Thanks," he said.

We stepped out of the office and into the locker room. I was apprehensive to say the least. I wasn't sure what was going to happen. I guess there were worse things than being removed as team captain. At least I'd still have most of my friends.

All my team-mates were sitting on the benches, or standing around in the locker room. Casper was there too, looking uncomfortable and a little edgy. I walked over and stood by him. Coach called for everyone's attention.

"I've been contacted by the president of the PTA," began Coach. "The call concerned Brendan and whether or not it is appropriate for him to continue as team captain."

There were angry murmurs around the room. Ben looked extremely uncomfortable and many of our team-mates were scowling at him. Everyone knew his mom was the president of the PTA.

"It is her intention to convince the PTA to contact the school board and demand that Brendan not only be removed as team captain, but be removed from the football team. Brendan and I have discussed the situation and want to know where the team stands. So, what do you think, gentlemen?"

The room erupted with shouts of "That sucks, Coach!", "Ben's mom can suck my nuts.", "We'll all quit if they try that shit!", "Fuck Ben's mom!", and various other declarations of disapproval. Coach held up his hand for quiet.

"Let's put this to a vote, men. All those in favor of Brendan remaining as team captain, raise your hand." Ben's hand shot up first. I looked around the locker room; there wasn't a hand that wasn't raised. I was so happy I felt like crying. Casper was smiling and fighting back tears. Only Casper could understand just how much the acceptance of my team-mates meant to me.

"Very well," said Coach, "I'll call the president and inform her that she will get no support from the team." The coach left and went into his office. Through the window I could see him picking up the phone and dialing.

The guys turned on Ben.

Derek grabbed him by the front of the shirt and pushed him hard against the wall. Some of the others closed in on him.

"Your mom's a bitch, Ben, and you're a fucking loser," said Derek.

I stepped forward. I was afraid they were going to start beating him. Ben's eyes were wild with terror.

"Guys! Guys! What Ben's mom is doing is not his fault. He doesn't like it anymore than you guys do." Derek slowly released him and the guys stepped back.

"Thanks, Brendan," said Ben. He looked at our team-mates. "I know, my mom's a bitch. At least you guys don't have to live with her!" Everyone laughed grimly.

The guys started talking about what they'd do if the school board tried to force me out. It didn't take them long to reach a decision. Ben himself knocked on coach's door and gave him the news. "Coach, we've all decided that if Brendan is forced out as team captain, we'll all walk. Tell the PTA president that, if she forces Brendan out, there will be no team."

I could see coach smile, then speak into the phone. Pretty soon he had to hold it away from his ear. I think Ben's mom must have been screaming at him. It wasn't long before he hung up the phone. He came out smiling.

"To make a long story short, boys, she's backing down." There were cheers throughout the locker room. It was the happiest day of my life.

Long after practice, I sat in the locker room with Casper and Brad. I'd been talking to the guys. They were full of questions like "How long have you known?", "What did your parents say?", and more other questions than I can even remember. What struck me wasn't the questions, but how much all of them supported me. Just about all of them expressed surprise, but not one of them was down on me. A few seemed a little stiff when talking to me, like they were a little afraid of being near me, but even those made an effort to let me know that it was cool with them that I was gay. I'd never have guessed they would react like that. I'd always thought that a few might stand by me, but I expected most to withdraw from me like I had some kind of disease. I really thought I'd become an outcast when they found out about me. I was wrong. I'd underestimated not only Brad, but all of my friends.

Casper

Brendan drove Brad and me over to *Phil's* after football practice. We got cheeseburgers, drinks, and fries. The three of us ate and laughed and kidded each other. Looking at Brendan, no one would have known that he was ready to kill himself less than twenty-four hours before. His mood was completely changed. He was happier than I'd ever seen him. I think it really got to him that everyone was so supportive. There were a few jerks at school of course that called us both names, but not many. Those who did call us "faggots" or "queers" were usually silenced by those around them. Brendan had a lot of friends and they were making sure neither of us had to put up with crap from anybody.

Brad was especially nice to me. He'd always been pretty nice, but now he was really going out of his way. I think he was treating me so well because he knew how much Brendan cared about me, and how much I cared for him. I was glad that Brendan had such a good friend.

My life had changed so much in such a short time. It had been bouncing around from bad to good and back again the whole time I'd known Brendan. On the very day it could have hit bottom, it rose to new heights. Suddenly, everything was looking up. I knew there were problems ahead, but everything was looking better than it had in a long time.

Brendan dropped Brad off at his house and I was next. Before I got out of the car Brendan pulled me to him and kissed me. I was surprised. He'd always been so secretive about our relationship before. I guess it shouldn't have surprised me, however. Everyone in town probably knew about us, so there was no use hiding something that everyone already knew. It felt good to be open about our relationship.

No one was home, so I got busy on my homework. I wanted to get it out of the way so I'd have some time later to walk and think. I had a lot to think about. It didn't take me long to get through all my schoolwork, but the shadows were lengthening as I stepped outside. I found myself walking toward the cemetery while I ran the past few days through my mind.

I thought about the future even more than the past. I wondered what life would be like for Brendan and me. He was rich and I was poor, but I knew that didn't matter. There was something special between us that would always be there. I just knew it. I started dreaming about us getting a little house together and living far away from my family. I didn't really care where we lived, so long as I could be with Brendan. That was what was important.

My day had been an eventful one. I was no longer the "invisible boy." I was about as visible as I could get. Wherever I went at school, people were looking at me, even teachers. I didn't mind. They weren't looking at me because I was poor. Thanks to Brendan, I had clothes as nice as anyone. They were looking at me because I was Brendan's boyfriend and they all knew it. I knew we were an unlikely pair. My classmates and teachers must have wondered how Brendan and I ended up together. I found that I actually liked the attention. I was proud that Brendan was my boyfriend. He was the best looking guy in school, and the nicest too. All the girls wanted him, and I'm sure a few of the guys too, but he was mine. I was even proud of being gay. Things had sure changed for me, and for the better.

I walked through the cemetery, remembering the times I'd hidden there from the terrible trio. They were once the terror of my life, but Brendan had taken that terror away. I thought too of the night that Brendan chased me into the graveyard, and how I'd thought he was going to hurt me. It seemed impossible now that I'd ever thought such a thing. I laughed to myself when I remembered how Stacey had taken Brendan out with a tree branch, although I guess it wasn't really funny. She'd hurt him. That was in the past though, so I guess it was okay to laugh about it now. Brendan had told me more than once that he sure wouldn't want Stacey for an enemy.

I sat down in front of my mom's grave and looked at her tombstone. As always, I felt like she was there with me. This time I didn't need her to quiet my fear. This time I just wanted to share my happiness with her.

"I met someone, Mom," I said. "I love him. I hope you won't mind me saying this, but I love him as much as I love you. I don't think you'll mind, however. I know you want me to be happy. I hope you're happy too. I'm sure you are. I wish you were here so I could hug you. I can feel you, though. I know you're here with me. I'm happy now and everything's going to be okay."

I sat there in silence for a long time, just listening to the breeze, the insects, and the sound of my own heart. I was at peace.

As a chill crept into the air, I let my feet carry me back toward the dilapidated shack I called home. Even it didn't seem so bad now that Brendan was in my life. He made everything worth while. I looked into the sky and saw the moon shining bright. I wondered if Brendan could see it too. I'd only been away from him for a little while, and I'd be with him again the very next day, but it still seemed that we were too long apart. I wanted to be with him every minute of every day. I'd once been disgusted by the thoughts running through my head, the thoughts about other boys, but now I knew that there was nothing wrong with that. What I felt for Brendan was something special. It was love and there could be nothing bad in that.

Brendan

I pulled the convertible into the drive. The day I thought I'd never survive had turned out to be one of the best in my life. I never dared dream that my friends and classmates would be so accepting. I'd heard so many horrible stories about what had happened to other boys when they were outed. I knew those stories were true, which made my own story that much more remarkable.

I felt a tremendous weight lift from my shoulders. I'd always wondered how many of my friends would still be my friends if they knew about me. I'd always feared that they'd leave me, even Brad. I'd underestimated them to be sure. I felt closer to Brad now than I ever had before. I'd long feared losing him if he found out I was gay, but he'd been the most supportive of all. I really don't think I could have walked into school if he hadn't been there with me every step of the way. I smiled. I had no doubts about my friends any more.

The moment I opened the front door, I knew something was seriously wrong. My parents were sitting on the couch, waiting for me.

"Sit down!" said my father, pointing to the chair directly across from them. I could tell by the tone of his voice that I was in deep shit.

"Mrs. Woolsey called earlier. You want to explain what she told us about?"

Fuck.

"If she called then you obviously know already," I said.

"I want to hear it from your lips, Brendan. Tell me it isn't true. Tell me you are not one of those!" My father was yelling. He almost never yelled.

"Listen," said my mother, "I know it can't be true. A strong, athletic boy like you, it's ridiculous." My mom was always the peacemaker.

"But it is true, Mom. I'm gay."

My mother started crying right before my eyes. She just broke down and cried. It made me feel about two inches tall. My own mother was crying because I was gay. I think it was worse than anything that could have happened at school.

My dad was so mad he couldn't even speak. He just sat there and steamed. He was like a smoking volcano, ready to erupt at any second.

"You're just confused, Brendan," said my mother between sobs. "It can't be true."

"I'm not confused."

"And just what does that mean!?" my father burst out.

"It means I know I'm gay."

"So it's true? You where caught…kissing that boy?"

"Yes," I said. I felt a certain defiance within myself. My own parents were attacking what I was. It made me beyond angry. "And we've done a lot more."

My father reached over and smacked me hard in the face. It hurt. I nearly attacked him, but I somehow managed to keep myself under control.

"I don't want to hear that! Here is what you are going to do, Brendan. You are going to stay away from that boy! You are never to see him again, never! You are going to find a nice girl. You're going to tell everyone it was all a mis-understanding and that you are not gay. You will go to a psychiatrist to have your sickness cured. You will…"

"The hell I will! I'm not doing any of that shit!" I yelled. "I love Casper. I'll see him if I damned well please. I'm not going to find a girl. I'm not going to live a lie anymore. I'm not sick. I don't need cured. I haven't got fucking cancer or some mental illness. I'm gay!"

My father drew his hand back and tried to smack me again. I grabbed his wrist and held it.

"Don't touch me," I warned him.

"Don't talk back to me, Brendan!"

My mother just stood back and watched. She looked horrified, but she was horrified that I was gay, not at the things my own father was saying to me. I couldn't believe it. I always knew my parents would have trouble accepting me if they knew, but I never dreamed they'd be so uncaring and unreasonable. I stared at them both.

"Listen, I'm gay. That's all there is to it. I'm not going to change. I am going to see Casper. He's my boyfriend and I love him. I don't care what you say."

My father was so furious I thought he was going to explode. He stood there trembling with rage, his fists clenched tightly at his sides.

"I think we all need to cool down," said my mother.

"Go to your room!" screamed my father. That was his solution for everything. He sent me to my room whenever I disagreed with him. He sent me to my room the time I dented the car. He sent me to my room if my grades weren't perfect. And now, he was sending me to my room because I was gay. I had news for him; some time in my room wasn't going to change things.

I considered saying something more to him, but I knew it was useless. I knew it wouldn't make any difference. He wouldn't listen, wouldn't even hear. I turned on my heel, ran up the stairs, and slammed the door behind me.

I sat down on the edge of my bed and started crying. My parents, and especially my father, had never been that caring, but they'd never treated me quite so harshly before. It was like they didn't love me at all. I was a good son. I knew I was. It didn't matter what I did; however, it was never enough for them. Even when I made captain of the football team, they weren't happy about it. All my father said was "You should have been captain last year."

I seriously thought about running away, but I had Casper to think about. I couldn't leave without him. I was certain he'd go with me, but what kind of life would we have on the run? I knew it would be a hard life. My father would cut me off from my funds the second he found out. He'd cancel my credit cards and lock me out of my own bank account so fast I wouldn't have a chance to get my hands on my own money. My father was a very powerful man. He could and would do it.

I lay back on my bed with my hands behind my head. I stared at the ceiling. I had no idea what I was going to do. There had to be some way to get my parents off my back. At the moment, it looked like nothing short of me renouncing my own sexuality would be good enough for them. I'd have to promise to stay away from Casper too, and that I would not do. He needed me, and I needed him.

I closed my eyes and tried to think of a way out of my situation, but nothing would come. I don't know how long I lay there with my eyes shut, wondering how I could make things better. If Casper had not been in my life I might have done something drastic. Casper *was* in my life, so that wasn't an option.

The door to my room burst inward and my eyes flew open. The room was bathed in red and white flashing light coming from outside. Two police officers rushed at me and grabbed me before I even knew what was happening.

They forced me onto my face on the bed and handcuffed my arms behind my back.

"Get off me!" I kept screaming, but they ignored me. They pulled me to my feet and through the bedroom door into the hall. I didn't know what the fuck was going on. Why were the police after me? The only thing I was sure about was that my father was behind it. I struggled to get free, but there wasn't much I could do handcuffed.

My parents were standing in the living room, looking at me. My father had a look on his face that said "I told you not to defy me, boy." My mother looked stricken.

"Mom?" I said.

"It's for you own good," she told me. "You're going to be cured."

"Cured of what!?" I was furious. I fought against the officers holding me, practically knocking them down. I went wild fighting and screaming. They dragged me toward the door. My father glared at me. I spit at him as I passed.

The officers dragged me down the front steps. I was fighting them every inch of the way. All the neighbors were in the yard watching by then. It was humiliating. The two officers pulled me toward a waiting ambulance. The lights were flashing like there was some big medical emergency. The officers, along with two guys from the ambulance, forced me onto a gurney and strapped me down. Before I knew it, I was inside the ambulance and we were speeding away.

I strained against the restraints, but it was no use. One of the guys in the back filled a hypodermic syringe with something and shot it into my arm. I began to feel sleepy and it was hard to focus my eyes. I gradually lost consciousness, wondering what the fuck was going on.

Casper

I looked all over, but I couldn't find Brendan anywhere at school. He didn't show up for lunch. It wasn't like him to miss school. I wondered if maybe he was sick or something, but then I started hearing the rumors. I couldn't believe them. They couldn't be true. Brendan, taken away in an ambulance to the *Cloverdale Center*? It was a mental hospital for kids. There was no reason for Brendan to have been taken there.

I was on my way to football practice when Jason cornered me in the hallway.

"I heard what happened to your boyfriend. So tragic," he said sarcastically. "I always knew he wasn't playing with a full deck."

"Shut up, Jason."

"You'd better be nice to me, little brother. Your big football stud isn't here to protect you anymore." He paused and looked me up and down. "See you tonight, Casper. It's been a long time. I've missed you." He made my skin crawl. I hated him. I was suddenly gripped with fear. Jason was right about one thing. If Brendan was gone, I was in danger. I'd have to watch my back. If it was true, I was damned sure not going to be home when Jason was there. I knew what would happen.

Brendan didn't show up for football practice, but I still couldn't believe what I'd heard. As soon as Brad walked into the locker room, I pulled him to the side.

"You know where Brendan is?" I asked him.

Brad confirmed that the rumor was true. He'd talked to one of Brendan's neighbors who'd seen them take him away. I grew angrier by the second as Brad told me what they'd done to him. I was frightened for him, and worried. I nearly lost it when Brad told me why they'd taken Brendan away. I simply could not believe it.

Brendan

I woke up in a hospital bed, wearing a flimsy gown that didn't cover my ass. I wondered what they'd done with my clothes. I tried to get up but I was held securely in place by restraints. I looked around and saw a boy in the bed next to me. He reminded me a little of Casper because he was blond and thin, but he was even taller than me.

"Where am I?" I asked.

"You're in the *Cloverdale Center*, dude." The boy sounded like a surfer from California and seemed just a bit simple-minded. His goofy smile made him seem even more dim-witted.

"*The Cloverdale Center?*"

"Yeah, you've heard of it, I bet."

"But that's where they put all the mental kids," I said without thinking. I looked at the boy, realizing what I'd said. "No offense."

"None taken." He smiled even more intensely than before. "I'm Chad." He got up and walked to my bed. He shook my hand.

"Brendan."

"Well, Brendan, what are you in for?" I wasn't sure I wanted to answer. I had a pretty good idea why I was there, even though it was totally wrong for me to be there for that. Chad peered at me.

"You gay?" he asked.

"Yeah," I said, looking at him curiously.

"Me too, that's why I'm here. My parents put me in right after I told them. They are determined to make me into a straight boy." He laughed, but there was no humor in his voice. His smile was gone. I looked at him. He had the saddest eyes I'd ever seen in my entire life.

"I guess that's why I'm here too. My parents found out about me and a few minutes later the cops were busting through my door."

"Sounds dramatic," said Chad. "My parents promised they'd only put me in here for a couple days, just for some tests. That was over two months ago. They lied to me. These bastards have been trying to make me straight."

"How?" I asked. I was feeling very nervous and afraid.

"A lot of counseling, dude—psychiatric bull-shit, hypnosis, drugs—lots of drugs."

I looked at Chad's eyes. They were kind of bloodshot. He looked like the boys at school who smoked a lot of pot. He had a nervous edge to him and his eyes darted around. He was a bit freaky and I had no doubt it was the drugs they'd pumped into him. That was probably why he seemed a little slow and goofy too.

"The worst thing is the ring, however."

"What's that?" I asked.

Before he could answer, a doctor came into the room. Chad went back to his bed.

"So how are we, um, Brendan," he said, looking at my chart.

"WE want the fuck out of here," I told him. "I don't belong here. I'm not sick."

"Now, Brendan, your parents placed you here so we could help with your problem."

"I don't have a problem!" I screamed at him.

"You need to calm down."

"Why should I calm down? I was kidnapped, drugged, brought here against my will, and strapped in this fucking bed!"

"It's all for you own good, I assure you, Brendan. We're here to help you. We're going to work with you to cure your sickness."

"I'm not sick! I'm gay. It is not a sickness!"

"You'll see things differently after treatment. Your parents tell me you're a fine young man. We'll get you cured and then you can go back home."

"I have no intention of going back there!" I yelled.

The doctor didn't respond to that. Instead, he went about his business.

"Now, the first thing we need to do is run a routine physical examine." He pushed a button by the bed and two burly orderlies appeared almost instantly. "You can come along with me quietly, Brendan, or these gentlemen will help you there. Which will it be?"

I eyed them suspiciously, but I knew I probably wouldn't get far even if I broke away from them. I had every intention of getting the hell out of that place, but I needed some time to plan and to scope things out. If I caused trouble, they'd just watch me that much more closely.

"I'll come quietly," I said.

The doctor released my restraints and I sat up slowly, rubbing my wrists. The orderlies were tensed and ready to act, but I made no move to cause trouble. I'd bide my time.

Casper

I waited until I was sure my brother was out of the house, then I went in and started packing. I took all the food I could find, which wasn't much. I also took as much money as I dared out of my dad's change jar, leaving just enough that he wouldn't notice. I went into the bathroom and took a wash cloth, towel, and bar of soap. I took my blanket and pillow and grabbed the spare blanket out of the hall closet. I also gathered up matches, old candles, and an oil lamp. There wasn't much to pack really, but I'd need everything I took.

When I was finished, I sat on the edge of the bed for a moment, unsure where to go. All I knew is that I couldn't stay in the house. It was far too dangerous. My brother was just waiting his chance to get me. I knew he'd pay me back for the things I'd said to him. I was in for a real beating the next time he caught me alone. I also knew he'd do things far, far worse. I shivered just thinking about it.

I was afraid to spend too much time in the house, so I threw the trash bag I was using for a suitcase over my shoulder and headed out the door. It was dark and I had no where to go, so I headed for the cemetery.

As I was walking along the sidewalk, I sensed someone following me. I prepared to run for it. I was sure it was my brother. I spun on my heel and there was someone there, but it wasn't Jason. It was just some guy. I turned back around and walked on. Whoever it was turned at the next street. I was getting paranoid. I was beginning to act as if everyone was my brother coming to get me.

It didn't take me too long to get to the cemetery. I sat on the bench and wondered what I was going to do, and where I was going to stay. I knew that Stacey would probably put me up if I asked, but I was too proud to ask her. Besides, I didn't want to ask her something like that. It was just too much.

The air grew quickly chill so I wrapped myself up in the blankets and leaned up against a tree. I was worried about Brendan. I wondered what was happening to him. I wondered what they were doing to him. I wished there was a way that I could at least talk to him, but I knew about the *Cloverdale Center*. I'd never get in there. My eyes grew heavy. I was tired and soon fell asleep despite my discomfort.

Sometime late in the night, or early in the morning, I awoke. I was shivering and I could see my own breath. I felt cold even with the blankets wrapped around me. There was frost on the blankets and on the bench beside me. I couldn't stop shivering. I was so cold. My teeth chattered.

I got up and walked around to warm myself. It didn't help much. As I paced around the graveyard I noticed that the door to one of the mausoleums wasn't closed all the way. I stood and looked at it for a bit, then walked forward. I pushed on the door and it opened. I went back and got my stuff, then returned to the mausoleum. I walked inside and closed the door behind me.

It was cold inside, but at least I was out of the light wind that stole the heat away from my body. I lit the oil lamp and held it up high. The mausoleum wasn't very big inside. There was a single stone sarcophagus sitting near the back wall with a space in front of it. I wasn't exactly thrilled with my accommodations, but it would be better than freezing to death. The air was a bit musty, but not too bad, really. I made myself a little bed on the floor, blew out the lamp, and lay down. The floor didn't make the most comfortable bed, but I was warmer than I had been outside. I lay there with the blankets drawn close about me, half to ward off the cold and half to ward off my fear. A tear rolled down my cheek. I missed Brendan and was beginning to wonder if I'd ever see him again. It was hard to get to sleep in my spooky surroundings, but I was so very tired that my eyes finally closed and I nodded off.

Brendan

"So how was it?" asked Chad as soon as the orderlies had escorted me back from my exam and the nurse had given me a pill.

"Not too bad, although I've never cared much for 'turn your head and cough."

"I think the doctors like doin' that one. It wouldn't be so bad if they weren't all so damned old and ugly."

I sat on the edge of my bed looking at Chad. My cooperation so far had earned me freedom. The orderlies didn't strap me down to the bed again.

"Wanna go look around?" asked Chad.

"Can we?"

"Yeah, you can walk around here, usually, as long as you don't try to leave."

"Cool." I intended to become as familiar with the hospital as I possibly could. I had every intention of escaping from that place as fast as I could manage.

"Okay, I figure we have about fifteen minutes."

"Why fifteen minutes?" I asked him.

"That's how long until that Thorazine you just took kicks in. Come on."

Chad led me out into the hall. There were a lot of rooms just like ours on either side of the hall, some with kids in them, some empty. It didn't seem quite like a hospital, more like a hotel in some ways. It had a bad feeling though, as if sinister things went on there. At the end of the hall was a big picture window looking out over a big, fenced in yard.

"That's where we can go in the afternoons if we don't cause trouble," said Chad. "Sometimes it feels good just to get outside and sit in the sun." His voice was so sad it brought me down. I looked out at the yard. It was park-like, with a few flowers and trees. It was surrounded on all sides by tall fences, however. There was even barbed wire across the top.

We made our way down another hall until Chad stopped at a room.

"Come here, I want you to meet Ian."

We walked into the room. There was a boy my age sitting on the edge of his bed. He was very handsome and well built. When he noticed us he scrambled backwards and bent his head down as if he expected to get hit. The sight of him scared me. He acted like a little boy, a little boy who'd been abused.

"Take it easy, Ian," said Chad. "You remember me don't you dude? It's Chad."

Suddenly, Ian looked up and smiled. The look on his face was vacant, like his mind was empty of thought.

"There's a river in my closet," he said, pointing across the room. I followed his gaze to a small closet.

"Is there, Ian?" asked Chad, humoring him.

"Yeah, the trolls put it in there. They wanna kill me."

I looked at Ian's eyes. It was like he wasn't even there. His eyes were distant. Even when he looked at me, I had a feeling he didn't really see me.

Chad moved toward the closet door.

"Don't man, you'll let it out, we'll all drown you know? That's what they want. They want us to drown. I got it all thought out though. See, I not openin' the door and the river can't get out."

Ian was obviously out of it. It was really freaky being in there with him. He was in his own little world. I felt sorry for him.

"That's a good plan," said Chad. "Thanks for looking out for us."

Ian smiled like a four year old that's just been told he's a good boy. Seeing that look on the face of a seventeen year old was hard to take.

"This is Brendan," said Chad.

I extended my hand to shake his, but he recoiled from me as if I were going to strike him in the face.

"It's okay, dude, he's cool."

Ian looked at me suspiciously.

"You're not with the trolls are you? You don't look like one, but still, can't be too careful you know."

"Um, no, I'm not with the trolls," I told him. The kid was obviously fucked up.

"Then you can be my boyfriend, you're cute."

I didn't know what to say to that. Ian was making me extremely uncomfortable. Chad saved me.

"We have to go, Ian, but we'll be back to see you later."

"Yeah, you come back," he said, staring at me with a hungry look. His eyes went vacant again after a moment and he curled up on his bed.

Chad and I left Ian alone, but I don't even know if he noticed we left.

"What's wrong with him?" I asked as we walked down the hallway.

"Drugs."

"He an addict or something?"

"No dude. They brought him in three weeks ago. He was just like you then. They keep pumping him full of drugs though, it's frying his brain."

"They really do that?"

"Oh yeah, they pump everyone full of drugs; Valium, Ritalin, Halcion, Mellaril, Elavil, Lithium, Thorazine, you name it."

"If they do it to everyone, then why aren't you like Ian by now? You've been here longer."

"Cause I don't take most of it," said Chad. "Except the Valium, I kinda like the Valium." The big goofy grin was back on his face.

"So you don't have to take it?"

"Yeah, you do. The nurse stands right there and makes sure you do, but there's ways around that dude! I'll show you when we get back to the room."

I started to ask him more about it, but I was suddenly extremely tired. I felt like I didn't even have the energy to move. My muscles felt useless. I drooped. I was so tired that I fell against Chad.

"Fifteen minutes, almost to the second," said Chad, looking at the clock overhead. "Your Thorazine has kicked in, dude. We gotta go back."

Chad led me through the halls. I was so tired I couldn't remember the way we'd come. It seemed to take forever to make it back to the room. When I got there, I crashed on the bed. I didn't sleep. I just lay there on my side looking at Chad.

"That's how they control you," he said. "Thorazine. Makes you real tired, gives you night sweats. No one causes trouble when they're on Thorazine."

I knew I wasn't in the shape to do anything. It was an effort just to move my arm. I'd never escape if that shit was running through my veins.

"How do you get away with not taking your meds?" I asked. I realized that Chad possessed some very valuable information.

"The nurse will be here in a few minutes. Watch me closely. When she's gone, I'll show you."

"I want out of here," I said.

"Who doesn't?" said Chad.

"Yeah, but I'm going to get out of here."

"Me too," said Chad. "I've been working on it. I'll help you." That gave me some hope. Chad seemed to know the score. I was sure he had a lot in his head that would help me escape, and I intended to take advantage of it.

"Good," I said, "I'm either going to get out of this place or die trying."

"Some have died trying," said Chad. "And some have killed themselves when they couldn't escape." There was no sign of his smile at all.

The nurse came in soon and handed Chad a small paper cup and another cup of water. He upended the cup into his mouth, and then swallowed the water. I watched, but I couldn't tell he'd done anything. The nurse came to me and gave me meds the same way. I swallowed them. As soon as I'd swallowed, the nurse was on her way.

"You do it?" I asked Chad.

"Yeah."

Chad walked over to me, put his hand in front of his mouth and spit out four pills.

"When you take the pills, you stick them under your tongue. It's not hard after you've tried it a few times. Then you swallow the water. When the nurse is gone, you just spit them out. Here, you can practice with these later," said Chad, handing me three pills that were still damp from being in this mouth. "This one's Valium," he said, showing me the fourth pill. "I like Valium." He popped it into his mouth and swallowed.

I looked at the pills in my hand. I was ready to start practicing. Holding pills under my tongue was a skill I'd definitely need. I put them in the paper cup and started to toss them back into my mouth. Chad stopped me.

"Not now, dude."

"Why?"

"Cause you took your meds."

I knew what he meant almost immediately. I started to feel sleepy and dizzy and happy all at the same time. I was seeing weird shit that wasn't really there.

"Go to sleep, dude," said Chad, pushing me down onto the bed. "You can work on it tomorrow."

My eyelids grew so heavy I couldn't keep them open. In moments I was asleep.

Casper

My life was miserable without Brendan. I went back to being the invisible boy, well, not quite. I'd never be the invisible boy again, but I did try. I guess things weren't quite as bad as they had been before I'd met Brendan. The guys on the football team looked out for me. The terrible trio tried to give me some shit right after school one day, but Brad and a couple of the other guys from the team came over and offered to break their noses if they didn't knock it off. I was happy that the boys on the team liked me, even without Brendan there.

When Brendan had been gone for about a week, Brad told me to wait for him after practice. I didn't mind at all. I didn't have anywhere to go. After practice I usually hung around in the park for a little while, then went to the grocery or somewhere and bought a little something to eat. I had the money I'd taken from dad's jar. Between the food I could buy with it and what I got at school, I wasn't too bad off. I was hungry sometimes, but I was used to that. Being hungry wasn't near as bad as trying to fill all those empty hours until it was time to go to sleep. I had trouble getting to sleep in the mausoleum, so I tried to get myself real tired so it wouldn't take as long. Every evening I took long walks in the shadows to tire myself out, and then I sat by my mom's grave long into the night. Sometimes I talked to her, and sometimes I just sat there in silence until my eyes grew so heavy I couldn't keep them open, and then I went to the mausoleum and lie down. Brendan was always on my mind when I walked, and when I sat by my mom's grave. He was on my mind all the time. I missed him and was worried sick over him. Every night I cried myself to sleep wondering if he was okay. I didn't mind waiting for Brad. It was a way to fill a few more empty minutes.

I was sitting on the bench waiting when Brad walked into the locker room. I'd already finished putting up all the wash cloths and towels. I'd even swept the floor and picked up after the guys.

"Come on," he said. "I'll take you out for a burger."

We sat down in an isolated booth at *Phil's* and Brad ordered us both cheeseburgers and fries and soft drinks and even chocolate milkshakes.

"I know you and Brendan are...close," said Brad "so I wanted to let you know what's going down. I'm going to get Brendan out of that fucking hospital."

"Yes!" I said. "What can I do to help?"

"Nothing," he said. I frowned.

"I want to help."

"I know that, Casper, but you can't." He held up his hand to hold off my protest. "Brendan's dad knows about you. He has someone watching you."

I started to tell Brendan how ridiculous that was, but then I remembered the guy that always seemed to be hanging around wherever I was. At first I hadn't noticed him, but once I did, he was everywhere. Sometimes I even saw him on my walks at night. I'd seen him as Brad and I walked into *Phil's*. I hadn't really thought much about it before. He wasn't my brother, so I wasn't worried about him.

"Why is he watching me?"

"In case you try to do something like I'm going to do. So you see, you can't be involved. The best way you can help is to stay out of it."

I didn't like the idea, but Brad was probably right. I didn't want to risk messing up the chance of getting Brendan out of that hospital just because I wanted to be a part of things.

"Okay," I said. "I understand."

"Good," said Brendan. "My cousin works in the *Cloverdale Center*. He's going to take messages back and forth between Brendan and me. I'm sending the first one tonight."

"He works...there? You sure you can trust him?"

"Yeah, I can trust him. He's a good guy. He wouldn't be working there if he didn't need the money bad. I know a couple of things about him that makes it extra safe, things that would be bad for him if they got out, if you know what I mean."

"Okay," I said. My world had become more exciting, filled with secret plans, and possible blackmail.

"If I know Brendan," said Brad, "and believe me I do, he's already trying to get out of that place. I'm going to set up a time with him for it. When he breaks out I'll be there waiting on him."

"When are you going to do this?" I asked.

"Don't know yet. I'm sending the first message tonight. Brendan is going to have to disappear fast when we do it, however. His dad will have cops everywhere looking for him. If they catch him, we may never be able to get him out a second time. I'll get him out of town as quick as I can."

"I'm going with him," I said. Brad smiled.

"Somehow I already knew that. I'll tell you as soon as I find out when we're going to do it. Brendan and I will pick you up somewhere. It needs to be somewhere out of sight."

"The cemetery," I said. I didn't tell Brad I was living there in an old crypt, but it was somewhere I knew I could be.

"Yeah, that's good. We'll pick you up there. You've got to be ready because we won't have any time to spare, so make sure you have whatever you're going to take with you."

Our food arrived and we ate and schemed. It was all rather exciting, like being in some spy movie, but the whole thing made me nervous. This wasn't a movie, it was real. If we failed, Brendan would be locked up in that hospital for who knew how long. I hoped we could do it soon. I couldn't bear to think of him in there. I missed him horribly too.

When Brad and I parted ways, I felt better. At least now there was hope, and I could communicate with Brendan. I'd given Brad a note for him, written on a paper napkin. The note told him how much I loved him.

I walked long in the moonlight that night, all nervous and excited inside. I just hoped that Brendan and Brad could pull it off. I didn't know what I'd do if they couldn't.

Brendan

I slipped the pills under my tongue, just like Chad had taught me, and then swallowed the water while the nurse watched. She left us alone. It was just like Chad said; it was easy when I got the hang of it.

I was just getting ready to spit out the pills when an orderly came into the room. I thought I'd been caught, or that he was coming to take me away for some damned treatment or other, but instead he handed me a piece of paper and a napkin.

"I'll be back in an hour," he said, then left without another word.

I opened the paper. It was a letter from Brad.

"What's that?" asked Chad.

"It's a message from my best friend," I said. Chad came over and read over my shoulder.

Brad told me how the orderly was his cousin and that I could trust him. He also asked if I had a plan to escape and said that he'd be waiting to help me get away when I gave the word. He told me a lot of other things in the message too. It was the first news I'd had of the real world in days.

"You sure this is from your friend?"

"Yeah," I said. "No doubt about it."

"Okay, just checking. You never know what these dudes in here will try."

Chad seemed rather paranoid, but from what I'd experienced in *Cloverdale* so far, his paranoia was probably justified.

"We can do it now, dude," said Chad excitedly. "We might really pull it off."

Next I looked at the napkin. The message was simple:

> *"Brendan, I hope you're okay. I miss you so much. Don't worry about me, the team is looking after me. I'll be waiting*

when you get out. I'm going with you, wherever you go. There's nothing for me here without you. I love you. Please hurry. Casper."

Tears flowed from my eyes.

I read through both messages again, and then flushed them down the toilet. I wrote out a lengthy message to Brad, telling him to be waiting for me at 10 p.m. on Thursday night. Chad and I had been working on our escape plan and, with a little help from Brad's cousin; we just might be able to pull it off. My heart pounded in my chest. I had a real chance to escape at last. I'd only been in the hospital for a few days, but it seemed like an eternity.

I wrote a message to Casper as well. I told him that I was fine, which, of course, wasn't true. I also told him that they hadn't done anything bad to me in the *Cloverdale Center*, which was another lie. I didn't like lying to Casper, but I didn't want him to worry about me. I told him how very much I loved him, and that couldn't have been truer.

The orderly was back right on time. He took the notes and quickly hid them away.

"Let me know if you need anything," he said. "I'll do what I can to help." Moments later, he was gone.

I turned to Chad.

"Thursday night," I said. "That's when we're getting out of here."

"You know, dude, you've turned out to be a better room-mate that I thought," he said smiling.

We didn't waste any time. We'd been planning and scheming almost since my arrival and Chad had been working on ways to get out of there even before I arrived. Sometimes Chad seemed too spaced out to even think straight, but he was a smart boy. He'd figured out how to avoid taking the drugs they tried pumping into him every day and that had allowed him to figure out a whole lot more. In the time he'd been in *Cloverdale*, Chad had learned the schedule for the security guards, the schedule for the nurses and doctors, and even the schedule for trash and laundry pick up. He kept his eyes open for any means of escape. One of his most important discoveries was that a small window in a storage room in the basement wasn't connected into the alarm system and had only a simple lock. He'd explained that it would be a tight fit, but that we could squeeze through.

There were three main problems standing between us and freedom. One of them was being able to get away from the center quick enough to avoid recapture after we'd escaped through the fences. Brad would take care of that one, however. Once we made it out, he could speed us away. That left us with two problems. One of these was getting through the fence. It was far too tall to climb and even if we could have, the top had barbed wire on it. It was only the day before that this problem had been solved. Chad had been saving up his drugs for weeks and he'd managed to trade them to one of the maintenance men for a pair of bolt cutters. He'd stashed the cutters in the little basement storage room. That left us with just one problem, but it was a big one.

After stashing the bolt cutters, Chad had been caught in the basement. He faked being totally high and out of his mind. That kept him out of trouble, but his presence in the basement had drawn attention to the fact that it was easy for him to get down there. The old locking mechanism to the basement door had been replaced with a high security lock that Chad couldn't pick. Opening the door would require a key.

We'd seemed so close when Chad got the bolt-cutters, only to be faced with a new obstacle in our path. We'd already been working out ways to get our hands on a key when the note from Brad arrived and a new opportunity presented itself. His cousin had a key.

Brad had long been my best friend, but if our attempt at escape was successful, I'd owe him a debt I could never repay. Without help from the outside, I don't think we'd have ever managed an escape.

I owed Chad a lot too. Without him, I wouldn't have been able to keep all the drugs the nurses pushed at me out of my system. I'd have been as doped up as everyone else and wouldn't have had a chance. That was the real reason the center handed out drugs like candy. All the kids in the center were so out of it they couldn't even think about escaping. Ian was a prime example of that. The drugs had fried his brain. I knew that without Chad's help, I'd have been like him in a short time.

I wanted nothing more than to escape from that place. In the short time I'd been there, I'd learned what it was all about. Parents sent their kids there in a fucked up, delusional attempt to make them straight. Chad and I had checked around. Kids had been committed to *Cloverdale* for all kinds of reasons supposedly, but every last one of them was gay. That was the real reason they were there; their parents couldn't deal with their kid's sexual orientation, so they put them in the *Cloverdale Center*. That was bad enough, but what the doctors and nurses did in there was worse. It was criminal. It was nothing less than psychological, and sometimes even physical, torture. After what I'd seen, I had no doubt that the center was all about sadism for profit.

* * *

Brad's cousin came into the room the very next day with another note. This one simply said that Brad would be wherever we told him to be at 10 p.m. on Thursday. I quickly wrote out instructions to Brad, while I talked to his cousin.

"On Thursday night, we need you to get us into the basement, is that a problem?" I asked.

"You sure don't ask for much, do you?" he said, acting as if I'd ask him to walk us out the front gates.

"Can you do it?"

"Yes, but it will be risky. You boys understand I can only cover your butts so far?"

"Yeah."

"As long as we understand each other. I'll get you into the basement, then I'm out of there and you're on your own."

"Thanks," I said. "That's all we'll need." I paused, then realized I didn't even know the guys name. "What's your name?"

"Jason." How ironic that his name was the same as that of Casper's brother.

I handed Jason the note for Brad and he carefully hid it away. He agreed to come for us the next Thursday at 9:45 p.m.

* * *

There were only a few days until our planned escape, but it seemed like forever in that place. Those were the worst days of my life. I had to endure hours of psychological battering from doctors intent on "curing" me. It was enough to drive me out of my mind. Every time they came for me, I cringed. I knew what was coming, a verbal and psychological attack meant to beat me into submission. If I'd been on the drugs that they continued to poke at me, I think I really would have lost it in there. It was a psychological horror house.

Chad and I were sitting on the edge of my bed talking when the door opened and Brian, one of the orderlies, walked right in. No one ever knocked. Privacy meant nothing at *Cloverdale*. Brian gave us an amused look.

"I guess you boys haven't learned much from your sessions," he said.

"What's that supposed to mean?" I asked.

"I know what you boys do when no one is around. Just look at how close you're sitting together."

"Give me a break, dude," said Chad.

"Come on, queer boy," he said, looking at me, "it's time for a session with your new shrink."

I got up and followed him. What I really wanted to do was beat him senseless. Most of the orderlies were real dicks, but Brian was the worst. He lived for putting us down and for slinging sexual innuendo at us. He loved calling me "queer boy." I thought about telling him what a hypocrite he was. He never failed to devour me with his eyes. I could tell just by looking that he wanted me bad. It made me dislike him that much more. I had no doubt he was gay. What kind of guy would be a part of the *Cloverdale Center* when he knew what went on there, and was gay himself? I knew he had to be one sick puppy. I was afraid of him. I feared that he'd attack me some night. It was one more reason for wanting to get out of that place.

Brian pushed me toward an open door.

"This is it, get in there you little pillow biter."

I could feel a draft as Brian pulled on a sting at the back of my gown. I could feel him staring at my bare ass. I wanted to slug him, but I didn't dare. I'd been working on my "good boy" reputation so I could move about *Cloverdale* freely. It wasn't easy to be passive when I really wanted to tear the whole fucking place apart.

I stepped into an office and there was an elderly man sitting there. I hadn't seen him before. He gestured to a leather chair across from him and I sat down, I inhaled sharply as the cold leather touched my naked skin where my gown was open in the back. Brian smirked at me as he leaned against the wall and watched.

For a few moments, the doctor just sat there looking at me. I looked back at him, and at his diploma hanging on the wall. He'd graduated from some school in the Cayman Islands. It figured. I knew no real psychiatrist would be working in a place like *Cloverdale*.

"Brendan, I'm Dr. Starke," he said, looking through my file. "It looks like you've been cooperative so far, that's a good sign, a sign you are willing to change. You'd be surprised at how many of the boys here are not."

"I've seen how they act," I said. It wasn't what I wanted to say at all, but if I spoke my mind I'd probably end up strapped to my bed.

"Do you know what this is?" he said, indicating a machine with a lot of wires coming out of it and a graph that looked like some kind of earthquake detector.

"No sir."

"It's a lie detector. Honesty is very important if you're to get well. I'm going to hook you up to the machine and then ask you a few questions."

I looked at the detector apprehensively.

"Don't worry, it is quite painless."

Pain wasn't exactly what I was worried about, although the thought that it might hurt had crossed my mind as well.

"Please pull the top of your gown down," said Dr. Starke.

I untied the bow at the back of my neck and pulled my gown down. I shivered as the cold air hit my bare chest. I felt awkward sitting there practically naked.

Dr. Starke taped sensors to my head and various parts of my upper body. They were cold at first, but they didn't hurt. I still flinched when he turned the detector on.

"First some simple questions," said Dr. Starke. "What is your name?"

"Brendan."

"Very good."

"How old are you?"

"Seventeen."

"Now, I want you to lie on this question. What year were you born?"

"1970."

"Excellent, now we can get down to business."

"Are you a homosexual?"

"Yes."

"Are you a virgin?"

"No."

"Have you preformed oral sex?"

The questions were becoming increasingly uncomfortable. Dr. Starke was asking things that were none of his business. I thought about telling him so, but I had to maintain the farce of cooperation.

"Yes."

"Have you preformed anal sex?"

"No."

He kept asking question after question, each one more intimate than the one before. Brian was all ears. I'm sure he loved every second of my session. He was discovering just the kind of things he wanted to know. I bet he would have paid big to be in on my session. I hated it that he was there; it made it much more difficult. He kept leering at me and boring into me with his eyes. I felt naked before him. My face was getting hot and red with embarrassment.

"Do you hope that our sessions here will cure you of your homosexuality?"

I hesitated. I didn't hope that at all, but I couldn't say that to Dr. Starke. The lie detector would tell him if I didn't tell the truth, however.

"Yes," I said and swallowed hard. Dr. Starke looked at the readout.

"That isn't true, is it, Brendan?"

"No sir."

"So you have no desire to be cured?"

He was pinning me down and I didn't like it. He was going to ruin everything.

"It's just that I don't think it is possible to be cured, sir. I don't think it's a disease. To cure me, you'd have to alter my genes."

It wasn't really an answer to his question, but I think I surprised him.

"I see."

There were more questions and I was sweating it. Dr. Starke was finding out a lot more than I wanted him to know. I was half afraid he'd tell Brian to strap me into my bed when he took me back. Dr. Starke didn't look happy with me at all as he pulled the sensors off, but he didn't say anything to me about it.

"Escort Brendan back to his room," said Dr. Starke.

Brian pulled me out of the chair before I even had time to pull my gown up. It slipped and I was standing there naked for a few moments before I got it back on. Brian took the opportunity to enjoy the view. He leered and smirked at me. I hated him. He made me walk in front him. I did my best to keep my gown closed but my ass was still showing. I'm sure Brian loved that.

"That guy gives me the creeps," I said to Chad, as soon as Brian was gone.

"Yeah, he's a dangerous one, dude. I've heard some rumors that he…well; you don't need to hear about that. The less you know the better." I wasn't sure about that. What was going through my mind was probably worse than reality.

I almost asked how they could have someone like that working at *Cloverdale*, but considering what was done at the center, it was a stupid question.

"You know the orderly with the black hair, Tracy?"

"Yeah."

"Well you should hear what he's done with some of the girls. It's sick dude."

"I don't want to hear about it," I said.

* * *

I sat my tray down beside Chad and Ian in the lunch room. It was a whole different world from high school. Instead of being surrounded by team-mates and friends, I was surrounded by other boys and girls who had been cruelly committed to *Cloverdale*. There was an overall sense of fear in the air that I understood only too well. No one had rights in *Cloverdale*. There was no knowing when someone would come to take you away, or jab a needle in your arm. I tensed every time someone in white walked near. Some of the kids did a lot more than that. I'd seen some of them flinch as if they were expecting to be stuck whenever an orderly got close.

I forced myself to eat the bland food they gave us. I always thought the food at school was bad, but it was fantastic compared to what we got in the *Cloverdale Center*. I ate it to keep my strength up. I knew I'd need it to get out of that place.

Ian suddenly ducked down and hid between Chad and I.

"Trolls," he whispered hoarsely. He was actually shaking. Chad and I put our hands on him to comfort him.

"It's okay, dude," said Chad, "they can't see you. Just stay down for a minute. We'll tell you when they're gone."

Ian was so pitiful. It infuriated me when I thought about what they'd done to him in there. In an effort to force him into being straight, they'd fucked up his brain with drugs so bad he'd probably never be okay. Seeing him scared me too. He was way too much like me. I knew that I could easily end up like him if I wasn't very careful. I was able to avoid taking most of the drugs they pushed at me, but there was no way to avoid the injections. There was nothing to stop them from messing up my brain with drugs like they'd done to Ian.

"Okay, they're gone." I told Ian.

He lifted his head cautiously and looked around. He went back to eating, playing with his food like a six year old. A tear rolled down my cheek for Ian. It was a tear for me too, and for everyone stuck in that horrible place. I missed Casper, and Brad, and the all the others so bad I felt like bawling right there.

"Trolls! Trolls!" said Ian, and ducked his head again.

"Here, dude, take this," said Chad, slipping Ian a pill.

"What's this?"

"It's a pill. It's magic. You take that and the trolls can't see you, makes you invisible to trolls, dude."

Ian looked at Chad like he thought Chad was a fruitcake. It would have been funny in another situation. "I'm serious, dude. Brendan and I both took one and now the trolls can't see us. Brendan, stick your tongue out at that big one over there."

"No don't!" Ian nearly screamed.

I stuck my tongue out at an imaginary troll. Ian trembled with fear.

"See, dude. It works. They can't see you. Swallow it."

Ian did as he was told. I wondered what Chad was really giving him. He seemed to have every kind of drug known to man.

"See, it's working already. They can't see you dude. Now you don't have to worry. Just one of those pills will keep you invisible forever."

Ian smiled slyly, content to be safe from the trolls. I wished we could keep him safe from the real horrors of *Cloverdale* so easily. It's too bad there wasn't a pill that could keep the staff away.

* * *

I had a session with Dr. Starke, or some psychiatrist or other, every single day. I was asked so many questions my brain was numb. The psychiatric sessions weren't nearly the worst of it, however. On what would hopefully be my last full day in the center, I was awakened early by Brian and another orderly and taken to a sterile looking room with a steel examination table in the exact middle. I felt like I was in some kind of concentration camp or something.

The orderlies stripped me naked, their hands wandering about my body. Brian's touch lingered, he touched me in private places like I was his to do with as he pleased. It struck terror into my heart when I realized that I really was his to do with as he pleased. Brian leered at me as he touched me, making me feel as if I was some boy he'd lured into his car with candy. I knew about some of the horrible things that happened to kids in the center. I was glad I'd be getting out of there soon. From the look in Brian's eyes, I had a feeling that something very horrible would be happening to me soon. If I stayed in the center much longer, he'd get me. The orderlies strapped me down to the table so I couldn't move. The metal was icy cold on my naked backside.

A doctor I'd never seen before, and a nurse, entered the room. The nurse shot something in my arm that made me feel like I was dead. The doctor and nurse put on plastic gloves and started prodding my body all over. I felt so vulnerable lying on that table, naked and unable to move. The orderlies watched as the doctor and nurse touched me in places that no one ever had before, determining if I had been sexually active or not. I'd never felt so violated in my entire life. My privacy meant nothing to them. They prodded and touched me like I was some kind of specimen and not a human being. I was more than half afraid that they were going to operate on me or something.

When they were finished, I was taken into another room and strapped into a chair, still naked. The nurse put a little ring around my penis. It was humiliating to have her touch me there. The ring had wires that led from it to some kind of machine. I was terrified. Chad had never told me about the "ring," but he'd spoken with a shudder when he'd mentioned it.

"We will do a few test slides first," said the doctor.

I didn't know what that meant until the nurse dimmed the lights and pictures began to appear on a screen in front of me. There were slides of trees and flowers and puppies at first, but then there were slides of naked women.

"No reaction," said the nurse, looking at some kind of readout on the machine.

The next slides were of naked men, most of them real hunks. I started to get excited.

"Definite reaction to slides of nude males," said the nurse with a disapproving tone in her voice.

"Begin the correction procedure," said the doctor.

More slides appeared on the screen, of all kinds of things. A slide of a really gorgeous blond boy appeared. I yelped. The ring gave me a painful shock.

Painful doesn't even really begin to describe it. It was excruciating. It was a hundred times worse than the time I'd accidentally been kicked full force in the nuts during football practice one day.

The next couple of slides were of animals and then there was one of a cute shirtless wrestler about my age. I cried out in pain as another shock was delivered.

"Whenever you begin to get an erection," explained the doctor, "you will feel a painful shock. In time, this negative stimulus will alter your inappropriate reaction to the stimulus of a nude male body."

He made it sound so clinical, so logical. It was neither. It was nothing less than torture. They were trying to torture me into being straight. Every few seconds I felt the excruciating pain assault my manhood. I was afraid there would be permanent damage. No one there cared for my welfare. All they cared about was changing me so that I wouldn't be attracted to boys. I tried not to cry out with pain, but I couldn't help it. It was just too intense. Tears flowed from my eyes.

"Please stop," I said. The doctor didn't answer. I received another shock that made me writhe on the chair. "Pleeaaaase stop," I begged him. The pain was too intense. I couldn't take it. I felt humiliated for doing so, but I kept begging the doctor to stop.

"I'm sorry, Brendan, but this is a necessary part of your treatment. If you cooperate with your psychiatrist more fully, we'll be able cure you faster, and there will be less pain."

I knew he wasn't sorry at all. I was sure he liked dealing out pain to boys. He was some kind of sadist or something. I felt as if I were being blackmailed too. What he was really saying was "Do what we want and we'll stop hurting you." I hated him. I hated the whole *Cloverdale Center* and all the doctors and nurses in it. They were worse than monsters.

After what seemed an eternity, the ring was removed and I was unstrapped. Brian threw my hospital gown at me.

"We're scheduling you for another session next week," said the doctor as I departed. With any luck, I wouldn't be there to re-enter his chamber of horrors.

The orderlies led me back to my room, making jokes at my expense about fried wieners. I didn't think it was very damned funny. I was still in pain and could barely walk. I wondered about Brad's cousin, Jason. How could he work in such a place? I tried not to judge him harshly. He was helping Chad and me out after all.

The orderlies pushed me onto my bed and left me there, doubled over from the pain. Brian gave me a slap on the ass and said "I'll be seeing you later, queer boy" so that only I could hear. His voice struck terror into my soul.

Chad hopped up as soon as they left. He grabbed a cup of water and pulled a pill out of his collection that he kept secreted away. He handed it to me.

"This will help ease the pain," he said. I downed it without comment. I trusted Chad completely.

Within a few minutes the pain eased enough that I could lie back on the bed. Chad sat on the side of the bed and brushed the hair out of my eyes. My eyes were still filled with tears. It wasn't just the pain either. I felt humiliated.

"Had a session with the ring huh?" he said.

"Yeah." I was still shaky. The experience had left me frightened and insecure. I felt like I wanted to cry. I wanted to be brave and defiant, but I lay there in fear, terrified that they'd come back for me.

"It was horrible," I said, looking at Chad, my eyes wide with fear. "I felt like I was being interrogated or something. It was like they were torturing me for information, but they never asked any questions." I was really upset. I didn't understand how anyone could do that to another person.

Someone passed in the hall. I jerked my head in the direction of the door and tried to sit up. I thought they were coming for me. I thought they were going to take me back to that room and strap me in that chair again. I was ready to fight anyone who came through that door, but no one came. Chad put his hand on my chest and pushed me back down.

"Take it easy, dude. Man, your heart's beating a mile a minute. Hey, look at me."

My eyes were darting around the room. I was breathing hard and my chest felt tight. I was pretty sure I was having a panic attack, even though I didn't really know what one was.

"Look at me, Brendan," said Chad, taking my head in his hands and gently forcing me to look at him. My eyes met his. Chad had that doped up look he always did, but I read sympathy and friendship there too. "Calm down, dude. It's over. They won't give you another session with the ring for at least a week. We'll be long gone by then, dude. You won't have to do it again. Understand?"

I nodded my head. I was still very frightened, but he was right. In just over a day, we'd be gone, if we were successful that is. I was more determined than ever to get out of that place.

"How many times…" I asked.

"They've done it to me four times," said Chad quietly. I pitied him. I pitied anyone who had to experience that. It was like something out of a mad scientist movie. It was so horrible that I almost couldn't believe it was true. The pain in my groin was a reminder that it was all too real. I was angry. This is what so called "normal people" did to boys who they labeled as "queer." We were tortured just because we loved someone of our own sex. It made me ashamed of the society I lived in. I wouldn't have wished what I'd gone through on the worst criminal, and yet it was done every day to innocent boys.

"We've got to get out of here," I said. "I can't take this. I always thought I was strong, but I can't take this."

"Dude, don't let them get to you. Don't get down on yourself. You are strong. What you've been through would shake up anybody. We're getting out of here. You won't have to face it again."

"I wish we could take them all with us," I said, thinking of all the other boys in that place, and girls too.

"I know, dude, but we can't. There's just no way. Someday they'll shut this fucking place down. Someday people will wake up and see what they've done here, and then they'll shut it down."

"I hope so," I said, and fell silent.

* * *

Very late that night, or perhaps very early the next morning, I stirred in my sleep and opened my eyes. My vision was blurred at first, but when I saw what was going on, I sat bolt upright in bed. An orderly was holding a cloth over Chad's face. I cried out and the orderly turned to me, it was Brian. He crossed the space between the beds in a flash and hit me in the face.

"Shut up, queer boy!" he hissed.

I was too frightened to call out for help. I wasn't even sure I'd get any if I screamed. I looked over at Chad's bed. He wasn't moving.

"A little chloroform goes a long way," laughed Brian.

At first I thought he'd smothered him or something, but he'd only knocked him out. As I thought more about that, I grew more afraid. Brian leered at me. He pulled a syringe out of his pocket. I tried to fend him off, but he was too fast for me. He pressed his weight down on me, trapping my arms, while holding one hand across my mouth to keep me from screaming. I felt the sting of the needle in my arm, then the greater sting of whatever it was he shot into me. Almost instantly, I felt very weak and groggy. I tried to push Brian away, but there was no strength in my body. It was as if my muscles didn't exist.

Brian threw away the syringe then ran his hands down my arms. He pulled my gown down to my waist and climbed on top of me. I was powerless to stop him. I was shaking with terror. My eyes filled with tears. I tried to scream, but he kept a hand clasped over my mouth. I don't know what it was he shot into my arm, but it made me so weak that he was several times stronger than me.

"You are a pretty one, aren't you?" he said.

He removed his hand from my mouth and replaced it with his lips. He kissed me forcefully, prying my lips open, forcing his tongue into my mouth. It made me retch.

He slapped his hand over my mouth again and ran his free hand all over me. He felt the muscles of my chest and abdomen then ran his hand lower still. I cried as he groped me.

"Don't act like you don't like it, queer boy. I know you do. This says you do," he said as he squeezed my manhood. I was getting aroused, but I didn't like it at all. I would have been willing to die right then to keep him from groping me.

Brian's body pressed into me. I tried to push him off, but I couldn't do it. I suddenly realized that this is what it must have been like for Casper. The thought of what his brother had done to him had always filled me with revulsion, but until that moment I'd never comprehended how truly horrible it was. I felt dirty, degraded, powerless, and weak. I couldn't imagine a worse feeling in all the world.

Brian pulled my gown all the way down. All I could do was cry. It made me feel impotent. Brian's eyes will filled with power and lust. I hated him. I wanted to kill him.

I heard footsteps coming down the hall. I was determined to bite Brian's hand and scream for help. Brian heard the footsteps too. He slapped the same cloth he'd used on Chad over my nose and mouth and I felt myself slipping into unconsciousness. I felt my gown being placed back over me and the cloth removed from my face. I turned my head to cry for help, but I was too far gone to speak.

"Is there a problem here?"

"No, I thought I heard noises, but as you can see, they're both fast asleep." It was the last thing I heard as I slipped into unconsciousness.

* * *

I slowly awakened. Someone was shaking me. Someone was on me. Brian, it was Brian. I screamed and pummeled him with my fists. I was frantic.

"Damn, dude, I don't like gettin' up early either, but you don't have to hit me. You were crying out in your sleep. I thought you were having a nightmare."

I saw Chad clearly for the first time. I looked up at him and just started bawling. I was shaking. I recoiled when he tried to touch me, but then I let him hold me. I felt so frightened and unsafe. It was a long time before he got me quieted down enough to tell him what had upset me.

"You sure you didn't just dream it?" he asked.

"Are you saying I'm making this shit up?" I asked angrily.

"No, no dude, it's just…I believe you, of course."

"I wish it had been just a dream," I said. "It was horrible."

"I can imagine. You're just lucky someone came along. It would have been worse."

"We've got to get out of here tonight. It isn't even safe to sleep here anymore."

"We'll get out, Brendan. Don't you worry about that. We'll make it."

Casper

It was Thursday night at last. Brad had already left for the *Cloverdale Center* to wait on Brendan. Soon Brendan would be out of that place and we'd be together again—if he escaped. I didn't even want to think about what would happen if he didn't. The days since I'd last seen him were like an eternity. I couldn't take much more. I never wanted us to be away from each other again.

Brendan was on my mind every moment. I tried not to think about what they were doing to him in that place. I'd heard stories, stories so horrible they couldn't possibly be true. I sure hoped they weren't. I couldn't bear the thought of anyone hurting Brendan.

I knew we'd be leaving that very night. My life was about to change forever. It was a change I welcomed. My life wasn't a life really. I lived in fear. It was better than it had been. The team looked out for me at school, so I didn't get beat up all the time the way I once did. Things were still pretty bad, however. I couldn't even stay in my own home, but had to hide out in a crypt in the cemetery. That was a life for a vampire, not a fifteen year old boy. Still, I wasn't bitter about my life. It could have been better, should have been better, but I knew I had it easier than some boys my age. That was the sad thing, that there were boys who would be glad to trade their lives for mine.

I knew the times ahead would be hard, but I'd be with Brendan and that's all that really mattered. I wondered how we'd survive on the road. We'd have nothing but what we carried with us. With that in mind I returned to the house; there were a few last things I wanted to get, things that would help us.

The house was dark when I returned. I picked my way through the living room, stumbling over dad's beer bottles. I paused for a moment, realizing that I'd never be in that house again. It was where I'd grown up. There were so many memories there. Sure, a lot of those memories were bad, but not all of them. I looked at the chair where my mom used to sit. My heart ached for her. I missed her so much it hurt. She was the one who really loved me. Sometimes I liked to sit in her old chair and remember when she'd sat in it, holding me in her arms. I'd never be able to do that again, just like my mother would never again hold me.

I pushed thoughts of the past out of my mind. I walked into the kitchen and turned on the light. I quickly went about my business. The house was silent, but there was always the danger of my brother returning. I didn't want to spend another moment in that house than was absolutely necessary.

I found a can opener in one of the drawers, and an old pocket knife in another. I also came up with more matches, and a lighter. There wasn't much food of course, but I did find a half-box of crackers and a real treasure—an unopened jar of peanut butter. I also took a box of salt and some pepper. I stuffed it all into a paper bag and walked to my room.

I flicked on the light and stepped toward the closet. The door slammed shut behind me and I spun on my heel, only to be slugged hard in the face. I landed on my ass. I looked up. Jason was standing there, leaning against the closed door, looking angry and resentful. What scared me most was the look in his eyes. It was back. I'd seen that look before. I knew what it meant. My heart pounded hard in my chest as he walked toward me. I scrambled backwards on hands and feet.

"You touch me and I'll tell Brendan!"

"I'll tell Brendan!" mocked Jason. "I'll tell Brendan! That's getting a little old you know. I've got news for you, little brother. I'm not afraid of your boyfriend anymore. He's nuts. That fag is getting just what he deserves now. He's gone and he's not coming back."

I stood. I wanted to tell Jason that Brendan would be back that very night, but I held my tongue. I scrambled to my feet so I could make a break for it when the time came. Jason closed in.

"You touch me and I'll tell the guys. The whole football team will kick your ass!"

"Yeah, right! You'll say anything to save your ass, won't you, little brother? How stupid do you think I am? Those guys won't do shit to me. You're just the fucking water boy. You're their bitch and nothing more. They don't care about you. No one cares about you. You're just a worthless little faggot. If you had any brains at all you'd have killed yourself long ago. You should be dead, you little fucker."

I hated him. I hated that his words hurt me. He was wrong; Brad and the other guys did care about me. They looked out for me. So what if I was just the water boy, so what if I wasn't a football jock? It didn't matter. They still liked me.

"They'll kill you," I said.

Jason got real quiet and it frightened me more than ever. I backed away from him as he advanced on me. It wasn't long before my back was to the wall and I had no where else to go.

"We have some business to take care of Casper. I've been waiting for you to come home. It's been a long time you know. I've needed you, little brother."

Tears filled my eyes and I slowly shook my head. I was shaking with fright.

"Why do you do this to me, Jason? Why? You don't even like boys, do you? You like girls, but you still…" I was crying. I couldn't speak.

Jason laughed. There was hatred in his eyes. I wondered when things had changed. There was a time when my brother loved me.

"I like girls," he said. "But then you're kinda like one, aren't you, Casper?"

I looked at him, hurt, and afraid.

He reached out to touch me. I bolted, running for my life. I flung myself at the door and jerked it open. Jason threw himself against it. I narrowly avoided getting my fingers crushed when it slammed shut. Jason grabbed me and shoved me back on the bed. I slugged him in the face, but he just laughed at me. I beat his chest with my fists, but he acted like he didn't even feel it. He slapped me across the face hard and it hurt. Tears welled up in my eyes. I screamed until Jason clamped his hand over my mouth. His free hand was all over me. He touched me and I felt dirty. He ripped my shirt. Tears streamed from my eyes. It was happening again.

Brendan

The hair on the back of my neck stood on end. I didn't know if it was because I was frightened, or because the back of my hospital gown was half open and my ass was freezing. I looked at Chad beside me. He had the same blood-shot eyes and doped up look as always, but I could read a touch of anticipation and fear there as well.

We followed Brad's cousin down the stairs. This was it. It was 9:50 p.m. and we were minutes from being free of *Cloverdale*. I just hoped we'd make it. I couldn't bear to think of what would happen if we didn't. I forced myself not to think about it. I had to keep my mind on the present. If we got caught, then I'd deal with it when it happened.

We were almost there. Only a few steps separated us from the basement doorway. Jason took out his keys and fitted one to the lock. He turned it and the lock clicked open.

"What are you doing down here?"

I jumped. Another orderly was standing behind us. He seemed to come from nowhere. I tensed, ready to jump him.

"I, uh…" said Jason, stammering a bit. He looked at me and Chad, and then back to the other orderly. "I just wanted to take these boys down to the basement for a little privacy, if you know what I mean." I was impressed. Jason was a cool liar. The orderly gave him a knowing smile. He reached out and took Chad by the chin.

"They are a couple of cute ones," he said, turning Chad's face. I could tell Chad was grinding his teeth, but luckily he had the sense to keep his mouth shut.

"You wanna…?" said Jason, motioning down the stairs with his head.

"No, no thanks. I never really cared for boys, although they have their uses. There's some hot girls on the third floor, though, wouldn't mind getting me one or two of them."

Jason smiled back at him.

"Enjoy yourself," said the orderly and went on his way.

I was so glad it wasn't Brian that had caught us. Jason's little ruse wouldn't have worked on him at all. He'd have been only too happy to take us down in the basement. He made my skin crawl.

We slipped through the door and Jason followed us to the base of the steps.

"You guys fucking owe me so big," he said, clearly disgusted with the conversation that had just taken place.

"We won't forget this," I said. "I don't know if our paths will ever cross again, but if they do, I'll remember what you did for us."

"Here dude," said Chad and handed Jason a mixed bottle full of pills. "It's all I got to give you. It's the last of my private stash."

"Thanks," said Jason. "You're on your own now guys. Good luck." He turned and left us.

"Was that really the last of your drugs?" I asked Chad.

"Yep," he said. "I know you think I'm a druggie, but I just took that shit while I was in here. I needed it man. I get through that fence and that's the last of it for me."

"I hope so," I said, not entirely believing him.

"Hey, I used to mess with that shit before I came here you know, but after seeing what I've seen, Ian and all, I'm not doin' it no more." I smiled at him. He seemed sincere. I just hoped he could handle it.

"Let's get out of here," I said.

Chad led me to the little storage room. He dug out the bolt-cutters from their hiding place and cut right through the lock on the window. I looked at the small window.

"We're supposed to fit through that?" I asked him.

"It'll be a tight squeeze, but we can do it. Your ass isn't that big, Brendan."

"Funny."

"I'll go first 'cause I'm thinner. If you get stuck I'll pull you through. Now help me up."

I hoisted Chad into the air and he caught the ledge and wormed his way out. When he was clear, I jumped up and pushed my way into the opening. My shoulders wedged in and I couldn't move for a moment, but Chad grabbed me under my arms and pulled until my gown ripped and my shoulders slipped past the window. My butt got stuck for just a moment, and then I was through.

"Hmm, guess your ass was too big," said Chad. I playfully smacked him in the back of the head.

We ran low across the open space that stood between us and a locked gate in the fence. I was terrified we'd be spotted. There was a big lock on it. Chad gripped the lock in the bolt-cutters and squeezed hard. He grunted, but couldn't cut through. I grabbed the handles as well and pushed them together with every ouch of muscle I had. I felt the lock give. It fell to the ground.

Chad and I slipped through the gate, carefully closing it behind us so it wouldn't be obvious the fence had been breached. We skirted the lights that surrounded the fence and ran down the grassy slope into the woods.

I was a little scared because everything seemed a little too easy. When escapes were too easy in movies, it was usually a set up. We weren't in a movie, however. The thought also occurred to me that the locks and gates weren't the main obstacle to escape. The main obstacle was drugs. Just about everyone in *Cloverdale* was pumped so full of drugs they probably couldn't have got past the locks with a key. The doctors were counting on that. We were making it because we weren't all doped up. I realized if it hadn't been for Chad and the tricks he showed me, I'd never have escaped from that place.

There was a little light from the moon, but it was still almost too dark to see among the trees. It was chilly and the thin hospital gowns we were wearing were no protection against the cold. I was shivering. Physical discomfort didn't matter, however. Getting away from Cloverdale did. I kept expecting to hear alarms sound at any moment, announcing the discovery of our escape.

Soon we were through the trees. There was a car parked on the little road at the base of the hill. It was Brad's car. The engine started as we raced toward it. We jumped into the back and the car took off as soon as the doors were closed. I was so relieved that I felt like crying.

"You guys okay?" asked Brad.

"Hell yeah," I said, "now that we're out of that fucking place."

It was only then that I noticed Stacey sitting in the front seat with Brad. She was looking at me concerned.

"Stacey?"

"Brad thought it would be safer with me along. That way if we got spotted they'd just think we were parking."

"Dude, you'll do anything to get a girl," I said to Brad, teasing him. He and Stacey looked at each other. I had the feeling that there was really something between them.

"Here," said Stacey, handing two stacks of clothing to us. "We thought you'd need these."

"They're mine so they might not fit quite right, but they'll be better than what you've got on."

"No shit. And thanks," I said.

Chad and I pulled off the hospital gowns and started dressing right there in the back seat.

"This is Chad," I said, trying to pull on a pair of jeans. "I couldn't have got out of that place without him."

"And we couldn't have got out of there without your cousin," said Chad. He was fighting to get into a shirt in the confines of the back seat.

"How's Casper?" I asked.

"He's cool," said Brad. "Me and the guys have been watching out for him. We knew you'd kick our asses if we let anything happen to him."

"Damn straight," I said. I was glad to hear that Casper was okay. The notes from him had helped set me at ease, but I was still worried about him. I loved him so much it hurt.

As we drove to the cemetery Chad and I filled Brad in on the rest of our escape plans. As soon as we picked up Casper, we'd be on our way.

"You mind driving us a little out of town?" I asked. "It will make it harder for them to track us down."

"Of course I don't mind stupid," said Brad. "What are best friends for?"

"I just don't want you getting in a lot of trouble."

"Hey, what are they gonna do to me? They can't arrest me for helping you. It's not like you're a convict or something."

We pulled up to the cemetery. I jumped out and ran past the gates.

"Casper!" I said in a loud whisper. "Casper!" There was no answer and I grew suddenly afraid.

I ran around the cemetery calling his name, but I couldn't find him. He wasn't there. I knew something was wrong.

I ran back to the car and got in.

"He's not here," I said. "Take me to Casper's house." Without question, Brad turned the car around. We were taking quite a chance, every moment counted, but I wasn't leaving without Casper.

* * *

I'd never been inside Casper's home; I'd only dropped him off there. As soon as the car stopped, I jumped out and ran to the house. It looked so lonely and forlorn. I rushed to the front door. I hoped Casper was there. If he wasn't, I didn't know where I'd find him. I was just getting ready to knock when I heard Casper scream from somewhere in the house. "Let me go! Get off me!"

Without thinking, I charged into the house. I followed the sounds of a scuffle to what I guessed was Casper's room. I burst through the door. Casper was lying across the bed. His clothes were torn. His brother was holding him down.

I launched myself at Jason and knocked him to the floor. We came up swinging. I was going to kill that fucking bastard. He'd hurt Casper for the last time. I punched him in the face as hard as I could. I didn't care if I killed him. He deserved to die.

Jason was tough. He took the pummeling I gave him and came right back at me. He swung his fist full force at my stomach. I tightened my abdominal muscles, but it still hurt like hell. I flew at Jason, catching him around the waist, sending us both crashing to the floor. I managed a quick jab to the gut before he got me in the face. My head snapped back. I don't think I'd ever been hit that hard before. Jason slammed me down before I had a chance to recover and pressed his knees painfully into my chest. He slugged me in the face over and over until I managed to punch him in the throat and get him off.

I came up swinging. It was all a blur after that. We slugged each other as hard as we could manage, fighting through the pain. All I really wanted to do was drop to the floor and moan and writhe in agony, but as long as I could stand, I was determined to keep fighting. This wasn't just any fight. It wasn't about something stupid. I was fighting to protect Casper. I'd die for him.

I was out of shape from all that had been done to me in the hospital and I took quite a beating. I gave better than I took, however. I was enraged. Jason had hurt Casper. There was no forgiving that.

Jason was no pansy, but he couldn't take the beating I was giving him. He was doing a lot of damage, but I was fucking him up good. I landed a good, solid punch to his jaw that sent him sailing back into the closet. The door collapsed under his weight. For a moment, I thought I'd killed him.

Casper ran to me, running his hands all over my body, making sure I was all right. I wasn't really, but it wasn't like I was going to die, it wasn't like I had any broken bones or anything. I wasn't so sure about Jason, he was barely moving.

"I'm okay, Casper." I looked down at him and the worried expression on his face. I hugged him close to me. "I love you. It's going to be okay now."

I let my guard down. It was a mistake. I caught movement behind Casper. I jerked my head up. Jason was just getting to his feet; he was pointing a double-barreled shotgun right at Casper.

"I told you you'd pay, little brother," he snarled. I'd never seen anyone look so menacing before, not only menacing—insane. I stared at Jason in horror.

Almost without thinking, I shoved Casper behind me, although I didn't know how much good that would do. I hoped that Casper would bolt for the door when Jason shot me. At least then he'd have a chance to get away. I knew what I was going to do. Jason only had two shots. When he fired, I'd push myself forward and grab the gun if I could. Maybe Jason would use his second shell out of fear. He only had two shots before he had to reload. Maybe he'd even blast me with both barrels at once. At least Casper would have a fighting chance to escape.

I knew even as I thought it, however, that it was a plan doomed to failure. The first blast would probably blow me off my feet. There would be no surging forward. I'd be dead. There was nothing else for it, so I'd do whatever I could manage.

"You're pretty brave for a faggot. Not that it'll help you much. Not so tough now are you? Those muscles aren't much good against this," he said, patting his gun. "This is gonna be a pleasure."

Casper tried to force his way in front of me. I knew what he was trying to do, but I couldn't allow it. I couldn't let him die for me. Even if I somehow managed to survive, I knew I could never live my life without him. I pushed him back. At the same moment a deafening shot assaulted my ears, sounding like a stick of dynamite had just gone off. I jerked my hands to my chest and looked down, but there was nothing to see. I looked up as quick as lightning and saw Jason falling to the floor, even as his shotgun blasted the air like a cannon. Jason hit the floor hard. Even as he did so, there was a loud thump in the doorway. I looked over to see an older man laying there, his stomach red with blood.

"Dad! Dad!" yelled Casper and ran to him.

I walked to Jason. There was a lot of blood. The sight of it made me sick. I expected him to be dead, but I could hear him breathing and see his chest rise and fall. He'd been hit in the shoulder.

Brad, Stacey, and Chad came running in.

"Oh my God!" said Stacey.

I took a shirt, waded it up, and pushed against Jason's shoulder. I took the sheet from the bed and tied it around his shoulder to help stop the bleeding. I wasn't quite sure why I was helping him, but I couldn't just let him lay there and die, even if he did deserve it.

I turned to Casper. He was holding his dad's head in his lap, crying. His dad was speaking to him, so quietly I could barely hear.

"I was never a good dad." he croaked out. "I'm sorry...no time to...you were a good son. I love..." His head fell over in Casper's lap and he was gone.

Casper looked up at me, his eyes filled with tears. He gently let his father's head slip to the floor, then ran to me and clasped me about the waist, crying. I held him tight.

"We've got to go," said Brad desperately. I looked at Jason lying on the floor, then back at Brad. I nodded my head. I knew he was right.

I led Casper out of his old home. We got in the car, and sped away, only to stop after a couple of blocks. Stacey hopped out and called an ambulance for Jason, and then we took off again. We'd done as much for Casper's brother as we could. It was way more than he deserved.

I held Casper as he cried. I couldn't imagine what he was going through. He'd seen his own brother and father shoot each other before his eyes. He'd lost his dad. Maybe his father wasn't a very good one, but he was still his dad. Casper's thin body was racked with sobs.

"Here." Brad handed a backpack to me as he drove. "I put some clothes and stuff in here for you. There are two more backpacks in the trunk, for Casper and Chad. All of them have clothes and stuff in them I thought you'd need."

Brad pulled his wallet out of his back pocket and handed it to Stacey. She pulled out a wad of bills and handed them to us.

"That's all the money I could get," said Brad. "I emptied my checking account and cleaned out my room. It isn't a lot, but it will help."

"I can't take your money, Brad."

"You're going to need it. Besides, it's a loan. You can pay me back when you get rich some day." He smiled.

"Thanks," I said.

"Just make sure I see you again. Otherwise I'll have to kick your ass."

"You'll see me again," I said.

"You're the best friend I ever had, Brendan. I don't want to lose you."

"You won't," I said. "I'll write. I'll keep in touch. Wherever we go, I'll let you know. Someday you can come and visit us. When I'm eighteen, I can come back and visit you. That's only a few months away. My father can't do shit after I'm eighteen, but until then, I've got to hide."

Brad's eyes met mine in the mirror, they were filled with tears. Mine were too. He was my best friend and I'd miss him. I told myself it was only temporary. I'd see him again.

"I made you guys cookies and brownies," said Stacey. "There's a big bag in the trunk. I went grocery shopping. I got you lots of stuff that you can carry with you."

"Thanks, Stacey," I said.

Casper and I were lucky. We had good friends.

We drove through the night, talking, trying to say everything that needed said before we were out of time. Casper was quiet. I could only imagine what was going through his head. The sight of his brother and father laying there was burned into my mind. It had to be ten times worse for him. I wondered if the paramedics got to his brother in time. I knew there was no saving his dad. He was already dead when we left. I hugged Casper close to me and he smiled weakly.

Before we knew it, the time had come to part. Brad pulled off at a little roadside park and we got out.

"You keep in touch with me or I'll track you down and whoop your ass," said Brad. The tears in his eyes shined in the moonlight.

"Like you'd have a chance against me," I laughed softly. "Don't worry Brad, we'll always be friends and I'll always let you know where I am. We'll be together again, just you wait and see." Brad hugged me tightly, and then he hugged Casper.

"You take care of him okay, Casper? You know he's just a big dumb jock. You're the one with the brains." Casper smiled despite all that had happened.

"We always take care of each other," said Casper, gazing at me with love in his eyes.

"I know we just met," said Brad to Chad, "but I consider you my friend. You ever need anything, you come to me."

"Thanks, dude," said Chad shyly.

"Wear your sweatshirt," said Stacey as she pulled one from Casper's backpack and slipped it over his head. "It's going to get cold out tonight and I don't want you catching anything."

"Sure, Mom," he said. I smiled that he was able to joke in that most serious of times.

"I love you, Casper," said Stacey and hugged him tight. "You keep in touch with me too. I'll miss you."

"I love you too, Stacey," he said, hugging her back as tight as he could.

"We have to go," said Brad, looking at his watch. "Take care of yourselves and write or call as soon as you get the chance."

"We will," I said.

"Bye," said everyone.

Casper, Chad, and I watched as Brad and Stacey pulled away and the taillights of the car faded into the distance. I felt as if my old life were disappearing before my very eyes.

I divided up the money Brad had given me between us. There was a little over $100 for each of us. I wished that I could have gotten to my own money, even if it was just what I kept in my room. I could've put my hands on a whole lot more and I knew we'd need it. That just wasn't possible. There was no way I could go back home.

I put my backpack on my shoulders and Casper and Chad slipped on theirs as well.

"You ready?" I asked Casper.

"I'm ready."

"You know you don't have to come."

"I know, but I want to. I couldn't live without you."

"I'm glad you feel that way," I said, "because I couldn't make it without you." I hugged Casper tightly and kissed him.

"Where are we going to go?" asked Casper.

"I don't know. We'll just have to figure that one out. It doesn't really matter where we go, however, because we'll always be together. As long as we're together, we'll be fine." I smiled at Casper and he smiled back.

"Then we'll always be fine," said Casper. He grasped my hand in his and smiled at me.

"I wish I had a boyfriend," said Chad.

"Maybe we'll find you one on the road," I said.

"About that," said Chad. "I think it's best if we don't travel together. They'll be looking for us you know. We're less likely to get spotted if we split up, and there will be two trails to follow. They won't be able to catch us both."

I was saddened by Chad's words, but I knew he was right. The time had already come and gone for the midnight bed check and the center surely knew we'd escaped. They'd be looking for us soon. I never wanted to go back there. I'd rather die. Splitting up was our best shot at making it.

"Stay with us tonight," I said. "We can go our separate ways in the morning."

The three of us walked in the growing darkness, scurrying out of sight whenever a car chanced to pass. When we grew too tired to walk further, we headed into a small knot of trees and hid ourselves for the night. It was chilly out, but we were all fast asleep almost as soon as our heads hit the ground.

Casper

I awoke early. At first I thought I was alone in the mausoleum, but then I saw the moon shining through the trees overhead. I looked to one side and saw Chad, the boy who had escaped from the *Cloverdale Center* with Brendan. He was sleeping peacefully. I looked to my other side and there was Brendan, also still asleep. I just lay there and gazed at him, smiling. I knew we were in a tough spot, but I couldn't help but be happy. We were together again, and this time we were going to stay together.

I wondered if that was really true, however. My boyfriend was a fugitive. He wasn't a criminal or anything like that, but until he turned eighteen, he belonged to his parents. It was like slavery. They owned him. They could do a lot of stuff to him against his will, like put him in that horrible center. I was worried that we'd get caught, and that they'd take him back there. I didn't think I could handle that. I didn't think Brendan could either.

I didn't want to be alone, ever again. If they came for Brendan, I'd do everything within my power to help him escape. I'd do anything. I loved Brendan. He was all I had.

I thought about my father and brother. It had been a long time since we'd been a real family. It had been ages since I thought that they cared for me. I guess my dad really had cared about me all those years, at least a little. He never showed it, but his dying words were all about how he loved me and how he was sorry. Part of me couldn't forgive him for the way he'd treated me, or the way he'd ignored me. Part of me mourned him. He wasn't the best father to be sure, but he was my daddy, and he was gone. I was without parents, an orphan.

I wondered if Jason was dead or alive. I didn't miss him. There was no sadness in my heart when I thought about him. If he was dead, it was no worse

180

than he deserved. He'd been cruel. He'd beat me and done horrible things to me. There was no excuse for it. I knew his life was hard, just like mine, but I didn't choose to hurt anyone like he did. True, I was small and not very strong, but even if I had muscles bulging out everywhere, I knew I wouldn't hurt anyone the way he'd hurt me. For a long time I thought maybe I deserved what he did to me in some way, but I didn't deserve it. No one deserved to be used like that. It was just wrong. My brother had been nice to me at one time, before our mother died, but he'd been abusive and cruel ever since then. Something inside him had made him go bad. He wasn't the same boy he'd been when Mom was alive. It didn't matter if he was alive or dead, he wasn't my brother anymore.

Brendan awoke and smiled at me. We smiled at each other all the time, it felt good. He sat up and stretched.

"What's for breakfast?"

"I made pancakes and fried some eggs," I said.

"Mmmm, that sounds good. Now what do we really have?"

"How 'bout peanut butter on crackers and some water?" I asked him.

"Peanut butter and crackers here sounds a whole lot better than pancakes and eggs back in the center, not that we ever got that," he said. "It sounds a whole lot better than the best breakfast I could imagine back in the center."

Our talking awakened Chad. He looked around confused for a moment, then it dawned on him where we were.

"Dudes!" he said.

Chad was an odd one, but I liked him. Brendan had said he couldn't have escaped without him, so that put me eternally in Chad's debt as far as I was concerned. I had to keep myself from laughing at the way he talked sometimes. He sounded like some kind of California surfer boy or something. He said 'dude' more than anyone I knew.

I got out a jar of peanut butter and some crackers from my pack. Stacey had even thought to put in a butter knife. Good old Stacey. I knew I'd miss her terribly.

I spread peanut butter on crackers and handed them out. We had ourselves a nice little breakfast under the trees. I felt like we were setting out on some great adventure. It was like we were alone on our own little island, just like in *The Lord of the Flies*, only without the sticks sharpened at both ends.

While we ate, Chad pulled a map out of his backpack. Brad and Stacey had thought of just about everything. Chad studied it for a few moments.

"About a mile on, there's another road that crosses this one we're following. I think I'll head out south from there, maybe go to Florida or Texas or someplace. It'll be getting real cold soon and I wanna go someplace warm. How 'bout you dudes?" he asked.

I hadn't really thought about it myself. We'd been so busy getting out of town that there just wasn't time to think about where we were going. "Away" was as much of a destination as we needed then. I looked at Brendan and he shrugged his shoulders.

"Maybe we'll head north for a bit, if you're heading south," said Brendan. "I don't really much care where we go, so long as it's away from where we were."

"Ain't that the truth?" said Chad.

We talked a bit more while we were eating and then hoisted our packs on our backs and set out. It was a fine and sunny day, perfect for a long walk. I grabbed a stick I found along the road and used it as a walking stick. I felt happier than I had in a long time. I felt like I was leaving behind all my troubles. I knew that wasn't quite true, but that's the way I felt.

The mile to the next road passed quickly and soon it was time to say "goodbye" to Chad. I didn't know him well, but I kind of wished he was going with us. He had his own ideas, however.

"Don't forget about me, dude," said Chad to Brendan.

"I don't think I could if I tried," he said laughing. They hugged.

"You take care of this guy, Casper. Without me around, he'll need someone to watch him."

"You don't have to worry about that," I said, looking at Brendan. I'd have done anything for him.

"Be careful," said Brendan.

"Oh I will. I know how to take care of myself. Don't worry, those dudes at the center won't get their hands on me again."

"I'll miss you," said Brendan.

"Me too, dude." Chad paused. "Well, I hate long good-byes and we've already stretched this one enough. Good luck, guys."

Brendan and Chad hugged once more, and then Chad turned and walked away, never looking back.

Brendan

Our first few days of traveling were pleasant enough. The nights were chilly, but Casper and I snuggled under our blankets and kept each other warm. His small body pressed up next to mine gave me a feeling of comfort and security that I'd never had before. The daylight hours were warm and sunny, just about perfect, not too hot and not too cold. My feet got tired from all the walking, but our journey seemed more like a vacation than an escape.

The ever present danger of being tracked down by the center, or by someone working for my father, kept us moving and out of sight. We were traveling north on an old country road without much traffic. Whenever we heard a car coming we hurried off the road and hid ourselves until it passed. I knew I was being a bit paranoid, but better that than end up back in *Cloverdale*.

I tired more easily than I should have. I knew it was the drugs that had been pumped into my body. I'd avoided most of them thanks to Chad, but I was still pretty drugged up. When we stopped for the night I crashed hard and slept straight through until the next morning. I wanted to just keep on sleeping forever, but I wanted to put as much distance between us and our former hometown as possible. The farther away we got, the safer I'd feel.

Casper was amazingly cheerful. I really thought he'd have a lot more trouble dealing with the death of his father. Of course, his father wasn't much of a father. I could understand why he wasn't worried about Jason; he was nothing more than a sadistic bastard. I didn't' really care whether Jason was dead or alive. I didn't tell Casper, but it wouldn't have bothered me one bit if we discovered that Jason had died. When we'd fought, I wanted to kill him. If it had stayed a fair fight, I might have done it. After what he'd done to Casper he deserved death, and worse. I still wasn't sure why I'd tried to save him at the end. I guess a little part of me just couldn't let him die helpless like that.

Casper's high spirits kept me going when I was tired. I was feeling pretty good myself. Just being free of *Cloverdale* was enough to make me walk on air. I felt like I'd awakened from a nightmare to find myself in a place so beautiful I'd never dreamed it could exist. I thought of the boys still stuck in the center. I wished that I could go back and free them all. I knew that task was beyond me, however. I was lucky to have made it out myself.

* * *

The rain pelted down on us, soaking us to the skin. I looked at Casper trudging along beside me, his blond hair plastered to the sides of his face. He looked very young and I wondered how wise I'd been bringing him on such a journey. I knew even as I thought it that I couldn't have made it without him. If I'd left him behind I would have pined away for him. Besides, it's not like he'd left much behind. His father was dead and the authorities would have probably put him in some foster home where no one really cared about him. I cared about him. I loved Casper so much it sometimes felt like my heart was going to burst right out of my chest.

Casper looked at me and smiled sweetly. He took my hand in his own and we walked like that down the side of the road. I was happy. The rain, the dreary weather, our never ending journey, none of that mattered because Casper was by my side.

Around six in the evening we came to a small town. I could see huge lights shining in the distance. As we grew nearer my suspicions were confirmed. There was a football game going on. I felt a tug at my heart as I looked at the distant field.

"Wanna go watch?" asked Casper. "We could watch, and then find some-place to sleep."

"Yeah," I said. "You don't mind do you?"

"Of course not. Besides, I'm tired and my feet could use a rest."

We headed off toward the football field and within minutes were seated in the stands with a big crowd of high school kids and their parents.

I watched with rapt interest as the quarterback of the home team did his stuff. He had a real arm on him and could pass the ball farther than just about any player I'd seen. He was pretty quick on his feet too, although he seemed to have a little trouble maneuvering. I found myself cheering along with the rest of the crowd as he cut through the defensive line and scored a touch down. His team-mates gathered around him, patting him on the ass, congratulating him. He was like a god or something at just that moment.

I don't think I realized until just then how much I missed playing football. I'd had it all. I was the quarterback and team captain and everyone looked up to me. My coach and team-mates had even stood beside me, and stood up for me, when they found out I was gay. Being a football star made me a celebrity at school and I'd be lying if I said it didn't make me feel damned good. There was just something about walking down the halls having everyone admire me that made me feel wonderful.

I looked at the players on the field and wondered if I'd ever get to play again. A part of my life was missing and it wasn't easy. It wasn't just the popularity and admiration either; it was just getting to play. A wave of sadness flowed over me.

"You'll get to play again," said Casper beside me. He was looking at me and probably had been for some time. He understood me. I loved him for that.

"Yeah, I hope so," I said. "I really miss it you know?"

"Yeah, I know."

The rain was still coming down and we sat closer, huddled under a blanket that Casper had dug out of his pack. I didn't let myself dwell on what I was missing. Instead, I just enjoyed watching the game while sitting with my boyfriend. When I looked at what I had, instead of what I didn't have, things looked a whole lot better.

6 Weeks Later

The December air was so cold that I could clearly see Casper's breath as he trudged along beside me. The ground was wet, my shoes and socks soaked. I didn't think I'd ever feel warm again. Casper coughed again, as he had more times than I could count in the last hour. His cough didn't sound good; it came from deep inside his chest. Casper didn't look well at all. He was pale and skinny and shivered in the cold. The jacket he was wearing wasn't enough to keep him warm. I was getting more and more worried about him.

It was only mid-afternoon, but I led Casper off the road. There was an abandoned barn not far away and we made for it. At least we'd have shelter from the wind and the heavy snow that fell from the air. It didn't take long to get there. I opened the huge door and we slipped inside. It was kind of dark, but light came through the cracks here and there. The old barn smelled of hay and had a pleasant feel to it. It reminded me of the old Highland barn on my parents' property.

I made Casper a bed out of hay and he sank into it. I covered him up with both our blankets. He closed his eye immediately, but did not sleep. His coughing didn't allow him that luxury. He was shivering. I pressed my hand against his forehead, the way my mother used to do when I was a little boy. He was too warm.

"Casper, I'm going to go get us something to eat. There's a town not far ahead. I won't be long okay? You just rest and I'll come back with something for us."

Casper mumbled something, but I couldn't make out what it was. I dug in the bottom of my back-back, seeking out the very last of our cash. I came up with a grand total of $45.58. The money Brad had given us was long gone. Casper and I had managed to scrape by doing odd jobs here and there as we went. I'd keep my eye out in town to see what was available; perhaps I could shovel snow for someone.

I closed the barn door behind me and walked back to the road. I followed it downhill toward a small town in the distance. My mind was filled with worry over Casper. He didn't look good. I was certain he had a fever. He'd picked up a cough several days before and it had grown steadily worse. I could tell he was growing weaker. We had to stop more often and halted a little earlier each evening. Our slow progress wasn't really a problem. We weren't going any-where in particular, so there was no reason to hurry. We were far, far away from the *Cloverdale Center* and I really doubted that anyone would find us after all this time.

It wasn't long before I was walking down the main street of Purity. I thought it an odd name for a town, but I guess it wasn't all that strange. Like most of the towns we passed through, it wasn't much. There were a couple of restaurants, some stores, and a motel on the edge of town. I spotted a diner across the street where I could get us something hot to eat, but I didn't head for it straight away. Just ahead was a doctor's office. I went there first.

I walked into a well worn waiting room. There was a nurse sitting behind a little window. I involuntarily shuddered when I caught sight of her white uni-form. It reminded me of the ones the nurses wore in the *Cloverdale Center*. I had to remind myself that I was far from the center and this lady wasn't any-thing like the ones who worked there.

"Can I help you, young man?"

"Yes," I said, "how much is it to see the doctor?"

"Office calls are $40. Do you need an appointment?"

It would take almost all our cash, but Casper needed to see a doctor. He'd just keep getting worse if he didn't.

"Um, yeah, for my brother—could he come in today?"

"Let me see," she said, looking through a large appointment book. "Yes, how about 6:30?"

"That will be great."

"Name?"

"Brewer," I said. "Casper Brewer." I didn't think it wise to give her Casper's real name. I kind of liked the sound of his first name with my last.

"Okay, Casper Brewer, 6:30 p.m."

"Thanks."

I walked back out into the cold and crossed the street. The doctor's appointment left us a grand total of $5.58 for something to eat. I entered the diner, sat down at the counter, and looked through the menu. A lot of stuff on it was too expensive. I thought fondly back to the days when I didn't have to think about cost and could order anything I wanted.

The diner was kind of pleasant inside. There was a little Christmas tree with bright lights in one corner and a scene of Santa Claus and his elves loading a sleigh painted on the front window. Christmas music played on the radio. It was cozy.

There was a woman sitting a couple of tables away. She kept looking at me. For a moment I was afraid she recognized me or something. Maybe my father had my picture sent out, like on a wanted poster. I knew that was silly, however. I was being paranoid. I looked in her direction, and she smiled at me. She was attractive enough I guess, but she had to be in her mid-forties.

I looked at the menu, then back at her again. She was still gazing at me. She was making me uncomfortable.

"What will it be?" asked the waitress.

"Um, two bowls of vegetable soup and two cups of hot cocoa. And that's to go," I told her. If I had calculated correctly, that would come to $5.25 with tax. I hoped I hadn't misfigured. It would be embarrassing if I was short of cash.

As I waited, I felt eyes on me, I looked back at the woman and she motioned me over to her table. I swallowed, and then walked over to her, wondering what she wanted.

"You're a fine looking one. What brings you here, hon?"

"Just passing through," I said. My words seemed so clichéd, but I didn't know what else to say.

"Have a seat."

I sat across from her.

"I'm Ellen."

"Brendan," I said.

"How old are you Brendan?" Her eyes roved over me, making me feel uncomfortable again.

"Seventeen."

"Have a girlfriend somewhere?"

"No."

"A good looking, well-built young man like you? Hard to believe."

I just shrugged.

"Now if I was a few years younger..." She smiled.

I smiled back, although I was really thinking that she'd have to be more than a few years younger to be anywhere near my age.

"Although," she said, "some boys your age like older women."

I was getting more uncomfortable by the second.

"Yeah, I guess some do."

"How about you, sweetie?"

"Um, not really," I said, trying not to offend her. She looked at me appraisingly.

It was then that I felt her foot sliding up my leg. Her shoe was off and her touch delicate.

"What if I was to ask you to help me carry these bags to my car?" she asked, nodding toward a large stack of shopping bags sitting near her. She paused, looking into my eyes. "And if I was to ask you to slip into the back seat for a moment..." Her foot found its way to the front of my jeans, she rubbed it against me.

"Umm...I don't..." I stammered.

"Just for a couple of minutes—just long enough for me to take a look at what you've got right here." She pressed her foot hard against the bulge forming in my jeans.

I was wondering how I got myself into such a situation. Me, a gay boy, being propositioned by a woman more than twice my age, it was almost funny. I racked my brains searching for a graceful way out.

"I'd give you a big tip for…carrying my bags to the car…" She said.

I couldn't believe it. She was treating me like I was some kind of rent boy. Part of me was insulted; part of me was just a little intrigued that she found me attractive enough to want to pay me when most boys my age would have given it up for free. Sure, she was old, but most boys would've been more than happy to let just about any female into their pants.

I was just about to give her a polite 'no' when she pulled two twenties out of her purse and pushed them across the table.

"Payment in advance," she said.

I looked at the money and thought about Casper shivering in the barn. With forty bucks I could get us a motel room for the night. Casper could sleep in a real bed, with warm covers, in a heated room. We could both have a hot shower. There might even be enough left over for some breakfast. I crumpled the twenties in my hand and stuck them in my pocket.

Ellen stood up and handed me most of her bags. I followed her out of the diner. She led me to her car parked out back. She opened the trunk and I dumped all her shopping bags into it. She opened the back door of her car and stepped aside for me to get in. I got in and slid to the far side. Ellen got in after me.

"Such a pretty boy," said Ellen, as she reached over and pushed my hair out of my eyes. I trembled slightly.

She ran her hands down over my chest and abdomen, then over the front of my jeans. I closed my eyes as she unfastened my belt and popped the button on my jeans. I kept thinking about Casper laying in the barn, and about Chad, and Brad, and Stacey, about anything but what was happening.

A slight whimper escaped my lips and I tried even harder to put my mind on something besides the present. I couldn't let myself think about what I was doing. Time slowed down to a crawl. I felt like I was in that backseat for an eternity, although it was probably no more than five minutes.

I was breathing hard. I threw my head back and moaned. It was over. Ellen leaned back. I pulled my boxers and jeans up and got out of the car. Ellen handed me a slip of paper.

"If you're interested in doing more, I'm willing to pay you well," she said. "You're so beautiful." She caressed my face.

"Uh, I'll think about that," I said and got out of the car.

I straightened my clothes and walked back into the diner. I picked up my order and paid the waitress. As I walked back through town, I felt like everyone was staring at me. I felt like they could all tell what I'd done, just by looking at me. I felt unclean. I'd just done something I thought I'd never do, I'd sold my body for money. I pushed the thought out of my mind and walked to the little motel on the edge of town and reserved a room for that night.

I walked back to the barn as quickly as I could so the soup and cocoa wouldn't get cold. Casper was lying right where I'd left him. He smiled at me weakly and sat up.

"Here," I said, "I got us some soup. It'll warm you up."

We sat close together. It was cold in the barn, but better than outside. Still, I could see Casper's breath, and my own. I was glad we had a motel room for the night and wouldn't have to make do in the barn. We'd been making do for so long that I could hardly remember what it was like to sleep in a real bed.

Casper and I finished our soup and cocoa. Casper coughed loudly. It sounded bad. That reminded me that it was getting close to time for his appointment. I helped him up and we hoisted our backpacks once more.

I took Casper to the motel first and we both had a quick shower. We left our backpacks in the room and walked to the doctor's office. It was almost 6:30 when we sat down in the waiting room. We flipped through outdated magazines while we waited. It wasn't long before a man who looked too old to walk came out and called Casper's name. It was unnecessary; we were the only ones in there. Casper followed him into the back while I sat and waited. I enjoyed the warmth of the waiting room.

Some fifteen minutes later Casper came back out. I walked up to the window with him and handed the nurse $40.

"Make sure you get plenty of rest," she said. "And make sure you get lots of fluids to bring that fever down. Here are some cough syrup samples. And here are your prescriptions." Casper took the cough syrup and I took the two small pieces of paper with writing on them that I couldn't begin to read.

"Thanks," I said.

I walked Casper back to the motel room, my mind troubled. I hadn't thought about Casper's medicine. Of course he'd have to take something to get well. The medicine would be expensive and I had less than ten dollars in my pocket. It wouldn't be enough. I slipped my hand into my right pocket and felt the small piece of paper there. It made me tremble. No, I didn't even want to think about it.

I put Casper into the bed and tucked him in.

"I'm going out," I said. "Don't worry if I'm late. I'm going to look around and see if I can find a job so we can make some money."

"Um hum," said Casper, more than half asleep.

I kissed his forehead and left. At least he was somewhere safe and warm. He could rest well for the night.

I walked uptown and went to the drugstore. I gave them the prescriptions and asked how much it would be.

"It will come to $78.67," said the pharmacist.

"I'll come back tomorrow," I said and put the prescriptions back in my pocket.

I knew there was no job I could find that would pay me enough for Casper's medicine. He needed it as soon as he could get it. He needed a place to rest and get well too. Sleeping out in the cold was no good for him. It made me sick to my stomach just thinking about it, but I knew what I had to do. I found a pay-phone, pulled the little piece of paper out of my pocket, and dialed Ellen's number.

Casper

I woke up screaming and sat bolt upright in bed. My heart was pounding like I'd run a marathon. I tried to calm myself by telling myself it was just a dream. The dream was about reality, however, and what had happened to my father and brother. I didn't have the dream very often, but when I did, it terrified me right down to my toes.

I lay back down. I felt too weak to even sit up for more than a few moments. I coughed so hard and long I could barely breathe. My throat felt raw. Each cough set it on fire.

I wasn't quite sure where I was for a few moments, but then I remembered that Brendan had brought me to a motel room. The soft mattress and sheets beneath me let me know I was still there, but where was Brendan? I seemed to half remember him leaving, but I wasn't sure why. Had he said he would be back late, or did he just say later? My mind was too foggy to remember.

I lay on the bed shivering and sweating. For a few moments I felt like I was burning up, and then before I knew it, I felt like I was going to freeze to death. Sometimes I felt hot and cold at the same time. I couldn't decide whether to burrow down deep under the blankets, or throw them off.

I was glad to be in a real bed for a change, but I felt so horrible I couldn't really appreciate it. I did appreciate being inside. It had been getting colder and colder with each passing day and I didn't know how long I could stand it. Wandering through the countryside with Brendan had been pleasant enough in the late fall, but winter had come, and had hit hard. I worried about what we'd do.

It was hard to keep thinking about anything for too long. My mind kept drifting. Sounds and images swam in and out and I wasn't always sure which ones were real and which imaginary. My body ached. I felt like even my hair

192

and fingernails hurt. I'd never been so sick before. I think if I could have wished myself dead I would have done so, just so I wouldn't have to feel so horrible anymore. I felt weak and had trouble breathing. I wondered if maybe I wasn't dying. At the moment, I didn't really care.

Brendan

I quietly crept into the motel room in the wee hours of the morning. Casper tossed and turned on the bed, but he seemed to be asleep. I tossed the wad of bills from my pocket on the night stand. There was over three hundred dollars there. It was more than I'd ever made in my life for only a few hours work. I was disgusted with myself. I was ashamed of what I'd done. I'd sold my body for money.

I undressed and got in the shower. I let the hot water fall down on my tired muscles. I soaped up and scrubbed myself all over. It didn't matter how much I washed—I still felt dirty. Nothing could take away what I'd done.

I dried off, and then slipped into bed beside Casper. I felt like I'd betrayed him. He was my boyfriend and I'd went out and slept with someone else. I felt like I'd betrayed myself too. I'd had sex with a woman.

I reminded myself why I'd done it. I sold my body to get money for Casper's medicine. Without it he would probably die. I didn't sell my body for pleasure, not even for cash for something I wanted. I did it because I had to do it. I did it to survive. There was no other way. It made me better understand the boys I'd heard about, the rent boys who sold their bodies just so they could eat. I'd heard about those boys living in the big cities, having sex for money, for food, for drugs. I pitied them. I had a little taste of what it must be like for them, a taste of the shame, the revulsion of having to touch someone that disgusted me, the knowledge that I was a whore. I'd done what I had to do, but it left me feeling unclean. I wondered if I'd ever lose that feeling.

I thought about the things I'd done with Ellen. It made me retch. She had kept telling me what a stud I was, complimenting me on my body, and my ability to perform over and over. She clearly had the night of her life. She paid me even more than she'd promised. The whole thing disgusted me. I wished that I could just wipe my mind blank so I wouldn't have to remember what it was like.

It was a pain I could share with no one. I'd already decided I'd never tell Casper what I'd done. Part of me just couldn't bear the shame of it. Part of me just couldn't stand the idea of him knowing. There was a bigger reason for keeping my secret, however. Casper would know I'd done it for him. He'd feel responsible. He'd feel like he'd made me do it. I didn't want him living with that on his conscience. I'd take my secret with me to my grave.

I awakened the next morning well rested. I turned and looked at Casper lying beside me. He still tossed and turned as if he had never stopped. He was covered in sweat. He moaned in his sleep. I felt his forehead and he was burning up.

I tried not to wake him as I slipped out of bed, but he stirred. He opened his eyes and peered at me.

"Hey," he said with a weak, hoarse voice.

"Hey, Casper," I said, as I leaned over and kissed his forehead. His damp skin was so hot it nearly burned my lips.

Casper smiled at me, but I could tell he felt like shit.

"I'm going to go and pick up your medicine," I told him. "Then I'll get us something good for breakfast. Anything you want in particular?"

"Chocolate milk and French toast," he said.

"You got it. Now you rest. I'll be back as soon as I can. We're going to stay here a few days okay? I'll be back soon."

I put on my clothes and slipped out the door. I headed straight for the drug store and had Casper's prescriptions filled. Next I went to the same diner I'd been to the afternoon before. I was half afraid Ellen would be there, but she wasn't. I breathed a sigh of relief. I didn't want to see her again. I didn't want to be reminded of what I'd done. I didn't want to look into her eyes, not with the things she knew.

I ordered both Casper and myself French toast and chocolate milk. I also got us bacon, juice, and hash browns. He needed to eat to get his strength back and I needed a good meal too. I'd dropped too much weight while we'd been traveling. I could hardly keep my jeans up.

Within minutes, I was sitting with Casper on the bed, chowing down on the best breakfast either of us had eaten in a long time. I gave Casper the first of his pills, and some acetaminophen I'd bought at the drug store. By the time we'd finished eating, he said he felt better.

I cleared away the mess, undressed again, and lay down beside Casper. He needed a lot of rest and I hadn't gotten much sleep the night before either. Both of us snoozed away as the cold wind whipped around outside. I was more comfortable than I had been in a very long time.

* * *

Casper got a little better each day, but it was almost a week before I stopped worrying about him. He often woke me up at night with coughing fits and I could tell it was coming from deep in his chest. I was worried he'd get pneumonia or something. People died from that. I made sure he took his medicine and made him eat even when he didn't feel like it.

I was glad we had a warm motel room to sleep in. The temperature dropped into the teens and the snow fell steadily. I don't think we could have made it outside. I guess we could've stayed in the old barn we'd slept in that one night, but it would have been miserably cold. Our room wasn't fancy, but it was comfortable enough. I'd slept outside on enough cold nights to just appreciate being warm.

* * *

A little over a week after first setting foot in the small town that had temporarily become our home, I awakened to find Casper out of bed and out of the room. There was a note on the nightstand.

"Brendan, went for a short walk, be back soon. Casper."

I'd little more than read the note when Casper returned.
"Hey, Brendan," he said smiling.
"You feeling better?" I asked.
"Much!"
Casper was back to his old self again. He was smiling and laughing. His brow no long felt hot and his cough was all but gone. To celebrate his recovery,

we showered, dressed, and then walked to the little diner where I'd been getting all of our meals.

"Hey Brendan," said Susie, the waitress, as we entered.

"What's up boy? asked Alec, the cook and owner. I'd gotten to know them both well since I was there so often.

"Ah nothin' much," I said.

"Is this your friend?" asked Susie. I'd told her a lot about him.

"Yeah, this is Casper. Casper meet Susie." Casper smiled sweetly.

"You didn't tell me what a cutie he was," said Susie. Casper blushed and it made him even cuter.

"Whatca doin Alec?" I asked. He was drawing on a large piece of paper.

"Putting up a help wanted sign," he answered. "My bus boy quit last night and Rachel is leaving too." Rachel was the other waitress, but I didn't know her well.

I thought to myself for a moment. Casper and I were going through our money much faster than was wise and it had grown so cold we couldn't possibly survive outside. The help wanted sign provided an opportunity.

"I don't think you need that sign," I said.

"Why not?"

"Because your new waiter and bus boy are sitting right here. What do you think?"

Alec looked me and Casper over.

"Think you can handle it?" he asked.

"Yes," I said. "I've already got your menu memorized. I've ordered everything there is on it. Casper can clear tables and wash dishes. I'll help when we're not busy with customers too."

"You know the pay isn't even quite minimum wage," said Alec. "Of course you get your meals free, and tips, so that helps."

"Sounds good to me, how about you Casper?"

"Great," he said.

"I'll tell you boys what I'll do. I'll hire you on approval. We'll see how you work out. If all goes well the first week, then you've got a job as long as you want it. If not, then I'll put up this sign."

"Fair enough," I said. "When do we start?"

"I could use you right now."

"Then now it is."

"Well, you can have your breakfast first. You're on the payroll now, so it's on me."

"Thanks Alec."

Casper and I ordered some French toast and sausages, with chocolate milk. We ate quickly, eager to start our new jobs.

"I guess since I'm the busboy it means I have to wash these dishes," said Casper laughing.

"Yeah," I said, "and since this place is none too busy right now, I guess I get to help."

Not long after finishing breakfast, I took my first order. I had a little trouble writing everything down fast enough, but I knew I'd get the hang of it quick enough. Casper seemed to like his job. He wasn't quite recovered from his illness, but I think he felt so much better that he didn't mind working.

I did a little calculating as I waited on orders to be filled. With our combined salaries, we could afford to live in our motel room. The rates were cheaper by the week. Getting our meals free at the diner helped too. We wouldn't be out anything for food. That would allow us to save up some money for whatever lay ahead. I felt more secure than I had in a long time.

Casper

The snow fell gently as I walked downtown. Brendan was back in the motel room resting. I'd told him I wanted to walk and think, but I had more purpose in getting out by myself than that. Christmas was less than a week away and I wanted to get Brendan something nice.

I took my time walking to *Driskle's*, the only department store in town. It was growing dark and all the lights in the store windows blinked in a multitude of colors. There were decorations in the windows and wreaths on the doors. It was beautiful. It reminded me of the home town I'd left behind. Every Christmas there I walked around looking at all the decorations on the houses and shops. We didn't even have a tree at home, but the town was always decked out for the season. Oddly enough, I didn't miss it. I was more content to be right where I was. I was far happier with Brendan in that cheap motel room than I ever had been at home.

I stopped outside the window of *Driskle's* and peered through the window. There was a giant tree surrounded by lots of wrapped packages. Its lights twinkled and its tinsel sparkled. A mechanical Santa Claus waved at me through the window. There was even a fireplace with stockings hung by the chimney. It seemed almost magical.

I pushed open the door and walked inside. I looked all around me while I listened to the Christmas music playing. I wanted to get Brendan just the right thing. I knew I shouldn't be spending very much of the money I'd made, but I wanted to get him something. There had been no Christmas presents at my house since my mother died. I was excited to have someone to buy something for, and especially someone I loved so much.

Driskle's sold just about everything. I looked at some records, but that wasn't very practical since we didn't have a record player. We could hardly take such a thing with us when we moved on either. I looked through a few books too, but it seemed a little wasteful buying a book when we could get lots of them from the library for free. I wandered all around the store, racking my brains to think of something cool that would actually be useful.

I walked into the clothing section and my eyes lit on just the right thing. There were some nice winter coats hanging there on display. I liked one in particular. It looked thick and warm. I tried it on and it felt like it was stuffed with goose down. It was real comfy. It had been more than a hundred dollars, but it was on sale for only sixty-five. It was a lot of money, but it was something practical. Brendan didn't have a winter coat, only a jacket that was more suited to early fall. I picked out one in his size and paid for it with money I'd earned at the restaurant. I even had it wrapped in pretty Christmas paper with little Christmas trees all over it.

I couldn't help but smile as I walked out the door. I knew Brendan would be really excited on Christmas morning when I gave him his present. I held the box tight against my chest and once again gazed at all the lights and decorations as I walked through the sleepy little town. It wasn't a bad place to live. It was sure a lot better than where I'd come from.

This would be my first Christmas without a family. Things hadn't been so good at home, however, so there wasn't that much to miss. I did miss Christmas back when my mom was alive. She always baked all kinds of Christmas cookies. The whole house smelled like Christmas when she'd been baking. About a week before Christmas she'd start in baking and Dad, Jason, and I would go out and get a tree. By the time we got back, there would be freshly baked cookies and hot chocolate waiting on us. Then we'd all decorate the tree together and I got to put the star on top. It had been a long time since I'd had a Christmas like that. This Christmas would be the best one in years.

Brendan was in the bathroom when I returned to the room, so I quickly hid the package behind the dresser. I wanted it to be a surprise. He came out of the bathroom and gave me a great big hug and kissed me. Yeah, it was going to be the best Christmas ever.

* * *

After supper in the diner, Brendan and I walked through town and out into the countryside. It was snowing and very cold and I wondered where Brendan was taking me. He cut off the road and we waded through deep snow into a small wood. I could see my breath clearly as we stepped under the trees. Brendan stayed just ahead until he spotted a large pine tree.

"What do you think?" he said, pointing at it.

"If you're thinking about taking that home, you're crazy," I told him. It had to be fifty feet tall.

Brendan just laughed. He pulled out his pocket knife and began sawing off a low branch. It was about three feet long. Pretty soon it was free of the tree. Brendan stood it on end.

"Now what do you think?"

The branch looked like a little Christmas tree standing there. I looked at Brendan and smiled.

"I think it's perfect!" I said.

Brendan picked it up and we walked back toward town. In just a few minutes we were inside our warm motel room setting up our little Christmas tree. A towel wound around its base kept it standing up with no problem at all.

I turned on the television and *A Charlie Brown Christmas* was playing. It was one of my favorites. I got all excited when I found out there would be Christmas specials on all night long. I loved watching those programs. It seemed more like Christmas than it had in years, with the snow falling down outside and Christmas music coming from the television inside.

We didn't have much in the way of decorations, but Brendan had brought some colored paper from the diner and we sat down and cut out little ornaments. We made most of them round, but Brendan managed to cut out some angels and I made some bells and sleighs. I tried for a reindeer, but couldn't quite get it right. I ended up saying it was a dog.

We hung our little ornaments on the tree and stood back and looked at it. It was surprisingly attractive. It was special because it was our tree, me and Brendan's. I wrapped my arm around his waist and pulled him close as we looked at it.

"It's the best Christmas tree ever," I told him.

* * *

We worked in the diner until six p.m. on Christmas Eve. It was usually opened later, but Alec closed it up early. Brendan and I spent much of the evening just walking around town and looking at all the lights. It had warmed up into the high twenties, so it wasn't as cold as before. We passed house after house all decorated with bright lights. We could see Christmas trees in some of the houses, but none were prettier than ours. We'd gone all out and even bought some icicles for it. When we grew tired, we went to our motel room and settled in for the night.

I awoke early on Christmas morning. I was excited. I couldn't wait to give Brendan his present. He was barely out of bed before I pulled it from its hiding place and pressed it into his hands.

"What's this?" he asked.

"It's a present, silly."

He turned it over and shook it.

"Open it!"

Brendan ripped the paper off the box, and then lifted off the lid. He pulled the coat out and laughed. It wasn't quite the reaction I was expecting.

"You don't like it?"

"No, no, I love it! It's just…" Brendan rummaged under the bed and came out with a wrapped box. He handed it to me.

I unwrapped the package and opened the box to find a coat identical to the one I'd given Brendan. I understood why he'd laughed when he saw his coat.

"I guess I've got good taste," I said giggling.

"Try it on."

I pulled it on. It was warm and comfy. It was the perfect present. I needed a coat badly. Brendan put his on too. We were a matched set. I grabbed him and hugged him, although it was hard to feel him through both of the coats.

"Merry Christmas," I said.

"Merry Christmas, Casper."

* * *

We had a quick breakfast of donuts since the diner was closed, and then went out into a snowy Christmas day. Everything was covered in a blanket of the purest white. It was cold, but my new coat kept me all warm. We walked to the park and started throwing snowballs at each other. There were some other boys there and pretty soon there were about a dozen of us having a big snowball fight. I got smacked right in the face with one real hard, but I didn't care. I couldn't remember when I'd had so much fun.

We called a truce and divided into two groups and built forts. Most of the boys were younger, so Brendan was in charge of building our fort. We made the walls real thick under Brendan's direction and left little places to look out and throw snowballs. Our opponents made a fort with much higher walls, so high they could stand up behind them and not be seen.

After about an hour of fort construction, the truce ended and both sides opened fire. I had to keep down to avoid getting another snowball in the face. I just whipped snow balls out the openings, and then jerked back before I could get hit. It worked, most of the time.

We fired snowballs back and forth for several minutes, and then Brendan made a few especially large and well packed balls. I knew they were too heavy for me to throw more than a yard or so, but Brendan was strong.

"Watch this," he told me and the other boys, then whipped one of his snow balls at the walls of the enemy fort. It smashed right through the wall, leaving a big hole. Brendan threw another heavy snowball and part of the front wall of our opponent's fort collapsed.

"Too tall, not thick enough," he said as he continued his attack. Each snowball wiped out part of the enemy fort until most of it was down. The rest of us fired snowballs at our opponents, really pounding them hard. Brendan took out more and more of their wall until there wasn't much left. The boys fighting us had to hide behind piles of snow that weren't big enough to protect them. We really let them have it. They couldn't take it and retreated. We jumped from behind our fort and attacked them. Soon we'd driven them away. We jumped up and down whooping with victory.

Some of the boys invited me and Brendan to go sledding and we followed them to the edge of town. There was a big hill there that looked more like a mountain. We all took turns using the sleds and it was a blast. Brendan even dared to go down the part called "The Devil's Backbone." It was a really steep section of hill that had a sudden drop near the bottom. Brendan sailed down the hill at break-neck speed then shot into the air when he reached the drop. He must have flown ten feet before he hit the snow again. He slid to a halt without being thrown from his sled. The boys said it was quite an accomplishment and I didn't doubt it one bit. I wasn't about to go down that part of the hill. It was too much for me.

We went back to our motel room and got out of our wet clothes. Brendan turned up the heat and I went in and took a hot shower. The hot water felt so good and warmed me up. It was Brendan's turn next and I dressed while he was showering. The room had warmed up nicely and only the snow falling down outside reminded me it was winter.

Brendan came out of the bathroom a few minutes later with a towel wrapped around his waist. I looked at him. He was beautiful. I admired his powerful muscles. He was so strong, and tall. I loved him so much. I walked over to him and hugged him close. I lay my head against his chest and could hear his heart beat. We just stood there, holding each other.

I leaned back and looked into Brendan's eyes. They were warm and inviting. I got up on my toes and kissed him on the lips. It made me feel wonderful. I felt a rush of excitement throughout my entire body. I took Brendan's hand and led him to the bed. I was amazed at my own boldness, but I gently pushed him down on the bed and lay on top of him, still kissing him. He was my boyfriend. I loved him, and he loved me. I pulled off my clothes and pulled Brendan's towel from his waist. We lay on the bed and made love to each other. I was happier and more content than I'd ever been in my entire life.

Brendan

The days slipped by until weeks had disappeared. The bitter cold of late December and January gave way to more comfortable temperatures and soon there was little more than a chill in the air. Casper and I spent most of our days working in the diner and our evenings in our motel room. Often we got out and walked around town and on weekends we spent a lot of time in the park, sometimes playing with the other boys there. One day seemed much like the next in the quiet little town. It was too quiet really and didn't take long to become boring.

The only real excitement was when my path crossed Ellen's, and it was excitement I did not want. I didn't like being reminded of what I had done and I didn't like the way she looked at me. I couldn't help but be resentful, even though she had done nothing bad to me. I guess she had taken advantage of me in a way, but I knew what I was doing. I guess it could just as easily be said that I took advantage of her.

She found me sitting alone in the park one Sunday. Casper was back at the motel room resting, but I wasn't tired. I needed to get out and stretch my legs. I ended up in the park since there weren't many places to go in town. I tensed as she approached and sat beside me on the bench.

"Have you been avoiding me Brandon?"

"It's Brendan, and no." She'd had sex with me, but she didn't even remember my name. I was lying about avoiding her. I avoided her like the plague—seeing her brought up too many unpleasant memories.

"Yes, that's right, Brendan. I've missed you." Ellen put her hand on my leg. I tensed and politely moved her hand to the bench.

"Who is that blond boy I see you with?"

"A friend."

"He's a real cutie isn't he? I wouldn't mind taking him home with me."

"You stay away from him!" I realized I was shouting angrily.

"Calm down, Brendan. I was just saying I thought he was cute."

"Uh huh."

"So he's a friend?"

"Yeah, that's right." I was beginning to get uncomfortable.

"Just a friend?"

The tone of her voice frightened me. Her words were something between an accusation and a threat. I didn't answer for a moment. It was a pause that spoke volumes.

"We're good friends," I said. It was a non-answer, but I didn't want to tell her the truth and I didn't want to deny the truth either. It's not like I owed her any kind of explanation. I was angry that she was prying and it came through in my voice.

"No need to get hostile, Brendan," said Ellen. "I like you a lot and I sure enjoyed our night together. You're quite a talented young man."

I could feel my face turning red. She was playing with me. She stood.

"Call me if you want to spend the night again. I'll pay double if you bring that cute little friend of yours with you, maybe more than that."

I was so mad I couldn't see straight, but I thought it wise not to go off on her like she deserved. She had information about me that I didn't want to get out. I especially didn't want her saying anything to Casper. I couldn't afford to let her know how desperately I wanted to keep what I'd done from him. I was sure she was the kind that would use such information to her advantage.

"I'll think about it," I said, when what I really wanted to say was "Fuck you, bitch."

She smiled and walked away. I felt shaky. I'd made a lot of money for the night I'd spent with her, but it had cost me in more ways than one.

* * *

I sat at the counter in the diner early one morning in mid-April. It wasn't time to open up yet and I fixing myself some cereal. I grabbed a carton of milk and began pouring it into the bowl. Suddenly my heart was in my throat and I dropped the carton, spilling milk all over the counter. I just sat there and stared at it as the milk ran out.

"If you think I'm cleaning that up, you're crazy," said Casper. He was behind the counter sweeping.

He stopped and looked at me.

"Brendan, what's wrong?" From the way I felt, I'm sure all the color had drained from my face.

I picked up the milk carton, and just stared at the side. Casper came around the counter to see what I was staring at. His eyes grew wide when he saw it. My picture was on the side of the milk carton. Right under it was my name, my birth date, and a description of me. I was on a milk carton. I couldn't believe it.

I looked at Casper. He looked back at me, uncertain as to exactly what it all meant. I wondered how many other people in town had seen my picture. I wondered if any of them recognized me. I thought of Ellen.

"We've got to get out of here," I said.

As if on cue, Ellen came into the diner. She ordered pancakes and sausages. She also ordered a glass of milk and put so much emphasis on the word "milk" that I knew it was meant as a warning. She knew. Any doubt I might have had was erased when she told me she wanted to talk to me that evening. She had a proposition for me. I shuddered to think what that proposition might be. I feared I already knew.

Less than two hours after discovering my photo on the side of a milk carton, Casper and I were packed and heading out of town. I felt really bad for leaving Alec short a waiter and a buss boy with absolutely no notice at all, but there was no way around it. Alec was very understanding when I told him we had to go, even though I didn't tell him why. He even sent us on our way with a big bag of donuts and rolls. I think he always knew that Casper and I were running from something.

As we walked north along the side of the road I wondered if anyone besides Ellen had recognized my picture, and if they'd called the number on the side of the carton. If they had, the police would be after us in a flash. Every step made me feel a little safer, but I must admit I was scared. The possibility of being taken back to *Cloverdale* was just too much for me. The old fear was back.

When we'd been walking for several hours, I looked at my watch. It was six p.m. That's when I was supposed to meet Ellen. She'd know pretty soon that I wasn't coming. I wondered what she'd do. I wondered if she'd call the police, or just come after us herself. I was afraid of her. I knew she would do something far worse than just turning me in if she got the chance. She'd threaten to turn me in if I didn't do what she wanted, and there was no doubt in my mind about what she wanted. I cringed when I thought that she might even want Casper involved. I couldn't handle even thinking about that. We were leaving Ellen farther and farther behind, however, so that danger was disappearing fast.

"I kind of wish we could have stayed," said Casper. "I liked it there. I was beginning to think of our little motel room as home."

"Yeah, I know what you mean," I said. I didn't completely share Casper's opinion, because of Ellen. I knew I'd never be comfortable with her around. She was a reminder of the worst moments in my life. I was glad to be leaving her behind.

"So where we headed now?" asked Casper.

"North," I said, as if it were a destination. "We'll find us a place to stay, Casper. We find someplace where we can stay for good. I want it to be someplace kind of isolated, however, so it will be less likely that someone will recognize me."

"I got something in my pack that will help with that," said Casper. "I picked it up when I went out and bought us groceries."

I was very curious. Before we left town, Casper made a last trip to the grocery store to get us some supplies. I'd stayed back in the motel room and packed because I was afraid I'd be recognized. I guess that was pretty stupid though. It was a small town and everyone had already seen me countless times.

"What is it?"

"Hair coloring. You're gonna be blond like me by tomorrow. You'll be like Ponyboy in *The Outsiders* when he had to bleach his hair so he and Johnny wouldn't be recognized."

"No way! You're not touching my hair!"

"It'll only be blond until it grows out, and it will make it a lot harder for anyone to recognize you. You don't want to go back to that hospital again do you?"

"No," I said. I didn't want my hair changed like that, but Casper was making a lot of sense. It would be a lot better being blond for a while than going back to the *Cloverdale Center*.

We walked on and on. I'd forgotten how my feet and legs got tired after walking for a few hours. It would take time to get myself back in shape. It was far more pleasant traveling in April than it had been in December, however.

Instead of cold and snow, we had reasonable warmth and sunshine. It would still be chilly at night, but nothing like it had been in the winter.

We camped out by a stream that night and Casper colored my hair. I wasn't at all thrilled with the idea, but it was better than the alternative. By the time he was done, I was just as blond as my boyfriend. At least that's what Casper told me. We didn't have a mirror and I couldn't see for myself. Casper said I looked really good, but I wasn't sure if I believed him or not. I suspected he'd lie to make me feel better about my appearance.

I awoke in the night thinking I was in our motel room. The stars overhead brought me quickly back to reality. We were on the run again. I wondered if we'd ever be able to stop running and settle down. The world seemed a very unfair place.

The morning light awoke us early and we set out once more, determined to put more distance between ourselves and the little town we'd called home for a few months. The miles wore on beneath our feet as we passed the forests and fields of central Indiana. It was the beginning of spring and the trees were just beginning to leaf. It was a time of year I loved and our journey was far from unpleasant. Had our future been a little more secure, I could have thoroughly enjoyed our flight as a little adventure. As it was, I had no idea where we were going to, or what we'd do when we got there.

Casper

After four weeks and more of continuous travel, the novelty of it began to wear off. I wanted nothing more than to stop somewhere, anywhere, and stay right there forever. Sleeping in a different place each night was its own kind of excitement, but I was more than ready to give it up. If I hadn't loved Brendan so very much, I don't think I could have taken that kind of life.

Brendan and I walked past a sign that read "Verona" and soon came to a graveyard on the edge of town. We walked in and seated ourselves for a rest, and a bit of lunch. It might seem an odd place for a picnic, but it was daytime, during school hours, and we didn't want to arouse suspicions by being seen. We could be alone in the cemetery, out of sight and mind among the weathered tomb stones.

Not all the tomb stones were weather-beaten, however. Right before us were two that looked as if they'd just been placed there. They certainly hadn't been there long; the dates of death were just the previous fall. I gazed at the stones as I chewed on a stale roll and immediately began to wonder about those buried there.

"Look at this," I told Brendan. "The guys buried here were our age, and they were both born on August 21, 1964 and both died on November 3, 1980. Isn't that weird?"

"Yeah, I wonder why they're buried side by side like that. Think they were brothers or something?"

"No, look at the names; Mark Bailey and Taylor Potter. They couldn't have been brothers."

"Maybe step-brothers?"

I looked at the stones but there were no answers there, just the names and dates of birth and death. I nibbled on my roll and let my mind drift to other things.

"Brendan, could we stay here?"

"What, in the graveyard? Want to keep Mark and Taylor here company?"

"Funny. You know what I mean. Stay here in this town, like we did in Purity before. I'll go anywhere you want, of course, but I'd like to find a place to settle down. I'm getting tired of just walking all day, every day." I was getting tired. In the last few weeks we'd covered well over two hundred miles.

"I know what you mean. Our funds are getting kind of short too. Tell you what, let's stay here and rest up; then, when it's late enough that school has let out, we'll walk into town and see what we can find."

We finished our lunch, then lay down side by side and took a nap. It felt good to rest in the shade of the big cedar trees.

I had a dream as I lay there, although I couldn't remember much about it later on. It was a dream about Brendan and me, and yet it wasn't about us. There was a boy with dark hair, very handsome, but not Brendan. There was a blond boy too, but he wasn't me. He was taller and had very long hair. He was so beautiful he seemed like an angel. They were looking at us as we slept, and they were smiling. I felt very safe. They took each other by the hand and then just kind of faded away.

When I awoke, it felt like no time at all had passed, but it was nearing four in the afternoon. It was safe for us to walk into town. We left the graveyard and followed a street into the heart of Verona. It was a nice little town, with just a few restaurants and shops, not too big, but big enough to have something to offer. Everyone was really friendly and said "hi" to us as we passed. I thought to myself that it was the kind of place I'd like to live.

We didn't pass a single "help wanted" sign, so Brendan went into the drugstore and bought a copy of the *Verona Citizen*. There wasn't much to it. The front page story was about the local baseball team defeating their long time rivals. There wasn't much to the classifieds either, but one ad immediately caught Brendan's eyes.

"Here, listen to this," he said. "Help Wanted: Looking to hire strong, dependable man to help with spring planting and other farm work. Room and board provided, plus small wages. Possibly a year round position. Apply in person at the Selby farm."

"Sounds pretty good," I said, "but it does say "man" and they're only wanting one person."

"Yeah, but I bet I could do it. It couldn't be that tough. Maybe we could both get hired. There's got to be stuff both of us could help with on a farm. We ought to at least check it out. If we can't get it, or decide we don't want it, we won't be any worse off than we are now."

"That's true," I said. "So let's do it."

It didn't take us long to find out where the Selby farm was located. The very first person we asked was able to give us directions. The farm was located not too far outside of town and we walked there in a matter of minutes.

We passed a mailbox reading *Selby* and followed a long drive up to a big, white farmhouse. Not far beyond it was a huge barn and all kinds of farm buildings. Fields stretched out for miles in every direction.

Brendan knocked on the door and an old, somewhat gruff looking man answered. My hopes fell. I knew that old guy would never hire us. He looked like the no nonsense, all business type. There was no doubt he was a farmer. He was wearing overalls and looked like he'd just come in from the fields.

"We, uh, came about the ad?" said Brendan.

The old man looked at us as if he was thinking of sending us away. Instead, he smiled ever so slightly and invited us in.

He showed us inside to a big living room, with a television in one corner, a sofa along one wall, and a couple of big recliners. It was nothing fancy, but it was homey and comfortable.

"Hey Jack, did you…" A boy who looked not more than fifteen entered the room and fell silent when he saw us. He was blond and just about as slim as me.

"They've come about the ad," said Jack in explanation.

"Oh, yeah, right."

The boy looked at us somewhat perplexed as well, as if we couldn't possibly be there looking for farm work. I don't know if it was our age, or that we probably didn't look like farmers in the least. He seemed a touch uncomfortable, but was friendly enough. He stood in the doorway for a few moments looking at us until he remembered why he was there.

"Jack, Ethan wants to know if you fixed the radiator on the tractor. He wants to get in some plowing before supper."

"Yeah, I got it patched up again. Tell him to go at it."

The boy was gone as quickly as he came.

"I'm Jack, as I guess you've figured out."

"Brendan."

"Casper."

"So, you boys came about the job?"

"Yes sir," said Brendan.

"I was really looking for someone a bit more mature. I don't suppose you have any experience with farm work?"

"No sir, we don't," said Brendan.

The old man looked at us appraisingly. It made me extremely uncomfortable and Brendan too. I knew we were being sized up.

"I guess maybe we're wasting your time," said Brendan, getting up. I got up too.

"Sit down, boy. I'll tell you if you're wasting my time."

Brendan sat back down quickly, as did I. The old man had a commanding tone that made me do what he said automatically.

"We've just added a whole lot of new acreage to the farm, and me and the boys could just barely keep up with what we had. Spring planting is coming up fast and we either need to hire help, or let all our new acreage lie fallow. I'd much rather get it planted. Wheat should bring a good price this year. I've also got a mind to start raising sheep, in addition to our cattle."

"Both Casper and I are looking for work," said Brendan. "We aren't experienced with farm work, but I'm sure we can pick it up fast and we'll both work hard. We really need a job and a place to stay. You won't be sorry if you take us on."

Brendan seemed to have found the courage to talk with the old man. I think the old guy was impressed by it.

"You are awfully young, both of you," said Jack.

"I'm seventeen, Casper here is fifteen." Brendan looked a bit frightened.

"So you need a place to stay? What about your parents?"

I knew this question was coming and wasn't looking forward to it at all. Brendan didn't answer.

"My parents are dead," I said. My mom died when I was little and my dad just died a few months ago."

"I'm sorry to hear that," said Jack. He looked back at Brendan.

"You a runaway son?" Brendan looked as uncomfortable as I'd ever seen him. I waited to see what he would say, and if he'd make up a story or not.

"Yes, sir. I had to run away. I promise that I didn't do anything bad though."

"Well boy, I'm not one to pry into anyone's personal business, but if I'm going to take you boys on here, I need to know what I'm up against. Both of you are underage and that can create a whole heap of trouble. I'll take you at your word, but I expect you to be honest with me. If I find out you aren't, you'll be out of here fast. I don't put up with liars. I'm not calling you one either, I'm just letting you know how it is."

The old man was definitely the straightforward type. I was afraid of what was going to happen next, but his words gave me hope. He made it sound as if we at least had a shot at staying. I looked at Brendan. He was so scared he was practically shaking.

"Okay, the truth. Just one thing, though. Promise me you won't turn us in. I swear we haven't done anything illegal. If you don't want to hire us, that's fine. Just let us go on our way. Okay?"

"Fair enough."

I could tell that Brendan was deciding if he could trust the old man or not. I could also tell he decided pretty quickly that he could.

"Well, uh, my parents had me committed to this hospital, right after they found out that I was, uh, gay."

Brendan looked at Jack fearfully, as if expecting him to order us both out of the house immediately.

"I'm beginning to wonder if any of you young boys like girls. We may be facing under population soon," said Jack.

It seemed an odd thing to say and it made me wonder about a lot of things. I could tell it made Brendan wonder too.

"That hospital was a terrible place. You wouldn't believe what they do to kids in there."

Brendan went on explaining just what had gone on in that hospital. I listened very closely because he was telling a lot of things I'd never heard before. Brendan didn't like to talk about what happened to him in there, so I never pressed him. He glanced at me now and then as he spoke. I could tell he was very uncomfortable.

The old man sat there and listened as Brendan poured his heart out. He told him everything about the hospital, how he broke out, about our travels and hardships. I was kind of surprised that he told him everything, but maybe he kind of needed to get it off his chest. Maybe he needed to tell it to an adult; even if it was someone we didn't even know.

I began to grow afraid as Brendan went on. I could tell he was afraid too. He kept speaking faster and faster until the old man told him to slow down. I was scared of the look on Jack's face. He looked very angry, like he didn't approve at all of us running away. Finally Brendan finished and there was dead silence in the room.

"That really burns my ass," said the old man. I feared he was getting ready to go off on Brendan and me and order us off his property.

"Some people would do anything to have children," said Jack "and then others abuse theirs like that. You were right to run away son, you too," he said, looking at me. "You should have gone to someone about it, however. You boys can't handle something like this yourself and you can't keep running forever."

"Yes, sir," said Brendan.

"I promised I wouldn't turn you in and I certainly won't. I'm a man of my word. A man isn't anything if he doesn't keep his word. You boys are going to have to deal with this situation, however, and sooner or later that's going to mean confronting your parents."

"I'll be eighteen in just a couple of weeks," said Brendan. "Once I turn eighteen they can't put me back in that hospital."

"True, true," said Jack, "you'll legally be an adult then. I guess the best thing may be for you to stay out of sight until your birthday."

"Yes, sir."

"You, however," said Jack, looking at me, "you're another matter entirely."

"Sir?" I said.

I didn't like having his attention focused on me. I felt like I was under a microscope or something. I was scared.

"Do you have any relatives?"

"Well, I have a brother and a grandmother on my dad's side, but that's it."

"No aunts or uncles?"

"No sir. I just had one uncle, my mom's brother, but he died before she did."

"Where's your grandmother?"

"She's in Florida. I never saw her much. My dad didn't get along with her, so I don't know her very well."

The old man looked like he was thinking very hard.

"You have to have a legal guardian, and your brother or grandmother would be the most likely to be granted that."

"Not my brother, sir! Please!" Brendan had told Jack that Jason abused me, but he'd left out the gory details.

"Calm down, boy. I'm just telling you how it is. We can talk more about this later, but if you two are going to stay here, you'll have to go to school. Brendan can enroll on his own, without his parent's involvement, when he turns eighteen, but the school is going to want to know who has custody of you. If we don't get that settled, social services could take you away and put you in a foster home. Most likely they will too."

Tears welled up in my eyes and I started to cry.

"Maybe we should just go," said Brendan.

"Don't be dense, boy. You can't keep running from your problems forever. We can work through all this. It will just take time."

I stopped crying. It sounded a lot like we were going to get to stay.

"Now, about the job," said Jack, "depending on what we can work out with your grandmother or brother, I don't see any reason why I can't at least give you boys a try."

I smiled, and so did Brendan.

"You certainly look strong enough," he said, looking at Brendan. He glanced at me for a moment and I know he was thinking I was puny. He didn't say anything, however.

"The job doesn't pay much in cash, but I'll give you each a room here in the house, all the food you can eat, and say…$20 each a week for spending money. There are conditions, however. As soon as you turn eighteen Brendan, you will enroll in school."

"Yes, sir."

"And you, we'll have to try and find your grandmother. We've got to get things straight with her."

"I know her address, if she hasn't moved. She sends me a Christmas card every year."

"Good. We've got to get this whole custody thing settled right away. I know you don't want to deal with it, but it's got to be dealt with, and now. Understand?"

"Yes, sir."

"So that's the deal. Take it, or leave it."

Brendan looked at me and I nodded.

"We'll take it, sir," said Brendan.

"Good, just don't make me sorry. I'm running a farm, not a house for wayward boys, although sometimes I'm not so sure."

I wondered what he meant by that.

"Yes, sir," said Brendan.

"And one more thing, stop calling me sir. The name is Jack."

"Yes, sir, I mean Jack," said Brendan.

When I looked at the clock, I was amazed to see how much time had passed. I didn't realize Brendan had been talking so long, but I guess it shouldn't have surprised me. He had a lot to tell.

Less than an hour later we sat down to the best supper we'd had in a long time. There was fried chicken, mashed potatoes, green beans, corn, bread, and even apple pie. An older boy came in before we started eating. He was the Ethan that Nathan had mentioned before. He looked to be about Brendan's age and was powerfully built, as well as very handsome. He was very friendly and I liked him a lot. He didn't look anything at all like Nathan however, so I wondered how they could be brothers. I found out later they weren't. Jack didn't have any kids. Ethan was his nephew and Nathan was working there kind of like Brendan and I would be. Jack's comment about running a house for wayward boys began to make more sense. I wondered how Ethan had come to live with him, and even more about why Nathan was there.

A boy of about nine joined us and we soon learned that he was Nathan's little brother, Dave. I would have immediately guessed it without being told since he looked like a smaller version of Nathan. He was a friendly little boy, and very lively. Jack had a whole house full of boys and not one of them was his own.

After supper, Nathan showed us to our rooms. We stopped in to look at Brendan's first. It was big with windows looking out in two directions over the yard and fields around the house. Mine was right next to it and had a great view as well. It was light and airy and had an old double bed that looked very comfy.

"The bathroom is just down the hall," said Nathan. "There's only one, so we'll have to share."

"Not a problem," I said.

"I'll let you two get settled in, and then I'll give you a tour of the house and show you where everything is. If you need me, I'll be downstairs."

Nathan left. Brendan and I checked out our rooms some more.

"It's nice isn't it," I said, looking at his room.

"Yeah, and big. I hope this works out."

"Yeah, me too. I guess we'll see."

"I wish we could share a room, and a bed," said Brendan meaningfully.

"Me too, but we better not push it."

"Yeah. I'm not so sure what Jack would think about that. I don't know what the others would, either. I think we'd better keep us being boyfriends a secret, at least for a while."

"Well, we don't want to lie."

"I'm not talking about lying. I'm talking about not telling. If one of them asks, we'll tell the truth, but if they don't, there's no need to volunteer it. Let's scope things out before we tell anyone."

It sounded like a good enough plan to me.

* * *

That evening, Brendan and I sat on a wooden swing on the big front porch as the sun set. The sky was all oranges and purples over the empty fields. I felt like I was in that Robert Frost poem we'd read in English class, "Nothing Gold Can Stay." We just sat there, and talked, and swung back and forth. It was beautiful.

For the first time in a long time, I felt safe. Our future was still uncertain, but yet it didn't seem so uncertain anymore. I had a feeling deep down inside that everything was going to be okay. Somehow I just knew that we wouldn't have to run anymore, that we'd be safe. I'm not sure why I felt that way. There was sure a lot of stuff to deal with, but I felt it all the same, and it felt good.

We were alone, Jack was out checking on a field, Ethan and Nathan were working in the barn, and Dave was inside doing his homework. I took Brendan's hand in mine and held it as we swung. A gentle breeze brought the scent of new mown grass and freshly tilled earth. In the distance I could hear insects I couldn't name calling to one another, and frogs singing their song. I looked at Brendan and smiled. Our eyes locked, our lips met, and I kissed him, feeling all the love in our hearts. We drew back and smiled at one another again.

I knew that everything was going to be okay. There were troubles before us without doubt, but they didn't seem so impossible to deal with anymore. Jack had a lot to do with that. I knew he was the kind of guy that got things done. I knew that he wouldn't let anyone hurt us. I just felt safer with him around.

We'd come to the farm looking for a job and a place to stay, but we'd found much more. We'd come to a better place.

PART 2

Nathan

I looked toward the farmhouse and saw Casper and Brendan sitting together on the porch swing. I wondered what had brought them to our farm in the middle of nowhere. There was an edge to them, a certain tension or fear as if they were waiting on some unpleasant fate to befall them. And yet, there was a sense of relief about them too, as if they had been in great danger that had now passed. I was sure their story was an interesting one, and I hoped to hear it when they'd settled in a little.

"Can you help me with this for a minute?" asked Ethan.

I picked up a wrench and held a bolt in place while Ethan tightened the nut on the other side. He was doing a few repairs to the plow that would soon be seeing heavy work. The light wasn't the best inside the barn at night, but the bulb overhead illuminated the machinery enough that Ethan could work on it without difficulty.

Wuffa whinnied and I walked over to the partition that separated us and gave him a pat. Fairfax wasn't about to be left out and came up for some attention too. I loved those horses and had even learned to ride them pretty well. I wasn't an expert rider like Ethan, but then again I hadn't been riding since I was eight.

The chickens were settling in for the night. I looked over and saw Henrietta, my little brother's pet hen, situating herself on her nest with great care. She seemed almost like a little old lady adjusting the blankets on her bed just so. After a bit, she settled into the soft straw and lay her head back on her wing. She was one chicken that would never see the frying pan. Dave loved her more than anything. He had ever since Ethan had given her to him, before Dave and I had come to live on the farm.

I looked at Ethan and almost laughed. He had smudges of grease on his cheeks that looked almost like war paint. He was beautiful, even in the dim light of the barn. Sometimes I still couldn't believe that he was my boyfriend. His looks were the least reason that I loved him, however. Ethan was good to me, and to Dave, and he loved me with all his heart. I knew that we had something special, something that most people searched their whole lives for without finding.

I picked up a clean rag and wiped off Ethan's cheeks. He looked at me and smiled. He wrapped his strong arms around me and held me tight. That's what I loved the most, just being held by him. It was wonderful when he kissed me, it was beyond description when we made love, but having Ethan hold me was the best of all. The feeling of loving, and being loved, is the greatest feeling that can ever be. I wished everyone could experience it.

Brendan

I woke up not quite sure where I was. I thought at first that I was sleeping out-side under the stars with Casper, as we had done so often since leaving Purity. Then, for a few terrible moments, I feared that I was still back in the *Cloverdale Center*, trapped in that hellish nightmare of a hospital where they tried to turn gay boys straight. I relaxed as I looked around my unfamiliar room in the old farmhouse. Casper and I had arrived there only the afternoon before, but it was a safe place and I felt more secure than I had in a long time.

I looked beside me. There was no Casper. I felt a twinge of loneliness, but I knew he was in the very next room. He was probably sleeping peacefully for the first time in a long time. We'd had a long journey, weeks of running from my parents and the *Cloverdale Center*, weeks of trying to avoid being hunted down and put back in that horrible place. A cold chill ran through my body. Fear still touched my heart when I thought of the things they did to me in there.

I got up and opened up the closet. It didn't take me long to chose what I wanted to wear. I had a grand total of three shirts, two pairs of jeans, a light jacket, and a heavy goose-down coat. The last was given to me as a Christmas present by Casper. I smiled when I remembered that I'd picked out the very same thing for him.

Before dressing I took a look at myself in the mirror. I was out of shape. I'd lost too much weight and I'd lost my muscle tone too. I hadn't worked out in months, and it had been equally long since I'd been through a football prac-tice. The drugs they pumped into me at the *Cloverdale Center* probably weren't any good for my body either.

I flexed my muscles. I wasn't in the best of shape, but the muscles I'd built up from lifting weights and playing football were still there. Muscles didn't go away in a few months time. I was sure I'd get my muscle tone back fast enough, farm work was sure to be as strenuous as working out.

I pulled on my clothes and wondered how Casper and I would do as farm boys. One thing was for sure, I was going to do the best job I could. I knew that Jack was really going to a lot of trouble to take us on. We were strangers, but he'd taken us in like lost puppies. Most people would have sent us on our way, but not him. I'd told him our whole story when he pressed me for it and I wasn't sorry in the least. Casper and I had our first real chance to take care of our troubles because of Jack. I wasn't about to let him down.

I pulled on my shoes, and then looked in on Casper. He was still sleeping, looking like a little blond angel as he lay there in his bed. He was far too thin. He'd always been thin, but weeks of hard travel had taken its toll. We'd sure get enough to eat while living at the Selby farm, however. That was part of our pay for working there, all the food we could eat, as well as a place to stay and $20 a week. After what we'd been through, it was a dream come true.

I walked downstairs to find Nathan frying eggs and bacon. It smelled so good. My stomach rumbled.

"Hey there, um, Brendan, right?"

"Yeah, Brendan."

"I keep getting confused and can't remember if it's Brandon or Brendan, but I'll get it down I promise." Nathan smiled and it made me feel right at home.

"So where is everybody?"

"Uncle Jack and Ethan are out getting a few things ready for today. They want to get started plowing."

"Should I go help?" I asked. Casper and I had been hired as farm hands and I wanted to make a good impression from the start.

"No, they'll be coming in soon. Jack said to let you sleep in since you looked like you needed it. We usually get up earlier around here, but it's Saturday, so we don't get up until eight or so," said Nathan.

"Do you mind me asking you something? I mean, I don't want to be nosy, but I was wondering about you and Ethan."

"What about us?" Nathan looked slightly uncomfortable as he sat a kettle on the stove.

"I was wondering how you both came to live here. I thought Ethan was Jack's son at first, but then Jack said he didn't have any kids."

"Oh that," said Nathan. "You mind setting the table? Most of the stuff's in that big step-back cupboard over there."

"Glad to help," I said. As I pulled out plates and forks and knives, Nathan talked.

"Ethan's parents were killed in a car wreck when he was little. He didn't have any other family, so Jack took him in. Jack's his uncle. I think Ethan's more like a son than a nephew, however. Jack was married, but he never had any kids and I think he really feels kinda bad about that.

"I've only been here a few months. I started in last year. At first, I just worked some after school, and on Saturday's, but then things got pretty rough at home and Ethan got Jack to let Dave and me come and live here."

"Don't your parents mind?"

"No, our parents don't care about us much. I don't really want to talk about it, but they weren't very good to us at all."

I didn't press him for more. I had no doubt we were getting into a touchy area. I had a few things I didn't like to talk about myself. Nathan looked at me with a question in his eyes. He paused, as if considering if he should ask what was on his mind.

"What's your and Casper's story? How did you come to end up here in Verona? I mean, this is the middle of nowhere."

"Well, that's a really long story, but it's kind of like yours. I had to leave home because of my parents. They weren't too good to me either. Casper had a lot of trouble at home too, more than me. His mom died a long time ago and his dad never paid much attention to him. His older brother beat on him a lot. We left right after his dad died. I needed to get away from my parents and Casper needed to get away from his brother."

I wasn't telling Nathan the whole truth, but I told him enough of it to explain why we were there. I wasn't lying either, I was just leaving out a lot of details that I wasn't ready to talk about yet. I didn't want to talk about why I'd had to escape from my parents. I wasn't at all sure what Nathan or Ethan would think if they knew I was gay. I wasn't sure what they'd think if they knew that Casper was my boyfriend either. I could just picture them freaking out about it. Jack knew that I was gay, I had to tell him to explain why I'd run away. He seemed pretty understanding, but I wasn't sure how comfortable he was with it. Jack didn't know that Casper was my boyfriend. I'd left out that little detail.

Casper came into the kitchen just then and helped me finish setting everything out for breakfast. It was a good thing the old kitchen table had extra
leaves, because there were six of us all together. Casper and I helped Nathan
finish getting breakfast ready while we talked. I really liked Nathan; he was
friendly, good natured, and funny too.

It wasn't long before Jack and Ethan came in. They washed up and we all sat
down at the table.

"If you don't get down here I'd giving your breakfast to the dogs," yelled
Nathan. A very short time later, his little brother Dave came running downstairs and into the kitchen. He plopped down in a chair and helped himself to
some biscuits and gravy.

"Just grab whatever you want," said Jack. "We all serve ourselves here. Don't
be shy."

Casper and I looked at each other for a moment, and then dug in. I reached
for some bacon and some of that biscuits and gravy. I took a few bites.

"This is so good!" I said.

"Yeah, it's even better than your cooking," said Casper, looking at me.

"You do a lot of cooking?" asked Ethan. I looked at him. Ethan was very
handsome, and strong. He was built even better than me. He had muscles
bulging out everywhere.

"Yeah, Casper and I worked in a little diner for a few months. I learned how
to fix everything on the menu. Casper got pretty good at it too."

"Good, we could use some more cooks around here," said Nathan. "I've
been doing most of it. Ethan isn't the best at it, and Jack, well…let's just say he
could burn cereal." Nathan and Ethan laughed, so did Casper and I.

"Watch yourself, boy!" said Jack, but the crinkles in his eyes got very close to
indicating a smile. He wasn't quite as gruff as he pretended to be.

The laughter and pleasant talk really made me feel at home. It was a good
feeling, and one I hadn't experienced in quite a long time. I looked at Casper. I
could tell that he could feel it too.

"So what are we doing today?" I asked. "Nathan said you're getting ready to
start plowing?"

"You're eager enough," said Jack.

"I just want to get at it. I really appreciate you taking us on and I don't want
to let you down."

Ethan bent his head down and encircled the end of his nose with his fist, silently calling me a brown-noser. It was all in fun though, his smile made that clear. He knocked it off before Jack had a chance to see him.

"You'll be helping Ethan this morning. I have a few things to talk over with Casper, and then Nathan is going to show him the ropes."

"Yeah, today I teach you how to drive a tractor city-boy, think you're up to it?" asked Ethan.

"What makes you think I'm a city-boy?"

"You're from the city, right?"

"More like a small town."

"Same thing."

"Well anyway, I'm up to it. You'll see." I was a little apprehensive. I wasn't so sure I was as up to the task as I claimed, but I was excited none-the-less. The farm was a whole new world to me.

We finished up breakfast, and then Ethan and I headed out for the barn. Casper stayed behind to help Nathan clean up, and to have a talk with Jack.

Nathan

After breakfast, Casper helped me to clear the table and clean up the breakfast mess. I was glad to have the help. I was accustomed to doing it myself and it went a lot faster with two of us. I'd known Casper less than a day, but I already liked him, Brendan too for that matter. I was glad Jack had hired them to help out with the farm and I was glad they'd be living with us. I knew it would complicate things between Ethan and me, but I also knew we'd manage to find plenty of time to be alone.

Casper looked a little like me. He had the same blond hair and slim build. He was even thinner than I was which was surprising. He was just a bit shorter too. He looked very frail and I wondered if he was up to farm work. I figured he could do it, if I could. I'd put on some muscle in the months I'd been working on the farm, but I was nearly as puny looking as Casper when I'd started.

Jack sat at the table and had another cup of coffee as Casper and I cleaned up. He was usually out the door as soon as breakfast was finished, but I knew he had things to discuss with Casper.

"So boy, you say your brother and grandmother are your only relations?"

"Yes," answered Casper nervously. I could tell Jack intimidated him a little. That didn't surprise me. Jack had a heart of gold, but he could be as intimidating as hell until you got to know him. He could be pretty frightening at times even when you knew him well.

"And you don't think we should try to contact your brother?"

"No, absolutely not. He's horrible. He did really bad things to me. He hurt me. I don't want anything to do with him."

Jack looked as if he were going to ask about the things Casper's brother had done, then thought better of it. I was curious as well. The fear in Casper's voice and eyes spoke volumes. I could tell he was holding back, as if what had happened was too terrible to even say out loud.

"So that leaves us with your grandmother. You understand I have to contact her? We have to get things settled or there is no way social services will allow you to stay here."

"I understand."

"Can you write her address down for me?"

"Sure," said Casper.

I dug out a scrap of paper and a pencil and handed it to Casper. He scribbled his grandmother's address and gave it to Jack.

"I don't really know how all this works, but I'll find out, and I'll get a hold of your grandmother. I can't make promises, but we'll see what we can do. Now if you two are finished in here, there's lots of work to be done outside."

"Come on," I said, "I'll show you some of the chores we do here every day. You'll be taking care of a lot of them."

I took Casper out to the barn. His eyes roamed everywhere and especially over the chickens wandering in and out of the barn.

"My brother takes care of gathering the eggs every morning, so you don't have to worry about that. There's lots of other stuff to do, however."

I led Casper around as I checked the water troughs, making sure the cattle, horses, and goats had plenty to drink. Casper helped me dump feed into the feed troughs.

"The horses and cattle do a lot of grazing, but we still need to feed them some, even at this time of year. In the winter we feed them a lot more, but there's plenty for them to eat in the pastures now. The goats pretty much take care of themselves. They'll eat about anything."

For the next hour, I showed Casper around the farm and pointed out all the little tasks that needed done every morning. I could tell Casper was surprised that there was so much to do. It was obvious he'd never been on a farm before. He looked around like he was on some kind of school field trip or something.

There was a lot to show him. I took him around to the outbuildings and sheds. He seemed especially interested in the silos for storing corn, wheat, and soy beans. They were empty now, but would be as full as could be after the harvest.

We walked back toward the house and I showed Casper the garden. His eyes grew wide when he saw how big it was. I'd already tilled some of it with the old garden tiller and set a few tomato plants, but I was really just getting started.

Practically the entire garden was bare. I led Casper to the little shed near the garden and showed him the worktable where I had all kinds of packets and bags of seeds laid out.

"I tilled some of the garden yesterday after school. You can start planting the green beans, peas, cabbage, and carrots. It's just starting to get warm enough to plant those. We'll have to wait before we can plant some other stuff, but it won't be long now."

We grabbed up seeds and I showed Casper how to hoe a straight row and how far apart and deep the seeds had to be.

"If you forget, just read on the packages and they usually tell you what you need to know," I said.

I left Casper to himself. He smiled as he started to work. I could tell he genuinely liked working in the garden. I rather enjoyed it myself. I walked into the shed and wheeled out the old garden tiller. I started it up with a few tugs on the rope and began tilling up the earth where it hadn't been worked yet. The tiller was loud and drowned out the sound of the tractor that Brendan and Ethan were riding in the near distance. The sun was warm overhead and it felt good on my back. The farm was peaceful, even with the tiller running loud and giving out a small cloud of smoke. There was something about being on the farm that I loved. It just made me feel at peace. I looked over at Casper and had little doubt that he shared my feelings. I was glad to have him there. It made me feel good to show him the ropes, just as Ethan had shown me when I was the new boy on the farm.

Brendan

I stood behind Ethan on the tractor, gripping the seat as if I were hanging onto the edge of a cliff. I was just sure I was going to fall off and be cut to bits by the plow behind us. The old Ford tractor chugged on as we finished our first pass in the field to the north of the house. Ethan turned the steering wheel hard and brought the tractor around for the second pass. The muscles in his arms and shoulders flexed with the effort. I tried to pay attention to everything Ethan told me, but he was shirtless and his muscular body was distracting. He had a beautiful build.

On our left were hundreds of yards of untouched field, while to our right were a few feet of freshly plowed earth. I loved the smell of the damp soil. It was a scent I'd never experienced before. I thought about what the field would look like later in the season, when it would be filled with tall corn. It was empty now, a blank canvas for nature to paint.

"Think you're ready to give it a try?" Ethan asked.

"Yeah, just guide me through it, okay? I've never driven one of these things," I said.

Ethan stopped the tractor, turned it off, and he and I switched places. Ethan bent low over my bare back as he showed me the controls. I could feel his hot breath on my neck.

"First you turn the key, just like you are starting a car." he told me. I tried it.

"Nothing happened," I said. I wondered if I'd done something wrong.

"It's not supposed to yet. See that little, round piece of rubber near your foot? Step on it." I did so and the tractor started right up. "This lever here," he said, showing me one near the steering wheel, "controls the throttle. It's set to just keep the tractor running right now. Push it up about a quarter of the way." I did so and the engine surged to life. "Okay, put it back where it was. See where the gear shift is now? That's neutral. Always make sure it's in neutral when you start the engine. If you don't, the tractor will take off and you might get thrown off if you aren't paying attention, or you'll just kill the engine. The gears are real simple, kind of like a truck. Have you ever driven with a clutch?"

"Yeah."

"Then you should be okay. Just remember, don't put it in reverse while anything is attached to the tractor, not until you've learned how to back up with the plow or discs on. Okay, now put it in gear, and then push the throttle forward just a little."

The tractor moved forward down the field. I didn't keep it quite in line, but I did pretty well as we crept along.

"Man, this thing is hard to steer!"

"That's because it has manual steering, not power steering like on a car. It's a little difficult until you get the hang of it. Turning is the worst of course, that takes some muscle. When you are ready, give it a little more power. Don't push it more than three-quarters of the way up though, we can't go too fast if we're going to plow the field right."

I gave the old tractor some more power and smiled.

"I like this," I said.

"Yeah, it is kind of cool. Uncle Jack always did most of the plowing and disking, but I'll be doing a lot of it from now on. We'll have a lot more plowing to do, so it'll take us both. I'm sure you'll be a big help too."

I started to veer off course a bit as my attention wandered. Having Ethan so close to me made it hard to concentrate.

"Make sure you keep the wheels straight or part of the field won't get plowed."

"Sorry."

"Don't worry about it. You're just learning. You'll get it down in no time at all."

I hoped that he was right. We slowly made our way down the field. It was late April and the sun was already beginning to feel nice and warm. I felt a small trickle of sweat flow down my bare chest. It was a sign of things to come. In a few weeks time summer would come and I knew I'd be sweating up a storm as I worked under the sun. I wouldn't mind that. I loved the feel of sweat running off my body. It made me feel alive.

"You're really getting the hang of this," said Ethan. "I'm sure glad. I don't mind telling you that we'll need your help desperately if we are going to get all the fields plowed and disked and the crops planted on time. Some of the new acreage hasn't even been cleared of brush yet. I'm sure glad you and Casper showed up. I don't think Jack, Nathan, and I could handle this by ourselves. Without you we'd have a lot of new farmland we couldn't use."

Ethan and I talked as I plowed the field. I told him that I was seventeen and Casper fifteen. I also told him that I was into football and had been the quarterback and team captain back home. I learned that Ethan was a wrestler. That made sense. He sure had the build of a wrestler. I was a little jealous of his build, in a friendly way. I was thrilled to learn that he had a weight machine. He even said I could work out with him, Casper too if he wanted. I was looking forward to that. I was definitely out of shape.

I could tell that Ethan wanted to ask me some more personal stuff, but he was nice enough not to pry. I was relieved. There were certain questions that I didn't really feel like answering, at least not yet. I was especially worried about what Ethan and Nathan would think when they found out I was gay, and Casper too. They seem like pretty cool guys, but I knew finding out we were gay could change that pretty fast. We couldn't keep something like that a secret forever, but I wanted to keep it quiet as long as I could. If Ethan and Nathan had a chance to get to know Casper and me before they found out about us, then maybe they wouldn't take it so bad.

"Slow up when you get to the end. The turn will be hard."

I felt my muscles bulge as I struggled to turn the steering wheel and bring the tractor around. It was a lot harder than I was expecting. Driving that tractor would be sort of a workout itself.

"Yeah, that's it, you got it. Now check behind you and line us up so that we aren't missing any areas. There you go. Just steer straight ahead now. Pretty soon you'll get the hang of the spacing and you won't even have to check."

I smiled. I was worried about a lot of things, but I really liked working on the farm. I really liked Ethan, and Nathan, and Dave and Jack too. I just hoped that everything would work out. I wanted to stay.

Nathan

I closed the door to our room before slipping into bed beside Ethan. We often closed the door for privacy, but with Brendan and Casper in the house I was uneasy. I really liked Casper, and Brendan too, but I knew that a lot of boys would freak out if they discovered that Ethan and I were boyfriends.

Maybe I was being paranoid for nothing. When Ethan came out to his wrestling team, that day after defeating Zac for the championship, I really thought there was going to be big trouble. I figured Ethan's team-mates would turn on him like a pack of wolves. I know Ethan was afraid of that too. It made me admire him all the more when he had the balls to tell his entire team face to face. They'd been really cool about it too. Every single one of Ethan's team-mates had stood by him, except for Zac, but that was no surprise.

"I wonder why they left home." I said. Ethan knew I was talking about Brendan and Casper.

"Me too. I guess we'll find out in time. I came close to asking Brendan today, but I didn't want to seem too nosy. He kind of stiffens up when I ask him anything the least bit personal."

"Yeah, I did ask Casper, but he just said they both had trouble at home. He didn't volunteer any details and I didn't press him. It must have been something pretty bad for them to leave home though."

"Yeah."

"He seems really afraid of his brother. Casper gets this fearful look in his eyes whenever he's mentioned. He must have done something horrible to him."

"Well, they're safe from that here. Jack won't let anything happen to them, neither will you or I for that matter."

"Jack is really a nice guy, isn't he? I mean, I know we needed help around here bad, but I think he took Brendan and Casper on to help them, more than to get help with the farm work."

"I was thinking that too. Jack's kind of rough on the outside, but he's a big old softy on the inside. I guess you know that already, though."

"Yep. I still wouldn't want to cross him."

"Me neither."

"Just think, Ethan, in a little over a month, school will be over. I can't wait."

"Same here. With wrestling season over, it's not as fun."

"I'm tired of all of them looking at me too. I mean, everyone has been pretty cool about everything, but I still feel like I'm some kind of sideshow freak sometimes."

"Yeah, I feel that way too. I wonder what they're thinking about us sometimes. At least no one's been giving us any trouble."

"Devon and Zac would if they could."

"No kidding. I think we've got them cowed for the time being, however. I really thought Brandon was going to kill Devon that night."

I knew that Ethan was remembering the night that Zac, Devon, and three of their buddies jumped us. I'd never been so scared in all my life. I had good reason to be scared too. They would have killed us if Jon and Brandon hadn't come to our rescue. Sometimes I still had bad dreams about it. Ethan did too.

"Well, at least they're off our backs for now."

"You know Brendan will probably be starting school in a couple of weeks."

"Yeah."

"You know he's going to find out about us pretty fast. We're still big news, the only openly gay boys in the whole school."

"True."

"You think maybe we should tell him and Casper before they find out?"

"Probably, but let's not tell them quite yet okay? They've only been here for a day. We don't have to tell them right off, do we?"

"Nah, it can wait, but it can't wait long."

I turned to Ethan and looked into his eyes. I loved him so much it almost hurt. I ran my finger down his chest, and then kissed him. We lie there and kissed, until we fell asleep in each others arms.

Brendan

The phone rang. Nathan answered it, and then handed it to me. I smiled. There were only two people who could possibly be calling me, and I'd be glad to hear from either of them. It was Brad, my best friend.

"How are you farm boy?"

"I've only been here a week, Brad, I don't think that qualifies me as a farm boy yet. I'm loving it though. You should see this place. I plowed this big ass field all by myself yesterday. It must have been like fifty acres or something."

"You sure sound like a farm boy to me."

"How are you doing? How are the guys?"

"I'm great and the guys are too. Everyone's still wondering what happened to you. Some of the guys ask me about you now and then, but I just tell them I don't know any more than they do."

"Cool. You won't have to keep lying for long. My birthday is in a couple weeks and then my parents can go screw themselves."

"You coming back here after your birthday?"

"No, not right away anyway. My parents and the *Cloverdale Center* can't touch me after I turn eighteen, but I still won't have any money, or any place to live."

"I'm sure my parents would let you stay here, and can't you get your hands on your money once you turn eighteen?"

"Thanks for offering, but me moving in would be a bit too much to ask of your parents. As for my money, I'm sure my father has it tied up in enough legal knots that I won't be able to get at it for months. Besides, I won't leave Casper and I don't think it would be good for him to go back. There are too many bad memories there, especially after what happened to his dad. He doesn't talk about it, but it bothers him. Sometimes he has nightmares. I'll come and visit you sometime, but I don't plan on moving back, at least not for a long, long time. Casper and I really like it here."

"It's about Casper that I called," said Brad. "Jason's been cleared by the District Attorney's Office. They've decided that him killing his dad was self defense."

"You can't be serious!?"

"I'm afraid I am. Casper's dad didn't have too good of a reputation. He'd been picked up for disorderly conduct a few times when he was drunk. The school made some reports to social services about him too. You know teachers have to report when they think someone is being abused. I guess they saw Casper's bruises a few times and turned his dad in. Anyway, Jason put on a big act while he was in the hospital, and after. He claimed his dad abused and molested him. He claimed that his dad was going to kill him and Casper the night he killed him. He said he killed him in self defense."

"That's total bullshit, Brad! You know it!"

"Yeah, I know it, but the D.A.'s office bought it."

"Didn't you and Stacey tell them what really happened?"

"Yeah, we did, but we were really telling what you said happened. We weren't in the room at the time you know. If you were down here to testify it might have been different, but coming from me and Stacey it was just hearsay."

I guess I could understand that. It still sucked big time though.

"Jason claimed he had Casper down on the bed because he was trying to get him to leave the house before their dad came. He said you got the wrong idea when you came in. Oh, you should have heard him. He even said he didn't blame you for attacking him. He said he was glad that you were looking out for his little brother like that, but that you just had the wrong idea about things. To hear him talk you'd have thought he was Casper's guardian angel or something."

"And how did he explain threatening to kill me?"

"He said he knew his dad was coming soon, and that he was desperate to get Casper out of there. He said he threatened you because it was the only way to get away in time, that he would have never really shot you."

"I can't fucking believe it."

"Jason told them his dad came in just then with a shotgun. He said his dad shot first. He fired back because he knew his dad was going to kill him and Casper, and probably you too."

"They did fire at about the same time," I said. "I couldn't say for sure myself which one fired first."

"Jason made it a real convincing story. Hell, I'd have believed him if I didn't know better. He kept fucking crying over what had happened, about how sorry he was to have to kill his own father. He kept saying he'd never get over it, that it would haunt him forever. He kept crying about Casper too, about how he missed him and how worried he was about him."

"Shit."

"Yeah, Jason's one good actor. Stacey and I told what we'd seen, but we didn't really see all that much. It was pretty much over when we ran in. Jason was able to twist it all around until he was the victim. I think what really clinched it was that there was lots of evidence that Casper's dad was abusive, but nothing on Jason. The school records showed he'd been in lots of fights, but there was nothing about him abusing Casper. It's too bad Casper didn't march into the principals office every time Jason did something to him and report it, then there'd have been a record of it."

"Yeah, but Jason would have hurt him that much more if he did."

"Anyway, Jason's been cleared of everything. He's living on his own and he's being real smart about it. He never misses school and you'd think he was all perfect when anyone is around that counts. He hasn't changed though. He gives me a look now and then that tells me he's as up to no good as ever. I'm sure he's still pissed at Casper too."

"Thanks, Brad. I don't like it, but I'm glad you told me about it. I'm glad we're a couple of hundred miles or so away too. Casper's safe here."

We went on talking and it was good to hear from my best friend. I missed him terribly, but until I turned eighteen I just couldn't risk seeing him. At least I could hear his voice, that alone was something.

I hung up the phone and looked at Nathan. He was only a few feet away where he was getting lunch ready. I knew he'd heard everything, but politely acted as if he hadn't.

"I guess you're wondering what that was all about?"

"Well, I didn't mean to listen, but it was kind of interesting."

"That's all right. I think it's time me and Casper told everyone what happened the night we left."

A few minutes later we all sat down to lunch. I told Casper about the phone call from Brad and he was cool with telling everyone what had happened. Together we explained how Jason attacked him (leaving out the sexual details, but I have little doubt they guessed). I told them about my fight with Jason and how he was all ready to kill me when Casper's dad shot him, and got shot himself. I also told them about Jason being cleared of his crime.

"Sounds like someone you need to stay clear of," said Uncle Jack to Casper. Both Casper and I had taken to calling the old man "Uncle Jack." It just seemed right.

"Oh I plan to," said Casper. "I'm glad to be away from him."

Uncle Jack, Ethan, Nathan, and Dave now knew just about everything about our reasons to flee, except the big one, that we were gay. I wasn't at all looking forward to telling them that.

Nathan

"She's coming here?" asked Casper.

"Yes, the day after tomorrow," said Jack.

I knew something was up when I saw Jack walking toward the garden where Casper and I were working. It was after supper and Jack was usually busy at work in the fields at that time of day. He'd stayed in the house after supper, however, and I guess he'd been busy talking to Casper's grandmother on the phone.

"She's a little put out with you boy. Well, more than a little, let's say she's furious. She said she was relieved beyond belief when she got my letter that you were okay. She's been worried sick about you. The authorities called her months ago when your dad was killed and told her you were nowhere to be found. She's been expecting you to show up, or to at least write."

Casper swallowed hard.

"I didn't think she cared that much about me."

"Boy, she's been turning the country upside down looking for you. As soon as she got my letter she called straight away and, like I said, she'll be here the day after tomorrow."

"But you sent that letter out two weeks ago, or more," said Casper.

"True, but your grandmother was in Kentucky trying to figure out where you could have gone."

Jack left and I could tell Casper was doing a lot of thinking. He looked slightly afraid, but there was a little smile on his lips that made me feel warm inside. I understood it. If I'd just found out that my grandmother loved me when I thought that she didn't, I'd have been smiling too. That wouldn't happen for me, all my grandparents were dead.

"You know my grandmother used to come every Christmas and bring up presents," said Casper. "She made these great cookies too. They were so good. They had chocolate chips, and pecans, and something chewy in them too."

"That does sound good."

"Yeah, she was the best, until my mom died. After that she just came once at Christmas and her and dad argued a lot. That was the last time I saw her. I thought she didn't care about me anymore, like Dad."

Tears welled up in Casper's eyes and I hugged him. I knew all about having parents that didn't care. Casper wiped the tears from his eyes and smiled.

"I guess I was wrong about that, though. She did send me Christmas cards every year. They probably had money in them too, but I bet Jason took it. He always got to the mail first and handed me Grandma's cards already opened."

"What a rat."

"Worse than a rat."

"Yeah."

Brendan's words as he told about the night Casper's dad had been killed were still fresh in my mind. I was pretty sure that Jason had done some really nasty things to Casper, sexual things, like my mom had done to me. Brendan hadn't said, but then he wouldn't have. I understood all too well. It made me feel for Casper all the more. I was sure glad his grandmother was coming. I wanted Casper to be happy.

We continued with our planting and Casper seemed happy enough. I would've known he liked the farm even if he hadn't told me so several times. The two of us got on well and Ethan liked him too. I really liked the way Casper spent time with Dave. It reminded me of how Ethan treated him, like he was his little brother.

What I noticed most of all was how Casper acted around Brendan. There was something between those two and I was pretty sure I knew what it was. My fears of them finding out Ethan and I were boyfriends were growing less and less. I was pretty sure that Brendan and Casper were just like us. There was something in the way they looked at each other, something in the way their hands lingered when they touched. It was in the eyes mostly, however. I could see the love in their eyes. Maybe they were just really good friends, but I had a strong feeling they were much more.

Brendan

I grabbed the sapling and pulled it out of the earth with brute force. I was sweating up a storm in the afternoon sun. My bare torso was positively slick with sweat. Casper's chest and back gleamed in the sun. If I wasn't mistaken, he was already beginning to put on a little muscle.

I tossed the sapling onto the stack of brush and went in search of the next. It didn't take me long to find another to rip out of the earth. It was a weekday. Ethan, Nathan, and Dave were in school, and Casper and I were working on clearing some of the new land to make it suitable for farming. It was one of those tasks that never ended. Whenever any of us weren't working elsewhere on the farm, we spent our time clearing land. It was hard work, but I liked it. I could tell Casper did too.

I took hold of a small tree and pulled. It wouldn't budge so I went for the shovel and ax. I dug around the base until I could get at the roots, then I hacked them away until I could pull the entire tree out of the ground. There were a lot of small trees that required considerable effort to get out, but all the bushes and saplings were really easy. Thanks to the sandy soil of northern Indiana, most of the smaller growth could just be ripped out of the ground with a good tug. The soil was a lot different from the heavy clay where I'd grown up. In Kentucky, getting even the smallest sapling out of the ground required a lot of digging and chopping.

The task ahead of us was still considerable. There were a lot of big trees that had to be cut down too. We only worked with those when Uncle Jack was around. It was dangerous felling a tree and he liked to be there to at least supervise. Ethan knew how to notch the trunk so that the tree would fall in the right direction, and I was learning. It was still dangerous though. I'd learned that just the day before. Ethan had notched a big oak and cut through the trunk. We were all watching the huge tree begin to topple when the bottom of the trunk flew back several feet with the force of a freight train and crushed another tree to the ground. Ethan said trees did that sometimes when they were coming down. It was called "kicking back" and was the reason no one ever stood behind a tree when it was falling. All of us always stood well beyond the reach of the tree when it was going down, except the one doing the sawing, of course. That was always Uncle Jack, or Ethan, and both of them were experts at getting out of the way. I was eager to try my hand at it. Jack said it wasn't dangerous if you used common sense.

The stack of brush grew higher and higher. It was already well above my head. Casper and I kept adding to it and it grew slowly, like a mountain rising out of the depths of the earth. We took a break from clearing and went to check on the progress of one of the many stumps that we were burning out. The stumps of the really big trees were just too big to dig out, so they had to be burned away. We took some of the larger brush, and some wood cut from one of the trees, and stacked it against the stump. That kept the fire eating away at the wood. Jack said it would take days, but that finally the stump would burn low enough that the plow wouldn't hit it. There were several stumps smoldering away around us and it made the air smoky. I loved the smell of a wood fire and didn't even mind when it burned my eyes now and then.

Casper and I went around and added fuel where it was needed to keep the stumps burning then went back to work clearing away brush and saplings. There was something satisfying about manual labor. I felt good about what we were doing. We were accomplishing something real.

I was feeling physically fit. Farm work was like a good workout. Several days of it had managed to tone my muscles. I was pretty sure it was adding on muscle too. I could see it in Casper's slim form and feel it in my own. Ethan and I hadn't had the chance to start working out with his weights yet, but we hardly needed to lift weights with the work we were doing. Chopping out roots was as good as barbell curls any day.

I looked up and saw Uncle Jack approaching in the distance. He wasn't alone. There was an old lady with him. I knew it had to be Casper's grandmother.

"Hey, Casper," I said.

He looked up and saw her coming. She was still at some distance. We both retrieved our shirts from where they were hanging on a limb and slipped them on. I smoothed out my hair as best I could and hoped that I wasn't all dirty.

Casper looked nervous. His grandmother's arrival was no surprise, we'd been expecting her, but it was still a bit of a shock to look up and see her walking toward us.

The pair got closer and closer. I wanted to take Casper's hand and reassure him that everything would be okay. I couldn't do that, however. The last thing he needed was to explain to his grandmother that he had a boyfriend. If she knew that, she might take him away with her. That was my secret fear. I hadn't told Casper about it, because I didn't want him to worry, but I was afraid that she'd take him away from me. I knew Casper wouldn't let that happen if he could help it, but I also knew that it might not be his choice. Casper was fifteen, and that meant he wasn't really free. Neither was I. I'd learned that lesson the hard way. I was on the brink of freedom, but Casper was still three years away.

In mere moments, Uncle Jack and Casper's grandmother were standing before us. She was a kindly looking woman, probably in her early sixties. There was something to her that told me I didn't want to cross her. I had no doubt she could be as tough as nails if she needed to be.

She and Casper just stood there and looked at each other for several moments. Casper was trembling, but whether it was from fear, or something else, I could not tell. Without warning he crossed the small space between them, hugged her tight, and started crying. The old lady hugged him and petted his hair.

"I've been so worried about you, Clint. I never thought I'd see you again." It was the first time I ever heard anyone call Casper by his real name.

Casper stopped crying, leaned back, and looked up into his grandmother's eyes.

"I'm sorry I didn't write you or anything, but I thought...well, I thought you didn't care about me."

"Not care about you? Where'd you get an outlandish idea like that?"

"Well, you never came to see me. You never called. You only wrote me at Christmas..." His voice trailed off.

"We have a lot to talk about, honey." The old lady's eyes were filled with tears.

"This is Brendan," said Casper. "He's my best friend in the whole world. He's been watching out for me this whole time, so you had nothing to worry about."

"We've been watching out for each other," I said, as I took the old lady's hand. That wasn't enough for her; she took me in her arms and hugged me. It almost made me cry as well.

"Thank you, young man." Her words were filled with more meaning than they seemed. I really liked Casper's grandmother. I nearly thought of her as my own.

"I think you two have done enough for today. Let's go inside and have a talk," said Uncle Jack.

Casper and I each grabbed a quick shower. Actually we took a quick shower together, but no one knew that. When we came downstairs just minutes later, Uncle Jack and Casper's grandmother were sitting at the kitchen table. They were having tea, which was odd for Jack, he was a coffee man. No doubt he was going out of his way to be polite. I also noticed that he was dressed better than usual. He must have fixed himself up to go and pick up Casper's grand-mother.I poured Casper and myself some tea and got out a few cookies as well.

"Would you like some more tea...um..." I didn't know what to call Casper's grandmother.

"You can call me Ardelene," she said. "And yes, I'd love more tea." She smiled as she spoke. I liked her a lot.

Uncle Jack explained our predicament in detail, concerning me and Casper staying on the farm and the whole custody question. Ardelene wanted to know exactly what happened the night her son was killed, so Casper and I told her the whole story. Well, not quite the whole story. We explained how Jason attacked Casper, but not that the attack was sexual in nature. We left out that little bit. I knew Casper wouldn't want his grandmother hearing about that. I did most of the talking because it was hard for Casper. It was hard for Ardelene too. Tears filled her eyes as I told her how her son had died. Uncle Jack handed her his handkerchief.

We also told her about our travels and our long stay in Purity. Some of what we were saying was news to Jack, but most of it he'd already heard. I left out the parts about Ellen, of course. Not even Casper knew about her. I wasn't proud that I'd sold my body for money, and I never wanted Casper to know I'd done it to buy his medicine. I pushed it from my mind. It was something I did-n't want to remember, but I wasn't sorry I'd done it. If I hadn't, Casper would have died for sure. Anything was worth saving his life.

Ethan, Nathan, and Dave came in from school as we talked. Uncle Jack introduced Ardelene and she remarked on what handsome boys they were. Nathan especially turned a little red at her compliment. Dave sat right down by her and took up with her immediately. Casper and I continued the tale of our journey and pretty soon we'd talked our way up to the present.

Casper needed some time alone with his grandmother, so all of us excused ourselves and went off to our various chores. I liked Ardelene, but I was nervous about her being there. I tried to reassure myself that everything would be okay.

Nathan

Ethan helped me wash up after supper. It was a great meal, and I'm not just saying that because I did most of the cooking. Having Casper's grandmother there made things different somehow, and it was a good change. The biggest change I noticed was in Uncle Jack. He was far less gruff and even smiled now and then.

"Did you notice Jack at supper?" I asked.

"He was positively charming wasn't he?" said Ethan.

"I think he likes Casper's grandma."

"I don't know. Maybe. He was awfully nice to her. Maybe he was just trying to put her at ease. Maybe he's just being nice because he wants Casper to stay here."

"I think it's more than that. There was something in his eyes."

"You might be right. I noticed he didn't take off to do any farm work after supper. He took Casper's grandmother out to show her around the farm instead. Not working after supper isn't normal for Jack, but then we never had visitors before either."

"I think something's up with him, and I don't think it has anything to do with him wanting Casper to stay and help with the farm work."

We dried our hands and went outside. It was getting quite dark. As we came around the house, there was Uncle Jack and Ardelene sitting on the swing on the front porch, talking quietly. They looked almost like young lovers and I was surer than ever that Jack really liked Ardelene. She didn't seem to mind his company either.

We walked on to check on how things were going in the field that we'd all been working so hard to clear. Brendan and Casper had gone out right after supper to build up the fires around the stumps. As we neared, I couldn't see them anywhere. It wasn't until we were almost on top of them that I noticed them. I don't know who was shocked more, Ethan and I, or Brendan and Casper.

The boys were lying on the ground, wrapped in each others arms. Their lips were pressed together. They were making out like nobody's business. They became aware of our presence almost the instant we walked up. They broke apart and jumped to their feet so fast that it was all a blur.

"Fuck!" said Brendan.

Both boys were clearly frightened. I don't know exactly how they were expecting Ethan and me to react, but I could tell they didn't think we'd take it well. Brendan positioned himself a little forward of Casper, protecting him. I guess he planned to fight us off and keep us from hurting Casper if we attacked them.

"Guys listen…" said Brendan.

"It's okay," said Ethan, cutting Brendan off. "It's all right, really."

Ethan was sparing Brendan and Casper the pain of standing before us in fear. I know those boys had to be thinking we'd hate them for being gay. I was proud that Ethan was moving so fast to put them at ease.

"It's okay," repeated Ethan. "It's cool with us. Nathan thought you guys might be like us. We understand."

Brendan and Casper visibly relaxed, although they seemed a little taken back. I think Ethan's words shocked them, especially the "you guys might be like us" part. Brendan moved out of his protective stance and stood by Casper's side.

"So are you boyfriends?" I asked.

"Yeah," said Casper.

"Man, how likely is this, four gay boys on the same farm?" laughed Ethan. What little remaining tension there was dissipated in an instant.

"So are you guys…?" said Brendan, looking at me and Ethan.

"Yeah, we're boyfriends," said Ethan. He put his arm around my waist and pulled me close.

"Does Uncle Jack know?" asked Brendan.

"Yeah, we told him months ago."

"And he's cool with it?"

"Yeah, about as cool as he could be," said Ethan. "I don't think he's entirely comfortable with it, but he was accepting, and understanding, right from the start. I can tell you that was the biggest surprise of my life. I expected him to send us packing."

"Yeah," said Brendan.

"I think he has more problems with it than he lets on. Sometimes I catch a look from him when Nathan and I are together that's kind of, I don't know, a little disapproving. He's cool though."

"I told him I was gay," said Brendan, "the evening we came here. I had to tell him to explain why I had to leave home. I thought he'd boot me and Casper out for it too, but he didn't. I didn't say anything about Casper and me being boyfriends though. I didn't know how well he'd take that. We were going to tell you all that later on, when the time was right."

"Sounds like our plan for telling you guys about us," I said, smiling at Ethan.

"So your parents kicked you out when they found out about you?" I asked.

"Worse than that," said Brendan, "much, much worse."

Brendan told us his story. What his parents had done to him was far worse than just kicking him out. I couldn't believe they had him taken away by the police and put in a hospital. I couldn't believe that hospitals like that even existed. The tale Brendan told was like some kind of horror story, about a place where mad doctors used drugs and pain to try to turn him straight. It sounded like something out of fiction, but it was true. I could read the pain and fear on Brendan's face as he relived the past.

"I can't even imagine going through something like that," said Ethan. "I think I'd wake up screaming."

"Sometimes I do," said Brendan softly. "Sometimes I have nightmares that I'm back there again." Casper hugged him close, comforting him.

We talked more, in low voices, telling things we'd never told before. For the first time, all the little pieces of the puzzle began to fit and we started to understand one another as we never could before.

"There's something I didn't tell you guys about me," said Casper. "I don't want to go into details, but the night my dad was killed, my brother was raping me. It wasn't the first time he'd done either."

I could tell it took an immense amount of courage for Casper to speak those words. He looked at us somewhat fearfully, as if we'd think badly of him for what had happened to him. I could tell he was embarrassed about it too.

It was a night of trust, and telling secrets. I told Casper and Brendan why Dave and I had to leave home. I told them about what my mom did to me. It wasn't as bad as Casper's brother raping him, but it was close. I told them how my mom made me have sex with her, and how I was afraid she'd do the same thing with my little brother. It hurt to tell them. Like Casper, I felt embarrassed and ashamed, although it wasn't my fault. Tears welled up in my eyes and Ethan hugged me close to him.

"I'm so sorry," said Casper. He understood, better than anyone else there, what I'd gone through. I'd never told anyone, except Ethan, about what had happened with my mom. It was painful to speak of it, and yet it felt good to have someone understand. Hearing Casper's story made me feel better about my own bad experiences. It let me look at myself through his eyes in a way. I'm sure hearing my own tale helped him too. That's why I told it. I wanted to help him. I discovered that in helping him, I helped myself.

Not all secrets were revealed that night, but we shared our deepest pain. It made things easier and made us all feel closer. I liked Brendan and Casper even more than I had before. They were more than friends now. They were brothers.

Brendan

"She what!?" My eyes filled with tears and I started shaking.

"She wants me to come home with her," repeated Casper quietly.

I'd heard him the first time, but he had spoken the words that were my secret fear. I tried to rein in my emotions, but I couldn't handle it. I just sat down on the edge of the bed and cried.

"Hey, Brendan," said Casper, taking my chin in his hand and making me look at him. "I told her I didn't want to go. I told her I wanted to stay here, with you."

"And?" I asked hopefully.

"She still wants me to come home with her, but she said she's not going to force me into anything. It's my choice."

"What did you decide?" I was pretty sure of the answer to my question, but I needed to hear it out loud. I needed to be reassured that Casper wasn't going to leave me.

"It would be nice to go and live with her in Florida. I like her a lot, Brendan. I love her and she's my grandmother. It would be nice to have a home like that." Tears started welling up in my eyes again. "Living with her would be nice, but I'm staying with you. I'd never leave you, Brendan, you know that. I love you, more than anything, more than anyone. I'd never leave you."

I was so happy I cried some more, feeling a little silly for doing so. I hoped that Casper didn't think I didn't have faith in him, but I couldn't help but react the way I did. The thought of losing him was just too much for me.

"So what happens next?" I asked.

"After Ethan, Nathan, and Dave take off for school, Grandmother and Uncle Jack are going into town to see this lawyer Jack knows. My grandmother is going to try and get custody of me."

It was time for breakfast, so I finished dressing, washed the tears off my face, and headed downstairs with Casper. The kitchen was noisy with everyone filling their plates and talking. Anyone walking in would have thought we were just another farm family. Well, just about. Nathan and Casper, the blonds of the group, looked a bit out of place. That was just as well I guess, since Nathan was Ethan's boyfriend and Casper was mine.

The bacon and pancakes were sure good. Breakfast was always big in the Selby house. Nathan and Casper took turns being the main cooks, but the rest of us helped out. There was no real schedule to it, but everyone did their part. Dave always supplied the eggs. He was in charge of the chickens. He fed them, he watered them, and he gathered the eggs. He loved them all and especially the little hen he'd named Henrietta. It was a good thing the chickens were kept for eggs and not for frying. I don't think Dave could have handled that. We had chicken now and then, but it came from the supermarket. Uncle Jack said that killing and plucking all the feathers off a chicken just wasn't worth it. He was probably right, but I suspected he didn't want to upset Dave either. Dave was like his grandson.

Now that I knew about Ethan and Nathan, I saw them differently. Before I'd thought that Ethan treated Dave like a little brother, but now I saw that he really treated him more like a son. It was kind of like Dave was Ethan and Nathan's kid, and Jack's grandson. I liked thinking of them like that.

Casper's grandmother fit in well. She insisted on helping out around the farm. I could tell she liked it. She made the most delicious bread I'd ever tasted. She especially liked working in the garden. I'd seen her helping Casper and Nathan with it a few times. Of course, she liked being near Casper. It was clear she cared about him very much. I could see why she'd want him to come and live with her. I felt a little sorry for her that he didn't want to do that. I guess it wasn't quite true that he didn't want to live with her; he just wanted to live with me more.

"I guess we'll be having a party tonight," said Dave.

"What for?" I asked. I was thinking it might have something to do with Ardelene attempting to get custody of Casper.

"Not too bright, is he?" said Ethan to Nathan.

"Hey!" I yelled.

"Duh! It's your birthday, Brendan," said Nathan. "It looks like you'd be able to remember that. And people think I'm dumb because I'm blond." He laughed.

"Hey, the blond guys are the smart ones," said Casper. "They just have all those blond jokes because they're jealous."

"Nah, you know why they have blond jokes, don't you?" said Nathan. "So brunettes have something to do on Friday nights." I'd heard that one before, but it was still funny.

I'd completely forgotten it was my birthday. The shock of Casper telling me his grandmother wanted him to come and live with her drove it right out of my head. Dave started singing "Happy Birthday" and Ethan and Nathan joined him. The others would have too, but they were too busy laughing. The boys were singing off key on purpose and it was exceptionally horrible.

"If you guys are gonna sing like that then I'm not having any more birthdays."

"You'll get to hear us again tonight," said Ethan. "It comes with the cake and ice cream."

"I can hardly wait," I said, rolling my eyes.

It felt good to be surrounded by friends who cared about me. I felt like they were family. It was funny, I felt more at home there than I ever had in my real home. I'd never realized it before, but even when things were good at home, there was a distance between me and my parents. Something had always been missing. I didn't know what that something was, but it was present on the Selby farm.

Nathan

Supper was beyond good. It was Brendan's birthday, so Casper and I cooked all of his favorites. Luckily, they were also mine, for the most part. We had barbecued ribs, mashed potatoes, sweet potatoes with marshmallow on top, and some sage stuffing. Casper's grandma made some wonderful bread and baked Brendan a big chocolate cake with the best icing I'd ever tasted. We hadn't had any of the cake yet, but I'd managed to sneak a taste. That was one of the advantages of being a cook.

After supper, we didn't return to our work like we usually did. Instead Jack got out the ice cream freezer and put in all the ingredients for vanilla ice cream. We all went out to the porch and us boys took turns turning the handle on the freezer. It took a lot of turning to make homemade ice cream, but it was way better than any that came from the store.

"So what happened in town?" asked Brendan.

We were all eager to hear what progress Jack and Ardelene had made toward getting custody of Casper.

"Well," said Jack, "it's going to take weeks to get through all the paperwork, and there will be a hearing before the judge, but it doesn't look like there will be any problems, since Casper has no other family, except for his brother. As I suspected, there is another difficulty, however."

"What?" said Casper, fearfully. Brendan looked scared.

"Don't get worried, it's not a big one. Until the hearing, Casper, you have to either stay with your grandmother, or be placed in a foster home."

"You said it would take weeks," said Casper. He turned and looked at his grandma. "This means I have to go back to Florida with you, doesn't it?" He glanced sideways towards Brendan, who looked like he was going to be ill.

"No, Jack has been kind enough to offer me a place to stay while we're waiting for the hearing."

"Really!? You're staying here? That's great Grandma! It's not that I don't want to be with you, it's just that I don't want to leave here, you know?" He looked again at Brendan and Ardelene didn't miss his glance.

"I know."

Casper ran over to Ardelene and hugged her. "I love you, Grandma."

"I love you too."

I looked over at Jack. He looked a bit sheepish.

"How's that ice cream coming, boy?" he asked Ethan, who was taking his turn at the freezer. Ethan lifted the lid and checked on the contents.

"Just about ready."

"Then it's time for presents!" said Dave, and ran inside. He came back moments later with a stack of presents for Brendan.

"This one's from me!" he said, "and Uncle Jack."

"You didn't have to get me anything," said Brendan surprised. Dave ignored him and pushed a package that he'd obviously wrapped himself into Brendan's hands.

Brendan opened the package and drew out a new pair of jeans. He smiled.

"Thanks, I can sure use these."

"This is from Ethan and me," I said, as I handed him another package. He unwrapped it and pulled out a new shirt.

"This is great. I don't have hardly any clothes." That's something we'd noticed. It made it easy to pick out presents.

"This is from Grandma and me," said Casper. He handed Brendan a package that was too small to have any clothes in it. I waited to see what was in it. Brendan opened it and almost looked like he was going to cry when he saw what was inside.

"*The Lord of the Rings*," he said. "These are my favorite books. Thanks so much Casper, and Ardelene. Thanks everybody!" Casper told me later that Brendan had to leave almost everything he owned behind when he left. He'd told him how he especially felt bad about leaving his *Lord of the Rings* set behind. He loved to read those books over and over.

Ardelene and Casper went inside and soon returned with the chocolate cake. On top were eighteen candles.

"Make a wish," said Dave. Brendan closed his eyes for a moment, and then looked at Casper before blowing out the candles. He blew them all out at once.

Ethan, Dave, Casper, and I broke into a bad rendition of "Happy Birthday." We did our best to make it sound worse than the one we'd sung in the morning.

"I'll tell you what I want for my birthday next year," said Brendan. "I want you guys NOT to sing happy birthday." That made everyone laugh.

Ardelene cut the cake and handed out pieces while Ethan scooped out ice cream. It was a beautiful spring evening and we sat on the porch, and ate, and laughed, far into the night. Brendan said it was the best birthday he'd ever had.

Brendan

Casper sneaked into my room after everyone else had gone to bed. It felt good to have him lying next to me. Most people believe that all boys ever think about is sex. We do think about sex a lot, but there is a lot more to us than that. Sex didn't enter my mind as I lay there with Casper. I just enjoyed being with him, I enjoyed the closeness, and the intimacy. I enjoyed sex as well, boy did I enjoy it, but it sure wasn't the most important part of the relationship between Casper and me. I think what most people really crave is closeness and not sex at all. They just want to be loved, and feel secure. Sex is just a way of expressing that. When Casper and I made love, I always had this sense of oneness with him. It was like we became one being when we made love. That feeling didn't disappear when the love-making was over either, it continued on as we lay together. Often, I didn't even need the sex to have the feeling of oneness. My body usually had other ideas, but my heart and soul were content to just be with the one I loved.

"You're eighteen now, Brendan. Your parents can't touch you. They can't ever make you go back to that awful place. No one can." He hugged me close.

"It's definitely a load off my mind. Our days of running are really over now. I'm legally an adult and your grandmother will get custody of you soon. Everything just might be okay."

"I hope so. Things are sure a lot better than they were."

I was quiet for several moments.

"What are you thinking?" asked Casper.

"I was just thinking that I'll have to go to school now. It almost doesn't seem worth it with only a month left to go. I can't believe we missed most of the school year. I wonder if we'll have to redo the whole thing."

"That wouldn't be so bad, would it?" asked Casper.

"I guess not, as long as the school here is cool. I wouldn't mind trying out for the football team next fall."

"And maybe they could use a water boy." Casper giggled.

"You think your grandmother will really let you stay here after this whole thing is settled? I know she'd really like you to live with her."

"Don't worry, Brendan. Grandma and I talked about it a lot, and she's talked to Uncle Jack about it. She thinks this place is good for me, and she knows I'll be safe here. She said I could stay here as long as I wanted. Grandma did say that I had to come and live with her if I stopped working and living here. That would be okay too though, 'cause you're eighteen now and you could just come too. I'm sure I could get Grandma to let you live with us."

"I don't know about that."

"I do. Anyway, don't worry about it, because I'm staying with you. No matter what, we are going to be together always." I smiled. It was the best birthday present ever.

Casper and I wrapped our arms around each other. We didn't mean to, but we fell asleep like that. I awoke with a jolt the next morning when I felt someone shaking me.

"Time to get up you sleepyheads." It was Nathan. I was still frightened by the whole thing. I kept wondering what would have happened if it was Ardelene who found Casper and I sleeping together, instead of Nathan. All we were doing was sleeping, but I was afraid of how she would react.

"Hurry up and come help me with breakfast," said Nathan.

"Sure," said Casper sleepily. He rushed to his room and I heard him jogging downstairs just moments later.

I was wondering a lot about what Casper's grandmother would think about Casper being gay, and about us being boyfriends. I was eighteen now, and free, but Casper was still fifteen and still very much under the control of others. When I thought about our ages, a new problem came to mind. When I was seventeen and Casper fifteen, the age difference seemed a bit big, but not too bad. Eighteen sounded so much farther away from fifteen. There was three years difference between us. Well, not really three years, more like two and a quarter, but anyone doing the math by our ages would come up with three. Casper's grandmother might think I was a cradle robber. If I was twenty-eight and Casper was twenty-five, it wouldn't be a big deal, but at eighteen and fifteen I was afraid it would be.

I was legally an adult now. In the eyes of the law, anything I did sexually with Casper was illegal. I didn't like thinking about that. It made it seem like we were doing something wrong. Ethan and Nathan would soon be in the same spot. I thought about talking to Ethan about it. I wondered if Uncle Jack had given it any thought. He didn't know about Casper and me, of course, but he might have guessed, and he sure knew about Ethan and Nathan.

I pulled on my clothes and went downstairs, feeling more than a bit uncomfortable about the whole thing. I just hoped it wouldn't cause any trouble. I always thought that turning eighteen would mark the end of my problems. I guess I was wrong.

*   *   *

I sat in a chair outside the Assistant Principal's office feeling very uncomfortable. Casper was sitting right next to me, and his grandmother next to him. I was eighteen, and technically didn't have to attend school, but I knew I was going nowhere in life without a high school diploma. Casper, on the other hand, did have to go to school.

"Mr. Montgomery will see you now," said the secretary.

I went in, alone. My first impression of Mr. Montgomery was that I didn't care for him all that much. It wasn't anything in particular. He didn't do or say anything that made me dislike him, it was just a feeling.

I had to endure questions about why I hadn't been in school in recent months and what I'd been doing all that time. I told Mr. Montgomery about the trouble with my parents and explained why I had to run away. I carefully avoided any mention of my sexual orientation.

"*Cloverdale Center...*" said Mr. Montgomery, thinking. "I've heard of it. I've..."

He looked at me and I had little doubt he'd remembered that it was a hospital where they sent gay boys to be "cured." There was something disapproving in his glance, but he didn't say anything.

Mr. Montgomery got on the phone and called my old school, requesting my transcripts. Luckily, my school records also indicated my date of birth. I had no way of getting hold of my birth certificate. He asked me more questions, most of which I didn't think had much to do with me enrolling in school. I was glad to leave his office when he sent me off to see Mr. Kerr, a guidance counselor who would help get me enrolled. I passed Casper on his way in with his grandmother and rolled my eyes at him. He smiled.

I walked through the halls, making my way to the guidance office. Classes were just switching and the halls were filled with kids I didn't know. They looked pretty much like the kids from my old school, of all shapes and sizes. I wondered which ones were on the football team. I knew football wouldn't start up until after summer vacation, but part of me was just itching to get back into it, even if that only meant talking to the guys on the team.

"Hey punk, watch where you're going!"

Someone pushed me roughly from behind. I turned; ready to give him a piece of my mind, or a good shove, when I realized it was Ethan.

"Hey!" I said; glad to see at least one familiar face.

"Where you headed?"

"Guidance office."

"Oh, what fun," said Ethan.

"I'm sure it will be. I'm tired of answering questions."

"Hey, I gotta run, but I'll see you after school," said Ethan.

He was gone as fast as he had come, but I felt more at home there after seeing him, even if it was just for a few moments. I found the guidance office and stepped in. Soon I was talking with Mr. Kerr.

I liked Mr. Kerr as much as I disliked Mr. Montgomery, but with more reason. Mr. Kerr was friendly and put me at ease. He didn't start right in with questions either. He just talked to me. He found out I was a football player and talked to me quite a while about that.

"We could sure use a good football player. Don't get me wrong, the boys try hard, but they just don't quite have it down."

"I was the quarterback and team captain at my old school. We were undefeated when I left."

"Oh, Coach Jordan is definitely going to want to talk to you. I'll tell you now; you can expect him to hunt you down."

"Guess it will save me the trouble of finding him," I said.

We got down to the business of figuring out what to do with me for the rest of the school year.

"How many credits had you earned with your sophomore year?" he asked.

I told him and he did some figuring with his calculator. He stopped for a minute, looked up a few things, and then did some more figuring.

"This will be tight, but I can get you partial credit for your junior year based on your grades at your old school, and what you'll be able to squeeze in during the remainder of the school year here. You get good grades at your old school?"

"Oh yes, all A's in fact."

"Good. Good." Mr. Kerr did some more figuring.

"Okay, you have two options. If you take a course instead of a study hall in your senior year, you'll have just enough credits to graduate; with the partial credit we'll be able to get you for this year. You'll have to get good grades for what's left of this year, but I don't think that will be a problem, based on your past performance. The teachers will also take into consideration that you're starting in very late in the year. Or, if you'd rather, you can attend summer school, and ease up your senior year schedule a bit."

"I think I'd rather have a tougher schedule and no summer school."

"Personally, so would I," said Mr. Kerr laughing.

Mr. Kerr set me up with a schedule for the rest of the year, then we sat and talked for a few minutes. I really liked that guy.

* * *

That evening, Casper told me he'd been to see Mr. Kerr too. Casper was only a freshman, so he'd have plenty of time to get enough credits to graduate. He had to endure even more questions with Mr. Montgomery than I did, but Ardelene was there with him. It had taken a lot of calls, but Casper was all set to start attending school the next day, just like me.

"I'm not sure if I'm going to like it or not," he said. "I never liked our old school. I got picked on too much."

"Yeah, but this isn't our old school. It's all new. There's no terrible trio. No one knows you got picked on. It's a chance to start all over again." I could tell that set Casper at ease.

I wondered about starting all over again myself. I'd been very popular at my old school and it gave me a weird feeling to be entering a new school where no one knew me, except Ethan, Nathan, and Casper, of course. No one knew I'd been the quarterback and captain of the football team. No one knew I'd been one of the most popular guys in school. It made me a little uneasy, but I was determined that I'd be just fine. My parents had stolen my life from me and this was just part of taking it back.

Nathan

I didn't have any classes with Brendan or Casper, but they had the same lunch period as Ethan and I. I think they were glad to sit with us. I knew it must be hard starting in at a new school, especially so late in the year. Ethan introduced them to a bunch of the guys on the wrestling team. He also told them how Brendan was the quarterback of the football team at his old school. That made him some points, jocks had it easy.

I introduced Casper to some of my friends. I didn't have nearly as many as Ethan, but I had made a few. Before I met Ethan, I kind of kept to myself, but after we became close I got a bit more outgoing. It felt good to have friends of my own. Ethan's buddies were really nice to me and I considered them my friends too, but it was still nice to have a set of friends I'd made all on my own. It was great to be able to introduce Casper to them. He reminded me a lot of myself. I knew he was nervous about not knowing anyone, so I wanted to help him out all I could.

I was glad that Brendan and Casper already knew that Ethan and I were dating, because our secret wouldn't have held long. Pretty much everyone was cool with us being gay, so no one made any attempt to keep our relationship a secret. Sometimes I still couldn't believe that everyone in school knew we were boyfriends. I also couldn't believe that we didn't get our asses kicked for it daily. The guys had a lot of respect for Ethan though, and after the terrible loss of Mark and Taylor, everyone was much more accepting. It was just too bad that two boys had to die to make everyone realize that abuse could kill.

I worried about Ethan sometimes. He'd been a lot closer to both Mark and Taylor than I had. He took their deaths very hard. They'd died in early November, but the pain wasn't over just because a few months had passed.

Occasionally, I still expected to see them in the halls and then I remembered. It just wasn't right that they weren't there.

I visited their graves with Ethan sometimes and he often cried while we were there. I know he felt a lot of guilt over their deaths, although he shouldn't have. He told me more than once how sorry he was for not standing up for them more when he had the chance. I know that Ethan believed that if he'd stood up for them sooner, they'd still be alive. I tried telling him that he didn't know that for sure, but I don't think it helped. I tried to just be there for him when he was thinking about it. I knew it was something he'd carry with him for the rest of his life.

It was sure crowded in the old pickup truck after school, although I didn't mind being squeezed up against Ethan. We made a stop at the feed store before heading home. Jack wanted us to pick up the first load of seed corn, and some other stuff. The guys in the feed store always looked at Ethan and me kind of funny when we went in there. I know it was because we were gay. They gave Brendan and Casper the same look and I know they were wondering if they were gay too. I just hoped it didn't make Brendan and Casper uncomfortable. The feed store guys never gave us any trouble. We spent a ton of money in there every year. We bought pretty much all of our seed and fertilizer from them, as well as a lot of other stuff. With a farm the size of ours, that added up to a sizable amount of money. They couldn't afford to be rude. I sometimes wondered if Jack didn't have more to do with it than the money, however. He was an easy going guy, but heaven help anyone who crossed him.

It was a lot easier loading the heavy bags of feed with four of us working on it. Ethan and Brendan tossed around the hundred pound bags like they were five pound bags of sugar. I admired their strength, and their muscles. Casper and I worked together and the bags were still almost too heavy for us. I was a lot stronger than I used to be though.

While Ethan and Brendan got the rest of the things on our list, Casper and I walked down the street to get something to drink. As I was sticking quarters into a soda machine, my mom walked around the corner. She stopped when she saw me. I forgot about what I was doing. It was the first time I'd seen her face to face since I left home. I'd seen her and Dad at a distance a couple of times, but they hadn't seen me. Mom ran her eyes up and down my body and it made me feel uncomfortable.

"You're looking very...well," she said.

"You too." I didn't know what to say to her. I didn't really want to talk to her at all.

"I heard you were living out on that farm, with that…boy," she said. She didn't say it out loud, but I knew she was talking about Ethan being gay. She meant it as an insult.

"Yes, I am. I like it there. Ethan and his uncle treat me and Dave real well." I aimed my words at her, reminding her that we'd never been treated well at home.

Mom kind of smirked, and then moved on. Only when she was gone did I realize that I was standing there as if I was lost in space.

"Are you okay, Nathan?" asked Casper. "You're shaking."

"Um. Huh? Yeah, I'm okay," I said and resumed sticking quarters in the soda machine.

"Who was that woman?"

"That was my mom," I said, turning a little red in the face.

"Your mom?" I knew Casper couldn't tell from the way we acted toward each other that we were mother and son. I knew we didn't act like it at all. Of course, most moms didn't do to their sons what mine had done to me. It made me sick to my stomach just thinking about it. Casper could tell that I didn't want to talk about it. He changed the topic.

"Hey, is Zac from school one of your friends? He came up and started talking to me just after last period."

"Zac? Zac Packard?"

"Yeah, I think that was it. He was really nice."

"He's not nice," I said. "He's not nice at all. What did he want?" Casper looked uncomfortable.

"He just asked if I was staying with you guys and about where I'd come from and all that, just stuff, you know."

I think I scared Casper a little when I grabbed him by the wrist and pulled him back toward the feed store.

"What's wrong?"

I didn't answer right away. Instead, I hurried along. When we reached the feed store, Ethan and Brendan were just coming out.

"Zac was talking to Casper," I said. Ethan stopped dead in his tracks. Brendan and Casper were looking at us, confused.

"What's wrong?" asked Brendan.

"We'll explain in the truck," said Ethan.

When we were all in the old green Ford and driving toward the farm, Ethan explained why Zac was bad news.

"I'm not going to tell you who you can and can't talk to," said Ethan, looking over at Casper, "but I suggest you steer clear of Zac."

"He seemed really nice," said Casper.

"Believe me, he's not."

Ethan told Brendan and Casper about the notes that Zac had left in his locker during wrestling season, and how he'd tried to blackmail him into throwing the wrestling finals so he could win instead. Both Brendan and Casper looked completely shocked when Ethan told them about the night Zac, Devon and some of their buddies had attacked us out on the soccer fields.

"They held me while they tied Nathan to the soccer goal, then they started beating me up. If Brandon and Jon hadn't showed up, we'd have been dead and I don't mean that figuratively. Zac and his buddies had planned to kill us."

"Fuck," said Brendan. "And these guys aren't in jail or something?"

"No, they probably should be, but Brandon got really nasty with them. He was so mad he just about killed Devon. We had those boys pissing their pants. We scared them so bad they haven't dared to say shit since then."

"Shit," said Casper.

"So it's best if you don't talk to Zac," said Ethan. "He's fishing for something I'm sure and up to no good. He's probably found out you're gay, or suspects it. Zac, Devon, and their little group don't like gays. They're too afraid of me and Brandon and Jon to do anything about it, though. I don't trust any of them. The best thing to do if you see them coming is run."

Casper looked scared. I hated to see him frightened, but I sure didn't want Zac to get him alone either. Zac was a wrestler and was way built. He could do anything he wanted to a little guy like Casper if he got him alone, or me for that matter.

Ethan's eyes met mine. I could tell he was worried. He was right; Zac was up to no good. I didn't know if it involved Ethan and me, or Brendan and Casper, or all of us, but Zac talking to Casper wasn't a good sign at all.

Brendan

I went to bed troubled. The things Ethan had told us about Zac Packard made me uneasy. I didn't like a guy like that taking an interest in Casper. He'd had enough troubles in his life. Ethan said he'd make sure that Brandon and Jon kept an eye out for Casper, and so would he. I sure would as well, but I was still uncomfortable. I loved Casper and I couldn't bear the thought of him getting hurt.

Sometime late in the night, or perhaps early in the morning, I woke up crying. I had bad dreams now and then, but this one was different. Most of my bad dreams were about being back in the *Cloverdale Center*, or about my parents, but this one was about something else entirely.

In my dream I was me, but not me. It was like I was me and someone else at the same time. In the dream I was sick with worry over Casper, but Casper wasn't just himself either. He was Casper, and someone else. Part of the time he looked like Casper, but part of the time he looked different. When I tried to remember what he looked like, I couldn't picture it. I couldn't really remember much about the dream at all, except that I was so much in love with Casper that it hurt, and that I was so worried about him it was making me sick. I was afraid of losing him, but I didn't know to what. It was all very fuzzy and got more so as I tried to think about it.

The dream bothered me so much that I got up and went to Casper's room. I looked in through the doorway and he was sleeping peacefully. He was safe. I knew he would be, but I still had to make sure. One part of my dream was certainly true; I loved Casper so much it hurt. It was a hurt I was happy to endure; a hurt I hoped lasted forever.

* * *

Casper and I walked by the garden on our way to help Ethan clear brush. Ardelene was tenderly planting flowers. She'd said that the garden needed a few flowers in addition to all the vegetables to brighten it up. Uncle Jack had readily agreed. Ardelene liked to work in the garden. She seemed to belong there. If I hadn't known better, I'd have thought she'd lived on that farm forever. She waved as we passed and smiled. Casper was lucky to have a grandmother like her.

"You see anything of Zac today?" I asked Casper quietly.

"Yeah, he started to come up to me, but Brandon came out of nowhere and stared at him until he walked away. He's really afraid of Brandon. He was shaking."

"Well if Zac comes around, you look for me or Ethan or Brandon or Jon."

"I will. Don't worry so much."

"After what Ethan told us about him, I'm not taking any chances."

"Brandon seems really nice," said Casper.

"Yeah, he does," I said. "I'd like to get to know him better. Anyone that looks out for you is cool in my book. Brandon has been nothing but nice to me. As soon as Ethan introduced me, he treated me like we'd been friends forever."

"Yeah, he's like that with me too. I've only talked to him a few times, but he made me feel the same way," said Casper.

We caught up to Ethan in the field we were clearing. We'd made really good progress. Ethan was chopping away at some roots. I just stood and watched him for a few moments. The thick muscles of his chest tensed and flexed and his biceps bulged as he swung the ax. Ethan definitely looked good without a shirt. He had the best build I'd ever seen on a boy of his age.

I forced myself to look away when Casper glanced sideways at me. I knew I shouldn't be looking. I felt guilty. I loved Casper. He didn't have a body like Ethan, but I loved him and it made me feel bad to even notice another guy. Casper was my boyfriend. Ethan was my friend, and nothing more. I looked at Casper, hoping I hadn't made him feel bad by checking out Ethan. I hugged him, and told him I loved him.

Ethan greeted us with a smile and we joined him in the never ending work of clearing the land. There was a time when I'd have dreaded working that hard, but times had changed. I found I actually liked it. It made me feel good to accomplish something with my own sweat and toil.

In the distance, I could just barely hear the tractor running. I looked up to see Uncle Jack plowing a field, far enough away that both he and the tractor seemed small. That tractor sure got a workout. Uncle Jack was usually on it when we left for school. When we returned, he was still riding the tractor as if he'd never gotten off it the whole day. In the evenings, Ethan or I usually took over and sometimes plowed until it was almost too dark to see. This evening, Jack wanted us to concentrate on getting as much brush as we could cleared away, so all three of us were hard at it as he plowed the dark earth.

Nathan joined us not long after. With the four of us working together, the pile of brush grew and grew. We talked and laughed as we worked and the minutes slipped by. It didn't seem like any time had passed at all before it was time for supper. I felt like I always had all the time in the world on the farm, but time had a way of speeding past sometimes too. I almost felt like fifty years could zip by if I blinked my eyes at the wrong moment. I sure hoped that wouldn't happen. I was happy. I loved Casper. I had a family on the farm, a family that wouldn't reject me for what I was and send me away. I was even making new friends at school and starting to feel at home there. I didn't want the next fifty years to zip past. I wanted every minute to last forever.

We had a quick, but wonderful supper, then it was back to clearing the field. Little Dave finished all his chores and joined us. The brush pile towered over our heads by the time the evening shadows were growing long. Ethan set it on fire and the flames lit up the sky like day. The heat was so intense at first that we had to throw on more saplings from a great distance, tossing them in the air like a boomerang. As the fire died down a little, it cast a golden glow on our faces. The night air was cool and felt refreshing on my naked skin. I actually got a little chilly as it cooled the sweat that covered my torso. I found myself drawing near the fire to catch a bit of warmth now and then. For the most part, the work kept me warm, however. Even without the sun above, clearing brush was still hot work.

Casper's grandmother came out carrying a big tray with drinks and a bag of marshmallows. We were all thirsty and gulped down the iced tea and cold water. Ethan whittled us all sticks for toasting marshmallows and soon we were all standing around the fire, attempting to get our marshmallows a golden brown. Nathan had a real knack for it and his marshmallows always seemed to come out perfect. Some of the rest of us weren't so talented. Every time I just about had mine right, it burst into flames and charred. I didn't mind. I kind of liked the taste of burnt marshmallow.

Uncle Jack joined us as the fire burned low. He talked quietly with Ardelene as he watched over us. I really liked the old man. There were times when I felt like hugging him, the way a grandson hugs his grandfather. I didn't, however, because I didn't know how he'd react. Jack didn't show much emotion and could be stern at times. I didn't know how he'd feel about such a display of affection from a boy he'd known only for a short time. It didn't matter. I knew he liked me, and I sure liked him.

Nathan

Another school day was done. I walked to my locker to get rid of my books. I arrived just in time to see Brandon slam Devon back up against the lockers. Devon's head hit hard and he looked dazed.

"You stay away from him you hear? I don't know what you are up to you sick fuck, but you and your buddies keep clear of Casper. Remember what I said I'd do to you if you messed with Ethan or Nathan? Well, the same goes for Casper."

Devon swallowed hard. He was panic stricken. There was anger in his eyes too, but mainly fear.

"So you gonna stay away from him, or do I fuck you up now?" Brandon was breathing fire. It was a terrible sight to see. I'd only seen him look that way once before, the night he'd come close to killing Devon for the things he'd done to Taylor and Mark, and for the things he'd done to Ethan and me.

Devon was terrified. He actually wet his pants as he stood there pressed up against the lockers.

"I'll keep away," he said quietly.

"Huh? I didn't hear you. Say it louder."

"I'll stay away!"

I could tell from the look on Devon's face that he would've liked nothing better than to beat Brandon senseless. I could also tell he knew he didn't have a snowballs chance in hell of managing it alone. I would have feared for Brandon, feared that Devon and his buddies would gang up on him, but Devon knew what would happen if he tried that. Ethan, Jon, and their friends would hunt Devon down and make him pay.

Devon still scared me. I knew the kinds of things he was capable of; I knew what he'd done to Ethan and me, and what he'd planned to do. Devon was sick. I shuddered to think what he'd be like when he grew older. I wondered if Hitler was anything like Devon when he was young.

Brandon let Devon go. I caught a glimpse of Brandon's face. He had a look of pure hatred on his features as he stared at the back of Devon's head. That look seemed out of place on Brandon's face. He was one of the kindest, most considerate boys I knew. He blamed Devon for the death's of Mark and Taylor, however, and he hated Devon for it. If Ethan hadn't stopped him, Brandon would have killed Devon the night that he and his buddies attacked Ethan and me. I knew he probably would kill him if Devon pushed things too far. Devon knew it too, which explained his mortal terror of Brandon. I was surprised that Devon even dared to get near Casper if he knew that he had any connection with Brandon.

"Hey," I said.

Brandon turned. The look of anger on his face was gone. Tears streamed down his face.

"I miss Mark so much," he said. "Taylor, too."

"I know," I said. "I know you do. I miss them too and I didn't know them near as well as you, or Ethan."

"I hate that fucker," said Brandon, looking in the direction that Devon had gone. "He should be dead instead of them. Why should an evil bastard like him get to live when they didn't?"

It wasn't a question I could answer. Brandon knew that.

"What was all that about? Did Devon do something to Casper?" I asked.

"No. I'd have kicked his ass if he so much as touched him. He just talked to him, like Zac. I don't like it. They know he's your friend, and Ethan's, they've singled him out. They want something. I don't like it at all."

I frowned. I didn't like it either.

"Brendan told me Zac and Devon tried to talk to him too. They were acting all nice, but he brushed them off. He knows what they tried to do to us, so he doesn't trust them," I said.

"We'll just have to keep an eye on them."

"You going to be okay?" I asked.

"Yeah."

Just then, Jon walked up. He looked at Brandon and knew something was wrong.

"Devon," I said. The name explained it all. I headed out to the parking lot to meet up with Ethan and the others, while Jon took Brandon under his arm and spoke quietly to him.

Brendan

"Brendan! Brendan wake up!"

"Taylor!"

I jerked up in bed, wide awake in an instant. I inhaled sharply in terror. I was trembling, and crying. Casper was standing over me, his hands on my shoulders. Ethan and Nathan were standing just inside my room, looking at me.

"That's not very damned funny!" said Ethan. He was more upset than I'd ever seen him. He looked ready to march over to me and start punching. I had no idea why.

"Ethan, calm down," said Nathan. "You know he's not playing games. How could he?" I still didn't understand.

I was still wild-eyed with terror. I felt such horrible anguish that it was all I could do to keep from bawling.

"It was just a dream, Brendan," said Casper softly. "It's okay. It was just a dream." He turned to the others. "He's been having bad dreams lately."

"About that hospital place?" asked Nathan.

"No, about something else," said Casper.

"Why did you say Taylor?" Ethan asked me, still visibly upset.

"Taylor." I repeated. "Yes, Taylor. I saw you," I said, speaking to Casper. "But it wasn't you. It was and it wasn't. Oh, it's all so confusing."

"Just tell us what you've been dreaming," said Ethan. He was clearly very interested. He and Nathan had drawn closer.

"I've been having these dreams at night. I'm myself in the dreams, but I'm someone else too. It's like I'm them and me at the same time. Sometimes I look like me, and sometimes I look like someone else. Casper is in my dreams, but he's not just Casper. He's Casper and some other boy. He looks like himself sometimes, and like some other boy sometimes too."

"What do you look like, when you're the other boy?"

"Brown hair, brown eyes, about my height, but a slimmer build, good looking." I paused. "It doesn't make sense, but I think I'm wearing a soccer uniform part of the time."

Both Ethan and Nathan grew pale at my words, but I had no idea why.

"And Casper, what does Casper look like when he's another boy?" asked Ethan.

"Taller, about my height too. Blond hair, but real long, blue or green eyes, beautiful, almost too beautiful to look at. Taylor. His name is Taylor."

Nathan looked visibly scared and Ethan looked half scared, half angry. I didn't understand.

"If this is a joke..." said Ethan. His voice was menacing.

"It's not a joke." I looked at him confused. He grew less belligerent.

"What happens in the dreams?"

"In most of them I'm just real worried. I'm afraid something is going to happen to the boy, the boy that's Casper and Taylor. I'm sick with worry. It's tearing me up. I almost can't go on it's so bad. But tonight, it was a hundred times worse. I was walking, walking toward the school, toward the soccer fields. I knew he was there. I knew he was lying there dead, but when I got there he wasn't there at all."

"When you got where?"

"Soccer goal," I said, swallowing. "When I got there, all I could feel was grief. I knew he was dead. Casper was dead, but he wasn't Casper. He was Taylor. I had something in my hand, something I pulled out of a bag I was carrying. It was a gun. Yes, a gun. I pointed it to my head and..."

"Stop it! Just stop it!" cried Ethan. I looked at him. I didn't understand why he was so upset by my dream. He ran out of the room. Nathan followed him.

"It was just a dream," said Casper, smoothing my hair. I looked at him.

"You were dead." I was so upset I could barely speak.

"It was just a dream," repeated Casper. "I'm here. I'm alive. It's okay, Brendan."

Casper stayed with me the rest of the night. I felt like a little boy who was afraid of monsters under his bed. I don't think I could have slept if Casper wasn't there. I knew it was just a dream, but it had seemed so real. I couldn't shake it. It terrified me. I thought about Ethan. Something about it got to him too. It didn't make sense. Why should my dream affect him so?

* * **

At breakfast the next morning, no one mentioned my dream. I knew that Ethan in particular wanted to talk about it, but no one breathed a word. I think the others didn't want to talk about it in front of Uncle Jack and Ardelene, but I'm not sure why.

Ethan looked at me oddly whenever our paths crossed at school that day. The look on his face was hard to comprehend. He seemed almost angry, but yet afraid, upset, and sad all at the same time. I didn't know what was going on with him, but I knew it had something to do with my dream.

Uncle Jack was doing some repairs on the tractor that evening, so we were all out clearing brush again. It didn't take long for Ethan to ask me about my dream, although he seemed almost afraid to bring it up. I had the distinct feeling he'd tried to bring up the topic several times on the way home from school, but just couldn't bring himself to do it.

"No one ever told you about Mark and Taylor did they?" he asked me.

"Uh no," I said, a little confused. Ethan looked at me closely, as if deciding if I was telling the truth or not. Apparently he decided I was being truthful.

"Mark was a really good friend of mine. Taylor was a pretty good friend too for that matter. They were like us, gay, and pretty much everyone at school made their lives a living hell for it. Devon was the worst, but there were others. It got so bad Taylor killed himself, by the soccer goal." He paused for a moment and the meaning of his words sunk in. I'd dreamed something that had really happened.

"Mark couldn't take it. He was torn up by it beyond repair. He went out to the soccer goal that very night and blew his brains out on the very spot where Taylor was found that morning."

"I was dreaming about them," I said. "But how? I never knew what you just told me. I've never even heard their names before."

"We saw them," said Casper.

"Huh?" I said, looking at him.

"Remember, the day we came to Verona? We hid out in the cemetery until school hours were over. We saw their names on the tombstones, side by side.

Remember? Mark and Taylor, they died the same day. We were wondering what had happened to them."

Nathan nodded. The graves were those of Ethan's friends.

"But how?" I stopped before I even finished the question. I knew it was a question that no one could answer.

"Maybe it was a warning," said Nathan. "Maybe something bad is going to happen, unless we stop it."

"Devon?" asked Ethan, to no one in particular. "Maybe it has to do with him and Zac talking to Casper. Maybe they have something horrible planned."

A shiver went up my spine and I looked at Casper. I couldn't bear the thought of anything happening to him. Casper looked scared.

Nathan

I felt someone looking at me as I opened my locker. I knew even before I turned around that I was being watched. My heart skipped a beat when I saw who it was—Devon. He just looked at me coldly, and then went on, but it scared me. I'd always been afraid of Devon, especially after that night he and his buddies attacked Ethan and me. I knew that Ethan, Brandon, and Jon were looking out for me, but he still scared me. I thought that after Brandon almost killed him he'd be too afraid to try anything else. I knew he was terrified of Brandon, but maybe he was off enough in the head that it wouldn't stop him. Maybe I was just being paranoid, but I was sure going to watch my back.

My thoughts of Devon were distracted by a couple of girls giggling at me. I couldn't catch much of what they said, but I thought I heard "boyfriend" in there somewhere. I turned a little red. Sometimes girls giggled at me like that. They weren't usually being mean or anything, but it kind of made me uncomfortable. It kind of made me feel proud too, having everyone know that I was Ethan's boyfriend.

It really surprised me when the girls walked right over to me. None of them had ever done that before. I didn't quite know what to think. They giggled a little more before speaking.

"Your boyfriend's really hot. You are so lucky," said one of the girls. I think her name was Cindy. I didn't quite know how to take what she said, but she seemed to mean it.

"I think so," I said shyly.

"He's so built. I used to have a crush on him," she admitted. "Well, I kind of still do, but I guess I don't have a chance with him."

"Sorry," I said "you're not quite his type."

"I know."

"Not that you aren't pretty," I said. She smiled.

Ethan walked up just then and the girls giggled more. He said "hi" to them and they got all excited like he was some kind of rock star or something. It was kind of funny.

"Hey, I'll be just a little late after school. I need to talk to Brandon. Tell the guys, okay?"

"Sure," I said. I looked into Ethan's eyes. He leaned over and gave me a quick kiss on the lips. The girls just stood there and watched. I think Ethan did it for their benefit. I saw a little smile on his lips as he left.

"Gay boys are so hot!" said the girl with Cindy. I turned a little red, but I liked what she said. I agreed with it too.

Having the whole school know Ethan was my boyfriend was quite an experience. At first, I was kind of scared. I think the most difficult times were those few moments when he was telling his wrestling team that he was gay. I stood by him then and I'm sure they suspected I was his boyfriend. We didn't make any effort to keep it a secret after that and in a few days they knew for sure. Ethan's team-mates had been really cool about it, however, and that gave me hope. As time passed, I realized that it wasn't that big of a deal to anyone. Everyone had been shocked when they found out Mark and Taylor were gay. Those two boys had a very rough time. What happened to them taught everyone a lesson about acceptance, however. Because of them, I could walk down the halls and not be harassed or called names. It's just too bad they had to die for everyone to understand.

A few guys gave me a bit of a rough time, but nothing major. There were a few snickers and I've heard them say things like "fairy boy" under their breaths as I passed, but that was the extent of it. After Mark and Taylor killed themselves, it just wasn't cool to give gay boys a hard time. A lot of people felt responsible for their deaths, and they were right.

I think that most of the boys at school would've been too afraid to cause trouble, even if they wanted to. Ethan could kick about anyone's ass that crossed him and they knew it. Ethan had some good friends that stood by us, and they'd become my friends. Anyone that messed with Ethan or me had to deal with Brandon, Jon, and Ethan's teammates as well. All of Mark and Taylor's old friends looked out for us too, even the one's we didn't know all that well.

The girls were the ones I really noticed. They had the most interesting reactions to Ethan and me being gay, and being boyfriends. I think a lot of them were surprised to find it out, especially since Ethan was such a jock. After Mark and Taylor, they shouldn't have been so surprised. Both of those boys were major soccer jocks and they were lovers.

Some of the girls giggled when we were around, like Cindy and her friend. Most of them just watched us. That always made me a little uncomfortable, but it wasn't too bad. I never felt like they were making fun of us, or putting us down in any way. They just seemed curious. I still couldn't believe Ethan had kissed me in front of those girls, however. He'd never done something like that before. I kind of liked it. It was uncomfortable, but it was fun too. I was wondering if maybe we shouldn't just make out right in front of them and see what happened. The shock value would sure be interesting.

Stephanie walked by just then. She was another one that had been torn up by Mark and Taylor's death. She had been Tay's "girlfriend" for a while, when he and Mark were trying to hide that they were gay. She'd been real hurt when she found out the truth, angry too. Taylor's death had hit her hard. I saw her crying for days after he died. Despite everything, she must have still cared for him.

I'd noticed something about Stephanie, something peculiar. Stephanie was putting on a lot of weight. She'd been getting bigger and bigger. There were rumors going around about her, rumors that said she wasn't just getting fat. The more I looked at her, the more I was sure the rumors were true. I just wondered who the father was.

Brendan

I walked around the corner of the barn and nearly ran into Ethan. He was stacking some fence posts up against the wall. He took off his gloves and turned to me. It was a warm spring day and his bare chest glistened in the sunlight. I couldn't help but run my eyes over his hard, muscular body. Ethan had a beautiful build and I wanted more than anything to reach out and run my hand over the muscles of his chest.

Ethan's eyes caught mine and we gazed at one another. I saw his eyes shift quickly down my bare torso, and then back up again. We were standing so close I could feel his breath. There was a tension in the air. I knew at that moment that he was as attracted to me as I was him. I looked into his eyes; he was so powerful, so beautiful.

Both of us leaned forward, just a little. Slowly, our lips neared, growing ever closer. Each moment seemed to last a century as the distance between us lessened. I could feel Ethan's hot breath on my face and I became aware that I was breathing harder myself. We were so close our lips were almost touching.

"No."

It took me a moment to realize that Ethan had said the very same word that I did, at the very same time. We took a step back and looked at each other.

"You are beautiful, but I love Nathan," he said.

"And I love Casper." I smiled.

Ethan extended his hand and I took it. He pulled me to him and we hugged. It was the hug of a friend and not a lover. We pulled away from each other and I nodded my head. We both silently acknowledged that we found each other attractive, but that we'd never allow anything to come of it. If we had met in another place and time, we could have easily have become boyfriends. We were both in love with another, however, and nothing could overcome that. I was glad that we did not kiss, but I wasn't sorry for what had passed between us. I think it made us closer than ever before.

"Well, I've got to get back to work," said Ethan.

"I need to get at it too," I said.

Ethan continued with his task. I watched him for a few fleeting moments. His muscles bulged under the weight of a fence pole. He was beautiful, but I loved Casper.

I walked back the way I'd come. I needed to think. I walked into the barn and sat down on a bale of straw. I suddenly felt very guilty for what I'd done, or rather, what I'd almost done. How could I even think of kissing another boy when I had Casper? What was wrong with me? I started crying, sobbing so loud I was afraid that Ethan would hear me outside. I cried for several moments more, and then realized that I was not alone. I looked up and saw Casper standing above me, looking down at me from the hayloft above. I looked into his eyes with great sorrow. He climbed down the ladder and stood before me.

"I've done something terrible," I said. I had to be honest with him. I had to tell him what I'd done.

"No you haven't."

"You don't know. I've done something horrible."

"I do know, Brendan." The tone of his voice made me look up. "I didn't mean to spy, but I heard your voice, and looked down through the cracks. I saw you."

"I'm so sorry." I said and began crying anew.

"Brendan," said Casper, taking my chin in his hand. "You have nothing to be sorry for."

"But I almost kissed him."

"But you didn't."

"But I…"

"Brendan, you did nothing wrong. I'm not blind. I know how attractive Ethan is. You think I wouldn't notice a boy that gorgeous? It's only natural to be attracted to a boy like that. It would have broken my heart if you kissed him, but you didn't. You stopped yourself, because you love me. You didn't do anything wrong. If anything, it proves how much you love me."

I jumped up and hugged Casper tight. I cried onto his shoulder.

"I do love you, Casper, more than anything. You're more beautiful to me than any boy in the world. I want to spend my life with you." I hugged him so tight I nearly squeezed the breath out of him.

"I know, Brendan, and I feel the same about you. I love you so much it hurts sometimes."

Our lips met and we kissed, passionately. We prolonged our kiss, making it last. I never wanted that moment to end. I'd been tested, and I'd passed. I had my chance at another boy, and an incredibly gorgeous one at that, but I'd been faithful to my Casper. Ethan had been faithful to Nathan too. I felt good about us both.

"I'm forgiven?" I asked when our lips finally parted.

"There's nothing to forgive."

We hugged again and kissed once more. I had the most wonderful boyfriend in the entire world.

* * *

I talked to Ethan later that night and told him that Casper knew what had happened. Ethan said he'd told Nathan about it and all was cool between them. Nathan understood just like Casper. He understood Ethan's attraction to me. He'd even commented on how hot he thought I was. That made me feel pretty good. It was a situation that could have been a disaster for us all, but Ethan and I were faithful to the ones that we loved, and they understood. What could have torn us apart brought us all closer together.

Nathan

Ethan, Brendan, Casper, and I all ran out of the doors of the school. The last day of the school year was over and we had all of summer before us. We hopped in the truck, calling and waving to friends. Ethan peeled out of the parking lot and headed for the farm. Brandon and Jon were close behind us in Brandon's car. There would be no farm work that evening, it was time to celebrate.

It took us no time to get home. All of us were bursting with energy, so after a quick raid on the refrigerator, we headed outside for a game of three on three football. Brendan split us up. It was him, Jon, and Casper against Ethan, Brandon, and me. Ethan and Brendan were the quarterbacks, and the rest of us played all the other positions. We faced off. Ethan had the ball. Casper was right across from me. I was glad it was him and not Jon; because I knew Jon could send me flying. Ethan yelled "hike!", although there was no one to really hike the ball. He plowed into Brendan. Casper charged me, trying to get to Ethan. We collided hard and he pushed me back. He was definitely getting stronger. Ethan used brute force to push his way past Brendan, but he didn't make it very far. Brendan tackled him before he could get free and took him down.

We tried a pass next and that worked better. I caught the ball and made it several yards before Jon nailed me. I went down hard. I didn't mind that, however. I hadn't played much football, but it was sure fun. I could see why Brendan was so into it. I couldn't imagine what it must be like to be the quarterback of a real team. It must've been awesome!

Later, Brendan had the ball. It was obvious that he was an experienced football player. He plowed right through Jon and would have made a touch down if Ethan and I hadn't tackled him from both sides and taken him down. On the next play, Brendan passed to Casper. Man could that boy run. Not only that, but he could change directions faster than anyone I'd ever seen in my life. Ethan grabbed for him and I thought Casper was a goner for sure, but he darted around Ethan so fast he was a blur. I went after him, but he outmaneuvered me without even trying. Jon tore after him at full speed, which was way fast because Jon is a soccer player. Even he couldn't catch him. Casper moved like lightning. He scored the first touchdown of the game.

Dave joined our team when he got home. That made it four against three, but Dave was only nine and Brendan's team had a clear advantage. Between Brendan's football skill and Casper's moves, they had us beat easy. Jon was no slouch either. I didn't do too badly for our side, and Ethan and Brandon made some powerful blocks, and some great moves. Dave even did pretty well.

Jack and Ardelene came out and watched us for a little while. Jon almost knocked me down because I wasn't paying attention. Jack was dressed in his good clothes, the ones he hardly ever wore. Seeing him dressed up was a bit of a shock. Ardelene was dressed nice too. She looked real pretty.

We took a short break for drinks and Jack called Ethan and me over.

"Ardelene and I are going out for a while. Will you boys be okay?"

"Sure we will, Uncle Jack," said Ethan. "Where are you going?"

"We have a few groceries to pick up, and then we thought we'd get something to eat and maybe catch a movie."

Ethan and I exchanged a quick glance. I think the last movie Jack went to see was *Gone With The Wind*.

"You boys will be okay for supper?" asked Ardelene.

"Sure we will," I said. "You two have fun."

"Hey, Uncle Jack, you mind if Brandon and Jon stay over?"

"Of course not, just stay out of trouble." Jack turned to Ardelene. "Well, we better get going if we're going to catch that nine o'clock show. There may be a wait at the restaurant."

Ethan and I stood there and watched them go. The others returned as Jack and Ardelene were leaving.

"Where they off to?" asked Casper.

"Dude, your grandma is going on a date with Uncle Jack," I said.

"Ah, come on!"

"Dinner and a movie," said Ethan. "Sounds like a date to me."

Ethan and I had noticed that Jack went out of his way to be nice to Ardelene. There seemed to be something between them, but we weren't quite sure what. We thought that maybe Jack was just glad to have someone his age around. He liked us boys, but I'm sure he wanted someone to talk to besides teenagers. It was becoming clear that there was more to it than that, however. He'd taken a real liking to Casper's grandmother and she seemed to return his affection. It was still hard to believe though—Uncle Jack on a date!

We started in again and played for another hour or so. I had the best time ever. School was over, the whole summer was ahead of us, and I was surrounded by my friends. It was one of those times I wished could last forever.

As the sun began to fade, we all began to think about supper. We decided it was time for a cookout of sorts. Casper and I went out and set one of the big piles of brush on fire, Ethan and Jon went inside and gathered up hot dogs, buns, chips, cookies, drinks, and everything else they could lay their hands on. Brendan and Brandon busied themselves with setting up a makeshift table and chairs.

The fire roared so fiercely at first that no one could approach it, but it soon burned down enough that we could attempt to roast hot dogs. Brandon wasn't very good at it at all. He said he'd only tried it once before, when he went on a trip with Mark and Taylor.

"I wish they could be here," he said. "We had such a good time at Mark's aunt's place." Ethan gave Brandon a little hug.

"They're here," said Jon. Brandon nodded.

"Here's to you guys," said Brandon, looking up into the sky. He took a big swig of soda.

I felt sorry for Brandon. Ethan had a tough time dealing with the loss of Mark and Taylor, but it hit Brandon harder than anyone. He was Mark's best friend. I know Ethan had talked to him a lot about it. Sometimes Brandon drove out to the farm and he and Ethan walked out into the fields alone. Most of the time, I could tell that one, or the other, or both, had been crying when they came back. I think talking about their loss helped them both, though.

We started talking and joking around to get Brandon's mind off things and he cheered up pretty soon. We all stood around roasting hot dogs and laughing. There was a mountain of food on the makeshift table. I took a seat on one of the logs serving as chairs and helped myself to some sour cream and onion chips and a bunch of chocolate chip cookies that Casper's grandmother had made. I sure liked having her around. I liked her for a lot of reasons, but the cookies and cakes and pies she made were reason enough.

It's a funny thing, but good times like that night don't take long to tell about, and aren't very interesting to hear about, while unpleasant times make for an interesting tale and take a good deal of telling. I enjoyed that night, however. It might not be much to hear about, but I had a great time.

We stayed up late, well past when Jack and Ardelene came home and that was nearly midnight. We finally all made our way to bed. Jon took the spare bedroom and Casper gave up his bed to Brandon. I knew Casper didn't mind giving up his bed for the night, since that gave him an excuse to share with Brendan. It's too bad they couldn't sleep together every night like Ethan and me, but I understood why they couldn't risk it. I don't think they minded. Living under the same roof was enough for them.

Brendan

I knew Casper was crying even before he got close. I was driving the tractor, planting soybeans, when I saw him coming in the distance. I stopped, shut off the engine, and met him. He cried harder when he saw me. He couldn't even speak for a few moments. When he settled down a bit, he looked at me. I didn't know what it was, but I could tell it was bad, just from the look in his eyes.

"I overheard Grandma and Uncle Jack talking. They were saying how those social service people weren't going to give Grandmother custody of me if I didn't live with her." He sobbed some more. "That means I'm going to have to move to Florida with her."

My face fell. I wanted to be brave for Casper, but it was hard. We wouldn't be able to live on the farm together like we'd planned. Casper would be moving away.

"I meant what I said. I'll talk to Grandma. You can come and live with us. If she won't let you, I'll run away. We'll run away together again."

I was frightened. What if Ardelene wouldn't let me live with them? I wasn't looking forward to life on the run again. I'd been there, done that. I knew what it was like. It wasn't a life. I knew in my heart that Casper and I couldn't run away again. If his grandma wouldn't let me live with them, I'd lose him. I'd try to follow, try to find a job and a place to live near him, but I knew the chances of succeeding weren't good. I hugged Casper to me and cried. He couldn't see me crying, but I'm sure he could feel my sobs.

It was nearly too dark to plant, so I put Casper on the back of the tractor and we drove to the barn. After pulling the tractor inside, we got off and walked to the farmhouse. When we arrived, Uncle Jack and Ardelene were sitting at the kitchen table talking. Nathan and Dave were in the living room watching television, and Ethan was upstairs somewhere.

"What's wrong with you two?" asked Uncle Jack shortly after we entered. Casper looked at them guiltily.

"I didn't mean to eavesdrop, but I heard you talking about me," said Casper. Tears welled up in his eyes and I thought he was going to start crying again. He kept from it somehow.

"I know Grandma can't get custody of me unless I live with her. I love you, Grandma, but I wanted to stay here, with Brendan and Ethan and Nathan and Dave. I love you, but I don't want to leave Grandma!"

Casper was getting frantic. Nathan and Dave came in from the living room to see what was the matter.

"Casper, come here," said Ardelene. She hugged him. He started crying. It was all I could do to keep from crying too. Casper was really upset. So was I. It felt like we were being ripped from each other—again.

"Calm down, boy, everything's going to be okay," said Uncle Jack. He looked at Casper's grandmother for a long moment. I could tell a silent communication was passing between them. "I guess we should go ahead and tell them Ardelene." She nodded.

"Ethan! Get down here!" called Uncle Jack. Ethan came running down the stairs half dressed. He'd been in the shower. He practically fell down trying to pull on his pants. In another situation, it would have been funny.

"We weren't planning on telling you boys quite so soon, but I guess it's best," said Uncle Jack. He looked at Ardelene. "You go ahead."

"Casper, what you overheard is true. Social services won't give me custody of you unless you live with me, but you don't have to worry, honey. You can still live here. I'm not going back to Florida. Jack and I are getting married."

There was complete, stunned silence in the room. We all knew Jack and Ardelene were getting on well. We all knew they were getting close. But none of us had suspected this. We'd joked about it, but we never really thought it would happen, not for a long, long time anyway.

"That will make you my grandfather," said Casper looking at Jack. "And you my um, um…some kind of relative," he said, looking at Ethan.

"I guess this means I get an aunt," said Ethan.

Everyone started talking all at once. It was a big change in the Selby household. Some of us would be having new relatives and everyone's life would be changed. I smiled. I wasn't gaining a new relative, but my worries about losing Casper were over. Just when it looked like I was going to lose him, it became certain that we could stay together forever. With Ardelene and Jack getting married, Ardelene would get custody of him. Jack might even adopt him. I somehow felt that I'd gained a family too. Everything was working out this time around.

I looked over at Uncle Jack. He was actually smiling, a real smile, and a big one. I'd never seen him smile like that. According to Ethan, he never smiled. The closest he came was when the corners of his mouth turned up a bit and the little wrinkles around his eyes crinkled.

* * *

"I still can't believe it," said Casper.

"Who can?" I asked.

We were walking between newly planted cornfields, holding hands. It was already dark, but the moon was bright and cast everything in a blue hue. Insects sang all around us, and frogs croaked in the distance. Other than that, there was not a sound to be heard. The Selby farm was peaceful. At that moment, I was content to stay there forever. I knew Casper and I would move on someday. Maybe we'd even get our own farm. But, for the next few years at least, we'd be staying right where we were, and I was happy about that.

"You know I never even knew my grandpa," said Casper. "He died about a year before I was born. I always wondered what he was like. I wonder if he was like Uncle Jack." Casper laughed.

"What's funny?" I asked.

"I guess I've have to quit calling him Uncle Jack if he's going to be my grandfather."

"Yeah, guess so. It's cool you'll be related to Ethan, even if it is just by marriage."

"I wonder if there's a name for how we're related. His uncle will be my grandfather, and my grandmother will be his aunt. That's not cousins exactly."

"I don't think there is a name for it," I said.

"Doesn't matter I guess. I was just thinking about it."

I stopped and turned toward Casper. I pulled him close to me and held him tight. I leaned down and kissed him. I loved him so much.

"You know this takes care of about all of our troubles," I said. "My parents can't touch me now, and you'll be safe with your grandmother. Even if something happened to her, God forbid, Jack would have custody of you, if he adopts you, and I bet he will."

"I guess all we have to worry about is if Grandmother finds out about us and doesn't like it."

"You know you're going to have to tell her you're gay," I said. "Jack knows, everyone knows. She's going to find out soon, one way or another. Even if everyone tries to keep it a secret, someone is bound to slip up sooner or later."

"I guess I do owe her the truth, but I'm not looking forward to it at all."

"I'll be there with you when the time comes," I said.

"I know." Casper smiled and held me even closer. We kissed some more in the bright moonlight, then walked on through the quiet of the farm.

* * *

I jerked upright in bed, gasping for breath. I was drenched in sweat and shaking. I'd had another dream. It was like the others, Casper and I were in it, and we were the others boys too, Mark and Taylor. In this dream, Devon had us cornered. I don't know how he had us cornered, but I knew we were going to die. The dream got mixed up with the night that Casper's brother had nearly killed us, the night Jason had killed his father. The dream shifted back and forth until I didn't know which way was up. There were other things in the dream too, but I couldn't remember them now that I was awake. One thing I could remember is that Taylor had turned to me and said "beware."

I knew it was just a dream, but I was frightened. I had half a mind to go and crawl into bed beside Casper. I don't think it would have bothered me so much if it weren't for Mark and Taylor in the dream. Their presence made it too real. I'd dreamed of them even before I knew about them. It was just too weird. Casper had told me he'd dreamed of them once too, on the very day we came to Verona. As we were napping in the graveyard, he dreamed that they were watching over us. He didn't know who they were then, and didn't think a thing about it, but later he realized who had been in his dream. There was too much to it for it to be a coincidence. That scared me. I was afraid something bad was going to happen. Maybe it meant that Casper's grandmother would take the news we had for her badly. Maybe it meant she'd take Casper away and never let me see him again.

* * *

The time to tell Casper's grandmother about us came soon. Not knowing how she'd react made me nervous and I know it had the same effect on Casper too. It made us uneasy and clouded otherwise bright and happy days. As long as we held the truth from her, we couldn't live our lives as we wanted. We had to hide that part of ourselves that we feared she would not understand. I felt as if I was living a lie and I didn't like it. What Casper and I had was special and wonderful and it seemed a shame to keep it a secret.

We sat near Casper's grandmother as she swung on the big wooden swing on the front porch. Everyone else was out and about, so we were alone. She smiled at us in that grandmotherly way she had and that put me a bit more at ease. I was still frightened, however, and I was glad that Casper would be doing the talking.

"Grandma, there's something I've got to tell you," said Casper. Ardelene looked suddenly serious and gave him her full attention. There was something in the tone of Casper's voice that meant business. "I know you love me, and I love you too, but there's something you don't know about me. It's something you may not like. It's what I am though, so I hope you can accept it."

I could tell that Ardelene was growing apprehensive. She wasn't the only one. I had butterflies the size of vultures flying around in my stomach. I was amazed that Casper had the courage to keep speaking. He wasn't exactly the outgoing type. He hung right in there, although I know he was afraid. I took his hand in mine and held it. I could feel him trembling faintly.

"Go on, Clint," said Ardelene. I knew she was taking the conversation seriously. She almost never called Casper by his given name.

"I like boys, Grandma. Well, one boy." Casper squeezed my hand. "I'm gay."

Casper looked into his grandmother's eyes, searching for her feelings, hoping for acceptance and love. Ardelene's eyes narrowed a bit and the corners of her mouth turned down.

"Gay," she said as if it left a bad taste in her mouth. The level of fear I felt began to rise. "I think you are too young to be making that kind of statement, Clint."

"I'm not too young, Grandma. I'm not confused. I'm not uncertain. I know."

"How could you possibly know? At your age?"

"I know it, Grandma. I feel it. It's what I am."

Ardelene's gaze fell upon me. I was more uncomfortable at the moment that I ever had been in my life. Her eyes fell down to my hand holding Casper's. Her gaze was withering. I felt as if I were silently being accused of being a cradle robber, or worse, a child molester.

"Is this your doing?" she asked me.

"I uh, no..."

"It's not his doing, Grandma. It doesn't work like that. No one made me gay. This is what I am."

"I don't like this," said Ardelene. "I don't approve." She looked at me harshly.

Casper got upset. His eyes filled with tears. He grew angry.

"Well I approve!" he shouted and ran off the porch, toward the fields.

I didn't immediately follow. I lingered for just a moment.

"I know you don't understand," I said to Casper's grandmother. "I know you don't like it, or approve, but Casper is what he is and nothing can change that. If you don't accept him, all you can do is hurt him. Please don't hurt him. I know you don't think very highly of me right now, but I love him, I love him more than anyone ever has, and I don't want to see him hurt."

I stepped off the porch and hurried after Casper. He'd already disappeared between the fields of corn. I caught up with him after a few hundred feet. He's eyes were watery and he was softly crying. I took him in my arms and held him.

"I thought she'd be nicer," he cried.

"It's just hard for her to understand, Casper. It's just hard for her to accept. Give her time."

"I didn't like her looking at you like that, like you'd done something wrong."

"Casper, she's confused. She loves you and doesn't want to see you hurt. She's protective. Right now she probably thinks I'm some kind of bad influence on you because I'm older, and obviously the 'boy' you mentioned. She'll come around."

"You really think so?" asked Casper.

I wanted to comfort him, but I didn't want to lie to him. I wasn't quite sure if I believed my own words or not. I wanted everything to be okay, but I wasn't sure that his grandma would ever come around. My heart told me she would, but my mind worried. I decided to believe my heart.

"Yes, I really think so." I pulled Casper close and kissed him. "We'll be okay, Casper. Don't you worry."

* * *

I awakened with a start, as I had so many times in the past few days. I'd been dreaming again. The dreams were coming more often now and I felt a greater sense of urgency within them. As in all the dreams, I was myself and Mark, while Casper was himself and Taylor. We merged in a crazy dream world, but I was always filled with worry. I felt like the dreams were some kind of warning, but I could never figure out what the warning was about. I knew that this most recent dream had been the most frightening, and disturbing, but I couldn't remember it. All I could recall was Casper or Taylor looking at me and saying "He's coming."

Nathan

Ethan and I walked between the cornfields, making our way toward the little lake in the woods. It was mid-July. Where had the time gone? So much had changed in the last year that it didn't even seem possible. I'd come to work on the farm, and ended up living there. I'd met Ethan, and he'd become my boyfriend. Then Brendan and Casper had come along. And now, just a week before, Jack, who no one ever thought would remarry, got married to Casper's grandmother. In less than a years time I'd left my old family, and found a new one. I was much happier with my new family. Dave and I were safe here. We were cared for, and loved. My whole world had changed, and for the better.

I looked at Ethan walking by my side, looking like Huck Finn wearing overalls and carrying a cane pole over one shoulder. I guess I looked much the same. I was wearing overalls too, with no shirt underneath, just like Ethan. I suspect we would have looked like a couple of hayseeds to city boys, but I didn't care one bit. Nothing mattered, but how we felt about each other.

We walked under the eaves of the forest and soon passed the old log cabin. I remembered the night Ethan had taken me there. He'd filled it with candles and flowers and that night we made love. Everything was so special with Ethan. I sometimes couldn't believe he really loved me, but I knew he did.

We walked on to the little lake. We usually rode the horses when we came back so far, but we wanted to fish and the horses would have disturbed the waters. We sat on the grassy shore, baited up our hooks, and swung our poles out over the water. I sat and watched my red and white cork floating lazily upon the surface of the lake. For a long time it moved only with a gentle breeze, but then it gave a little bounce, followed by another, and another. Quite suddenly, it was pulled under and I felt a tug on the pole. I pulled it up to find a blue gill attached to the hook. It wasn't of much size. I was surprised it had the strength to pull the cork under like that. I took the hook out of its mouth and let it go.

Ethan and I fished for a couple of hours. We both caught several little blue gills. A couple of them were pretty big, but we didn't keep any of them. We weren't out to catch supper. We just wanted to fish.

We grew a little lazy in the afternoon sun. I liked the feeling. It was Sunday and one of the rare afternoons when we weren't busy with farm work. The workload had lessened. All the crops were in and busy growing, or at least trying to grow. A drought was forming and the corn and soy beans weren't doing so well. We'd managed to get several acres of the new ground planted, but with the general lack of water the fields were beginning to look wilted. Hopefully, there would be rain soon.

We were still working on getting more of the new land cleared, but that work was coming along nicely with the help of Brendan and Casper. The work would pick up when harvest time came, but for a while, the farm wasn't quite so demanding.

We pulled our lines in and set our fishing poles on the grass. Ethan and I figured we'd caught enough fish for one day.

"I don't know about you, but I'm hot," said Ethan.

He'd barely said it before he was slipping out of his overalls. He was wearing only boxers underneath and those were soon gone too. There was a time when seeing Ethan naked would have embarrassed me, but that time was long gone. I watched as he dove and his muscular, white butt disappeared beneath the surface of the lake. I slipped out of my clothes and joined him.

We swam in the cool waters. It was refreshing after the hot sun. I loved swimming naked. It was invigorating. Most of the time we just tread water, or floated on our backs. Part of the time we wrestled, and sometimes we stood in the water and made out. Feeling Ethan's naked body pressed against mine was the most wonderful feeling in all the world. I loved standing there, kissing him, feeling him against me. I felt loved.

The sky began to darken, although it was not yet time for the evening shadows. We lingered in the lake, even when the wind got up and it grew darker still. We could hear the rumble of thunder and see the sky lit now and then by distant lightning. Reluctantly, we stepped out of the water and dressed. Nothing could last forever.

The wind grew heavy as we walked under the trees. I felt we were in some danger of having a limb fall upon our heads. We picked up our pace and were soon in the open fields. The corn swayed in the wind, which had grown heavy enough that we walked with some difficulty. I looked overhead. The sky didn't look right. It was a bluish-green and unnatural looking. I'm not afraid of storms, but I felt fear, as if I were aware of something bad that was about to happen. I began to run and Ethan with me.

As we neared the farmhouse, the wind was so strong that we had to fight to keep moving forward. The sky had become darker still and the clouds churned as I'd never seen them do before. I saw Jack holding open the door to the storm cellar, herding Ardelene, Brendan, and Casper inside. Dave came running from the barn, his hen Henrietta cradled in his arms. If I hadn't been so frightened, I'd have laughed at the sight of him trying to run without the use of his arms.

Jack helped Dave down the steps, and then motioned to us with his arm, beckoning to us to hurry. The wind grew so fierce that I feared we wouldn't make it. I actually felt myself being lifted off my feet by the wind and only Ethan holding tightly onto me kept me from losing my balance. We fought and fought against the wind, but made little headway. Suddenly, the wind stopped dead and utter silence fell. It was as if all the wind and noise had come from a fan of colossal size that someone had turned off. The silence was more frightening than the noise. Ethan practically jerked my arm off pulling me to the storm cellar. I could tell by the look on his face he was scared.

We dove inside. Jack fastened the doors of the cellar shut and it hit—a wind so hard I thought it was going to rip the doors right off the hinges. We descended to the bottom of the concrete steps and saw the faces of the others lit by a kerosene lamp.

"Tornado," said Jack.

Uncle Jack alone did not look frightened, but then nothing ever frightened him. His calmness put me a little more at ease.

"No need to worry," said Jack, looking around. "We're safe down here. I built this cellar myself. The walls and ceiling are concrete, eight inches thick. Not even a tornado can come through that."

I grew even less frightened. I suspected Jack was quite capable of lying to put us at ease, but I was pretty sure he wasn't. The walls did look sturdy. I had my doubts about the wooden doors at the top of the stairs, but the cellar was designed like an L, so even if the doors were ripped away, we'd still be safe.

I jumped as something slammed hard into the doors. Whatever it was, it sounded big. I wondered if maybe the wind hadn't picked up the tractor or a large section of the barn and hurled it at us. The doors held. I just hoped we weren't trapped inside.

I checked on Dave, but he didn't seem particularly frightened. He just sat along the wall petting Henrietta. It figured that he'd go and get her. He loved that little hen. I'm glad he brought her down into the cellar. I could just imagine him hysterically screaming that he had to go and save her if she was out in the wind.

A sound like a freight train practically deafened me. I'd heard that tornadoes made a sound like a train, but I never guessed that one would sound that much like one. It really sounded like a big train was speeding past.

The noise outside grew less until it was little more than a light wind. In a few minutes more, there was nothing to hear. Jack went to check on things and came back moments later, telling us that all was safe.

I didn't know quite what to expect as I stepped outside. I more than half expected the house, the barn, and all the outbuildings to be gone. My eyes fell on the house first. It looked the same as always. My eyes went next to the barn. It too seemed sound, except for a couple sections of tin on the roof that had come loose. I caught sight of something big about a hundred yards into the cornfield to the west of the house, something that didn't belong there. It looked like the twisted wreckage of an airplane. Only when I looked closer did I realize it was the silo that until a few minutes before had stood a hundred yards away on the other side of the barn. The tornado must have ripped it right up off the ground, carried it over the barn, and dropped it in the cornfield.

Other than the silo, there was little damage. Even the corn itself seemed to have faired well. Everything was in amazingly good shape, considering what had happened. The crops had even got a little rain, too bad it wasn't more.

"Take a look at this," said Jack, pointing to a telephone pole. I didn't know what he was talking about until I got up close, but then I saw it. There were pieces of straw driven right into the pole. I'd heard that could happen in a tornado, but I'd never really believed it until I saw it myself.

I looked at Ethan. I was glad he was safe. The tornado was a reminder that the unexpected could happen at any moment and that life was uncertain. If we'd lingered a bit longer at the lake, we might have both been killed. Or worse, maybe Ethan would have been killed and I would have lived. I didn't like thinking of living without him. I forced the morbid thoughts from my head. Ethan was safe, we all were, and for that I was thankful.

Brendan

Uncle Jack took Ardelene and Dave into town, leaving the rest of us boys to see to the farm. Casper went off with Nathan to do some work in the barn, while Ethan and I took a look at the twisted hunk of metal in the cornfield that had once been the silo. It was a real mess. If I hadn't known what it was before it was destroyed, I could never have guessed. I thought that we might have to cut it up with a blowtorch, but Ethan thought we might be able to pull it out with the tractor, without cutting it up.

Ethan and I went to the barn. We got out the tractor, a log chain, and a big hammer and a chisel to cut into the metal. I backed the tractor up close to the remains of the silo, while Ethan knocked a hole in a section of metal big enough to get the chain through. It didn't take him long to get the chain attached to the silo, and the tractor. Ethan took my place and inched the tractor forward until the chain when taunt. Once the slack was gone, he powered it up. At first, not much happened. I figured the wheels would start spinning and that would be that, but the twisted wreck began to move forward slowly. Ethan added on a little more power and the whole mass moved along at a slow, but steady pace.

It was a good thing that the silo landed close to dirt road that ran between the fields, because it completely destroyed the corn as it was pulled over it. Not too much was lost, just a section about fifteen rows across and maybe twenty feet long.

Ethan pulled the twisted metal along the road until he had it even with some abandoned farm machinery. He unhooked it and left it there. In years to come, it would be the only evidence that a tornado had visited the Selby farm. I was still surprised that it did so little, especially when it totally wiped out a farm down the road and flattened a few homes in its path. Uncle Jack said tornadoes were like that. They could destroy one building, and leave the one next to it untouched.

I hopped on the back and rode to the barn with Ethan. We pulled the old tractor into its customary parking place and stepped off. I heard a deafening "bang" and the wood above our heads splintered and showered down upon us. I jerked my head in the direction of the noise and saw there what I least expected. I was instantaneously filled with dread.

"Miss me, stud?"

I just stood there gaping. It was Casper's brother, Jason. He has his arm around Casper's neck. Nathan was standing just in front of him and a bit to the side.

"You seem surprised," he said. It was an understatement. Jason was the one person I never expected to see again. I'd never given him a moment's consideration after the night he'd tried to kill me and Casper. He wasn't a part of my life after that. I couldn't believe he was there. I had no idea how he'd been able to track us down. Unless…But no, how could Zac or Devon have had anything to do with it? Still, there was a suspicion in my mind as if I somehow knew they were connected.

My dreams came back to me as I looked at him. I remembered the last of them and the warning I'd been given, "He's coming." I should have known it meant Jason. Like a riddle once solved, it was absurdly simple. How could I have been so stupid? Why hadn't I been able to figure it out? If I hadn't been so dense I could have done something. Now we were doomed. I'd figured out the warning, only too late. I was filled with fear.

"You and your butt-buddy get over there," he said, pointing the pistol he was holding to a spot in the middle of the barn. "You too," he said to Nathan as he shoved him roughly from behind.

I started to step toward him, but he whipped the pistol around and pointed it to Casper's head.

"I wouldn't try that, Brendan, or things could get messy."

I stood there glaring at him, my muscles bulging. I wanted to tear him apart. Ethan was standing next to me. He looked like he wanted to do the same thing. I saw Nathan looking around. I could tell he was thinking of what he could do. There was nothing any of us could do, however. Jason had the gun, and Casper.

"We've got a score to settle, little brother," he said. "Your friends caused me a lot of trouble; almost got me put in jail. Luckily, I was able to convince the judge that I was only looking out for my poor, baby brother." His voice was dripping with sarcasm and menace.

"Casper saved you," I said. "We could have just let you lay there and die, but he called an ambulance for you." That wasn't entirely true, Stacey had called the ambulance, but Jason didn't know that.

"So he's stupid, as well as a little queer," said Jason. His features were filled with hatred. He looked at Casper. He grabbed him by the front of the shirt and made him face him. He pointed the barrel of the pistol right between his eyes.

"Show your friends how you can beg, Casper. Beg me not to blow your brains out."

It was all I could do to keep from pouncing on Jason, but I knew Casper would die if I did so. Jason would pull the trigger. I'd be just as guilty of Casper's death as if I'd shot him myself. I hoped that Ethan and Nathan wouldn't try anything stupid.

"No," said Casper. I knew he was scared, he had to be, but Casper stood right there and defied his brother. I couldn't believe his courage. It infuriated Jason.

"You'll beg me, you little fucker!"

He forced Casper down onto his knees and put the barrel of the pistol right in his mouth. I wanted to close my eyes. It was too horrible to watch. I was crying. I wanted to jump Jason. I'd have done anything to stop him, but I was powerless.

Casper looked up at his brother and shook his head. I thought that was going to be the end. Jason screamed in rage and smashed Casper in the face with the pistol. I leapt forward, so did Ethan, but Jason whipped the pistol around and leveled it on us in an instant.

"If you won't beg for yourself, then maybe you'll beg for your friends. I was going to let them live Casper, but now I'm not so sure. Which one should it be first little brother?" he asked.

Casper was still on his knees, he was trembling and the side of his face was turning purple where Jason had hit him.

"Maybe this one," he said, pointing the gun at Nathan. "He looks kind of like you, Casper. Shooting him will almost be like shooting you. Want to watch him die before I kill you little brother?"

Casper didn't answer.

"Or maybe this one," said Jason, pointing the gun toward Ethan. "Damn, he's got even more muscles than your boyfriend. I bet you and him are real close, aren't you Casper? You like 'em built, don't you little brother?"

"No," said Jason, pointing the gun at me, "I think it's got to be Brendan. I think killing him will pay you back more than anything else I could do to you. I might spare him if you beg me Casper. Do a good enough job and you'll be the only one that dies today." He turned and looked at Casper, smiling.

"Oh," he said, "I almost forgot. I already did a little paying back, just before I came here. Remember your little friend Stacey? Do you Casper? I paid her back good." Casper's heart broke and he bawled.

"I hate you," he said.

"And Brad," said Jason, turning to me, "He begged. He squealed like a girl begging me not to kill him. Too bad he didn't beg quite hard enough."

I trembled. I didn't know whether to believe him or not. I feared the worst, however. Jason was a sick bastard. Something in his eyes made me believe it was true. I slowly shook my head slowly as tears flooded my eyes. My best friend, Brad, who had stood by me when I'd needed him the most, gone, killed by that evil bastard. It was more than I could take.

Jason pointed the gun square at my face. He turned to Casper. Beg me not to kill him little brother. Beg me not to turn his pretty face into goo. Beg me!"

Before I knew what had happened, Casper launched himself at Jason. He didn't punch. Instead he bit Jason right in the nuts, clamping down with his teeth full force. Jason screamed. He whipped the gun around toward Casper. I flung myself at him. Ethan and Nathan launched themselves at him too. All three of us smashed into him at practically the same time. I feared the sound of the pistol. I feared it would fire and at least one of us would fall dead. It flew from Jason's grasp, however, and landed harmlessly on the hay.

I slugged Jason hard in the face. I threw him onto his back and just kept slugging him. I would have beaten him to a bloody pulp, but Ethan pulled me off him. Ethan tied Jason securely and I ran to Casper to make sure he was safe. He was crying, so was I. He was unharmed, except for the bruise already forming on the side of his face.

"It's really over this time, Casper," I said. "He won't get away with it this time. It's over." I held him as he cried. I cried too.

Nathan ran in and called the sheriff. Minutes later Jason was handcuffed and was tossed cussing and fighting into the back of a squad car. I was glad that Ethan was there. I really think I would have killed Jason if he hadn't have been. I would have had to live with that guilt.

As soon as they had taken Jason away, I ran inside and dialed Brad's number. Casper was right behind me. Each ring took an eternity. I shook with fear.

"Hello." I smiled; it was Brad's familiar voice.

"Hey," I said, "it's Brendan." I looked at Casper's worried face. "How's Stacey doing?" I gave Casper the thumbs up. Brendan had seen Stacey less than an hour before. She was safe. Jason had just been tormenting us. I filled Brad in on all that had just happened.

Uncle Jack, Ardelene, and Dave returned a bit later. We had quite a story to tell. I was just glad it had a happy ending. I thought we were all going to die. I thought they'd be coming back to find our lifeless bodies lying in the barn. Even when we jumped Jason, I was sure that at least one of us would fall to the ground dead. I think all of us thought that. One of us dead was better than all of us, that's what was going through my mind. I can't even begin to describe how I felt when I realized we'd all made it.

Nathan

We all took turns telling Jack, Ardelene, and Dave about our adventure, although nightmare might have come closer to describing it. I hadn't been so scared since the night that Zac, Devon, and their pals jumped Ethan and me. I hoped I'd never have to experience anything like that ever again. Ethan did most of the talking, because he seemed the least shaken up by it. Casper didn't say much at all, but then if I'd had a gun pressed between my eyes, and put in my mouth, I wouldn't have been in much of a talking mood either. Brendan added in some details that Ethan left out, but he was pretty shaken up as well.

Brendan was more concerned with making sure that Casper was okay, than with relating what had happened. Casper was practically sitting on his lap and Brendan was holding him close and petting his hair. Casper seemed to feel pretty secure in his embrace.

One good thing did come out of the attack and that was a change in Ardelene's attitude toward Casper's sexual orientation, and his relationship with Brendan. I think knowing that she just about lost him made her feel differently. I watched her as she watched Brendan holding Casper. Before, she'd always had a look of distaste when they were the least bit intimate, but that had changed. I think she finally realized how much they loved each other. Looking at them, it was obvious that they cared about each other deeply. I think seeing Brendan take care of Casper warmed her heart toward him.

Ethan didn't fail to point out Brendan's bravery. He'd risked his life for Casper. In that split second when we all rushed Jason, it was Brendan who took the lead. I remembered cringing, expecting any moment to hear the boom of the gun, and to see Brendan fall dead. He must have known he would probably die trying to save Casper, and yet he did it anyway, without hesitation. Ardelene didn't fail to realize that either. From that night on, she loved Brendan as if he were her grandson too.

I for one was tired of excitement. Ethan and I had experienced more than our share in the past few months. I hoped that this was the last of it. A little boring would suit me just fine.

When Ethan and I crawled into bed that night, I pulled him to me and hugged him close. I didn't need to almost lose him again to appreciate how much he meant to me, but I held him tightly none-the-less. I didn't know what life had in store for us, but I knew it would be a good life, because Ethan would be at my side.

Brendan

I awakened in the middle of the night, but I wasn't sweating or shaking. I wasn't gasping for breath as if I'd just seen the terrors of hell. This time, I felt peaceful. I remembered less of this dream than all the others, but I knew it had been as different as night from day. I strained to remember it, not because I thought it held some warning, but because it was so peaceful and beautiful that I felt I'd learn the secret to happiness if I could recall it. It stayed just beyond my grasp, slipping through my fingers like mist.

I turned, and saw Casper lying beside me. For the first time, he was openly sharing my bed. I didn't touch him. I just lie there and looked at him sleeping peacefully. I couldn't believe how lucky I was to have him. All the bad things that had happened didn't matter. I'd go through them all again if it meant that I could reach this moment. Perhaps I didn't need the secret to happiness. Perhaps I already had it.

Some Weeks Later

I smiled as a familiar car pulled up to the Selby farmhouse. Brad got out and walked toward me. Casper went running to Stacey. She barely had time to climb out the passenger side before he clasped his arms around her and hugged her tightly. Brad and I exchanged a bear hug that nearly left me breathless.

"It's good to see you," I said.

Moments later, we were all seated on the porch. Ethan and Nathan had joined us. I looked at Brad and asked the question that was on all our lips.

"Well, what's the news?"

"Jason's trial won't come up for a few more months," said Brad, "but he's not being held in the county jail anymore."

"They didn't let him out, did they?" asked Casper, fearfully.

"No. He's not free. You don't have to worry about that. He's been sent to the *Cloverdale Center* for treatment."

I couldn't help but shiver when Brad said it. No one but me really understood what that place was like. If anyone deserved to go through something like that, Jason did. I couldn't help but think that maybe even he didn't deserve it, not even after all he'd done. I knew that Jason was about to enter a hellish nightmare from which he would never escape. Despite everything, I felt for him. He'd made his own choices, however, and now he had to live with them.

Casper looked sad. I knew he was thinking of his brother, before he changed. It had to be hard for Casper. Jason was still his brother after all. I could tell that Casper pitied him. He had to be wondering what had changed Jason so, for there was a time when he was a good brother. I knew as I looked at him that Casper was feeling a loss, as if that brother of long ago had died.

I reached out and grasped Casper's hand. He gave my hand a little squeeze and looked into my eyes. I knew he was silently telling me "I love you."

"I guess it's really all over now," he said.

"Yes, it's over, Casper," I said.

It felt like I was at the end of a very long story, but I knew it was only the beginning. I knew that Casper and I had many, many years ahead. I looked around me. They were all there, everyone I cared about. Well, not quite. Ardelene, Jack, and Dave joined us just then and I felt complete. This was my family.

Casper hugged me tightly and gave me a loving kiss on the lips. There wasn't a single disapproving glance. No one there cared that we were both boys. They knew that love was love, and that Casper and I loved each other as deeply as it was possible for two souls to love. We were meant to be together and nothing could come between us. Ardelene smiled at us and I knew everything was going to be okay. I knew I was in a better place.

The Adventure Will Continue...

About the Author

Mark A. Roeder is the author of the "Gay Youth Chronicles", a continuing series about gay youth dealing with the many problems associated with being gay. Information on his current and upcoming books can be found at markroeder.com. Those wishing to contact him may reach him at markaroeder@yahoo.com.

Other Books by Mark A. Roeder

Listed in Suggested Reading Order

Gay Youth Chronicles:

Ancient Prejudice Break to New Mutiny

Mark is a boy who wants what we all want: to love and be loved. His dreams are realized when he meets Taylor, the boy of his dreams. The boys struggle to keep their love hidden from a world that cannot understand, but ultimately, no secret is safe in a small Mid-western town.

Ancient Prejudice is a story of love, friendship, understanding, and an age-old prejudice that still has the power to kill. It is a story for young and old, gay and straight. It reminds us all that everyone should be treated with dignity and respect and that there is nothing greater than the power of love.

The Soccer Field Is Empty

The Soccer Field Is Empty is a revised and much expanded edition of *Ancient Prejudice*. It is more than 50% longer and views events from the point of view of Taylor, as well as Mark. There is so much new in the revised edition that it is being published as a separate novel. *Soccer Field* delves more deeply into the events of Mark and Taylor's lives and reveals previously hidden aspects of Taylor's personality.

Authors note: I suggest readers new to my books start with *Soccer Field* instead of *Ancient Prejudice* as it gives a more complete picture of the lives of Mark and Taylor. For those who wish to read the original version, *Ancient Prejudice* will remain available for at least the time being.

Someone Is Watching

It's hard hiding a secret. It's even harder keeping that secret when someone else knows.

Someone Is Watching is the story of Ethan, a young high school wrestler who must come to terms with being gay. He struggles first with himself, then with an unknown classmate that hounds his every step. While struggling to discover the identity of his tormentor, Ethan must discover his own identity and learn to live his life as his true self. He must choose whether to give up what he wants the most, or face his greatest fear of all.

A Better Place

High school football, a hospital of horrors, a long journey, and an unlikely love await Brendan and Casper as they search for a better place...

Casper is the poorest boy in school. Brendan is the captain of the football team. Casper has nothing. Brendan has it all; looks, money, popularity, but he lacks the deepest desire of his heart. The boys come from different worlds, but have one thing in common that no one would guess.

Casper goes through life as the "invisible boy"; invisible to the boys that pick on him in school, invisible to his abusive father, and invisible most of all to his older brother, who makes his life a living hell. He can't believe his good luck when Brendan, the most popular boy in school, takes an interest in him and becomes his friend. That friendship soon travels in a direction that Casper would never have guessed.

A Better Place is the story of an unlikely pair, who struggle through friendship and betrayal, hardships and heartbreaks, to find the desire of their hearts, to find a better place.

Someone Is Killing The Gay Boys of Verona

Someone is killing the gay boys of Verona, Indiana, and only one gay youth stands in the way. He finds himself pitted against powerful foes, but finds allies in places he did not expect.

A brutal murder. Gay ghosts. A Haunted Victorian-Mansion. A cult of hate. A hundred year old ax murder. All this, and more, await sixteen-year-old Sean as he delves into the supernatural and races to discover the murderer before he strikes again.

Someone is Killing the Gay Boys of Verona is a supernatural murder mystery that goes where no gay novel has set foot before. It is a tale of love, hate, friendship, and revenge.

Keeper of Secrets

Sixteen-year-old Avery is in trouble, yet again, but this time he's in over his head. On the run, Avery is faced with hardships and fear. He must become what he's always hated, just to survive. He discovers new reasons to hate, until fate brings him to Graymoor Mansion and he discovers a disturbing connection to the past. Through the eyes of a boy, murdered more than a century before, Avery discovers that all is not as he thought. Avery is soon forced to face the greatest challenge of all; looking into his own heart.

Sean is head over heels in love with his new boyfriend, Nick. There is trouble in paradise, however. Could a boy so beautiful really love plain, ordinary Sean? Sean cannot believe it and desperately tries to transform himself into the ideal young hunk, only to learn that it's what's inside that matters.

Keeper of Secrets is the story of two boys, one a gay youth, the other an adolescent gay basher. Fate and the pages of a hundred year old journal bring them together and their lives are forever changed.

Do You Know That I Love You

The lead singer of the most popular boy band in the world has a secret. A tabloid willing to tell all turns his world upside down.

In *Do You Know That I Love You*, Ralph, a young gay teen living on a farm in Indiana, has an aching crush on a rock star and wants nothing more than to see his idol in concert. Meanwhile, Jordan, the rock star, is lonely and sometimes confused with his success, because all he wants is someone to love him and feels he will never find the love he craves. *Do You Know* is the story of two teenage boys, their lives, desires, loves, and a shared destiny that allows them both to find peace.

This Time Around

What happens when a TV evangelist struggles to crush gay rights? Who better to halt his evil plans than the most famous rock star in the world?

This Time Around follows Jordan and Ralph as they become involved in a struggle with Reverend Wellerson, a TV evangelist, over the fate of gay youth centers. Wellerson is willing to stop at nothing to crush gay rights and who better to halt his evil plans than the most famous rock star in the entire world? While battling Wellerson, Jordan seeks to come to terms with his own past and learn more about the father he never knew. The excitement builds when an assassin is hired and death becomes a real possibility for Jordan and those around him. Jordan is forced to face his own fears and doubts and the battle within becomes more dangerous than the battle without. Will Jordan be able to turn from the path of destruction, or is he doomed to follow in the footsteps of his father? This time around, things will be different.

Printed in the United States
79785LV00005B/27